221

D0051051

MAY 1 3 2014
DEC 1 3 2014

DEC 0 6 2013

moonrise

also by cassandra king

Queen of Broken Hearts

The Same Sweet Girls

Making Waves

The Sunday Wife

moonrise

a novel

CASSANDRA KING

MAIDEN LANE
PRESS

Copyright © 2013 Cassandra King

King, Cassandra
Moonrise/by Cassandra King
ISBN 978-1-940210-00-1
1. Southern fiction. 2. Domestic Fiction. 3. Gardens-Fiction. 4. Psycho-
logical Fiction. 5. Gothic Fiction
Interior Design by Karen Minster

FIRST EDITION

10 9 8 7 6 5 4 3 2 1

Publishers Note:

For information on bulk purchases please contact:
SpecialSales@MaidenLanePress.com

You may book Cassandra King and other fine speakers for your live events
through the Maiden Lane/Rusoff Agency Speakers Bureau.
Contact speakers@rusoffagency.com

To Rebecca King Schuler,
and the beloved memory of
Nancy Jane King,
who will be with us always.
Always, sweet sister.

And yet to think of you!—such peace
Around me settles soon
As if—I'm puzzled how—my gaze
Were spellbound on the moon.

—GÖETHE

MOON GARDENS

I sit up with a start, my heart pounding. A noise like the scraping of a chair against the wooden floor wakes me, and for a brief moment, I have no idea where I am. The fire has died out, and a melancholy whiff of woodsmoke lingers in the cool air. Woodsmoke and something else, like the pungent aroma of sage. Pushing aside the crocheted coverlet, I swing my legs over the side of the bed, a bed so high that my feet barely touch the floor. I wait for a minute and listen for the noise again, but the room is quiet and still. The only sound is the soft snoring of my husband, who always sleeps like the dead. His back is turned my way, and I watch the gentle rise and fall of his bare shoulders. He is not one to be disturbed by things that go bump in the night.

I slip out of bed and stumble through the darkness toward the tall arches of windows just beyond the fireplace. Not once since we've been here have I closed the heavy brocade curtains, nor do I intend to. The lace panels provide just enough privacy for me to walk around in my nightgown, or wrapped in a towel after my bath. Tonight, however, I want light more than privacy, so I push the lace panels open. Like everything else in this place, the lace is antique, beautiful but fragile, liable to come apart in my hands if I'm not careful with it.

With the windows uncovered, the bedroom is bathed in

moonlight, and I breathe a sigh of relief. Hugging my bare arms against the cold, I glance toward the bed to see if the moon, or the movement of the curtains, disturbed Emmet. Oblivious, he sleeps on, and I turn back to the window. Every night that we've been here, I've had disturbing dreams, or been awakened by strange noises. Even the wind rustling through the treetops sounds like someone calling my name.

It's different in the daylight. I don't jump at shadows, or imagine ghostly voices whispering my name. A couple of nights ago, I'd worked so late in my makeshift office that Emmet came downstairs to check on me. I lost track of time, I'd told him, and he had leaned against the doorframe, smiling an indulgent smile. Our eyes locked, and Emmet lingered. Come to bed, sweetheart, he'd said finally, his voice husky. When I muttered that I still had lots of work to do, he frowned. He wasn't used to me turning away from him, or averting my eyes to avoid his gaze. Eventually he shrugged his shoulders and went upstairs alone. Because he'd think I was crazy, that he'd made a terrible mistake marrying me, I didn't tell him the truth: I have to wear myself out before I can go to bed. It's the only hope I have of sleeping.

The problem is, this is not my house, and won't ever be. Everything here, including Emmet, belonged to another woman before I came along. Foolishly, naively, I thought that wouldn't matter. I wanted so desperately to be welcomed and embraced that I believed I could make it happen. Wouldn't it be obvious that I not only loved Emmet but also everything else: this old house with its ruined gardens, the gently lapping lake below, the cloud-shrouded mountains surrounding us? I'd expected to be loved in return, and to be entrusted with their care. What I didn't expect was to remain apart, separated by a barrier of mistrust and suspicion. Instead I'm the outsider, the one who doesn't belong. And it's making me a bit crazy, especially at night, in this room. *Her* room. At times I even imagine she's the one who calls my name.

With a sigh, I lean into the window frame and stare down at the shadowy gardens below. They were once magnificent, I've been told. In their glory days, the gardens were known far and wide for their unique beauty. Pebbled walkways formed intricate paths through flowering beds, around fountains and statuary, beside koi-filled ponds before tapering off to terraces extending halfway down the mountain. Now the pathways are overgrown and indistinguishable from the weed-choked flower beds. Neglected, the koi have died, and the fountains dried up. Since the untimely death of Emmet's first wife, the once-glorious and much-heralded gardens tended for generations by her family have gone to ruin.

In stark contrast, the grounds in front of the house remain intact, the lawns manicured, the formal beds and topiary pruned to perfection. You can approach the house from the lake without even being aware of the ruined gardens in back. I certainly wasn't, when I got here at the beginning of summer. Coming up the long driveway through a leafy tunnel of rhododendron, you emerge to find the house suddenly looming in front of you. Set in the midst of wide lawns and stately hemlocks, the stone house with its ivy-clad walls appears to have sprung from the mountainside. It's a sight that once drew flocks of tourists to this area.

I had heard little of the history of Moonrise before I came here. Maybe I wouldn't have been so eager to come if I'd known more, though that's pretty unlikely. I've always been overly imaginative, and way too romantic for my own good. It's a part of my nature that has caused me not just a lot of disenchantment but also considerable grief. From the first moment I heard about Moonrise it became an obsession. Emmet grew alarmed when he saw my obsession taking hold, and who could blame him? After all, I was asking him to take me to a place he didn't want to go, a place and time he'd tried to put behind him. I think he finally agreed to bring me here as a sure way of curing me . . . or so he thought.

Maybe Emmet deserves some of the blame, too. If only he'd told me more about his former life, things might have turned out differently. I might not be huddled by the window, shivering in the cold after being chased out of my bed yet again by the night noises. I would've known more of what to expect here. Although Emmet is a verbose newsman known for his in-depth interviews, he clams up on personal matters. At first I was suspicious, sure he was hiding something from me, something too terrible to discuss. My overactive imagination caused me to wonder if I'd come to hate him after discovering whatever it was—a crazy wife in the attic, or a murdered one at the bottom of the lake. Then I wondered if I was being insensitive. Was his grief simply too raw, and his reluctance to discuss it only natural?

Emmet stirs in the bed, and I hold my breath until he settles back into sleep. I don't want him to catch me prowling around in the dark again. He's growing impatient with me, and I can't blame him for that, either. I was the one who insisted we spend the summer at Moonrise. He tried to talk some sense into me. Let's give everyone a little more time to get used to the idea of *us*, he'd said. His late wife had been dead less than a year, and our marriage had been sudden, unexpected. Everyone would come to love me, he was sure, but we should expect a bit of reticence at first. It was only natural, considering. At the end of August, said my sensible, reasonable husband, he'd take me to Moonrise for a week or so. Would that appease me?

No, it would not. Looking back, it astonishes me how stubborn I was, and how insistent. I've never been that way before. Like most women of my generation, I was raised to be a pleaser. Southern women don't make many demands, especially of their men. But I made it clear that I wanted the two of us to spend the summer at Moonrise, and refused to settle for less.

At home in Fort Lauderdale, I presented my case: A summer

away from the miserable heat of south Florida would be good for
both of us. Since Emmet had never lived in Florida, he had no idea
how brutal our summers could be. And I'd never spent any length
of time in the Blue Ridge Mountains. It'd be cool at Moonrise, bliss-
fully so, and wonderfully peaceful. Everything I'd heard about the
little town of Highlands, where Moonrise was located, enticed me.
And the house, I'd been told, had been vacant too long. The gardens were in ruins and the house was showing signs of neglect.
Give us three months, and I felt sure we could restore everything to
its former glory.

At that point in my argument, Emmet had placed his hands on
my shoulders and turned me to face him. "Helen," he'd said with a
heavy sigh, "I wish to *God* you'd never found that damned photo-
graph album."

I couldn't help myself. I laughed and embraced him, the tension
between us dissipating as it always did when we held each other. He
was right; that damned album had started it. I'd found it in a box of
his things I unpacked when we moved in together, a collection of
photos his late wife had begun putting into a scrapbook. Only a few
pages at the beginning were filled; the rest were conspicuously,
tragically blank.

Emmet's response to my discovery of the album had caught me
off guard. I'd been so sure he'd be pleased by my find that I'd barged
into his office, something I never did. When we first married, I'd
asked for photos in order to put faces with the names of his family
and friends, whom I had yet to meet. Although I'd force-marched
him through all of my family albums, his only contribution had
been a few framed pictures of his daughter. With a shrug, Emmet
told me that everything from his former life had either been put
away or given to his daughter. When I found the album and photos
I assumed he'd forgotten, he flinched but tolerated my questions.
Yes, that was Rosalyn by the lake, on the dock sunbathing, pulling

weeds in the gardens. And the others, their friends of so many years; couldn't I guess who was who by the descriptions he'd given me? His eyes softened at an old picture of his daughter on her pony. She was ten in the picture, Emmet told me with a smile, and that pony turned out to be mean as hell. Horses, it was always horses with Annie, even then. But that was the extent of his indulgence, and he pushed away from his desk abruptly.

No question, finding the album started my obsession with Moonrise, the grand old estate with the wonderfully romantic name. Until then, I'd known little about the place, just that it was where Emmet had "summered" in his previous life, before he moved to Florida and met me. Located in western North Carolina, the property had belonged to the family of Emmet's late wife, Rosalyn, and had become his by default when she died. I didn't know anyone with a *cabin* in the mountains, much less an estate. It shames me now to remember how impressed I was, and how thrilled at the thought of having a mountain home of my own. I admitted to Emmet that it was something I'd always dreamed of having. Florida does that to you, I think. Living in a perpetual state of summer makes you long for changing seasons.

Only after we married did Emmet admit that Moonrise was an albatross around his neck, a burden he didn't quite know how to handle. A magnificent estate in its day, it had lapsed into a sorry state after Rosalyn's death. The property was tied up in a trust that barely provided for its upkeep, yet made unloading it next to impossible. He couldn't afford it, nor could he bear to give it up. Although Moonrise held nothing but bad memories for him, Emmet wanted it for his daughter. And her mother would've wanted that even more. It had been Rosalyn, not Emmet or Annie, who had loved Moonrise so fervently, much more so than their home in Atlanta. Foolishly, carelessly, Rosalyn had not anticipated that Emmet, a few years older and in a highly stressful career, would outlive her and end up burdened with her beloved estate. If so, surely she wouldn't have brushed off her lawyers' pleas to take care of things lest the unthinkable happened.

Alone, poring over the snapshots in the album, I decided that Emmet had taken the pictures. Not only was he into photography, the pictures were black and white, his favorites to shoot. Most of them were taken from a distance, which I found so frustrating that I finally took a magnifying glass to study them more carefully, especially the ones of Rosalyn. This I did without a smidgen of guilt or morbidity, sure that any new wife would do the same. After all, this was the woman whom the man I loved had spent most of his life with, the woman he had loved with all his heart, by his own admission. She had died tragically, and too young. Naturally I was curious about her; who wouldn't be?

In most of the photos Rosalyn's face was obscured by a floppy hat or big sunglasses, but in one, Emmet had caught her perched serenely on the edge of an Adirondack chair with her fingers intertwined in her lap. She was smartly dressed in crisp white linen, a V-neck tunic over cropped pants, leather sandals on her shapely feet. This much was obvious: My predecessor was not a thing like me. That surprised me a bit, since I've been told that men tend to go for the same type. The only similarity I could see between Rosalyn and me was the color of our hair. Like me, Rosalyn had abundant dark blond hair, though hers was longer and a shade darker than mine, without the highlighted streaks. She was quite lovely, fine boned with long, elegant fingers and the graceful air of a prima ballerina. Her expression was serene if somewhat bemused, as though she and the photographer shared an intimate secret. Which, assuming it was Emmet, I suppose they did.

When I'd asked Emmet what his late wife was like, he'd given me a surprising answer. "You would have liked her, Helen. Everybody did. She was a wonderful woman." That part didn't surprise me; it was what he said next, after studying me for a long moment: "The two of you might look a bit alike, but you aren't, really. Rosalyn was more . . . delicate, for lack of a better word. You're a much earthier woman than she was."

Now what did *that* mean, I wondered. The image it conjured wasn't exactly appealing. I thought of big-boned peasant women bundling straw in the fields, or barefoot hippies, tiptoeing through the tulips. His observation sent me back to the photo album with my magnifying glass. Since Emmet was so reluctant to talk about his late wife, I'd had to piece things together on my own. Several weeks after our marriage, I'd finally met Emmet's daughter, Annie, who was in her early twenties. Naturally I'd been curious about her, wondering if she took after her mother, but Annie was more like her father in both appearance and temperament. As for Rosalyn and Emmet's close friends, I'd had phone conversations with them, but Rosalyn was rarely mentioned by any of them. Out of politeness, I'm sure, but their reticence only added to my curiosity.

Even if I hadn't figured out that Rosalyn Harmon Justice had been born into wealth and privilege, it would have been apparent from the photos. In every likeness of her, good breeding was as obvious as a birthmark. The way she dressed, the tilt of her chin and jaunty lift of her shoulders, her understated beauty—all spoke of class. But it was more than that. It was also obvious that she possessed an enviable air of confidence, and an innate poise. I say "enviable" because confidence is something I sadly lack, and what little poise I possess is as hard earned and slippery as the proverbial eel. Poise, confidence, social ease; all are qualities I admire and have worked hard to cultivate, even though they remain elusive at best. Not only am I ill-bred, I've always been gauche and graceless, never at my best in social situations. No wonder I studied the photos every chance I got. Rosalyn was everything I've always wanted to be.

What I didn't see in Rosalyn's pictures was anything suggestive of fragility or delicacy. Why Emmet would refer to her as delicate was a mystery to me. Unless he meant ethereal, or otherworldly, but those terms were even more confusing. Based on her unwavering gaze into the camera, Rosalyn appeared to be the no-nonsense type. A woman secure in her own skin, there didn't seem to be a thing hesitant or uncertain about her, unimaginable to someone like me.

Although I focused most of my attention on Rosalyn, I was almost as curious about the others in the album, the two men and three women who were Rosalyn and Emmet's closest friends. All of them had summer homes in Highlands, and lived in Atlanta the rest of the year, as Emmet and Rosalyn had done. When Emmet and I first started dating, he told me about his friends, as lovers do while getting to know each other. Everything I heard about them—by all accounts a rowdy, fun-loving bunch—made me eager to meet them on one hand, and nervous on the other. After our marriage, they had called me to offer their congratulations, which made me even more eager to know them.

With the photo album in hand, I could put a face with a voice on the phone, or with one of Emmet's anecdotes. There was one really good group picture of the six of them, dated the summer before Rosalyn's death. I'd later learn that Emmet had taken it at Bridal Veil Falls, a sixty-foot waterfall near Moonrise. The group was posed together with the falls a stunning backdrop, like a silver scrim. I studied the photo and better understood the reason it pained Emmet to talk about those lost days. Everyone in the photo looked so happy, with no way of knowing that tragedy was about to tear them apart.

It seemed appropriate that Rosalyn stood in the center of the group, her arms stretched out as if to embrace everyone. In this photo she wore the large, face-obscuring sunglasses, the sun against her blond hair creating a halolike glow. Again she was in fashionable summer whites: knee-length shorts with a hooded top, the sleeves casually rolled to her elbows. On her right was the woman Emmet pointed out as Rosalyn's closest friend, Kit Rutherford. Kit was the only one of them I hadn't spoken to yet, and the others made a point of telling me she'd been traveling a lot. Even though Kit'd sent me a congratulatory card, I wondered if the real reason for her silence toward me was an ongoing grief for her best friend. After all, acknowledging the presence of a new wife meant coming to terms with the former one's absence, and maybe she wasn't able to do that yet.

Because Kit was turned partly sideways and in profile, I couldn't tell that much about her. She, too, wore large sunglasses, and although her windblown hair obscured her face, she appeared to be quite attractive. She was a widow, Emmet told me, her much-older husband having died a couple of years before Rosalyn did. Kit and Rosalyn had been like sisters, he added, childhood friends who'd been inseparable since the day they met. As I'd suspected, he verified that Kit'd had the hardest time coming to grips with Rosalyn's death.

In front of Rosalyn was a scholarly couple, Dr. Linc and Myna Varner, he a highly respected professor at the University of Alabama, and she a Pulitzer Prize–winning poet. Emmet winced when I showed him the picture because it showed Linc partly kneeling, one leg extended for Myna to sit on. Things have changed drastically for the Varners since then. On the eve of his fifty-sixth birthday, Linc—who'd always been in perfect health—had suffered a debilitating stroke. Since it happened only a few months after Rosalyn's death, it was a further blow to the close-knit group. Although Linc's tanned and agile in the photo, Emmet explained that he was now frail, and dependent on a walker. When I asked if the Varners were the most normal of the group, Emmet snorted and said that normality was a relative factor with that bunch.

The man and woman on the other side of Rosalyn, Noel Clements and Tansy Dunwoody, were the ones I found the most intriguing—and certainly the most attractive. According to Emmet, the two of them had been together as long as he'd known them, yet they weren't lovers, and never had been. They were a stunning couple, especially seen next to each other. Noel was sunbright and tawny, a striking contrast to the dark-eyed, sultry Tansy. He had an arm crooked around her neck, and she was contorted in a playful pose. Despite their movie-star looks, it was their relationship that interested me. In Atlanta they lived at the exclusive Reid House, where each had their own flat (as they were called at such a ritzy place). In the summer, however, they shared a house together, right below Moonrise. And they're not lovers? I'd asked skeptically. Emmet had waved me off in exasperation and said they'd have to explain their relationship to me. And if they did, could I kindly let him know because it'd never made a damn bit of sense to him, either.

Another photo showed a young woman who didn't fit any of the descriptions of the folks I'd heard about. Judging by her startled expression, she'd been caught unaware as she hung a bird feeder from the eaves of a porch. Dressed in a flannel shirt, jeans, and work boots, this woman was strikingly different in appearance and demeanor from the rest of Emmet and Rosalyn's sophisticated group. When I asked Emmet about her, he frowned as he took the album from me for a closer look. "Oh, that's Willa McFee," he said as his face relaxed into a fond smile. "I'd forgotten taking it. Probably the only one we have of her, she's so camera-shy. A lot of mountain folks are." Handing the album back, he explained. "Willa's like family. Her mother was the housekeeper at Moonrise; now Willa's taken over. Well, not as housekeeper—she's the property manager, runs her own company. Matter of fact, she takes care of all of our places off-season, and does some housekeeping for us when we're there. Nice girl. You'll like her."

The remaining pictures were of Moonrise, and I couldn't get

enough of them. Emmet told me that the estate was on a mountain-side a couple of miles outside Highlands, and that it overlooked a lake. Looking Glass Lake, the original settlers of the area had called it, because of the way the water mirrored everything around it, or on it, so exactly. My favorite picture of Moonrise was one taken from the lake, looking up at just the right angle. Gothic in style and majestic in scope, Moonrise had the gabled roofs and turrets of a storybook castle. And the setting! A lifelong resident of south Florida, I peered longingly at the formal layout of shrubs and trees, many of which were unfamiliar to me. The foliage I was accustomed to was lush and tropical. Although I knew nothing about gardening, I could only imagine the upkeep of such majestic grounds.

A photo of the back of the house proved to be my downfall. Although I'd vowed not to bother Emmet with anything else about Moonrise, I *had* to know more about that one. The gardens in the back of the house had been photographed at night, in the light of a full moon. It was an eerily beautiful scene, unlike anything I'd ever seen. Although the leafy foliage of the garden was dark and mysteri-ous, the moon illuminated white blossoms that grew everywhere—in every bed, border, shrub, and tree. Arbors hung heavy with flower-ing vines; pale blossoms encircled fountains and statuary; moonlit blooms lighted the graveled pathways like torches. I'd heard of moonflower vines and night-blooming cereus, of course, but I'd never seen anything like this. Those gardens had clearly been de-signed to be nocturnal, seen only by the light of the moon. Then it hit me. *Moonrise!* Did the name come from the garden, or was it the other way around?

I could hardly wait for Emmet to get home to ask him about the photo, and he was surprisingly patient in responding—initially, any-way. No, he hadn't taken that one. He didn't have the equipment for night photography, so Rosalyn had hired a professional. The photo was taken a few years back, when she needed one for a poster advertising one of her garden tours. And I'd guessed correctly; the house got its name from the moon gardens planted by Rosalyn's great-grandmother, the original mistress of the house. Rosalyn took great pride in maintaining the unique gardens, a skill that had been passed down from her mother. The maintenance was so much work that few gardeners would've undertaken it without an extensive crew. At that point Emmet's face changed and took on that guarded, remote expression I'd come to dread. "But all that died with Rosalyn," he stated bluntly. "You've met Annie, so you know that, too. Rosalyn wasn't able to pass her skill on to her daughter because Annie never had the interest. Maybe later, she might've come around." He stopped himself and took a deep breath. "It would be better for all of us, Helen, if you'd let go of this obsession of yours. You're stirring up a lot of things from the past that are better left alone. Trust me on this one, okay?"

And I might have done so, if it hadn't been for a conversation I had with Noel Clements later that same night. It was early April, and I was still smarting from Emmet's abrupt end to my probing into the life he led before I became a part of it. I'd answered the phone reluctantly, and even more so once I recognized the voice on the other end. Funny, I chatted freely with Linc Varner whenever he called, but was uncomfortable talking with Tansy and Noel. They were too glib for me, their urbane banter off-putting. With Tansy, I stammered like an ignorant Cracker and said the most embarrassing things imaginable. "I can't wait to meet you, Tansy. I'm sure we'll be the best of friends!" My blabbering would be followed by awkward, deadly silences. Finally, mercifully, Tansy would drawl, "I can't wait to meet you, either, Helen. Ah . . . when did you say Emmet would be home?"

My conversations with Noel were worse, if possible. It never failed; I ended up gushing like a schoolgirl, then cringing at the sound of my voice. "Noel? Oh, hi! Hi! When will we ever meet face-to-face?" Noel was obviously the quintessential Southern gentleman, for he always made gallant attempts to rescue me from my blunderings. That evening, however, he had a ready comeback. Make Emmet bring you to Highlands this summer, he said, then all of us can meet the new bride. Not only would Moonrise fall apart if Emmet didn't soon take care of it, so would their group.

"Tell the son of a bitch that we miss him," Noel added gruffly. "The rest of us are taking the summer off, and we're spending it in Highlands, just like the old days. That way we can have one last summer together before we all lapse into senility and old age." Before he hung up, Noel threw in one last caveat. "And, Helen? If Emmet balks, tell him I said to think about Linc. We've lost one of our group, and come close to losing another. The truth is, none of us knows when our last summer will be. Tell him he owes it to Linc."

When I repeated Noel's message to Emmet, he dismissed it without further comment. He hadn't been back to Highlands since Rosalyn's death, though he'd halfheartedly promised to take me. But in dismissing Noel's request, Emmet made the mistake of using our jobs as an excuse, not realizing how I'd pounce on that. Seeing how badly I wanted to go, he hedged, he'd be tempted if only we weren't tied down to our work.

I began plotting the very next day. Surely if I set everything up with our jobs, made it easy for the two of us to get away for an extended period, Emmet would *have* to agree. Both of us worked at the same TV station, on the same show, even, which made it easier than if I'd had to deal with two different situations. Besides, Emmet was such a big shot at the station that they'd never deny their prized newsman anything. I moved quickly, and everything fell into place. I was given permission to tape my cooking segments in advance, and Emmet could do his news commentaries from an affiliate network, whichever one was closest to Highlands. Everything worked out so well I convinced myself that it had been intended. By the end of May, our town house had been sublet and our bags packed. We would be spending the summer in Highlands, North Carolina.

Yet here I am, several days into the summer I was so determined to have at Moonrise, huddled in the darkness and wondering what's wrong with me. I can't sleep; I'm hearing voices, and I lie to Emmet every time he asks me if I'm happy that we're here. He doesn't question my lies, and why should he? From his point of view, I'd wanted to be at Moonrise so badly that I was blind to the risks involved.

What he can't know is, I *had* known the risks; I'd just ignored them. The thing was, I'd just gotten through a really bad time in my life when I met Emmet Justice. It was a meeting that turned both of our lives around. He and I had little in common, and neither of us was looking for a relationship. Yet we'd fallen so deeply in love that we'd hastily—and some might say foolishly—cast our lots together. We were just settling into our lives with each other, and we were happy, goofily, giddily so. I was more at peace than I'd been in a long time, maybe ever, and I believed Emmet to be also. So what did I think I was doing, bringing Emmet back here? *Here*, of all places, where the ghosts of his past lived on? No wonder I was so restless. Emmet had been right. By bringing us to Moonrise, I've stirred up things that would have been better left alone.

2
tansy

A LITTLE
NEIGHBORLY SPYING

I tell myself that I'm not going to look this time. I tiptoe toward
the bathroom quietly so Noel won't hear me from his room
down the hall. And passing by the windows, I avert my eyes. After
doing my business, I make sure I don't bang into the dresser on my
way back to bed. Which is what woke Noel last night. Or was it the
night before? Whichever, I had no idea that Noel had heard me
banging around or cursing the damned dresser until he flung my
bedroom door open. He stood there wild-eyed and half naked, and
I screamed like a banshee. It was funny the next day, though neither
of us laughed at the time. Even less amusing was his accusing me, yet
again, of spying on Emmet and the Bride. He claimed to have caught
me in the act, as though I would've left my warm bed for the sole
purpose of doing such a thing. The very *idea*.

Tonight, I return to my bed quickly and snuggle under the covers. The thing is, I didn't really have to look. If a light had been on
at Moonrise, I would've seen it as soon as I turned off my bedside
lamp. A few years ago I discovered, quite by accident, that any lit-
up room at Moonrise, except those in the back of the house, is visible through my bedroom window. It happened after Noel had some
tree limbs cleared out around the cottage. Moonrise is such a distance away that I can't really see anything except the occasional

shadowy figure moving around a room. Even so, I teased Rosalyn by claiming I could see her and Emmet in bed together. Being Rosalyn, she had a ready comeback. "Trust me, sweetie," she'd said with a roll of her eyes. "After all our years together, there's not much to see."

The real, honest-to-God truth is, Noel *has* caught me turning the binoculars toward Moonrise a couple of times recently, and it's caused some problems between us. The first time, he was exasperated but also a bit amused, which he tried to hide from me. The next time he was utterly furious. Noel's like that. He's easygoing to a fault, and so laid-back he's practically in a coma, unless he gets pissed. Then you'd better watch out. Usually I know just how far to push him, but all this stuff with Emmet and his new wife has been a different matter. I can't quite figure out where Noel's coming from these days, and it's bothering me more than I've admitted to anyone. Even myself.

The tension between us started in Atlanta, before we came to Highlands for the summer. I know Noel so well, and we're closer to each other than I was with Rosalyn, or Noel is with Linc and Emmet, but in a different way. So I know I'm not just imagining this. Closing my eyes and hugging my pillow tight, I burrow under my deliciously warm quilt and try to remember when I first knew that something was going on with him.

I guess it was the time he called me to see how the packing was going, a few days before we closed up our respective flats for the summer and headed toward the hills. The packing wasn't coming along that well because my closet depresses me so badly. I stood inside it—easily since it's bigger than your average room—trying to decide what to take to Highlands, and I couldn't make myself continue. Since the day that Kit and I packed up Rosalyn's things so Annie wouldn't have to, I haven't been able to bear my closet, with its color-coordinated hangers and cubbyholes. Whatever made me think I wanted, much less needed, all that *stuff*? And what would happen to it after I was gone?

I almost didn't answer the phone that day because I knew it was Noel. I'd already snapped at him earlier, and wasn't ready to pick up our fight. After lunch I'd stopped by his office to tell him I was going home to pack. I didn't remind him that I'd finished the invitation design for the fall Tour of Homes, way ahead of schedule, and was exhausted. After all, a perk of being friends with the boss should be taking off when you want to. "You're *packing* for Highlands?" Noel had said, giving me a look of amused irony (which no one does better). "What could you possibly need to take, dear girl? Your part of the cottage already looks like a Goodwill store."

I told him to bugger off, that his royal ass had never been inside a Goodwill store to know what one looked like. Then I got out of there before he could start in on his favorite topic—me, and my neuroses. I'll admit, I have quite a few, and I'm rather prone to go on and on. After Rosalyn's death, all of us got downright morbid. Then Linc had a stroke and almost died, and our mortality became an obsession.

Linc, even as sick as he's been, has done his best to help me deal with my funk. After he got out of rehab, I drove over to Tuscaloosa and spent several days with him so he wouldn't be alone. That self-centered wife of his, who pretends to be *so* devoted to him, had prissed her fanny back to New York to do one of her New Agey poetry workshops. So I had Linc all to myself. I'm well aware of the irony, my calling Myna self-centered when I was there to take care of Linc, yet all I did was cry on his shoulder. Linc ought to be used to it, though. He's always been my Zen master, the one who will listen to me ad nauseam when I bore the others shitless.

With the calm reassurance that Linc's known for, he told me I would remain miserable until I accepted death as a natural part of life. Contradictory as it sounds, we only begin to live when we acknowledge that we're going to die. All the great philosophies teach the basic concept of birth, life, death, and rebirth; nature's ongoing cycle. On the day I was headed home, Linc had a rather bizarre suggestion. He reminded me that I used to spend a lot of time wandering around Atlanta's most famous cemetery, Oakland. Although it's a habit that makes me look even crazier than I am, Linc suggested that I pay another visit to Oakland as soon as I got back to Atlanta. It could very well help me get some perspective.

I thought it was a great idea, but found to my surprise that I couldn't do it. Instead, every time I drove past Oakland, I'd catch myself averting my eyes. It's true; I used to enjoy going there, wandering around and reading the old gravestones. I would take flowers to my mama's grave, then to the Clements plot, where I'd talk to Mr. Clements about whatever Noel and I were doing. Sometimes I'd bring flowers to the much-visited graves, like Margaret Mitchell's, or to those lonely plots that never had any. My favorite place was the mausoleum. I loved the way sunlight filtered through the wrought-iron entrance, and how appropriate everything seemed— the eerie light, the faint odor of decay, the chill of stone and marble. I'd spend hours sitting on a nearby bench and wondering about the stories of those resting there, how they lived and died. But after Rosalyn's death, my musing took a different direction. What difference does it make, I thought, the silly little ways each of us fritters away our lives? The graveyard is where all our stories end.

On the day I was supposed to be packing, Noel kept calling until I had to either answer or unplug the phone. I picked it up to tell Mr. Smarty-Britches that he was right, everything I needed was already at Laurel Cottage. Of course, he gloated for a long moment before asking, "So. Have you talked to anyone today?"

"Just Linc," I told him. "Big surprise. Myna's not staying."

"No." Although Noel said the word flatly, I heard the bitterness in his voice. "God forbid she give up anything for him. Her career has always come first, as we both know. Linc's the only one who can't see that."

"Yeah," I'd murmured in response. Then I'd reminded him that we were plowing old ground there. And that Linc was the most perceptive and introspective of men except when it came to his own life. Maybe we were all that way.

"Oh, I know," Noel agreed. "Just wish that . . ." He let his voice trail off, then it brightened up as he added, "Willa has signed on, though. I knew she would. She'll take good care of him."

Unusual for me, I kept my thoughts to myself, that one day Willa McFee would have to get a life and stop her selfless caregiving. She'd nursed her mama through Alzheimer's for years; she lived with a sorry alcoholic man, and now was taking on a stroke victim. Even so, I was overjoyed that she'd agreed to help us with Linc. The end of the summer would be plenty of time for Willa to find herself. To Noel I said, "Oh, yeah, forgot that I talked with Kit briefly. She won't be around till Memorial Day. How about you? Heard from Emmet or the Bride?"

"Dammit, Tansy, would you stop calling her that?" And just like that, Noel had done it again, gone from being warm and friendly to turning his wrath on me. "Give the poor girl a break, would you? I can only imagine what a formidable bunch we must be, and she's going to be slammed with all of us at once."

I responded to that ridiculous statement with the scorn it warranted. "*Us* formidable? That 'poor' girl, as you so gallantly call her, married Emmet Justice, the most formidable man who's ever drawn a breath. Compared to him, the rest of us are pussycats."

Noel's response had been a soft chuckle. "You and Kit might have claws, but no one would call you pussycats. The true softies are me and Linc. It's you girls that Helen had better watch out for."

"Oh, please," I shot back. "I don't care what you say, I will *never* understand why Emmet had to up and marry like he did. Whatever happened to a proper period of mourning? And if he was so dead set on marrying again, why couldn't it have been to one of his own? I don't like the sound of this woman, Helen. She's a nitwit on the phone. So eager to please it takes all I can do not to retch into the receiver."

"Tansy—" Noel's voice turned to ice, but I cut him off, waving my finger in the air as though he could see me.

"She's a *dietician*, Noel. How many dieticians do you know, pray tell? What kind of prissy, pious occupation is that? She's not going to fit in with us, you wait and see. She'll turn out to be sanctimonious and uptight, someone who uses every dinner party as an excuse to lecture us on trans fat and cholesterol. And she'll only allow us to have one glass of wine—*red* wine, of course—before dinner. If she allows anything at all. For all we know, she's already made Emmet quit drinking."

"If Rosalyn couldn't make him quit, no one can," Noel reminded me, but I ignored that.

"To top it off, her name is *Helen*. Helen *Honeycutt!*" I mocked. "What a stuffy, old-lady-sounding name that is."

Infuriating me even further, Noel had laughed. "You're just jealous because she's so cute. When I showed you her website, remember, you admitted that she was."

"I did not!" Before he could argue further, I conceded. "Well, maybe I said something like that, trying to be nice. You know me, ever the sweet Southern belle. The truth is, I thought she looked rather mousy, like a dietician named Helen ought to look. And, Noel? If anyone ever calls me *cute*, just shoot me, okay?"

With another laugh, he said, "No one would ever call you that, my dear." I didn't rise to the bait, but he couldn't let it go. "You can think what you want, Tansy old girl. Both Linc and I think that the new Mrs. Justice is quite a looker."

"Oh, she won't be called Mrs. Justice, remember?"

Noel sighed in exasperation. "Surely you're not going to hold that against her, too. She took her maiden name back after her divorce, Emmet told me, and now she's keeping it for professional reasons."

"Yeah, he told me, too. And I wanted to say, 'Well, la-di-da.' She has a cooking spot on a noon show in Fort Lauderdale, Florida, for God's sake. We're not talking Julia Child."

"That's for sure," he snorted. "She's a hell of a lot better looking than Julia Child ever was."

"She has bouncy hair," I said peevishly. "I've never liked women with bouncy hair."

"Maybe that's what Linc likes about her. Bouncy hair."

With a dismissive wave of my hand, I'd said, "Linc doesn't count. Any woman would look good compared to that wife of his, the skinny bitch."

Noel tried not to laugh, but couldn't help himself. It's what I love best about Noel. Although he's one of the movers and shakers of a very hoity-toity Atlanta society, and looks like he stepped off the cover of *Town & Country* magazine, the man has a truly wicked sense of humor. He would not have laughed, though, if I'd told him how I really felt after seeing the Bride's website. He would've scolded me instead, and sworn that I was neurotic about growing old. I catch enough flak about being the oldest in our group—well, except for Emmet, that is. The truth is, it shocked me to see how young Helen looked, even though there's only twelve or thirteen years difference in our ages. Her smooth, pink-cheeked face, the perky butt and bouncy hair—they reminded me of how much I resent younger women. Doesn't matter if they're pretty or plain, fat or skinny; in my present state I hate every woman in the world who's younger than me.

Noel startled me out of my reverie by asking if I was still there, and I'd blurted out, "The thing is, I will never understand Emmet, and this surprise marriage of his. After Rosalyn—" My voice caught in my throat and my eyes filled, but Noel wasn't having it.

"Stop it, Tansy," he'd said harshly. "You're not the only one who's still grieving for Rosalyn, you know. All of us are."

That was when I went too far. It's what I've been doing lately, pushing him to the limit. I know I do it, but can't seem to stop myself. With a snarl, I said, "Oh, yeah, right. Grief sure didn't stop Emmet from finding someone else, did it?"

With a sharp intake of breath, Noel'd hung up on me before I could retract my hateful words. I'm not sure I would have, anyway. Until this sudden marriage of his, Emmet—the grieving widower— had my unwavering sympathy. Kit and I had worried about him for months after Rosalyn died, and we'd made a point of checking on him every day. The three of us would cling to one another for comfort when he broke down. And break down he did, in the worst kind of way. Only a few days after Rosalyn's funeral, Emmet had ended up in Emory University Hospital with some pretty scary symptoms. Then a few months later, he'd worked himself into such a state of exhaustion that he landed in the hospital yet again. Following that had been the nights—and yes, days—of heavy drinking, the most destructive of all. We were actually relieved when Emmet decided his only hope was a change of scenery. First he sold the fabulous home that Rosalyn's parents had given them as a wedding gift, then he decided to relocate. Although none of us wanted Emmet to move from Atlanta, or to leave CNN where he'd made such a name for himself, we had no choice but to support his decision to do so. Otherwise, our group seemed to be in danger of losing him and Rosalyn both.

God, that was such an awful period of time, those first weeks after the accident! Looking back, I'm not sure that any of us handled it well. Sudden deaths, I think, are the hardest. As difficult as it is to see a loved one suffer from some horrible disease, at least we have time to prepare ourselves for losing them. And we can accept the loss better, I think. Both my mother and Noel's had died of cancer, and our fathers of heart failure, but they were older, their deaths more in the natural order of things. Rosalyn had only been fifty-five when her car skidded on ice and plunged down a mountain. It's been over a year ago now, yet I still can't believe that she's gone. I'm always reaching for the phone to call her, to tell her some stupid story about my stupid life. Kit's even worse. Not too long ago, she scared the crap out of me one night, banging on my door in hysterics. It was after midnight, and she'd driven all the way from Highlands to my flat. A dream about Rosalyn had upset her so badly that she'd gotten up, dressed, and driven to Atlanta. She stayed for only a few days that time; after Rosalyn's funeral she'd been here for several weeks because she couldn't stand to be alone.

In retrospect, I think that we should have joined forces to keep Emmet from leaving Atlanta so hastily. If only he hadn't taken that job in Fort Lauderdale! It was a step down for him, if nothing else. He'd had offers from all over, even the big networks in New York. In his younger years, Emmet had been ambitious enough to give consideration to each of them, though we knew he'd turn them down. A born-and-bred Atlanta belle, Rosalyn didn't want to live anywhere else. And why should she? She and Emmet were the golden couple, the undisputed royalty of an elite social scene that Rosalyn had reigned over since her debut into society. Rosalyn Harmon Justice was everything us lesser beings aspired to be. She came from an old family so well-off that Moonrise was a mere summer home for them. Classically beautiful, with a rare, old-fashioned charm, she also had a rugged, hotshot husband, and an adorable daughter whose trophy case overran with the blue ribbons she'd won with her show horses. For many years, Rosalyn was the envy of every woman in Atlanta.

I'd never tell Noel this, but despite my mean-spirited remarks about Helen, I can't help but feel sorry for the girl. I wouldn't want to be in her shoes, even though Emmet Justice is one of the most attractive men I've ever known (and that's saying a lot). I know for a fact that he's not an easy person to live with. Emmet even admits it himself. He's hard-nosed and opinionated, with such a sharp tongue he can tear you to shreds before you realize what's happened. I'm sure he's fully capable of giving a woman's heart the same treatment. I adore Emmet; we all do, but he's not anything like Linc, the dearest man on earth. Or Noel, who might be a maddening pissant, but is also disgustingly nice, as even I have to admit. No, Emmet would be thrilling to bed, but not to wed. I love him, but I wouldn't want to be *in* love with him, and I pity the woman who is.

———

IF MY BED wasn't so cozy and warm, and my eyelids weren't so heavy, I'd get up again to see if the lights are still off at Moonrise. Every night since we've been here, it's been the same. The Bride gets up from the bed she shares with her new husband, then slips downstairs in the dark. I know this because she always turns on a small lamp in the room that she's using as her office, writing that little heart-healthy cookbook of hers (just as I predicted!). One night recently, I watched her lamp come on, then suddenly the stairwell lit up. I couldn't really see him, but I knew the figure moving on the stairs was Emmet coming down to check on her. I don't care what Noel says about my spying; I'm convinced something's not right between them.

I haven't mentioned the strange goings-on at Moonrise to anyone else. Not yet, anyway. Kit would be terribly interested, I know, but I can't bear to do or say anything that might upset her more than she's been lately. She's having a harder time with Emmet's remarriage than the rest of us are, which is understandable considering how close she and Rosalyn were. All of us are close, but Kit and

Rosalyn had a deeper bond because they'd been raised together. They were childhood friends, then roommates at Agnes Scott College. Kit is Annie's godmother, and Annie like the daughter she never had. And no question, she's loved Emmet like a brother for all these years. To her, this too-sudden marriage is an insult to his daughter and a betrayal of Rosalyn's memory.

Kit might have accepted Emmet's new wife more graciously had it not been for what happened soon after the marriage, which she recounted to Noel and me. The marriage hit her hard, but to her credit, Kit called Emmet immediately to wish him well, as soon as he broke the news to us. She'd like to come to Fort Lauderdale to meet Helen, she told Emmet, and could arrange to do so during her upcoming trip to Coral Gables. Emmet had responded enthusiastically (or as enthusiastically as Mr. Cool can), and told Kit that he'd check with Helen. By the time he got around to calling her back with some lame excuse or the other, Kit's trip had come and gone.

Kit was hurt, and shared her concerns with me. She couldn't help but wonder if Emmet's new wife was to blame. What if she was trying to keep Emmet away from us, his nearest and dearest? After all, Annie didn't even meet Helen until several weeks after the marriage. Both of us knew women like that, Kit reminded me, jealous of their husbands' affection for others. Even when we heard that the newlyweds were coming to Highlands for the summer, Kit still worried. "I still wonder," she told me. "First they'd given us a definite no, then Helen finds that photo album of Rosalyn's. After that, she changed her mind. That bothers me." Then Kit added, "We don't know anything about this woman, Tansy! After seeing the pictures of Moonrise, she might be looking for a way to get her hands on Rosalyn's inheritance."

We went back and forth a bit about the trust, and how surely it was set up for the inheritance to go to Rosalyn's heirs, not whomever Emmet might marry should he survive her. Kit wasn't so sure, and since she'd had plenty of experience with trusts, I didn't argue. No point in getting her all stirred up over something out of our control, anyway.

One thing I won't say to Kit: If the Bride has set her sights on Moonrise, no one can blame her. It's one of the grand summer estates of the Highlands area, which is saying plenty. A lot of landed gentry "summer" in the Highlands-Cashiers area, so there are some spectacular homes here. What makes Moonrise so special is its history as one of the first, and the way Rosalyn preserved its unique character. She became an expert in all things Victorian, then turned the whole place into a museum and showplace. The work she put into those weird old gardens was just plain mind-boggling. I'm a devoted gardener, too, but nothing like she was. A crew of professionals kept up the yards at their Atlanta house, but not at Moonrise. Rosalyn wouldn't let anyone else touch it.

Actually, the preservation of Moonrise ended up being the driving force of Rosalyn's life. She insisted that everything stay as it had been for generations, since her great-grandfather built the place, a replica of their home in England. I was the one who talked her into installing a *dishwasher*, for God's sake. And Emmet, who indulged her in everything else, refused to spend another night there until the claw-foot tub was replaced with a shower. Eventually he came to resent the place because it was such a financial drain, even with Rosalyn's considerable family money. In a house like Moonrise, a restoration expert is necessary for every little repair, and old houses require constant work. Since Rosalyn has been gone, the place has gone down drastically. I don't know how Emmet will ever keep it. But he can't sell it, either.

I doze off thinking about Moonrise, and Rosalyn's obsession with it. Funny, the other night when we all went over to Moonrise for drinks and to meet the Bride, I asked her how she liked the place. She became so animated that it took me by surprise, considering what a skittish little thing she is. It was exactly the way Rosalyn had looked when she got on the subject of Moonrise. Helen's eyes took on that same feverish glow, and her voice grew breathless with excitement. Something about that spooky old place casts a spell on its occupants, evidently.

Maybe the spell is cast by the spirits who dwell there. Moonrise is haunted, I have no doubt. Rosalyn joked about hearing strange noises and seeing shadowy figures, but it's no joking matter to me. Because everyone thinks I'm crazy, anyway, some things I keep to myself. I'll never tell any of them what happened to convince me.

Until this summer, I'd only been back to Moonrise once since the week after we buried Rosalyn's ashes. Kit and I had taken it on ourselves to put Rosalyn's things away, both at the Atlanta house and at Moonrise. We couldn't bear the thought of Emmet and Annie seeing her clothes hanging forlornly in the closet, or the personal items she left on her dressing table. As painful as the task was, we did it methodically and thoroughly, with little discussion. Following Emmet's instructions, we donated a truckload of stuff to charity, kept a few mementos for ourselves, then stored the rest in the attic for Annie to go through at a later date. The attic at Moonrise is so creepy looking, Kit and I were anxious to do what had to be done and get the hell out of there. Leaving, Kit told me she'd never set foot in that attic again, and I had no intention of doing so, either.

As I was putting away some of my mementos, however, I realized I'd left the one that meant the most to me, a sunhat I'd decorated with flowers from her garden. Those suckers had taken me forever to dry, but Rosalyn had loved the hat. I'd spotted it with the summer things in the attic's cedar closet, but forgotten to get it. I asked Willa to fetch it next time she was there, but she kept forgetting it as well. (Which made me wonder if the attic spooked her, too, though she'd never admit it.) If I wanted the hat, I'd have to get it myself.

Which is what I went to Moonrise to do, one sunny afternoon in late spring. I was also missing Rosalyn and longing for a connection to her. The Atlanta house, grand and elegant as it was, never had that. "Let's walk up to Moonrise," I said to Noel, but he waved me off. It'd be too depressing, he said, which was the last thing I needed. I didn't relish going alone, but wouldn't have asked Kit to accompany me even if she'd been around at the time. Like Noel, Kit would've refused.

After retrieving the key from the most obvious place imaginable, one of the stone planters flanking the front door, I let myself in and ran up the stairs before I chickened out. At the top of the landing was the door to the attic, so I didn't even have to go down the dark hallway. Without glancing that way, I flicked on the light switch and marched fearlessly up the steep attic steps. Because of the eaves and slanted ceilings, the attic was dark and dreary even with an overhead light, but I reminded myself how Rosalyn pooh-poohed the notion of Moonrise being haunted. All old houses have strange noises. Even so, I dared not look around as I made straight for the cedar closet, grabbed the hat from its hook, and started back to the stairwell leading to the landing.

And that's when it happened. *Wham!* The door at the foot of the stairs slammed shut, and I let out a scream bloodcurdling enough to scare away the most frightful of spirits. I'd probably still be standing there if I hadn't convinced myself that I'd purposefully left the front door open, and strong breezes tended to whip up the mountain from the lake. Fortunately I didn't stop to wonder why a breeze would climb the stairs, blow the attic door shut, and leave the front door open; I just got down those stairs as fast as my wobbly legs could carry me. Safely on the landing, I leaned against the door clutching Rosalyn's sunhat like a talisman, then remembered I'd left the attic lights on.

Only one thing to do. Sitting atop an ornate table on the landing was an old Victorian vase, ugly as sin and twice as heavy, which I used as a doorstop. A hurricane couldn't move that thing, I told myself as I scampered back up the stairs. Just as I reached the top and turned off the lights, *wham!* The door slammed shut again, except this time the slam was preceded by another sound—the scrape of a vase against a wooden floor.

I almost busted my butt getting down the dark stairs, but not in fear like the time before. I was mad as hell. It had to be Noel, playing a trick on me, I thought as I flung the door open. Sure enough, the vase had been moved to the side, and I caught a glimpse of a shadowy figure disappearing down the main staircase. I keep myself in good shape and can move pretty fast, but I wasn't fast enough. Halfway down the staircase, I knew it was futile. No one was there, despite what I thought I saw. No one but me was in the dark, empty house, nor was anyone running down the driveway, laughing gleefully at having tricked me.

I knew then, as I know now, that no earthly presence slammed the attic door on me that day. Moonrise is haunted. And it's not a stretch to imagine Rosalyn as a ghost, returning to walk the halls of the place she loved so much. Before I convinced myself otherwise, I blamed Noel for scaring me that day, but it certainly could have been Rosalyn. She might've been having a little fun with me, or trying to let me know she was still around. I can't help but wonder if the Bride has seen her, or if she senses her presence. If the idea weren't so sad, it'd be rather deliciously gothic.

Something hits me and I sit straight up in bed, wide awake now. I wonder if Emmet has told his new wife that the gardens where Rosalyn spent so many happy hours are also her final resting place. Not only does Rosalyn's spirit still dwell there, her ashes are part of the grounds she once trod. Does the Bride have any idea that she shares Moonrise with her predecessor, and quite literally, too?

Then an even more troubling thought arises, one I suppress

each time it comes up. The rest of us do the same—or so I assume, since no one will talk about it. Will we ever know what really happened on the night Rosalyn died? It was early March, but still winter here in the mountains. Without letting any of us—even Kit—know what she was doing, Rosalyn left Atlanta late one afternoon to come to Moonrise. That in itself was strange enough, but what she did once she got here remains the true mystery. For some unknown reason, Rosalyn left Moonrise that same night, even though it was snowing and the roads iced over, to drive back to Atlanta. *Why?* Driving so late on dangerous, curvy roads was completely out of character for her. Until that fateful night, she had never done such a foolish thing. It torments me, and always will: Why did Rosalyn come to Moonrise so impulsively, and what on earth scared her away once she got there?

SUMMER FOLKS

It'd make more sense for me to start at Moonrise and work my way around to Laurel Cottage, but I don't. Never have. Old habits die hard, and I'd druther end up at Moonrise. Completes the circle, I reckon. Another of my foolish notions, Momma would say. She only had Moonrise, though, not the slew of houses I have. Sometimes I wonder what she'd think about me having my own property management company, with so much responsibility. Momma wasn't what you'd call ambitious. She was content with Moonrise, content to have me end up a housekeeper like her. It was her lot in life, something a good Christian woman like her would never question.

I know that Momma'd understand why I clean the houses at Looking Glass Lake myself, even though I've turned the other places over to my crew. Boss lady does the lake houses, I hear the girls telling one another. Most of them don't speak much English, but they're good girls, and good workers. Truth is, I do only three of the lake houses—Laurel Cottage, Moonrise, and the Varners' cabin—and all have plaques out front saying they're on the National Historic Register, which makes me proud.

The fourth of my lake houses, Kit Rutherford's, I've started sending Carlita to clean. Thank the Lord that Carlita pleased Kit 'cause *I* never could. Duff still works for her, though, which gets my goat. She's snippy with my helpers yet lets him get by with anything: sloppy work, showing up half crocked, borrowing money, whatever. I tease him, saying it's those tight jeans and wide shoulders of his. I let Duff think he's hot stuff, but in truth, I don't worry about Kit flirting with my fellow. That woman likes her men rich, with one foot in the grave and the other on a banana peel. After Kit's latest husband, Al Rutherford, kicked the bucket, she contested his will, and took his kids to court. Even though Al had left her well-off, she wanted more. No one expected the judge to take the Rutherford house away from those poor kids and give it to Kit, but that's exactly what happened. Next thing you know, she sent bulldozers in to tear up the yard with its beautiful old gardens so she could fix her some new ones. Folks in town are still wagging their tongues about that!

If I'm gonna finish today before everybody gets back from their outing, I better shake a leg. I don't like cleaning houses while the owners are home, getting in my way, talking to me, and normally it's not a problem. This summer, though, *everything* is different. Maybe it's because my folks have been here about a week and haven't settled into all the changes that's taken place since last year. And there's been plenty of changes besides that ugly house and torn-up yard of Kit's. Noel and Tansy arrived fussing and snipping at each other, worse than ever. But most of all, Emmet showed up with a new wife, then Linc in a walker. (Wish *he'd* been the one with a new wife.) Linc's doing much better than I expected, though, good enough that his friends were able to take him out sightseeing today.

Even though I hope to finish all three places before sundown, I can't hurry through Laurel Cottage. Too many antiques and whatnots, which I take my time dusting and cleaning. Every room in the house—even the bathrooms—has pictures hanging on the walls, and Oriental rugs on the floors so old they're about to fall apart. I've never counted, but I bet those hutches in their dining room hold three hundred pieces of china each. One time I asked Tansy if they had that many dishes in their Atlanta apartments, and she said, "Honey, you wouldn't believe it." She's right; I probably wouldn't.

It don't take me as long to finish Laurel Cottage today because Noel keeps everything nice and clean when he's here. Funny, him being more persnickety about neatness than Tansy is. Laurel Cottage originally belonged to Noel's family, though Mr. Clements left it to him and Tansy both. Momma didn't hold with gossip much, but she did tell me all about *that* situation. She said Mr. Clements didn't have to do such a thing, since he only courted Tansy's mama instead of marrying her, but that was the kind of man he was. Good-hearted and decent, despite him being rich as a lord. Mr. Clements treated Tansy like the daughter he never had. You'd think Noel would resent sharing his house with somebody who's not blood kin, but no. Momma always said that Noel was every bit as fine a man as his daddy. "Fine" has a different meaning these days, and Noel Clements is sure that, too.

Noel and Tansy have the most peculiar relationship of anybody I know, and that's saying a lot among the summer people. They live together, but not really. They date other people, or each other, and it don't seem to matter to them which. Both have been married to other folks, and neither came to Highlands much during those days. Well, Noel couldn't, I reckon, since he married a Frenchwoman and spent a lot of time overseas. Tansy's tied the knot twice, both times to men old enough to be her daddy. Seems like one—or both—of her husbands died recently. One of them was funny, I recall—"funny" like in homo, and Noel teases her about it. Not about the guy being homo—Noel's not like that—but about Tansy marrying him and not knowing. Peculiar as they are, though, Tansy and Noel are sure entertaining to be around.

Laurel Cottage is the prettiest of all the houses I manage, even Moonrise. Moonrise is more famous, but it's creepy to me. Plus

Moonrise is cold all the time, even in the summer. Laurel Cottage is more what a house in the mountains oughta be, but in a good way, not like those gussied-up ones with pictures of bears on everything, even furniture. Summer folks actually think bears are *cute*. You won't see any bear stuff at Laurel Cottage, cute or otherwise. It's been written up in a lot of decorating magazines, which Tansy frames and hangs on the walls.

Standing at the kitchen sink of Laurel Cottage, I arrange a bunch of white dahlias in a heavy antique vase. It's a personal touch of mine, fixing flowers from the owners' gardens after I clean their houses. I'm halfway up the stairs with the vase in my hands when my cell phone rings. Probably just Duff, aggravating thing. He knows I'm at work, and he's supposed to be.

I've just put the vase on Tansy's dresser when my phone goes off again. I pull it out of my pocket, and sure enough, it's Duff. "Hey. Whatcha doing?" he says.

"I'm at the Old Edwards Spa, Duff, getting my toenails done while I wait for the hundred-dollar massage," I snap. "What'd you think?" With an exasperated sigh, I add, "What'd you call for? I don't have time for your foolishness today."

"Just to remind you about us singing at the prayer meeting to-night," Duff says.

"You think I've gone senile?" I ask him. "We've been singing at every prayer meeting for a year now. Though all your church-going ain't done you a bit of good, far as I can tell. Every night you're not in church, you're at the juke joint." Then, hearing him sucking on a cigarette, I sigh again. "And you're smoking, ain't you?"

He tries to deny it but starts coughing, bad. "Naw. I quit, like I told you," the liar says.

"I'm going now," I tell him meanly. "I'm not listening to no more of your lies. After that doctor said you might lose your voice, I thought you might straighten yourself out."

I slam the little phone shut, cussing. But before I can get it tucked back into my jeans, it's ringing again. This time it's Helen.

"Willa?" she says, and I reply, "Yep, it's me." Then I worry that they're on their way home, and I haven't even made it to Moonrise yet. But they're still touring the Biltmore Estate, she tells me. "Listen," she says, "I called to see if you'd do me a favor when you get to the house." No surprise, she wants me to make sure the oven's off. They'd only been here a day or so when Helen smelled gas and had the gas company come out in a hurry. She'd turned the oven on, the guy told her, without making sure the pilot light was lit. Helen had a fit, swearing she did no such thing—she hadn't even been in the kitchen. It was pretty obvious that no one believed her.

I tell Helen not to worry, I'll check it out. "I didn't touch the oven this morning," she says with a nervous laugh, "but still. And Willa? I'd appreciate you not saying anything about my call, okay? Can't have everyone thinking I'm scatterbrained."

Another little laugh, and she's gone. We hang up, and I start back downstairs, shaking my head. Lord, that poor woman! Bless her heart. Last month, when she called to say she and Emmet had decided to spend the summer in Highlands, she asked if I could get the house comfortable for them. I wanted to tell her that I was the property manager, not a miracle worker. If there's anything comfortable about that old-timey place, I've yet to find it. Turns out she meant having it wired for the Internet and stuff, which was at least doable. She and Emmet couldn't stay, she said, unless an office could be fixed up for both of them, since they had a lot of work to do this summer. A working holiday, she'd called it, which tickled me.

Helen seems so earnest and is trying so hard to be liked, but I have my doubts. I like her fine myself, but she's gonna have a hard time fitting in here. I've been knowing these folks all my life, and they're not an easy bunch. I love 'em to death, and they're good to me, but they're strange. Linc's the best of them, but he's a college professor, and half the time he uses big words I don't understand. That Yankee wife of his thinks she's better than everybody else, especially me. I pure-tee cannot *stand* her. Noel and Tansy couldn't be nicer to me, but they talk crazy and act the fool. Kit Rutherford is a snot, though she tries to act like she's sweet as pie. Then there's Emmet. Momma used to say that Rosalyn Harmon was the only woman who could be married to Emmet Justice because she knew how to handle him. I find him pretty scary myself. Not mean scary, but scary the other way. He stares at you with those clear-colored eyes of his, then fires questions your way like he's interviewing you on his TV show. It makes me nervous, and I avoid him as much as I can. All I can say is, poor Helen's got her work cut out for her.

I got another worry besides Helen, though. Driving down the road to the Varners', I wonder what I've got myself into by promising to help out with Linc. I start next week, after that wife of his gets on her broomstick and flies back to Alabama. I love Linc to pieces but have problems with Myna. I can't figure out what Linc ever saw in her, even if she is a big-shot writer. All those years he'd been a bachelor, then Myna comes from New York City to speak at Bama, and next thing you know, she's got her hooks into him. And her not even pretty! Everything about her is sharp—elbows, collarbone, chin, eyes, and tongue.

Only good thing is, Myna don't like Highlands, so she won't be around much. Never is. She goes someplace—Maine, seems like—where her people have a summer home. She's always telling Linc how his house don't measure up to her family's "compound." If I was him, I'd tell her to keep her skinny ass up there, then. Although the Varner house is an authentic, old-timey log cabin, and sits right on the edge of the lake, Myna complains that it's dark, cramped, and smells like a fireplace. Shoot, that's what I like about

it! Actually, Linc's cabin is a lot like the old homeplace I was raised
in, which belongs to me now. Both of them have the same pointy
tin roof, blackened chimneys on the sides, and laurel rail porches.
And each has chinked log walls and fireplaces made of rocks from
the Cullasaja River. Only difference is, mine is the one *without* the
brass plaque.

Linc hadn't been to Highlands since his stroke, but the cabin
has handicapped rails and stuff now. Myna sent me a list of how she
wanted things done, but not many of her orders were carried out.
One weekend Noel met me there and changed everything on her list.
Just between us, he told me with a wink, and brought in his own
workmen. He was damned determined Linc'd be comfortable here,
he told me. Noel won't say nothing bad about Myna—not to me,
anyway—but it's obvious how him and the others feel about her. It
tickles me the way they all pretend to like one another, regardless.
Summer folks are bad about that, I've noticed.

I brought some of Tansy's dahlias to Linc's house, so I go outside
to get fillers, maybe a little buddleia and oxeye daisies. Summer
people *love* their flower gardens, and all over Highlands are the prettiest, showiest ones you've ever seen, with statues and waterfalls and
goldfish ponds. Odd thing is, men and women alike work in their
flower beds. Duff can't believe that the men belong to garden clubs
just like ladies do, but he thinks all summer people are weird. And
most of the locals feel the same way.

I gather a handful of buddleia from Linc's butterfly garden, but
gotta get the sprinklers going next—Linc's not happy with his garden, and neither is Tansy with hers; least they know I've done the
best I can. Western North Carolina is in such a bad drought that the
lakes are all down, and some of the waterfalls nothing but trickles.
The governor's been asking everybody to pray for rain. The Lord's
liable to tell us we can't keep on using up everything He gave us,
then holding out our hands for more.

Linc's yards are different from everybody else's. He's one of those professors who studies butterflies and teaches his students about them, so his garden's like a science lab. Used to, if you needed to find Linc, look in the yard. Day and night, he'd be squatting out there taking notes and pictures of caterpillars and cocoons. Wonder how much he'll be able to get around it now, with him in that walker. Part of my job will be taking him for walks to build up his legs, then he can start using a cane instead. Most of our strolls will be through the butterfly garden. I 'spect it's going to be tough, seeing him wanting to squat down and study things, and not being able to. Maybe taking notes is something else I can do for him.

Driving down the dirt road that circles Looking Glass Lake, I catch myself humming a little song. I can't help myself, being excited about the arrival of summer. Winters here are so gray and dreary. Seems like spring will never get here, then it's gone as quickly as a cheating boyfriend. Only excitement we have in these parts is when the summer folks roll in. Everything, and everybody, picks up then. Highlands is a small town, just a few blocks of downtown storefronts, but you'd never know it come summer. The newspaper wrote that the town swells with tourists, and that's what it feels like. Swollen, like a big ripe persimmon about to burst open. Excitement fills the air the first week of June, and it don't leave till the cold winds of winter blow back in.

The road leading up to Moonrise isn't much wider than a pathway, and I pray I won't meet another vehicle. If so, nothing to do but back out. The road winds through a laurel and rhododendron forest where pink-and-white blooms hang so thick and heavy overhead that you can't see the sky. Not seeing is good at certain spots, where the road hugs the side of the mountain. Looking down is not for the faint of heart. The drop-off's not near as bad as some, but it's still plenty scary. Sure hope Emmet's warned Helen about driving on mountain roads, especially after what happened to Rosalyn.

Helen told me she'd never spent any time in the mountains, nor been around anything higher than a sand dune.

Suddenly the rhododendrons clear out, and there's Moonrise. Big old ugly thing that it is, it never fails to take my breath away. The way it looms out of the clearing is a surprise, with its rooflines of different heights, and the round turret like a fairy castle. The walls are made of local river rocks, but they're about covered with ivy. Takes all me and my crew can do to keep it cut back so it don't cover the windows—why it's so dark inside. Everything here looks good, though, long as you stay in front. The back's another story. I kept telling Emmet how bad Rosalyn's gardens had got, but he won't let my crew, or nobody else, work back there. He don't want them moon gardens here, not ever again. Let them go to rack and ruin, he said, and they up and obliged him.

I brought more of Tansy's dahlias here, too, not wanting to wade through the overgrown gardens looking for blooms. I leave the front door open to catch the breeze blowing up from the lake, which is sharp and pine scented. No matter how often I air it out, the inside of the house is always musty and damp. And cold as a well digger's ass.

Even though it's broad daylight, I go around turning on lamps. My work boots sound like a mule clopping on the slate floor of the entrance hall, but I don't mind. It's way too quiet here. Always is. Turning on the lamps don't help much because they either have painted globes or dark, fringed shades. Not a plain, ordinary lamp on the premises, but then, it's not an ordinary house. After Momma got too sick to work here anymore, I took over. That's when Rosalyn showed me how to take care of everything, way more information than I gave a fig about. When the house was on garden tours and things like that, Rosalyn was the guide. She insisted I tag along until I learned the history of the house.

When I asked Rosalyn how come the furnishings were so fancy, she told me they were Victorian, as though that explained it. All I know is, the Victorians couldn't leave anything alone. Every dang thing in the house is gussied up with fringe, ribbons, scrolls, scallops, embroidery, flowers, feathers, or beads. Worse of all is the furniture. The tables, chests, and sideboards are as big and heavy as coffins, with deep carving you can't half dust. The fabric they used isn't easy to clean like the kind we have nowadays, either. Oh, no—nothing would do them but velvet and satin and linen and lace. If I was Helen, I'd yank down all these brocade curtains and let in some light! Then I'd get someone to haul off every last piece of the furniture, even if it did belong to Rosalyn's family.

I head down the hallway to the kitchen, carrying my basket. The stove's cold as a stone, with no smell of gas, but Helen was right to double-check. As old as that thing is, it could spring a leak, I reckon.

I notice that Helen's using the glassed-in porch as their sitting room now. The TV, something most summer folks don't even have, is in the back parlor. Rosalyn had to put one in for Emmet, who never misses the news. Unlike most kids, Annie wasn't bad about watching TV, but she wasn't here much. Always off at some horse-riding camp. Now she's grown into a young woman I barely know. She's nice enough, but kind of a hippie chick. I wonder if she'll visit here, get to know Helen. Even before her mama died, Annie and her daddy didn't get along so hot. He was always fussing about her dropping out of college, and not doing anything with her life. Last I heard, she's living in Boone and working on a horse farm.

I put my basket of homegrown tomatoes on the counter, and some fresh eggs in the fridge. I felt bad for Helen when she first saw the kitchen, and her a cook on a TV show. She tried to play like everything here was "quaint" and "charming," but didn't fool me none. I knew good and well that Emmet hadn't told her how old-timey it was, or how Rosalyn wouldn't change anything. Helen told me how she'd be trying out recipes for her new cooking show this fall, and how she's writing a cookbook to go along with it. She sure won't get much cooking done unless she fixes up this god-awful kitchen. Rosalyn didn't cook because they either went out to eat, or had stuff catered from town. It's obvious that Helen's gonna be a lot different, but especially in the kitchen.

Upstairs, I lay the wood in the marble fireplace of the master suite, then turn back the covers on the bed. The mahogany half canopy is draped in heavy old lace, and looks like it was made for the bride of Dracula. So does every other dark, ugly thing in here, including the wallpaper. Poor Helen was going to use another room until she saw this was the only one with a shower. She had a hard enough time talking Emmet into coming here, she told me with a sigh, to make him go down the hall to bathe. So she was stuck with it. After placing a vase of yellow dahlias on her night table—trying to brighten things up—I skedaddle out of there.

Coming down the shadowy hallway, just before I get to the landing, it happens again. I've never told nobody, but there's a reason this house spooks me. Even before Rosalyn died, I had some strange experiences here. I'd be by myself, maybe downstairs in the kitchen, and I'd hear something upstairs plain as day, clomping around. For the longest time I didn't think nothing about it, so I'd go barreling up the staircase like a fool, thinking a squirrel or coon had gotten in. I never found a thing, not even in the attic. What was more peculiar, the noises didn't happen for a while, and enough time went by that I forgot about them. I'd come and go without looking over my shoulder for shadows, or jumping at the least little sound from dark, empty rooms. That changed last year, after Rosalyn died. Her funeral was held at a big fancy church in Atlanta, but the next day, the family and her friends came to Moonrise for a smaller service. They wanted to bury her ashes in the garden she'd loved.

I'd only been to burials in the cemetery, not a person's backyard. But I was raised to pay my respects to the dead, so I went.

The service turned out to be real nice instead of weird like I expected. They didn't have a preacher, but Linc read a passage from the Bible and a pretty poem. Each of them said something nice about Rosalyn, then threw a handful of her ashes into the hole Noel had dug for that purpose. It's way in the back of the gardens, beneath a magnolia that Rosalyn planted. When everybody finished, Noel refilled the hole, then put some rocks on the mound so it wouldn't look so raw. Afterward, Emmet had a catered supper for everybody. I didn't stay for that but came back the next day to straighten up. I was wiping the kitchen counters when I heard it again, upstairs in one of the empty rooms. *Thump, thump, thump.* That did it. I just threw down my dishrag and hightailed it out of there. And didn't go back for several days, either.

Since then, there was only one other time I thought I heard the haints, and that was the day I first met Helen. It was over a week ago now, the official beginning of the summer season. I'd been on the phone with Helen on and off all day, tracking her trip from south Florida to Highlands. She and Emmet were driving separately so they'd both have their cars up here, and Helen had a couple hours' head start. She didn't know Emmet'd asked me to be at Moonrise when she got here. A house that old had too many quirks for anybody to figure out on her own, he said, especially after such a long trip. So when Helen called to say she'd cleared Atlanta, I headed over here. No cleaning since I'd done so already, but I brought her a welcome basket and some zinnias from my yard.

As I did earlier today, I'd laid a fire in the master bedroom and started down the hall when I heard a noise. Since I hadn't heard anything strange here since the day after Rosalyn's service, my knees went weak and my breath caught in my throat. I stood just short of the stair landing while a shiver ran up and down my spine. Oh, great, I thought. The new wife will be here soon, and who shows up to welcome her but those dad-blamed ghosts?

That's when I realized the noise was coming from outside the house, not inside. From where I stood on the landing, I could bend down and see beneath the stained-glass inset over the front door. And when I did, I felt like a pure-tee fool. A car was parked out front, behind my truck, and what I'd heard was the slamming of car doors. It was a little gray Honda, and a woman stood beside it, peering all around. She must've made that racket getting something out of the trunk. Even though it was a tad earlier than I expected her, the new mistress of the house had arrived.

I remember how I watched her curiously, glad to have a chance before opening the front door and meeting her eyeball-to-eyeball on the steps. It turned out to be a stroke of luck, because it gave me time to put on my best poker face. One thing for sure: Helen wasn't *anything* like I expected. Despite Kit and Tansy's gossiping, I expected her to be more like Rosalyn. I couldn't have been more wrong. At my first sight of Helen Honeycutt, I knew she was as different from the last lady of the house as any two women could be.

For one thing, she looked almost like a teenager standing there, the wind from the lake blowing hard enough to flatten her clothes against her, toss her hair every which way. Not many women could wear their hair that way, cut short and choppy with streaks of blond shot through it, but it suited her. She had a dark tan and a really good figure, like she exercised a lot. I expected her to be pretty and she was, but in a whole different way from Rosalyn. Rosalyn held herself like a queen, and turned heads wherever she went. I figured Helen turned a few heads, too, but for different reasons.

When people don't know they're being watched, they act more like themselves. That afternoon, Helen stopped just before she got to the stone steps leading up to the front door, and I got a better look at her. In spite of her sassy swing, she looked so anxious that I pitied her. Her sunglasses were pushed to the top of her head, and she was staring at the house with real curiosity. By the way her face lit up, I figured she was thinking, Good Lord, what a mansion. If she'd had any idea what she was getting herself into, though, she should've been thinking, Oh, shit. Get me out of here!

4

helen

THE GANG'S ALL HERE

My eyelids are so heavy that I dare not lean against the headrest. If I do, I'm liable to be asleep before we're halfway up the driveway. I steal a glance at Emmet. Brow furrowed, his attention is focused on keeping the Jeep within the ruts of the narrow drive. Without taking his eyes off the road, he says, "You enjoyed the trip today, didn't you, baby?"

"I had a great time," I reply, but he doesn't hear me so I have to repeat myself. Speak up, he's always reminding me. Look directly at the camera with your chin lifted, and don't mumble. If your audience can't hear you, you've lost them.

"I'd never heard of the Biltmore Estate before," I tell him, and glance over to see that indulgent half smile of his.

"No, sweetheart," he says patiently. "The 'before' is unnecessary. Try it, and you'll see what I mean."

Dutifully I intone: "I'd never heard of the Biltmore Estate." It sounds better with the "before," I start to say, but don't. I can't expect him to help me if I'm going to argue about every little thing.

As though reading my mind, he says, "I'm not doing this again when the others are around, Helen. That's why I stopped earlier. They already think I'm an asshole without giving them more ammunition."

I smile and place a hand on his arm. "Oh, Emmet. Your friends might think you're an asshole, but they still adore you."

Emmet snorts, then turns his attention back to his driving. Both of us are right, I think, on all counts: His friends adore him, even if he is difficult at times. And he shouldn't have corrected me in front of them, even though I'd asked him to. Begged him to, actually. Ever since the station manager called to say they wanted to expand my spot to a half-hour show, I've been in a panic. I'd just gotten comfortable with my seven minutes on the noon show, gotten to where I handled it pretty well, even when they threw this at me. Who would've ever expected "Fit to Eat," my gimmicky little spot where I transformed fat-laden dishes into healthier ones, to be such a hit? The viewers couldn't get enough of it, and suddenly I was in demand. Or, as Emmet put it, a hot item. At first I'd balked, terrified at the prospect of facing the camera for a whole show. Only after Emmet agreed to coach me did I think I could do it. I insisted that he be merciless in pointing out my shortcomings; otherwise, how would I learn? He didn't want to see me humiliated, did he? After kissing my cheek, the smooth-talking devil said that I'd given him an impossible task because I was perfect, but I couldn't afford to listen to his sweet talk. How about my tentativeness, I demanded, the too-soft voice, the way I bumble around searching for words? He'd reluctantly signed on, but was right that his coaching shouldn't be done around anyone else. It makes him look bad, and me even worse.

We clear the rhododendron tunnel, and suddenly there it is, Moonrise. The storybook castle that has turned into my own personal House of Horrors. Emmet heads toward the carriage house in back, which serves as the garage. At the front of the house, however, he suddenly brakes and looks my way. I tilt my head curiously.

"You know what?" he says breezily. "I've changed my mind.

Think I'll go back and have a drink with Noel after all. That okay with you?"

"Of course," I say as I reach for the handle, hoping I don't sound too eager. All day I've had to fake it as we traipsed around the millions of gardens at Biltmore, then through the hundreds of rooms in the mansion. I dutifully oohed and aahed over everything, but was so exhausted I barely remember it. The only thing that saved us from a tour of the winery had been Linc, who begged off by saying he was too tired. I'd been horrified when Noel, who'd pushed Linc for the entire tour in a wheelchair, stepped back indignantly to say, "*You're* tired? What about *me*, you ungrateful gimp?" Only when everybody else laughed did I realize that Noel was teasing. Linc caught my expression and shot back, "Look at poor Helen's face, Noel. Gimp that I am, at least I'm not an insensitive brute like you." I'd blushed like a nitwit, and Emmet had rolled his eyes my way. Unamused, he admonished me for taking everything that damn-fool bunch said seriously. "Don't pay them any mind, sweetheart," he'd said. "No one else does."

Throwing Emmet a kiss, I'm out of the car before he can change his mind. After our return from Asheville to Laurel Cottage where we fetched the Jeep, Noel and Tansy had invited us in for a drink. Or rather, Noel had; Tansy told him rather curtly that she had an "engagement" tonight and would have to excuse herself. I begged off, too, though I'd secretly hoped that Emmet would stay and keep Noel company. If I could just have a little time to rest up before dinner, I might make it through the rest of the evening without collapsing.

I wave my unsuspecting husband off with a mixture of guilt and relief, then force myself to wait until the Jeep disappears before turning toward the house. My exhaustion isn't just from my restless nights; the emotional drain is taking its toll as well. Walking up the stone steps to the house takes all the strength I possess. What I really want to do is get in my car and head straight back to Florida.

As soon as I reach the front door—propped open to catch the lake breezes—I realize that Willa is still here cleaning, and my heart sinks. I didn't see her truck, which must've been parked on the side of the house. I glance at my watch to assure myself that she'll be leaving soon. Stepping inside the entrance hall, I call out, and Willa answers from the back of the house.

Willa'd been the one who waited for me the first day I came here, a day that's imprinted on my brain—and not in a good way, either. So much has changed since then, and in such a short time! I'd come to Highlands with such hope, so thrilled to be at a place I'd dreamed of since finding the photo album. As soon as I laid eyes on Moonrise, it was obvious that the pictures hadn't even come close to capturing its astonishing beauty. The towering house and stately old trees, the parklike setting with its vast lake view—all of it was far grander than I'd imagined. The black-and-white photos failed to show how the slanted rays of the sun burnished the ivy-clad stone of the house, or how they reflected off the mullioned windows like thousands of crushed diamonds. Or the way the sun sent luminous streaks of light spilling across the grounds. Despite the silvery image of its name, Moonrise first greeted me silhouetted in gold.

Willa McFee had been another image from the photo album that turned out to be far different from what I expected. When she and I'd talked in preparation for my and Emmet's arrival, her voice had been as hesitant and faltering as mine, with a brogue so thick I had trouble understanding her. I'd formed a picture in my mind of a roughhewn farm girl, shy and awkward, maybe a bit simpleminded. That was shattered the minute she flung open the door and peered at me in undisguised curiosity. Bright-eyed and apple-cheeked, Willa McFee had the sort of lush, buxom looks rarely seen these days. Although she was clad in jeans, a flannel shirt, and work boots, I could imagine her in a Botticelli painting, with that vivid red hair and creamy complexion. I liked her on sight.

I don't think the feeling was mutual, however. Willa's greeting to me had been friendly enough, but guarded. Wary, even. Emmet had tried to prepare me for the mountain folks, whom he described as a breed unto themselves. Most of them are descendants of the original settlers who came from the highlands of Scotland, he'd told me, and are a clannish, suspicious lot. They take their time warming up to strangers. I offered my hand, which Willa had taken in her large, sunburned one with a grip so strong I tried not to wince.

Today I pause in the entrance hall as my eyes adjust to the dim light, then see Willa coming toward me. Her backpack is slung over her arm, so she's on her way out. "Y'all are back early," she calls out in a hearty voice. "Everybody have a big time?"

I assure her that everyone had a "big" time indeed, then wait by the marble-topped table where I've been leaving my purse, easy to grab on my way out. Since our arrival here, Emmet and I've been out every single day, and most evenings. No wonder I'm exhausted. I sneak a glance at myself in the massive, gold-framed mirror that dominates the entryway. My God, I look like shit! I watch Willa's reflection as she approaches, and her expression tells me that she agrees. She catches herself when her eyes meet mine, however, and she smiles.

"The stove wasn't on, Helen," she says as she hefts the backpack up on her shoulder. "But I still can't figure out how you're gonna cook fancy recipes in that thing, especially with the gas acting up."

I eye my reflection as I run my fingers through my hair, pretending the reason I paused by the mirror was to primp. I'd rather Willa think I'm vain than crazy, checking myself out to see if the services of an undertaker are called for. "Believe it or not, hon," I say in a light voice, "that's a very fine and valuable old Viking stove, better than anything I've ever used." Although her reflection is still smiling at mine, her blue eyes are troubled. I step closer to the mirror to smooth down an errant eyebrow. "Besides, none of my recipes are fancy."

Her face falls, either in surprise or disappointment. I don't yet know her well enough to tell. "Oh," she says. "I thought . . ." When I turn to her questioningly, she looks embarrassed, and I wonder what she's heard. It's only natural that everyone's curious about me, the new mistress of Moonrise, and I wonder what they're saying. I'd love to ask Willa, but I'd never put her in such a position. Not that she'd tell me, anyway. Another thing Emmet's cautioned me about, the fierce loyalty of the mountain people. If they like you, they'd die for you. If not, don't turn your back on them. I've gone out of my way to try to make Willa like me.

Today I'm too exhausted to stand and make small talk, so I mention a much-needed bathroom run. Willa's good-bye strikes me as a bit too hearty, then she pauses by the door to glance my way. "Helen? You okay?" she asks hesitantly.

It's my turn for the too-hearty smile, the dismissive wave of my hand. "I'm great," I tell her, practically pushing her out the door. "See you next week, okay?"

I stick my head out and wave as Willa crosses the driveway toward her truck, which I now see under the low branches of the hickory. I don't want her carrying tales to the others, telling them how tired I appeared, or how I look like I hadn't slept since I've been here. I can only imagine their response to *that* observation, considering the bawdy humor of that bunch. Emmet and I heard our share of newlywed jokes at the station. I wish to God that was the reason for my exhaustion, and I'm sure Emmet does, too. Despite his obvious bewilderment, he's been remarkably patient with my lamebrain excuses for avoiding him in bed. I can hardly tell him the truth: *Not tonight, dear. I can't with the ghosts watching.*

I close the front door behind me, only to stand lifelessly in the entryway for several weary moments. I wasn't lying to Willa; I'm heading upstairs to the bathroom, then to change clothes. After which, I'm going to the coziest place I've found in this tomb of a house. Which happens, not coincidently, to be outside it, not in. Taking a deep breath, I ponder yet again what I've wondered so often lately: How could a place this beautiful be so unwelcoming? It wasn't that way at first. I fell in love with Moonrise the moment I laid eyes on it. Entering the house, I marveled at everything I saw: the vaulted ceiling of the entryway; the diamond-paned windows with their stained-glass insets; the massive staircase looming through the shadows at the back of the hall. Stepping over the threshold of Moonrise was like taking a journey back in time, to another era, and I went eagerly.

Willa, my tour guide that first day, had been as keen to show me the house as I'd been to see it. My surprise at her knowledge of Victorian history and decor must've been obvious because she confessed that Rosalyn made her learn all that historical "stuff." As impressive as it is, Willa'd confided, Victorian decor was not to her taste. Matter of fact, she'd added, she found it downright god-awful. I agreed that it was overwrought and way too formal for me, too, yet perfect for this setting. The front parlor was crammed with furnishings: a velvet sofa and wing-backed chairs facing the black marble fireplace; curlicued tables topped by old-fashioned lamps; brocade curtains and lace panels framing windows. I could picture corseted women in bustled dresses seated in little groups as they sipped tea from china cups, white-gloved pinkies aloft.

In addition to the parlor and a turret room with unique curved windows, the downstairs contained a formal dining room, extensive library, two sitting rooms (one of which would become my office), and the old-fashioned kitchen with an adjoining glassed-in porch. My gushing enthusiasm had not only pleased Willa but also egged her on; her formal tour gave way to a chatty history of the place and its occupants. I noted that she caught herself before revealing too much about Rosalyn. As eager as I was to know more about her, I made myself tread carefully. Any comments Willa made about my predecessor came casually, in some detail or the other about the house.

Even so, that first afternoon I was able to learn things about Rosalyn Justice that I wouldn't have known otherwise. It's funny how much a house can reveal about a person, more than just his or her taste and tidiness. I walked through the cavernous halls of Moonrise and began to understand why it was more museum than home. Rosalyn would've been raised in a place like this, I thought, a showpiece to good taste and breeding. I figured her childhood home had been an extension of the Harmon family image rather than a place to kick off one's shoes and unwind. Although Emmet'd never admitted it, I felt sure that his and Rosalyn's house in Atlanta had been the same, the one he sold before the move to Florida. The things most of us associate with a homey atmosphere would've been lacking in any of Rosalyn's households: piles of mail and magazines; newspapers on the breakfast table or strewn around easy chairs; kids' drawings taped to the fridge next to the shopping list. There'd be few cozy nooks; Rosalyn and her breed chose furnishings for historical significance and aesthetics rather than comfort. Her houses would always be showy and formal, even the summer places where they went to get away from such trappings.

That day I walked the hallways in the forever-stilled footsteps of a woman I'd never know, and looked for her everywhere. I paused to study the furnishings of each room for clues. What did it say about my predecessor that she had favored dark jewel tones over pastels, even in her boudoir? Or that her signature scent was a bold, heady floral (lily, maybe) that still lingered in the air like a sad melody? It was obvious that her kitchen was rarely used, yet the cookware and serving pieces were the finest I'd ever seen. The butler's pantry was stocked with the most expensive liquor available.

Because Emmet's preference was Russian vodka, I knew the other bottles had been selected for their frequent visitors. To me, that meant Rosalyn was the perfect hostess, floating from guest to guest with the ease of a queen among her subjects. Did she enchant each of them with her beauty and elegance? And did her husband's eyes follow her with unmistakable pride and adoration?

Today, as on the first day of my arrival, I have to force myself to stop thinking such thoughts. If I'm not careful, I'll become obsessed with a dead woman—as I'm dangerously close to doing already. Sometimes, I go to the turret room and stare at a portrait of her, the one I initially failed to see. Only later did I realize that Willa'd stood in front of the portrait so I wouldn't notice it. The turret room's an extension of the library, which it leads to, and only has a small seating area against the back wall. The room's main attraction is the circular wall of windows, two stories high and with bookshelves underneath, where Willa led me that first day, and where I stood gaping at the panoramic view of the lake. Willa moved me quickly from there into the library; the following day I saw why. Hanging on the wall behind where she had stood was an oil painting of a young woman in a silvery-white ball gown, a sheer tulle wrap draped around her bare shoulders. It wasn't terribly large, as portraits go, being much too tasteful to be life-sized. Moving closer, I saw that the woman was Rosalyn.

I couldn't blame Willa for wanting to shield me from the portrait as long as possible, or to avoid my questions about the subject. I only wish I'd left well enough alone, that I'd not seen it until I was more firmly entrenched into my new life and its strange setting. In the photos I'd seen of Rosalyn, she'd been a lovely, poised woman in her early fifties; seeing her like this, young and still untouched by life, I realized with an unwelcome twinge of jealousy how utterly beautiful she was. I stood before the portrait and studied her flawless ivory shoulders; her swanlike neck, unadorned by jewels;

the tilt of her aristocratic chin; the silver-blond hair in that most elegant of styles, the chignon. The painter had captured a playful glint in her smoky blue eyes, a hint of a seductive smile on her lips. This was the woman whom Emmet had fallen in love with, the one I suspected he'd always love. Studying the painting, I could understand why. I'd heard from everyone that Rosalyn was near about perfect; that such a paragon should also be so beautiful told me all I needed to know about the fairness of life.

Every time I returned to the painting, I chastised myself for caring, for being intimidated by Rosalyn's beauty. Why do women do that? I wondered. Until I saw the portrait, I'd taken pride in my fit, trim body, the result of a stringent diet and exercise; in my smooth, bronzed skin; in my tousled and highlighted coif that cost me a month's salary with every trip to the salon, but gave me the confidence to appear before a camera. Looking at Rosalyn, I saw myself as I really was: coarse and blowsy, an overripe, sun-baked Cracker trying to pass herself off as someone of taste and refinement. What had I been thinking, prissing around town in a tank top with such a low-cut neckline? Sun-browned cleavage was not only tacky but so *Florida*. I studied my so-called shapely legs and firm upper arms, another source of pride, and realized I'd mistaken muscle-bound for fit. And whatever had possessed me to have a Celtic cross—tiny though it was—tattooed just above my right ankle? Rosalyn would've never done such a thing, nor painted her toenails a lurid shade of pink. I tormented myself by returning to the portrait of my predecessor over and over until I understood the difference between me and her. Rosalyn was a slender, single-stemmed white rose, while I was one of those passion flowers commonly found in ditches—purple, overblown, and going to seed, fast.

After changing into jeans and zipping on a hoodie, both blanket-soft from so much wear since my arrival, I hurry downstairs to catch the sunset from my newly discovered perch outside. I stop by the kitchen to grab a bottle of chilled wine and a paper cup, then exit the house through the side porch. The Victorians had been big on porches, according to Willa, which they called verandas and furnished like outdoor parlors. The porches of Moonrise are as formal and uninviting as the rest of it, so I pass quickly through the one on the far side of the house, overlooking the lake. It's quite grand with a stenciled ceiling, a fireplace against the stone wall of the house, and antique wicker decor, and I'll be entertaining out here again soon. But for now, I scamper down the steps and across an unused, neglected patio, then trod down a flagstone pathway that leads away from the house, toward the side of the mountain.

Whenever I'm outside, I'm careful to avert my eyes from the overgrown gardens in back. The sight depresses me more in the daytime than it does at night when I'm sleepless, and its sad, wild beauty calls out to me. In sunlight, the garden is unsightly but unremarkable, just another gone-to-seed backyard crying out for a Weed Eater. Being nocturnal, nothing much blooms there in the daytime, anyway. At night, however, the moon coaxes everything to life, with buds bursting forth from the dark earth like the souls of the dead on Judgment Day. It creeps me out, for some reason. The pathway veers away from the house and I raise my eyes in relief. Thankfully, the ruined gardens are now beyond my line of vision.

The flagstone path disappears into a sun-shot, shadowy tunnel of rhododendrons, much like the one at the entrance to the house. When I emerge, the pathway comes to an end on a secluded terrace nestled behind a copse of laurel. The terrace appears to be perched on the edge of the gently sloping mountain, in a cleared-off space that offers a bird's-eye view of the lake. I make my way to a small sitting area at the far end, taking care not to slip on the mossy stones of the terrace. I was exploring the grounds a few days ago when I came across this spot, and could tell that no one had been here in a very long time. There's only an old bent willow settee and chair here, and I plop on the settee gratefully. When I first stumbled on the terrace, I figured the seating was purely decorative, unable to imagine actually sitting on branches twisted into chair shapes without any cushions. Resting from my walk, I'd perched on the chair and found it surprisingly cozy, age having worn the willow as smooth as stone. I then dragged the old furniture to the edge of the terrace for a better view of the lake, making my own little tree house, and I had my refuge.

After pouring myself a cup of Chablis, I settle back into the settee, squirming until I'm comfortably situated. Funny, a house as grand and richly furnished as Moonrise at my disposal, and I can only relax when it's out of my sight. I sip the wine and look down at the lake, where the last of the day's sunbeams prance on its rippling surface like bright little seahorses. Looking Glass Lake is a long, spectacular body of water surrounded by woods; my lofty perch provides me a good view of the houses fronting its banks. A lot of them are hidden away in the woods; only the sight of a chimney or roofline above the treetops gives away their presence. Thankfully, the three houses that interest me the most are the ones most clearly in my sight.

Laurel Cottage is the closest, on the same side of the lake as Moonrise and right below us. Even from this distance, it's so charming it appears make-believe, the dwelling of the seven dwarfs, and I halfway expect to see Snow White waltzing down the garden paths, singing to the birds. Despite the drought, the gardens surrounding the cottage are riotous with blossoms and butterflies. It's a fanciful place, with koi ponds, a stone wishing well, and topiary cut in the shape of the Mad Hatter's tea party. I spot Emmet's Jeep parked in front. He and Noel are most likely having their martinis on the back porch, which has French country decor and is every bit as exquisite as the rest of the house. Laurel Cottage is the only one of the three that I've been inside.

Linc and Myna's cabin is a bit farther down, perched on a little cove that juts out into the lake. The porch appears to hang precariously over the water, and Emmet told me they used to dive directly into the lake from the porch railing. The house is an authentic log cabin that I'm dying to see, but Myna can't have guests over until Linc's comfortable with the new handicapped features. Which made sense to me, though I overheard Tansy and Kit saying that Myna couldn't be happier at having an excuse not to reciprocate dinner invitations. Emmet was amused when I repeated their conversation, and told me that Myna wasn't highly regarded by the others. She seems friendly enough, I responded, but of course I hardly knew her. For that, Emmet responded drily, I should consider myself fortunate.

Kit also has an excuse not to entertain because her house, located on the other side of Linc's, is in the final stages of a big remodeling project. She's talked of nothing else since I've met her, which is good since I'd wondered how she'd take to me. I'm still wondering. I've not only sensed her reticence at accepting me into the fold; she's made several remarks that could be interpreted as such. Plus she's always studying me curiously, sometimes not even turning away when I catch her. One of those times I felt sure she was regarding me with something like pity. Because she seems so sweet on the surface, there's nothing I can pinpoint as proof of her hostility. When we first arrived and everyone came over to meet me, I asked Emmet afterward if his friends had approved of me. His look was so scathing that I've dared not bring it up again. I should've known better than to ask him, of course. Emmet Justice is not a person to give a rat's ass whether he has the approval of anyone else.

I pour myself a bit more wine, thinking back on the day I finally met Emmet's group of friends face-to-face. Maybe enough time's passed that I can get some perspective on that occasion. Since that rather unnerving evening, we've been in such a whirlwind of activity that I haven't had a chance to process much of anything. Not only that, the long-awaited meeting happened the day after Emmet and I arrived in Highlands, before I even had time to get unpacked, or oriented to my surroundings.

My first glimpse of the Blue Ridge Mountains had been nearly a religious experience. The two-day drive from Fort Lauderdale was so long and tiring that when I hit the horrendous traffic of Atlanta on the second afternoon, I was sure I'd made a terrible mistake. What had I been *thinking*, insisting Emmet and I spend our first summer together away from home? There was no turning back; we'd already sublet our town house for the summer. But a couple of hours beyond Atlanta, the landscape began to change from rural to mountainous, and my despair lifted. Although still in north Georgia, I'd entered another world. At the foothills of the Blue Ridge, I turned off the four-lane highway and onto a narrow road that took me into North Carolina. For several miles, I clung to the wheel white-knuckled while the road, which appeared to be carved out of the side of a mountain, wound upward. At a scenic overlook halfway up the mountain, I pulled over, wide-eyed and weak-kneed. There I stood and looked down at a blue-hazed valley so beautiful that it brought tears to my eyes. I'd been born and raised by the sea, cradled by sun and salt water; but at that moment, I fell in love with mountain vistas.

The remainder of the journey only deepened my reverence. The dizzying mountain road continued through the storybook village of Highlands, then wound past Looking Glass Lake, a couple of miles outside town. Following Emmet's directions, I turned off just beyond the lake; later I'd learn that the highway followed the Cullasaja River for several miles as it roared and tumbled down a rocky gorge, the site of several well-known waterfalls.

My arrival at Moonrise, then Willa's informative tour, remains a blur to me. After two hard days of driving, I was exhausted, both physically and mentally. Moonrise was so much grander than I'd expected that I became irrationally angry at Emmet. Why hadn't he *told* me? Fuming, I swore to myself that I never would've married Emmet if I'd known he ran with the jet set. Palm Beach was full of jet-setters, and I didn't like them worth a damn. Fortunately I kept those foolish thoughts to myself, and Emmet attributed my sulky silence to exhaustion. To my further dismay, we ended up in the same bed he'd shared with his previous wife since the master bedroom was the only one with an adjacent shower. Why hadn't I thought of which room would be ours *before* we arrived? I fell into such an exhausted sleep that I didn't wake until noon the next day.

I awoke refreshed, my old self again, and bounded out of bed starving and eager for my first day at Moonrise. Following my nose to the kitchen, I made my way down the massive staircase to the back of the house. Emmet'd either just gotten up, or was brewing a fresh pot of coffee for me. More likely the latter; his years as an anchorman had made him an early riser. I paused at the kitchen door, stopped by the sight of Emmet at the old-fashioned stove, studying it in bewilderment. Because he was frowning in concentration and didn't see me, I was able to watch him unobserved, one of my favorite pastimes. Sometimes I'd lie in bed and watch him dress, mugging his reflection in the mirror as he patted down his springy, gray-streaked hair impatiently. If he caught me, he'd strike bodybuilder poses until I giggled, but he was clearly disconcerted by my scrutiny. He couldn't understand why I enjoyed simply gazing at him, watching him in action, and frankly I wasn't sure, either. Although attractive in a craggy sort of way, Emmet was hardly eye candy. He looked more like an ex-linebacker than the classically handsome, square-jawed anchorman of most news shows. When we first met, he appeared so gruff and unapproachable that I avoided him, and he proved to be as scrappy, combative, and tough as he looked. Yet I melted like candle wax under a flame whenever his eyes met mine.

Spotting me at the door, Emmet called out his usual greeting, "Hey, Honeycutt," and I responded with "Hi yourself, big guy." My vexation of the previous day was forgotten, and I went into his arms, loving him again.

My joy was short-lived. To my surprise, Emmet announced that he had invited the gang over for drinks that evening, only a few hours away because I'd slept so late. At least he had the grace to look apologetic when I went into full panic mode. I reminded him that we'd *just* arrived, that we hadn't even *unpacked* the car, and that I couldn't *possibly* entertain on such short notice—I didn't even know my way around the kitchen! Emmet knocked down my arguments one after the other. He promised to get us unpacked, and to help me get ready for the gathering. He'd already ordered a cheese and fruit tray from the caterer in town, and was about to make a run to the wine store. Plus, we'd entertain on the side porch, not inside the house, so I need not fret about fixing it up. With a defeated sigh, I gave in.

It had been surprisingly cool that evening, and I'd ended up changing clothes twice before our guests arrived. I'd never tell Emmet that the oh-so-smart black sundress I'd splurged on at one of Fort Lauderdale's ritziest boutiques had been with this occasion in mind, hoping to impress his friends. As it turned out, I might as well have saved my money. The only sweater I brought was coral colored, which made the black dress look like a Halloween costume. Didn't matter; I still had to wear it. Packing up, Emmet'd warned me about mountain nights being cool, but I hadn't understood that to mean freezing-ass *cold*.

Taking pity on me, Emmet built a fire. The fire made the open, spacious porch cozier, especially after he lit the wall lamps, which gave off just the right glow for a twilight evening. As the time for our gathering grew nearer, my trepidation gave way to excitement. I'd wanted time to throw an impressive party, to wow everyone with my entertaining skills, but conceded that Emmet'd been right. His friends were as eager to meet me as I was them, and they'd understand that our getting together was the important thing, not a fancy spread. Or so I told myself as I awaited their arrival. Emmet watched me with such amusement that I dared not look his way at the sound of a car in the driveway. Instead, I busied myself at the wicker table rearranging Willa's yellow zinnias, the only centerpiece I had.

Tansy was the first to appear. Emmet'd instructed everyone to park on the side and come directly to the porch, which would be easier for Linc than trudging all the way through the house. I had my back to Emmet, who was at the makeshift bar setup in the corner, when I heard him call out, "Tansy!" I turned to see him moving forward to greet the woman who was coming up the porch steps, her arms outstretched.

I watched as Tansy hugged Emmet, then stepped back to take his face in her hands and kiss him right on the mouth. Laughing, she used her pinkie to wipe the dark red lipstick from his lips. Their greeting gave me time to study her before she turned to me. As I'd feared, she was every bit as intimidating as I'd imagined from our brief, unsatisfactory phone conversations. As tall as Emmet, with glossy black hair in startling contrast to her magnolia-white skin, Tansy was the epitome of glamour and sophistication, the kind of woman who'd always made me tongue-tied and knock-kneed. Twirling around in a side-tied dress that showed off long, slim legs, she made her way from Emmet to me, and I gulped.

"So you're Helen," Tansy said as she eyed me with unabashed curiosity. "I'm Tansy Dunwoody." Her black eyes boring into mine, she grasped my hand with a grip as strong as Willa's had been.

"I guessed that," I said with a laugh. I hated my nervous little laugh, which I seemed to have no control over, especially in situations like this. "It's wonderful to meet you at last, Tansy."

With my hand still held firmly in hers, Tansy glanced over her shoulder at Emmet and hissed, "Cradle robber."

I was so taken aback I was speechless, but not Emmet. Eyes glittering, he raised his glass to her in a mock salute and said, "Ah, yes. My child bride."

I gasped and freed my hand from Tansy's as I cried out, "Oh, no—not at all, Tansy! I've always been told I look younger than I am. Emmet's just teasing you . . ." My voice trailed off and I looked toward Emmet helplessly.

To my further surprise, Tansy waved off my protests, swung her head back to me, and said as casually as if we had been discussing the weather: "So, Helen. How do you like Moonrise?"

I took a deep, bracing breath before spouting out such overwrought hyperbole in praise of the house that I cringed hearing it. Mercifully, the rest of the gang appeared before I could make a complete fool of myself, and I stopped to wait for them. Their entrance was preceded by much laughter, and the sound of shuffling feet and scraping wheels on the stone walkway that led from the driveway to the side porch. The deep, cultured voice I recognized as Noel's boomed out of the darkness: "Jesus, Linc—I'm *dying* here. Speed your ass up, man."

Linc's response was muffled, as though he held his head down, but we heard him say, "Hey, you wanna drive? Be my guest." When a woman gave a sharp retort that I didn't hear, Emmet and Tansy exchanged amused glances, and Emmet murmured, "Some things never change, do they?"

My initial impression of the others, Noel, Linc, Myna, and Kit, was a confused blur because everyone was talking at once when they emerged into the yellow circle of light spilling out from the porch. Pushing his walker, Linc led the way with Noel close behind as if to catch him if he got tripped up. Myna was at Linc's side, and slightly behind her was a shadowy figure that must be Kit

Rutherford. My eyes swept over them rapidly as I sorted out who was who and wondered if their greeting to me would be as unsettling as Tansy's had been.

Emmet moved swiftly down the steps to help Noel get Linc onto the porch, pausing first to give Linc and Noel the back-pounding kind of greeting that men give each other, followed by a hug for the two women. Seeing Linc, I understood why Emmet'd been so concerned about him. Hunched over the walker, Linc appeared so frail that I wouldn't have known he was the same man in the group picture by the waterfall. Since that photo was taken, he'd grown a sparse little beard that, like his hair, was heavily streaked with gray. Although his thin arms were still trembling with the effort of the walk, Linc threw back his head and whooped with laughter when Emmet and Noel picked him up, walker and all, and deposited him on the porch.

Noel Clements was a stunner, so impossibly good-looking that I had to tear my eyes from him to search out the others. I didn't exactly recognize Myna from her photo, but knew she was the one climbing the steps while Kit remained in the shadows. Even if I hadn't seen her picture beforehand, I would've picked Myna out as the artsy one of the group. Rail thin with a pale, sharp face, wire-rimmed glasses, and wild, frizzy hair, she had the look. I wasn't sure *what* she was wearing, but it appeared to be some sort of coarsely woven dashiki, set off by a bronze cross and dangling earrings much too large for her small frame. Studying her, I understood why she wasn't particularly liked by the others. Her strangeness set her apart.

Noel reached me first, wowing me by saying my name softly before bending his fair head to kiss me on the cheek. I flushed and fluttered like a schoolgirl, then took the arm he extended to lead me over to Linc. With a saucy toss of her head, Tansy left my side and headed toward the fireplace. I held out both hands to Linc, who had moved from his walker to sit in a sturdy wicker chair. "Helen!" Grinning, Linc grabbed my hands as though we were long-lost friends. "We meet at last. Please forgive me for not getting up."

Linc Varner was a small, fine-boned man; his twinkling eyes, playful expression, and wispy beard made him look like a leprechaun. When he introduced Myna, who was putting away the walker, I turned toward her eagerly. I'd purchased her books and pored over the poetry, which was way too obtuse for me, but I was still anxious to meet a famous poet.

"This is *such* an honor, Myna," I declared as I shook her hand. A huge silver ring on her middle finger jabbed my palm painfully. "I absolutely *love* your work."

There was no mistaking a guffaw from Tansy, and I flushed in response. Standing erect, Myna gave me a tight smile. Behind the wire-rimmed glasses, her pale eyes glittered. "Thank you, Helen," she said shortly. Her voice was clipped and nasal, definitely not Southern. "Always a pleasure to meet a fan," she added. "Especially around here." She glanced around at the others with something like malice.

As if to diffuse the tension, Noel moved in quickly. With a little bow, he handed Myna a glass of red wine, Linc a beer, and told me that Emmet was bringing mine over himself. Twirling around, Noel pointed a finger at the woman who had silently appeared to stand next to me. "Kit? Pick your poison."

"Red's fine," she responded in a cool voice, then held out a hand to me. "Hello, Helen. I'm Kit Rutherford."

With her hand in mine, Kit and I took each other's measure. Because she'd been half hidden in the photos, I wasn't expecting her to be quite so pretty. What a sight she and Rosalyn must have been together! A head taller than me and slender as a model, Kit had light brown hair, olive-hued skin, and hazel eyes. She was simply but stylishly dressed in a crisp white shirt, designer jeans, and sandals with heels, which struck me as the perfect attire for the cool evenings here. I had the sudden, unwelcome thought that Kit would've been a more suitable replacement for Rosalyn, her long-time friend and roommate, than someone like me. How had Emmet missed so obvious a match? Kit greeted me by squeezing my hands and saying it was a pleasure to meet me, and I forced those hurtful thoughts out of my mind.

This time it was Emmet who stepped up to diffuse the awkwardness. He strolled over to me with a white wine seltzer in one hand and his customary martini in the other. I took the wine from him gratefully, hoping no one noticed my hand trembling. Emmet placed an arm around my shoulder as he looked around at his friends, who had ended up in a semicircle around Linc's chair. They waited expectantly, and I watched them watch my husband. Managing to look both rakish and elegant, Noel leaned against the porch railing with an amused expression on his face and a frosted mug of beer in his hand. Across from him, Tansy held a glass of wine to her full red lips, which were turned up ever so slightly at the corners. Over the rim of the glass, her coal-black eyes were directed at me. Myna's eyes, on the other hand, darted from one of us to the other, while Kit's remained remote and unreadable. Only Linc regarded the rest of us with what appeared to be genuine curiosity, oblivious to the tension that had crept into our gathering like the fog from the lake.

Scowling, Emmet looked down at me in sudden irritation. "Damn! I should've gotten champagne, sweetheart. Why didn't you remind me?"

Before I could respond, the others chimed in. Linc hooted derisively and said, "Probably because she knows what a cheapskate you are, my man."

"Yeah, Emmet," Noel agreed. "Don't blame it on Helen." Turning to me, he added, "The cheap son of a bitch probably planned it this way. He's the one who went into town for the booze, right? Pretending he was helping you out?"

"Well, he did, but—" I began when Noel stopped me with a shout of laughter.

"I knew it!" he cried, then leaned over to click his mug against Linc's. While Kit and I were greeting each other, I'd been vaguely aware of a small drama playing out next to us. Myna had protested when Noel brought Linc a beer, and I heard Noel say curtly that the doctor had okayed one a day, if she recalled. Surely she wasn't implying that he'd give Linc anything harmful, he'd added, but I'd missed Myna's response.

Emmet turned to me and sighed in exasperation. "Now you see why I didn't want you to meet my so-called friends, Honeycutt?" The fondness in his voice softened his words, however, and the others laughed good-naturedly. Waving them off, Emmet held his glass high. "Our next get-together, I'll furnish the finest Moët. For now, we'll toast with what we have. Helen and I would like to thank each of you for coming over tonight. As you know, she's been quite anxious to meet everyone."

On the other side of me, Tansy murmured, "Beware of what you want. You might get it."

"Let me add a toast to the newlyweds," Noel interjected in a hearty voice, "from all of us."

With much clamor and clanking of glass against glass, we toasted old friends and new; Emmet and myself; the new bride (this from Tansy); our upcoming summer together; and at least a dozen other things. After so many refilled wineglasses (without the aid of my usual splash of seltzer), I got rather woozy, but at least the tension had dissipated. Or so I thought. Before another toast could be raised, I spoke up. "Before I get too smashed to remember my manners, please help yourselves to the food."

"I cannot *wait*," Tansy sang out as she waltzed over to the wicker table. "All Emmet's talked about is what a great cook you are."

Before I could explain that I hadn't made anything, Tansy had grabbed a plate and started piling it high. "Hey, Tans," Noel called out from his perch on the railing. "Don't forget the rest of us are hungry, too. Fix me a plate while you're at it."

"Actually," I began, "Emmet had to get the food from . . . ah . . . where did you say you got it, honey?"

But my voice was lost in the clamor of Tansy telling Noel to fix his own damn plate; Linc and Emmet laughing at their exchange; Myna announcing that *she'd* fix Linc's plate, thank you; and Kit slinking over to the table to inspect everything. I cleared my throat and tried again, but by then Tansy had popped one of the miniature cheese rolls into her mouth, declared it better than anything she'd ever gotten from the caterer here, and said she simply *must* have the recipe. When I finally made myself heard, Noel threw his head back and laughed.

"So, Tansy, those cheese rolls are better than the caterer's, huh?" he teased. With a bored expression, Tansy gave Noel the finger, and I let out a giggle, startled by the obscene gesture from such an elegant-looking woman.

Despite being catered rather than homemade, the party tray provided enough distraction to carry us through the cocktail hour. While everyone ate and refilled their glasses, they threw questions at me. Did I love the mountains, or find them claustrophobic? Did I think Moonrise was fabulous, or overwhelming? Were Emmet and I *really* working this summer, or had we made that up to get away from our jobs? And speaking of my job, what exactly did I do, anyway? So I actually *liked* to cook, then? Anything having to do with my and Emmet's relationship was taboo, I noted. No one asked how we met, how long we'd known each other, or any of the usual questions you might ask a newly married couple. Even less was brought up about my personal life. Linc inquired politely whether my son, Adam, would be visiting. Adam was spending some time with his father in Miami, I replied, before heading north for his first year of med school. Johns Hopkins, I added casually, to which everyone responded enthusiastically, as duly impressed as I'd shamelessly hoped they'd be.

Kit Rutherford had contributed little to the conversation the entire evening, except to complain about the remodeling of her house. Since I hadn't heard about it, I asked what she was having done. Making a face, Tansy cut me off with a dramatic wave of her hand. "Oh, God—don't get her started on that topic, Helen. We'll be here all night, and I'm sure you and Emmet are still exhausted from your trip."

It was the perfect segue to end our get-together, and thankfully the others took the hint and made noises to leave. Despite the subtle tension that had hung around like an unwelcome guest, the evening might've come to a fairly pleasant close if Kit hadn't insisted on helping me clear the table. I tried to discourage her, saying as forcefully as I could that Emmet and I would clean up after they left. Emmet, too, told her to let it be, and Tansy said if Kit was riding back with them, she'd better get her ass in the car. But Kit shook her head and said she wouldn't dream of leaving us to clean up the mess—her mama had raised her better. No *true* Southern belle would do such a thing.

Later I'd wonder if Kit had merely been looking for an excuse to go inside. Because a small bathroom is located near the porch, there hadn't been a reason for any of them to wander through the house. To my dismay, when Kit followed me into the kitchen, her arms full of dirty plates, she looked around wide-eyed before bursting into tears. Tansy came running in to glare at me, as though I'd said something to upset her friend. I stood by helplessly as Kit dumped the dishes into the sink with tears rolling down her flushed cheeks. Throwing me a look, Tansy enclosed Kit in her arms and led her out of the kitchen. From the porch I could hear the cries of concern, then Noel's voice. "Was the kitchen that big of a mess, honey?" he said, but no one laughed in response.

Before everyone left, Kit apologized, saying how she never imagined seeing Rosalyn's kitchen would affect her like that, but the harm had been done. The evening ended on a sour note, and I fretted as I cleaned up. Emmet was silent and unapproachable as he worked beside me. When I asked him if he thought it went well, he shrugged. "I guess so," he said tonelessly. "Didn't you?" Turning away abruptly, he announced that he was wiped out and hitting the sack. Before leaving, he stopped by the butler's pantry and fixed himself a nightcap—a double, I noted glumly.

I lingered in the kitchen as long as I could, putting off the moment I'd be forced to climb the long flight of stairs to our bedroom. Somehow I knew that the previous night, my first in the house—in *Rosalyn's* house—would be the last good night of sleep I'd have here. When I finally went to bed, I lay awake and listened to the strange noises of an old house. The sounds were unfamiliar and somehow frightening, as though they were whispering me a warning.

———

SHAKING OFF THE memory of that unsettling night, I see Emmet's Jeep pulling out of Noel's driveway and get to my feet, the wine bottle tucked under my arm. If the bright pink glow beyond the mountaintops is any indication, this evening's sunset will be something to behold. I hurry down the pathway to join Emmet for the viewing, a favorite ritual of ours. He'll be looking for me.

Just as I emerge from the suddenly dark rhododendron tunnel into the golden light of late afternoon I see it out of the corner of my eye and I blink in surprise. Someone is in the moon gardens, moving swiftly away from the house. From here, it appears to be a man.

Emmet? But what would he be doing out there? He can hardly bear the sight of the gardens; I can't imagine him suddenly deciding to wander through them. Plus, there's hardly been enough time for him to get to the house, much less around back.

I'm almost to the house and about to call out, but I no longer see the dark figure moving through the trees. Stopping in bewilderment, I wonder if I really saw someone, or if my mind was playing tricks on me. Exhaustion can do that to you. I stand and watch the back of the house, my eyes scanning the overgrowth, the shrubbery, the trees, for any sign of movement. Nothing. If Emmet was out there, he's back inside. Even as I think that, I know better. It wasn't Emmet I saw out there. It was only a play of light at the end of the day, I tell myself. I speed up, anxious to get back, to sit on the porch and watch the sunset with my husband, leaving shadows behind.

5

tansy

ARS POETICA

Naturally, Noel parks as far away from the building as possible, and I cut my eyes his way. "Wish I'd known we'd be walking all the way from Cashiers. I would've worn my hiking boots instead of heels," I say between clenched teeth. From the backseat, Kit giggles.

"Maybe Noel's trying to tell us we need the exercise," she suggests.

"Or maybe he's just being a turd," I retort.

Noel sighs heavily. "Tansy, Tansy, Tansy. Might I remind you that the last time we came here, you also wore those ridiculous shoes that make you look like an Amazon warrior—"

With a gasp, Kit leans forward to slap his shoulder. "Those are the best-looking Jimmy Choos she owns, Noel Clements! You don't know what you're talking about."

"Like that's ever stopped him," I mutter as I fumble with the latch of the door.

Noel continues as though neither of us has spoken. "—*and* I drove you up to the front door so you wouldn't have to walk on the gravel. You flat-out refused to get out because—according to you—nobody but blue-haired ladies are driven to the front door."

My cheeks flame, remembering. I'd totally forgotten. God, I

hate it when Noel's right. Trying to save face, I say haughtily, "Yeah, but that was different."

I get out of the car quickly before he can ask me why, because I can't think of a single reason. While I'm holding the seat up so Kit can get out, Noel slams out of the driver's side with a huff. One of his pet peeves, when I don't wait for him to open the door for me. His manners are so much a part of him that I feel a twinge of guilt, aggravating him like that. Then another twinge, witnessing Kit crawling awkwardly out of the backseat of Noel's little hybrid. When we stopped by her place to pick her up, I hopped out and held the passenger seat up for her to get in the back. Noel shot me a look of amusement, which I ignored. Good manners dictate that I go in the backseat, but Kit's half my size. Why should I fold myself up like a pretzel so she could have more room than needed in the front seat? By the time Kit has gotten herself out and smoothed down her knee-length skirt, Noel has come around the car to elbow me out of the way. Always the gentleman, he lends a helping hand as Kit adjusts the sheer shawl draped around her shoulders.

Kit tosses her head, and I note how pretty she looks tonight. A nearby streetlamp, as muted and understated as everything else at the art center, catches the glint of the exquisite diamonds in her earlobes. She could always sell those, I realize, if her situation gets any worse. Kit has never been good at finances, but she's really gotten herself in a mess this time. Somehow she's managed to blow every cent her last husband, whom we now refer to as Poor Old Al, left her. To be fair, a lot of it went to lawyers. Understandably, Poor Old Al's kids weren't exactly happy with the terms of their father's will, and Kit had no choice but to fight them in court. She's been in court more in the last few years than most judges have.

With a mock bow, Noel offers one arm to Kit and the other to me, but Kit freezes in place. Her eyes dart toward the entrance of the Bascom Visual Arts Center, then back to Noel and me. In a whisper, she says, "Don't look now, but you're not going to *believe* what she's wearing."

When Noel and I both turn our heads toward the entrance like spectators at a tennis match, Kit hisses, "I said don't look!" Since I'd expected to see Myna in one of her artsy-fartsy outfits that we love making fun of, I'm surprised (and a tad disappointed) to see Emmet and the Bride instead. He, of course, caring much more for the Bride than Noel does for me, has parked close, which gives us the perfect opportunity to watch from a distance as they stroll arm in arm toward the entrance. It shakes me up, the way Emmet is looking at his new wife, and I feel an almost unbearable pang of grief for Rosalyn. As long as I've known Emmet, that besotted look has been reserved for Rosalyn alone.

I glance at Kit, and the look on her face breaks my heart. Noel's gaze catches mine, and holds. He, too, has seen the grief in Kit's expression, but there's nothing either of us can say to comfort her. The cold, hard facts are simple: Rosalyn is gone, and another woman has taken her place. A flood of anger sweeps over me as I turn to stare at the newlyweds. Damn Emmet Justice to hell—how *dare* he flaunt his new love like this? It's bad enough how he rubs it in our faces, those of us who still grieve for Rosalyn, but to appear like this in Highlands, where she and her family were so highly revered, is even worse. Everybody in town had plenty to say about him remarrying with his late wife dead less than a year; I can only imagine the talk about the young wife and the way Emmet can't keep his hands off her. I reach over to pat Kit's arm, and she smiles at me weakly. "Well," she says in a small voice. "The show must go on, I suppose."

My eyes return to Helen, wondering what Kit meant about the Bride's choice of clothing. So far, it's been the tropical look of her wardrobe that Kit and I dish about—the skimpy sundresses and short little skirts, the tank tops and garish floral prints. I've longed to ask her if she's ever heard of Lilly Pulitzer, who does tropical with class. Think Palm Beach rather than the Daytona racetrack, I've wanted to suggest. But tonight, the Bride looks unusually presentable in a simple black sheath, a colorful but elegant shawl, and tasteful jewelry. When it hits me what Kit was referring to, I turn to her wide-eyed.

Kit nods grimly, her greenish eyes glittering. "She's wearing Rosalyn's necklace."

We've begun to walk toward the front, with Noel between us, and he pauses to look down at Kit. Uncharacteristically, the three of us pay no attention to the other well-dressed patrons as they glide gaily by us, chattering among themselves.

"Helen is?" Noel asks, looking genuinely puzzled.

"Of course, nitwit," I whisper. "Who the hell do you think she meant—Myna?"

Noel raises his head to study Emmet and Helen curiously, and his expression remains neutral. Because Kit's with us, he won't admonish me like he usually does for trash-talking Emmet's new wife, but his expression tells me more than he knows. Even Noel, cool and unflappable as always, is taken aback. Rosalyn had several pieces of fine jewelry, mostly heirlooms, but none she loved as much as an unusual gold locket that Emmet got her in Cuba. He'd bought it on the sly from a Cuban aristocrat who had hidden it away since the fall of Batista. Although Rosalyn never wore it—its heavy, ornate design didn't suit her—she adored both the necklace and the story behind it, especially the risks Emmet took smuggling it out of the country. That he would give Rosalyn's most treasured piece of jewelry to someone other than Annie is appalling.

"And isn't that Rosalyn's shawl, too? The one he got her in Cuba to go with the necklace?" I ask Kit, but it's Noel who answers me.

"Oh, come on, you two," he groans. "The necklace is one thing, but Rosalyn would never begrudge the poor girl a shawl. I for one can't stand to see her shivering every night. If Emmet hadn't gotten her some kind of wrap, I would've done so myself."

"At least the shawl's covered up the cleavage," I mutter, and Noel chuckles.

"That's the only reason I haven't gotten her a wrap," he says, and Kit pokes him with her elbow, giggling.

The three of us watch as Emmet and Helen disappear into the crowd inside. The front of the Bascom is solid glass, so we can observe them for a moment as they mingle with the crowd, Emmet taking Helen around to introduce her. It occurs to me that this is their first public appearance at a social venue in Highlands. Everybody is curious to meet the woman who made Emmet Justice forget his grief, especially since most of them know how close that grief came to killing him.

"C'mon," I say to Noel and Kit, motioning for them to hurry. "We can't miss this."

Dutifully, both pick up their pace, but Noel says, "What we cannot miss is poor Linc. We should've gotten here earlier to help him get settled, but I didn't think there would be such a crowd. We've never had a turnout like this for a reading. Even for the poet laureate last year, remember?"

I shake my head at his naïveté, unusual for Noel. "Poor baby. Everyone came tonight because they knew Emmet would bring the new wife." Another thought hits me, and I groan. "Oh, Jesus! Myna will think the crowd is for her, and she'll be more insufferable than ever."

"Not possible, my dear," Noel says drily.

"She's so transparent it makes me want to puke," Kit chimes in. "Noel takes Linc everywhere we go, except tonight for her poetry reading. Oh, no—she *insists* on doing it herself. I can only imagine how she carried on bringing him in, can't y'all? The long-suffering, devoted wife, taking care of her pitiful husband all by her lone-some! And where are those sorry friends of theirs, everyone will be asking? You'd think the least they could do is help the poor woman out with her burden."

"Beverly Howell and Keturah Paulk are right inside the door," I tell them breathlessly. "We can get the scoop from them if you two will just hurry your butts up."

"One good thing about Myna," Noel says with a sly grin. "She's managed to get the two of you to shut up about Helen."

"Not to worry," I call out as I make a rush for the front door. "Beverly and Keturah will have plenty to tell us about her, too."

Once inside the Bascom, Kit and I are surrounded by our women friends, eager to gossip about Emmet's new bride now that she and Emmet are no longer in sight, having left for the lecture room right before we entered. Kissing cheeks and pumping hands like a politi-cian up for reelection, Noel makes his way through the crowd to-ward the lecture room, where Linc is being held captive by his doting wife. It's Myna's big night, when she honors Highlands not only with her presence but also with a reading of her weird, obtuse poetry, and she's in full-bitch mode. Kit's right; Myna's insistence on bringing Linc herself doesn't fool anyone . . . except Linc, I guess. For the umpteenth time I wonder what happens to the brain of an otherwise über-intelligent man when a woman is involved. Say what you will about the dumb things women do for love, at least we don't think with our peckers, and wouldn't even if we had one, I hope.

As expected, the women, and even some of the men, are tsk-tsking about the Bride, now that they have Kit and me to commis-erate. "My God, Tansy—how *old* is she?" Beverly Howell asks in a horrified whisper. "I heard she wasn't much older than Annie."

"Surely she's not pregnant!" Keturah Paulk says, putting a hand to her mouth.

It's tempting to let that rumor float, but I reluctantly tell the middle-aged crowd gathered around us that Helen is older than she looks, in her mid-forties, with a son about Annie's age. It's safe to say that she's past childbearing age. "Guess it's healthy eating that keeps her so youthful-looking," I throw out casually. "She's a dietician, you know."

This brings about the reaction I'd aimed for, and I wish Noel were here to witness my vindication. John Jeffers, one of my closest—and gayest—buddies, guffaws in delight. "Emmet Justice married to a dietician? That'd be like me marrying a gay-bashing right-winger, wouldn't it?"

Eyes round, Kathy Manning leans forward to whisper, "Does she allow Emmet to *drink*? He's always been a heavy drinker, as all of us know."

"One glass of red wine at dinnertime," I tell her. It's a bald-faced lie, but I cannot resist, especially since Noel's not here to correct me, and Kit sure won't.

"Maybe I could send her over to straighten out my husband," Anne Sullivan says, and everyone laughs, including her husband, Claude. But Bootsie Woodruff, an influential dowager who'd been a close friend of Rosalyn's mother, silences our laughter.

With her great dignity and full-throated drawl, Bootsie grabs the attention of the crowd when she proclaims in a loud voice, "Frankly, I find the whole thing appalling—just *appalling*! Rosalyn Harmon was the finest woman I've ever known, and this much-too-sudden marriage of Emmet's is a *disgrace* to her precious memory. I refuse to speak to him or that *girl*, either one."

Over Bootsie's shoulder I see Noel motioning to me just outside the door of the lecture room, and I tug on Kit's arm. We make our good-byes and the whispers follow us. Even though we're out of earshot, I know the whispers are of sympathy and commiseration, unlike those that followed Emmet and Helen just moments before.

"Quit the gossiping and get your fannies in here," Noel hisses when Kit and I reach the door. "They're about to dim the lights."

"I thought we had reserved seats," Kit says with a frown as we make our way down the aisle, pausing only to wave at friends already seated.

"Oh, we do, darling." Noel's blue eyes twinkle with mischief. "The esteemed poet asked the ushers to reserve several for her dearest friends."

"That would be us, then," I mutter. "She sure as hell doesn't have any others."

Seeing Linc seated in the front row, his walker folded away next to him, I shut my trap. Emmet and Helen have already seated themselves on one side of him, Noel on the other. Naturally he hogged the end seat so Kit and I have to be next to Helen, and I signal Kit with my eyes that I'll go first. That way, I'll sit next to the lovebirds, and Kit won't have to endure the sight of them pawing each other like teenagers. Their fingers are entwined, I note in disgust, and his leg is practically on top of hers. At least Noel will be pleased; the fringed Cuban shawl has slid down on the Bride's tanned shoulders, exposing enough cleavage for the men seated near us to get an eyeful. Well, they'd better enjoy the view; there sure won't be any once the poet appears.

Kit and I both stop to greet Linc before we take our seats, and I linger for a moment with my face pressed next to his, nuzzling his beard. He's spruced up for the occasion, looking very professorial and distinguished. Those who don't know about the stroke probably can't see anything much different with him, especially with him seated. He's made a really good recovery, considering the shape he was in, but I have to remind myself that I was in the waiting room after his surgery, when the doctor warned us to be cautiously optimistic. After you've had one episode like Linc had, he told us, the chances of having another quadruple . . . as do the chances of one being fatal.

I sit down to fan myself with the program, which is better than having to look at Myna's picture on the front cover, grinning like a nun in a cucumber patch. Like everything else at the Bascom, the lecture room is top-notch, one of the classiest I've ever been in, and I've been in quite a few. A tuxedoed trio to the side of the stage area is playing Chopin's Étude op. 10 no. 3, and the lectern's decked with a spectacular arrangement of Casablanca lilies. After Kit and I take our seats, hypocrites that we are, both of us greet Emmet and the Bride with enough sweetness to gag a maggot. Up close, I'm shocked to see how tired Helen looks. If her exhaustion is from carrying out her wifely duties every night, she needs to plead a headache and get some rest. Otherwise, she'll lose her looks before she reaches fifty. Her big brown eyes are dark-smudged and weary, and for the first time I notice a fine web of wrinkles in the corners, faint lines on either side of her mouth. There must be a God after all.

Emmet, on the other hand, looks better than I've ever seen him. Even though I'm downright disgusted with myself, I can't help it—I like being seated near enough to watch him out of the corner of my eye. It'll give me something to do instead of listening to Magpie's reading. Besides, what's sauce for the goose is sauce for the gander. I notice the men around us ogling Helen; it's only fair that we women get to ogle Emmet. Emmet always attracts a crowd of admiring women. For a man who's not even remotely good-looking, he has the most magnetism of anyone I've ever known. My God, I've known the man forever and still find him hot as a Fourth of July firecracker! It's that intensity of his, I suppose, that draws women to him like bears to honey. Or maybe moths to flames would be a better analogy, for he's a danger if there ever was one. He leans forward to wink at me, and damned if I don't blush like a fool, fearing he read my mind.

The other chick magnet of our group, Noel the golden boy, is flitting around the room beside himself at the turnout. Naturally, goody two-shoes is helping the ushers (college kids who get *paid* to work here) set up extra chairs. You'd think the fool had never been on the board of an organization like the Bascom's, instead of chairing some of the most illustrious charities and foundations in Atlanta, including the High Museum. Noel's always been that way, so nice and humble it makes you want to throw up.

To my left, Helen lays a hand on my arm and bends over to whisper in my ear. While she asks me to identify some of the people around us, and I whisper my responses, my gaze is drawn to her neckline like a magnet. As bad as I hate to admit it, Rosalyn's locket looks great on her, and I can see why Emmet wanted her to have it. I've always wondered if it hurt Emmet's feelings, that Rosalyn never wore the necklace after all the trouble, and expense, it cost him to obtain it. His getting it made a good story, but the truth is, he could've been arrested for smuggling, and might still be locked away in a Cuban prison. I remember Rosalyn holding the necklace up to her throat and asking Kit and me what she should do. It wasn't *her*, she said, but she adored it because Emmet thought so. Wear it, anyway, I'd advised her, even if only occasionally, but Kit talked her out of it. Make a point of telling Emmet how much you like it, was her suggestion, but for God's sake, don't wear the thing! It was heavy and gaudy and totally unsuitable for Rosalyn's delicate frame. Since Kit always had more influence on Rosalyn than anyone else, that's who she listened to.

Instead of being the chunky piece of jewelry I remember, the gold locket is actually rather exquisite, I see now, suitable for the grand Spanish contessa who once owned it. The ornate inlay on the heart, which Kit called garish, is bold and eye-catching. Mainly, the necklace suits Helen in a way it never did Rosalyn, probably because Helen's warm coloring is more Mediterranean, while

Rosalyn's was pure Nordic. Dulcinea and Queen Gertrude, I think, rather enjoying my literary flight of fancy. Before I can take it any further, the lights dim, Noel takes his seat, and the audience settles in for an evening of high culture.

The ever-elegant George Landon, a close friend of Noel's and one of my favorite escorts, takes the stage to introduce Myna Fielding-Varner, a poet of such renown (to hear George tell it) that Highlands should be genuflecting at the mere mention of her name. With a nod toward those of us in the front row, George tells the romantic story of how Dr. Fielding came to the University of Alabama as a lecturer several years ago, and how she was hosted by an equally renowned scholar, Dr. Linc Varner, chairperson of the visiting scholar program. In a story to equal the most romantic of Shakespeare's sonnets, the poet and the lepidopterist fell in love, and the rest is history. When George says that New York's loss was Alabama's gain, I make a face at him. He knows what we think of Magpie. Kit pokes me with her elbow so often that I'm forced to scoot out of her reach.

After pointedly refusing to meet my eye, George reads a long, boring list of Myna's many publications and awards, the most notable of which is the Pulitzer Prize. I groan inwardly hearing it, even though I knew it was coming. Getting the Pulitzer a few years ago made Myna more insufferable than ever, which I didn't think possible. Noel, Emmet, and I often take bets on how long it will take Myna to "casually" drop it into a conversation: "I remember such-and-such because it was a few days after I was awarded the Pulitzer, wasn't it, Poopsie?" Following a properly reverent silence for everyone to absorb the honor, George Landon brings the prize-winning poet forward to thunderous applause. Without turning my head his way, I can tell that Linc is applauding with great enthusiasm, despite a gimpy arm. Fortunately I didn't eat anything before we came, or my stomach would be turning over like a turbine.

To my surprise Magpie looks almost pretty tonight, her face flushed at the sight of the large turnout and the welcoming applause. She's wearing makeup for a change, and her kohl-lined eyes shine behind the granny glasses, which are perched on the tip of her sharp little nose. Taking the podium, she smiles and nods again and again, like a bobblehead doll. I assume she selects her wardrobe to conform to her image of the serious artiste; at least I hope she has a reason other than the most appalling taste imaginable. Tonight she's draped in a gauzy black tunic with winglike sleeves, as if she's just flown in from a witches' coven. Her frizzy hair is piled chrysanthemum-like on top of her head, and elongated silver loops swing from her slightly protruding ears. I haven't seen the necklace before (just fortunate, I guess): an entwined black-and-silver cord that flaps against her flat chest. When she closes her eyes and raises both hands high over her head, I lean even farther away from Kit's elbow. Poor Helen; she's got Emmet practically in her lap on one side, and me on the other. It's going to be a long night.

Myna achieved poetic fame by her innovative use of a single word or two to create an image, somewhat like haiku boiled down to even fewer syllables. She's the darling of critics and the literary intelligentsia, but I don't care for the stuff myself. I like my poetry more . . . poetic, I guess. She begins her recitation in a loud, dramatic voice: "An eagle! The sky! A cliff! An eye!" With her eyes closed and arms upright, she tilts her pointy chin toward the ceiling and takes on a look of pure ecstasy. Saint Teresa couldn't have done it better. She proceeds to recite a much longer poem (also about eagles) with such intensity that when it reaches a crescendo, she shivers before slumping over the podium with arms outspread, spent. After a stunned silence, the audience bursts into startled applause. Emmet clears his throat, but I dare not glance his way. After enough time passes that I'm beginning to wonder if she's fainted, Myna straightens herself up and bows solemnly. No more smiles and flushed cheeks now; she's about the serious business of bestowing her poetic gifts on the masses.

I perk up when she launches into the next poem because it sounds suggestive, with tantalizing images of bees sucking dew from the shy petals of daisies. A few stanzas later, the bees are darting in and out of stamens, which seems to be giving the quivering daisies quite a buzz. About halfway through, however, she loses me, and I decide the poem is actually about bees, petals, and daisies instead of fornication. As expected, Myna moves on to the feminist poetry she's known for, and I suppress another groan. If anyone's ever been oppressed in a male-female relationship, it's Linc, but Myna's poems are so full of graphic images of female oppression, you'd think she'd gone through it. She goes from slavery, rape, and genital mutilation to the more common sins of job discrimination and housewifery drudgery. The idea of her being oppressed is ludicrous. I pity anyone, man or woman, who tries to hold that one down.

Big surprise: Myna's reading goes on way too long, and the audience begins to get restless, eager to get out to the candlelit terrace where Noel and I, with a little help from Holly the caterer, are hosting a reception to honor the esteemed Magpie Poet. Finally, mercifully, I can make my exit on the pretext of helping get things ready. I slip out while Myna stands in front of the podium to bow over and over, her chrysanthemum head almost touching her knees, arms outspread as though she's about to take off. The applause is as enthusiastic as it was when she entered, but this time it's from gratitude that the ordeal's finally over.

A couple of hours and several glasses of champagne later, I'm cornered by an old friend, Frank Grimes, who motions for me to follow him to a quieter area of the terrace. I noticed him trying to get my attention earlier, but every time I attempted my getaway, someone would detain me. The terrace is still full of folks, with Myna holding court in the center. Seated by her side and cradling the one glass of wine allowed him, Linc glows with pride at his wife's success. I hope he can make it for the duration. Highlands is a party town, and the revelers will stay until the booze runs out.

Like the rest of us, Frank Grimes loves to dish, so I figure he's looking for the lowdown on the Bride. To my surprise, his expression is solemn when he says to me, "Listen, Tansy, I need to ask you something. Do you remember last year, when you and Kit brought some things of Rosalyn's to the shop?"

Of course I do. Frank and his partner, Bill, manage the charity thrift shop downtown, where Kit and I took a lot of the stuff from Rosalyn's closets at Moonrise. Frank goes on to tell me that they always store their high-end donations away, then put out a few pieces at a time to sell. "The other day, I was going through the wardrobe where the remainder of Rosalyn's things are stored," Frank tells me in a low voice, "and I found something in one of her purses. Evidently you and Kit missed it when you cleaned out her things."

I gasp in surprise, and Frank winces at my reaction. "Oh, dear," he says ruefully. "I didn't mean to get your hopes up, like we found a long-lost heirloom. It's nothing, really, but it's monogrammed, so I thought you'd want to have it, you or Kit. I've tried to corner Kit a couple of times tonight, but she's been rather . . . ah, busy."

Both of us turn our heads to where Kit stands leaning against the railing of the terrace, deep in conversation with one of our friends, Jim Lanier. They've been in that same spot for most of the reception, much to my delight. Jim is another of my former lovers, a handsome, sophisticated jet-setter who would be perfect for Kit. Until tonight, she's resisted all efforts to be fixed up with him or anyone else. It's a funny thing about relationships. It's been almost four years since Poor Old Al's death, and Kit, whom I never considered the ever-faithful type, has shown no interest in another man. Emmet, on the other hand, seems to have attached himself to the first woman that came along. Go figure.

As if echoing my thoughts, Frank says, "I figured a lovely woman like Kit would've remarried long before now."

"Yeah, me, too," I agree, then remind him of the item he found of Rosalyn's. Can't let the talkative Frank get sidetracked with gossip, the main thing besides tourists and bears that Highlands has in abundance.

I'm taken aback when Frank reaches into the pocket of his sports coat and pulls out a small book. "I brought it with me, figuring all of you would be here tonight." He cuts his eyes toward another corner of the shadowy terrace, where Emmet and Helen huddle together with their plates of food. "As soon as I saw Emmet, though, I knew better than to approach him with this. It's obvious that he has other things on his mind." Frank wiggles his eyebrows meaningfully.

Poor Frank; he's caught me at the end of the evening, after I've about talked myself out on everybody's favorite topic, Emmet and the new wife. I'm suddenly tired, and don't want to hear yet again how young Helen looks, or what a short time Emmet knew her before they married, or how different she is from Rosalyn. Not only that, a strange thing has happened over the course of the evening. The tide has turned, and somehow, the villain of the story is now Helen. Originally, the town was incensed that Emmet had dishonored his beloved late wife's memory by remarrying so soon, and the new wife was mainly an object of curiosity. Now everyone has decided that Helen took advantage of a grieving widower and moved quickly to get her hooks into him. People are saying that Emmet was in no condition to make any kind of rational decision. They've got a point, but still. I turn my attention back to Frank and the book of Rosalyn's he holds, which is about twice the length of a deck of cards. Monogrammed *RHJ*, it's a brown leather pad with a gold pen attached to a loop on the side.

"Oh, it's Rosalyn's notepad!" I gasp when Frank hands it over. "Her Day-Timer was retrieved from the car, but not the notebook.

So this really is a treasure." Glancing at Frank, I explain rather breathlessly. "You see, she got a new one the first of every year. We teased her because she usually kept it in the car to scribble reminders to herself while driving. Not the safest of habits, especially in Atlanta."

My voice catches in my throat, and Frank pats my arm awkwardly. After thanking him profusely, I excuse myself and make a dash for the ladies' room. No doubt he's disappointed that I didn't hang around to talk trash with him, but I don't want curious eyes on me when I open Rosalyn's notepad. I pause for a moment to motion Kit to follow me. I hate to disturb her tête-à-tête with the delectable Mr. Lanier, which seems to be getting even cozier, but she'll want to know about Frank's discovery.

Waiting for Kit in the elegantly appointed ladies' room, emptied now of its usual crowd of bejeweled and perfumed ladies, I thumb through the notepad curiously. It's as painful to see Rosalyn's large, looping handwriting as it is to read the jottings of her day-to-day life: reminders to order tickets for the symphony or theater, to call the florist or cancel a dental appointment. Since only a dozen or so pages are filled, I'm sure this was her last notebook. Her habit was to purchase a new one after Christmas, fresh for the new year. It hits me like a punch to the stomach that this little notepad chronicles the final months of her life. She bought it the end of December, then died of injuries suffered on a cold night the first week in March. My breath catches in my throat. Could this unassuming little book answer some of the unsettling questions I've harbored ever since?

Hearing the click of heels outside the ladies' room and knowing it's Kit, I do something that I can't explain, even to myself. Without thinking it out, I quickly step inside the nearest stall. When the door swings open and Kit calls out my name, I flush the potty to cover the sound as I tear out the written-on pages of the notepad.

After stuffing them in my little evening bag, I smooth down my dress and exit the stall, as though I hadn't heard anyone enter. Arms crossed, Kit waits next to the lavatory looking peeved. "This better be good," she says. "After all your scheming, I finally hook up with Mr. Lanier, and now you're dragging me away."

"Oh, trust me, he'll wait," I scoff. "It's probably been as long since he's gotten any as it's been for you."

"If that's all he's after with me, he'll have an even longer wait," Kit says piously, and I roll my eyes.

"Trust me again——" I begin, but Kit waves a hand to stop me.

"Oh, no, you don't. I don't want to hear the salacious details of your assignations, or I might change my mind about having dinner with him tomorrow night."

Just to aggravate her, I say, "Huh! If I told you the details of my evenings with Mr. Lanier, you'd jump his bones right now."

"Tansy——" she begins irritably, but I stop her by holding up the little notebook. Kit stares at it as if she's seen a ghost, and I realize I should've warned her first. Quickly, I tell her how I came to have it, and she snatches it from my hand before I even finish my story. Her face falls in disappointment when she opens it to see nothing but empty pages.

"Oh, Tansy," she murmurs. "She never got a chance to use it."

Kit's eyes fill, and she twirls toward the marble counter to grab a tissue from a tortoiseshell box. Despite an almost overwhelming pang of guilt, I don't tell her what I'm keeping from her. And I have absolutely no idea why not.

6

willa

A PATIENT, AND PATIENCE

I can't think of a blame reason for me to be so nervous, but I know what Momma'd say if she was still here. If you don't feel right about doing something, then you'd best stop and ask yourself how come. Could the Lord be trying to tell you to think twice?

Well, I've thought not just twice but lots of times, and it keeps coming out the same way, that I'm getting myself into something I'm bound to regret. Just give it a try, Noel tells me, and if it don't work, all you have to do is say so. But you're gonna do fine, he always adds. He reminds me that they could hire a real nurse, but Linc won't stand for it. Only because it's me did he go along with the idea of hiring help. Noel's too polite to tell me so, but I doubt Linc gave in without a fight. He probably agreed just so they'd shut up and leave him alone. Summer folks love nothing more than minding each other's business.

I knock again, louder this time. I can hear them inside, and know dang well they heard me the first time. "Coming!" Myna sings out, and I sigh. If I can survive my first day, the rest oughta be a piece of cake. She wasn't supposed to be in town, but she outsmarted Noel by claiming she needed to show me the ropes. I told Noel flat out if she ended up staying longer than today then count me out, but he swore she couldn't even if she wanted to. She's teaching graduate classes at Bama this summer.

The door opens a crack, and Myna peeks out like I might be an ax murderer. I swear, for somebody who's supposed to be so smart, that woman don't have the sense God promised a goat. First she called out "Coming!" in a friendly way, now she acts all suspicious. I just stand there and don't even say good morning till she opens the door for me.

She looks a sight. That's either a white cotton robe she has on, or a sheet. Whichever, it's big enough to wrap around her two or three times, and her bushy hair's flying every which way. Holding a mug in her hand, she squints at me behind her little-bitty glasses. Eleven o'clock in the morning, and her just now getting up, the lazy heifer.

I don't see Linc, but heard his voice when I was on the porch knocking. Classical music is playing in his room behind the kitchen, so I figure Myna must've run him off so she can have a go at me first. Since Linc can no longer climb the stairs to the loft, the back porch was closed in to make a downstairs bedroom. Myna sent the orders, and Noel told her not to fret, he knew a good contractor who'd handle everything. First time I came to clean, I noticed that Linc had the new room to himself, and Myna's stuff was upstairs. Then I heard her squawking like a wet hen because the expanded room wasn't big enough for the two of them. She got on the phone and told Noel to get his ass over there, *right* then, and she by God meant it. I stayed hidden away cleaning the bathroom, knowing there'd be fireworks. Sure enough, Myna chewed Noel out good, going on and on about her *specific* orders for the new bedroom. Peeking out, I saw Noel, cool and unruffled as always, shrugging and telling her the contractor must've misunderstood. I hid both myself and my giggles till he left.

"So, Willa," Myna fires at me. She talks fast and through her nose, which makes her sound like a mule braying. "You're finally here. I'd given up on you."

I stare at her in surprise before stammering, "B-but—Noel told me eleven!" I glance at my watch to make sure I hadn't looked at it wrong earlier. Nope. Eleven on the dot. I pride myself on being punctual.

Myna scowls. "You must be mistaken. I specifically told him ten." When she watches for my reaction, I know she's lying. If she was expecting me earlier, how come she's not dressed? I'm not about to argue with her, though. Instead I mutter an apology, and she scowls at me again. With a sweep of her hand, she indicates a chair next to a little twig table. "Have a seat."

The living area's furnished with big, overstuffed chairs, a sofa piled with pillows, and a couple of rockers, yet she puts me in the only tiny, straight-backed chair in sight. Clutching her mug, Myna settles on the sofa across from me and somehow manages to fold her skinny legs under her and the big robe. Eyeing me over the rim of her mug, she startles me by saying, "So you're planning on playing nursemaid to my husband this summer?"

"No, ma'am." I'm bound and determined to keep my voice even, not let her know she's getting my goat. But something about her question sounds dirty, and my face burns. "Noel talked to me about helping him with his exercises, taking him for walks, stuff like that."

Her overplucked eyebrows shoot straight up. "Oh? What kind of exercise is Noel doing that he needs help?"

"Ma'am?" I blink in confusion, and she smirks at me like a possum eating briars.

"I assumed Noel was the antecedent to your pronoun," she says, and I get it then. Every time I'm around her, she pulls that grammar crap on me.

I clear my throat to say, "Uh, Noel said—" but Myna stops me. Her smirk becomes a snarl, her dishwater-colored eyes flash, and she bares her sharp little teeth. In a flash, she's gone from crane to weasel.

"Let me get something straight right now. Noel Clements does *not* give the orders around here. *I* decide what's best for my husband. And you are here *strictly* on a trial basis. You are sadly mistaken if you think otherwise."

I stand up so fast I almost knock my chair over. "No, ma'am. You're the one who's mistaken. I'm not here at all."

I flounce for the front door in a huff, but just as I reach for the latch, a sound from the back of the cabin stops me. I look around to see Linc making his way out of his room, and my heart sinks. If only he'd stayed put a few minutes longer, all he would've seen of me would've been heels and elbows.

"Willa!" Linc calls out. "I didn't realize it was you at the door. We overslept this morning, so Myna banished me until I could make myself presentable. As you can see, I failed rather miserably." There's some truth to that; he's wearing a stained robe over a pair of plaid pj's, and his hair, sparse as it is, is almost as bushy as Myna's, like it hasn't been combed in days. Plus he's barefooted, which don't seem safe for somebody in a walker.

As Linc makes his way toward the sitting area, I drop my hand from the latch. But I stand my ground. "Listen, Linc—don't feel like you need to come out on my account," I say pretty loud. "I was about to leave."

He stops in surprise, then swivels his head toward Myna. Sipping from her mug cool as a cucumber, she shrugs. "Willa came by to tell us she won't be able to help after all, Poopsie. I told her you'd be *so* disappointed, but she's adamant." Raising her head, her eyes meet mine. "Just too busy, aren't you, my dear?"

It's the "my dear" that does it. That, and the McFee pride, which Momma used to say would be the death of me. I'll be damned if a mean, skinny, sharp-tongued woman—and her a Yankee to boot—is gonna get the best of a McFee. I throw back my shoulders, step away from the door, and walk right over to a big, overstuffed chair, where I plop down my overstuffed arse. Staring straight at

Linc, I say, "You know what? I reckon I can do it after all, Linc. Seeing as how disappointed you'd be otherwise."

Myna sloshes what's left in her mug on her robe, she sits up so fast. "Oh, no, no, Willa," she squawks. "Linc wouldn't *dream* of asking you to overcrowd your busy schedule. He understands that you're a single woman who has to support herself, and—"

Without realizing it, Miss Smarty-Britches has outsmarted herself and I know how to settle this once and for all. Dropping my eyes, I say in a little-bitty voice, "Yes, ma'am, which is the other reason I'm not gonna back out on Linc." I raise my head to give him the most pitiful look I can muster. "To tell you the truth, Linc—I need the money pretty bad, so I can't tell you how much I 'preciate you giving me the extra hours."

Linc smiles his sweet smile as he settles himself into the chair next to me. "You're the one who'll be helping me out, hon, and don't forget it. I'm delighted that our arrangement will work out for both of us, then." He's still smiling when he turns to his wife to say, "How about fixing Willa and me a cup of that marvelous jasmine tea of yours, love? It smells divine."

———

AFTER THAT FIRST morning in the Varner cabin, I'd wonder if I won the battle but lost the war. The truth is I left scared I'd do Linc more harm than good.

After the three of us finished our watery tea, Linc suggested Myna demonstrate his range-of-motions exercises to me, then he'd excuse himself so she and I could go over her to-do list. To her credit—and my surprise—Myna quit picking on me long enough to make sure I understood what needed to be done. Because she's a teacher, I reckon, she was good at explaining it, too. A lot of Linc's exercises he couldn't do by hisself; somebody either had to hold him up, or push when he pulled. Even though Linc laughed and joked while she went through each of the exercises with him, I could tell how much pain they caused him. Seeing my expression, he told me not to worry, that his reward came afterward because he got a little nap. Sure enough, the final exercise was a foot massage, which put him right to sleep. Even though Linc loved the massage, it wasn't for fun, Myna explained, but to help with the leg cramps and curling in of the toes, which kept stroke victims from resting. When Myna finished she put these funny-looking separators between his toes, then motioned me out of his room. Linc lay curled on his side like a baby, snoring away.

Myna went over her lists like a drill sergeant, and I paid close attention. She was all business. Oh, she got in plenty little jabs, and talked down to me something awful, but I didn't let her get my goat again. I think I even surprised her somewhat, like when she aimed her pencil at me and said sharply: "This is crucial. When conversing with Linc, it's important that you clarify things as much as possible. Stroke victims have a slower cognitive process. Do you understand what that means?" When I said, "Yes, ma'am," she demanded that I repeat it back to her.

"Because of the stroke, Linc thinks slower now than he used to, and has trouble connecting the dots from one thought to another," I said. "So I need to make myself as clear as I can."

She eyed me kind of funny, then said, "The main thing is, you must not slow down the cognition even more with vague suppositions that require a connective process. Do you understand that concept?"

Again she made me repeat it to show that I understood. Most of the big words she used didn't mean pea turkey to me, but I could figure them out by using plain old horse sense. "Sounds like I need not only to be clear, but I also need to lay things out for Linc one at a time," I told her. "And to do so in a way that don't require him using thoughts that build on one another."

I couldn't tell if I got it right or not because Myna didn't say anything, just narrowed her eyes. But she moved on to the next thing, so I must have. When we finished, she handed me the list. "Well. I think we've covered the therapeutic exercises adequately for the time being. Let's move on to the next thing. I assume Noel discussed with you the nutritional needs of his diet?"

"Noel's on a diet?" I echoed innocently. Even though Myna's cheeks flushed and she looked like she could shit a brick, I kept my face expressionless. If she hadn't been looking, I'd have chalked one up for the home team. Pulling another list from her briefcase, she thrust it at me.

"I've worked with Helen to come up with an acceptable list of snacks, and I demand strict adherence to the plan as formulated. Linc has a deplorable sweet tooth that simply must not be indulged. He has a real weakness for ice cream—"

"Me, too," I blurted out. Her eyes traveled over me from head to toe.

"Obviously. But *he* cannot afford to carry any extra poundage." Leaning forward, she added, "This is a deal breaker, Willa. Absolutely *no* sweets for Linc, you hear? If you let him talk you into it, I'll get it out of him, I can assure you. Linc and I signed a covenant on the day we married that there would be no secrets between us."

I left that day worrying myself plum sick about remembering everything on Myna's lists, so I sat up half the night putting them to memory. If I messed up and Linc had another stroke, I'd never forgive myself. Myna'd drawn little pictures showing how to do the exercises, so I felt pretty confident about them. It was Helen's list that bothered me, with its measured servings of lean meat, leafy green vegetables, and whole grains. It was up to me to make sure Linc got a "balanced and nutritious" lunch, she wrote. And Helen agreed with Myna: sweets must be strictly monitored. To satisfy

Linc's sweet tooth, a piece of fruit, a bowl of berries, or a slice or two of melon would be acceptable.

Yet the next day what does Linc do but ask me to drive him to Kilwin's, the local ice cream parlor. He's got a hankering for their Highlands Hash, a rich chocolate that's full of almonds, fudge ripples, and marshmallow creme. Seeing the look on my face, Linc reaches over to squeeze my hand, and his eyes twinkle like the stars on a dark night. "Aw, come on, Willa! I know all that crap my wife told you, and the ridiculous list Helen made. This will be our little secret, okay?"

"B-but—your wife told me y'all had a covenant never to keep secrets from each other," I cried, and Linc chuckled.

"Oh, we do, honey. But I guess she failed to read the fine print. That thing's only good in Tuscaloosa."

———

THE FIRST TIME I sat at the foot of Linc's bed and massaged his feet liked to have embarrassed me to death. I was glad he dozed off because I couldn't meet his eye. The week before, when Myna had showed me how to do the massage, I hadn't thought nothing about it. Matter of fact, I figured that part of his exercise routine was bound to be the easiest, since you didn't have to worry about hurting him. But doing it by myself was different. There I sat, all by my lonesome in a man's bedroom rubbing on his feet, and all I could think about was what Duff'd say. When Myna showed me what to do, she'd sat on a stool beside the bed. I couldn't get my much-bigger fanny situated on the stool, though, so I ended up on the bed with Linc's feet in my lap, which made my embarrassment even worse.

Only thing that made the situation bearable was Linc's attitude, the way he joked about everything. He must've seen how uncomfortable I was, but he said nothing. Or rather, he didn't say nothing about me being embarrassed; he said plenty otherwise. Which suited me, because I've always loved listening to summer folks talk. When I was a girl, one of my favorite pastimes was eavesdropping on grown-up conversations. Sometimes Momma had to take me with her when she worked at Moonrise, a place where I loved eavesdropping more than anywhere else. I heard a lot of stuff there, too, stuff I've never told anybody. One thing Momma drilled into me at an early age: If you work in people's houses, you keep your mouth shut. Repeat stuff you hear, and you won't be working there long.

Mainly it's just kinfolks, or the grown-ups at our church, who I listen to. The difference is, the conversation of the summer people's a lot more appealing than what mountain folks talk about. Summer people don't go on and on about not being able to pay their light bill, or getting enough work during the winter months, or rain for the crops in the summer. They don't talk about who got saved or baptized or spoke in tongues last Sunday, or what all they ate at the fellowship supper on Wednesday night. Instead, they talk about interesting things, like why people act the way they do. Shoot, some of them talk for hours about nothing but their feelings!

While I was working on Linc's feet, he got to where he wouldn't nap until afterward. Instead, he'd talk, and I'd listen. All I had to do was bring up something to get him started. The first week, it was butterflies. Only problem was, the things he told me were so interesting that I'd have to remind myself to keep massaging. I'd catch myself as wide-eyed and frozen in place as a young'un hearing a ghost story. Not only that, I'd get so lost in his conversation that I'd blurt out questions, then blush like a fool. Linc never fussed or told me to get back to work. Instead he'd be real patient answering, even when my questions were dumb. I'd always wondered where butterflies go when it rains, I told him, and how come they love to play in mud puddles. Sometimes he wouldn't answer me directly. Instead, he'd show me the answers during our daily walks through his garden. It was a better way of learning, Linc said.

In a few weeks, I'd relaxed enough with him not to be embarrassed anymore. Quite by accident, I discovered something that made the foot massages even more relaxing. Afterward, Linc swore I missed my calling. I could make a living as a conjurer woman, he claimed, like my Momma had been. Momma was no such thing, but she did know how to make potions with things growing in the woods, 'sang and mushrooms and wildflowers. Even some of the weird plants in the moon gardens ended up in her potions, which tickled Rosalyn's mother. I never was particularly interested in stuff like that, though Momma showed me how to make a few things.

One of them was a healing oil made from camphor and mint, and I took to using it for the foot rubs. Linc asked me not to mention the oil to Myna if she should call. (Which she'd taken to doing, calling up all the time to fire questions at me about how things were going.) She was particular, Linc added, about anything that wasn't approved by his team of doctors. "Huh!" I said in response. "What does she say about your ice cream, then?"

"That's our little secret, Willa," he murmured, his eyes closed. "Remember?"

"I remember all right," I told him, shifting my weight around on the bed. Since I'd started using the oil, I had to fold a towel under his feet to protect my blue jeans. His left leg was pretty strong, but the right one was deadweight in my lap. "Your wife'd fire me before you could say jackrabbit if she ever found out about the ice cream."

"Then we'll have to make sure she never finds out, won't we?" His voice was playful as always, and I wondered if the man ever let anything rattle him.

———

IT TAKES A while before Linc talks about the others, Noel, Tansy, Kit, Emmet, and Helen. First time he mentions them—the day after Helen's big dinner party—I hold my breath so he'll keep talking. Since I helped Helen get everything ready, I'm dying to know how the party went, but would never ask. When Linc tells me what all Helen fixed for supper, it's the opening I need.

"She told y'all about her new TV show, I reckon?"

"Indeed she did," Linc says, eyes still closed. "Sounds like quite an undertaking to me, converting all those recipes." With a drowsy chuckle, he adds, "The dishes she served were low everything."

"Bet she sells a lot of cookbooks, though. Most folks would eat healthy if they knew how, don't you think?"

Linc opens an eye, then smiles that devilish smile of his. "Actually, I think most of us would rather die an early death than eat that shit."

Startled, I giggle and tweak his big toe. "*Linc!* I hope you didn't say that to Helen."

He settles back on the stack of pillows and closes his eyes again. "Naw. I told her it was good. I wouldn't hurt her feelings for the world."

I suspected as much, but study him to make sure. From what I've gathered, him and Noel are on Helen's side, while Tansy and Kit blame her for everything. Just the other day, I overheard Kit saying to Tansy that Emmet would've never married so soon if he'd been in his right mind. It wasn't Emmet's mind that led him astray, Tansy shot back.

I think Linc has dozed off, so I jump when he says, "Helen and Emmet's marriage has been the talk of Highlands this summer. Were you as shocked as everyone else?"

I couldn't be more surprised if he asked me to buck dance down the middle of Main Street. None of the summer people have ever asked me what I think about their doings. Before I can answer, Linc waves a hand in the air as if erasing his words. "Forgive me, my dear. Because you are both one of us and outside our group, you have a unique perspective. But my curiosity has put you on the spot, and I apologize."

"It's okay, Linc. To tell you the truth, I was as surprised as everybody else to hear that Emmet had married so soon. He was . . . you know . . . so crazy about Rosalyn and all."

Yet again, Linc's quiet for a long time, then he says in a low voice, "People can do strange things when they're lonely, Willa."

I study on it. "So you think Emmet rushed into this marriage?" But Linc, eyes still shut, starts shaking his head before I even finish.

"Not necessarily," he says. "I'm reserving judgment for the time being."

Clearing my throat, I dare ask, "Do you think it's good or bad that Helen's so different from Rosalyn?"

"Hmm. That's an intriguing question, and one I haven't considered. My gut reaction is negative, because we're more comfortable with what we're used to, even if it's unhealthy. It's the reason people are drawn into one dysfunctional relationship after the other. Subconsciously, we tend to seek out what we know best. Don't misunderstand me—I'm not implying that Emmet and Rosalyn's relationship was unhealthy. On the contrary, they had an unusually good one. It might not have worked for anyone else, but the two of them"—he stops himself to search for the right word— "understood each other. And thus were able to meet each other's needs. Which is the dirty little secret of relationships, my dear—having one's needs met. Never forget that."

I chew on that a minute before asking, "How come you know so much about relationships? Are people a lot like butterflies?"

Linc laughs. "God, no. They'd be a hell of a lot better off if they were." His speech isn't near as slurred as it used to be, and I listen real careful when he goes on to say, "Most of us create our own misery, Willa, by making unwise choices that we have to live with. Then an unexpected event will happen out of the blue, like my aneurism, or Rosalyn's accident, and one's whole life will change in a nanosecond."

I finish with his right foot and pick up the left one. I'm using the mint salve today, which Linc says smells like summertime and juleps. Before I can stop myself, I blurt out, "What puzzles me more than anything is the way Rosalyn died. I don't reckon I'll ever understand it."

There's no taking the words back once I've said them. Linc's eyes fly open, and he pulls himself up on an elbow to look at me. My face burning, I say, "Oh, Lord—I can't believe I said such a thing. Don't pay no attention to me—" but Linc isn't having it.

"So I'm not the only one who's wondered," he says after a while.

I swallow, hard, and lower my eyes. "She never came up here in the winter months without letting me know." I give up on the massage, and his feet lie still as stones in my lap. "It was the same when Momma worked for her, and I was a girl. Back then, Atlanta TV didn't give the weather for the mountains, so Rosalyn would call Momma to see if the road was bad, or if snow clouds were building. After I took over, she took to calling me to check on firewood, or things like that. But she always called."

"She didn't let you know that night, then," Linc says. It's not a question.

I shake my head. "Tansy and them said afterward that Rosalyn must've been coming up to surprise Emmet, but that made even less sense. Everybody knew that Emmet was off somewheres doing a news story."

Linc nods. "Well, he was, though not that far away. That week he was in the Asheville area with a film crew, doing a special on that guy—oh, what's his name?—who bombed the Olympics and hid out in the mountains. Remember? After the accident, we figured that Rosalyn had been on her way to Asheville, maybe to that spa she frequented, and decided to spend some time at Moonrise first. And just as impulsively, got up here, changed her mind, and decided to go home. She's not around to explain herself, so our theories are purely conjecture."

Again, I shake my head. "But that's just it, Linc! I said Rosalyn didn't call me beforehand, not that she didn't call me at all. The night of her wreck, she called to say she was at Moonrise, which surprised me since it was starting to snow, and the roads could get bad. Did she have any trouble driving up, I asked, and she said no, she'd made it fine. I do recollect her mentioning it was a spur-of-the-moment trip, so I asked if she needed me to bring her something, since it was late and the stores were closed. No, no, she said; she wouldn't dream of me coming out after dark, just wanted me to know somebody was at the house. But here's the most peculiar thing—what's been eating at me ever since."

I pause to take a breath, and Linc waits with a curious look. " 'But you already knew, didn't you?' Rosalyn said. When I said, 'Ma'am?' she said it again. 'You already knew somebody was here, so I shouldn't have bothered you.' Didn't make a blame bit of sense to me, Linc, because it was just the opposite—I knew nobody was at Moonrise because I'd been by the day before. Before I could ask what she meant, she'd hung up. I should've called her back, I know now, but I just shrugged it off."

I don't tell Linc why I didn't call back, that Duff was drunk and acting the fool, and I had other things on my mind. I clear my throat to continue my story.

"It was barely light the next morning when one of the nurses at the hospital called to tell me about the wreck, knowing I worked at Moonrise. Rosalyn was in bad shape, but still alive. First thing I asked was about the family, if they'd been called yet. The nurse wasn't sure, she said, since the law was taking care of that. She'd called so I could come be with Rosalyn. It didn't look like she was gonna make it, and the nurse hated that nobody was with her. You know, until some of the family arrived. I hightailed it over there, but I never got to see Rosalyn."

Linc looks surprised to hear this. "They wouldn't let you be with her?"

I sigh and look down at my hands, stilled now and folded in my lap. "It wasn't that. The deputies who worked the wreck were waiting for me soon as I walked in. They needed Emmet's cell number. Everybody knew he worked at CNN, so they'd called there, but the switchboard operator told them he was on assignment in a remote location. Which made me scared they wouldn't be able to reach him at all, even on his cell."

"But they did, right?" Linc asks.

I nod. "Emmet answered on the first ring, and they told him to come to the hospital quick since his wife was critical. Then the nurse told me that Rosalyn kept asking for Kit, so I tried her cell, but couldn't get her. The nurse was fixing to take me to be with Rosalyn when a doctor came out to tell us that she had just passed. While the deputies tried to reach Emmet again, I called Noel." Deep in our memories of that morning, both of us keep quiet until I blurt out, "I won't ever know what Rosalyn meant."

Linc rubs his face like he's real tired. "Jesus! My own unanswered questions have more to do with her being here at all, then suddenly leaving to return home. You've added a new dimension with the suggestion that someone else might've been at Moonrise." He goes quiet, thinking, then shakes his head. "Kit's closer to Rosalyn than anyone, yet even she didn't know Rosalyn was coming here. Matter of fact, when Noel finally got in touch with her, Kit thought the accident had happened in Atlanta. All of us did, initially."

"I stayed at the hospital until Emmet got there. Came in on a CNN helicopter later that morning, and with everything going on, I never heard where they'd brought him from. It was so awful, him getting there and thinking she was still alive, then having to call Annie to say she'd passed while he was on the way. Tell you the truth, the rest of that day's a blur to me."

"Yeah, me, too," Linc agrees. "I'd just finished up my first class when Noel reached me." I feel his eyes on me, then he says, "Rosalyn's question to you could mean a couple of things, couldn't it? Either that you knew *she* was at Moonrise, or you knew that someone else was. What's your take?"

His eyes bore into me, and I squirm uncomfortably. With another big sigh, I say, "The way she asked me, Linc? She made it sound like someone else was there. Only afterward, when I was questioned about our last conversation by the deputy writing up the accident report, did anything else occur to me. At the time, though, it sounded like Rosalyn got to Moonrise, and found someone there. And because I'm the one who checks on the house, she figured I knew."

His gaze holds mine for a long time until Linc says in a quiet voice, "But no one was. Right? No one was at Moonrise except Rosalyn."

I nod. "That's the thing. As far as anybody knows, wasn't no one there but her. I had to make sure, though. At the hospital, I asked Emmet what I could do to be of help, and he said just go on home, but could I keep my phone nearby. He'd let me know when he knew more. He left then with the helicopter crew to pick Annie up, and from there on to Atlanta where they were sending Rosalyn's body. I couldn't help myself, Linc—I went to Moonrise on my way home. And there was no sign of a soul being there except Rosalyn."

Linc snaps to attention. "Let me make sure I'm following you. You could tell that she'd been there the night before, though?"

"Oh, yeah. Probably no one else would've noticed, but I know the place so well. If you'd gone through it, or, say, Tansy maybe, y'all wouldn't have seen anything out of place."

"Rosalyn was a fanatic about that," he agrees. "The house never looked lived in, even when they were there. Emmet complained that he couldn't even put the paper down without Rosalyn snatching it up. But how can you be sure it was Rosalyn who was there? They let friends or relatives stay sometimes. Remember Noel was there a few days last fall when the plumbing at the cottage went out, and Kit while some of her remodeling was going on?"

"No one but Rosalyn was at Moonrise that night. I know the signs, like the towel from her bathroom being in the clothes hamper. And the fireplace—she'd made a fire in her room." When Linc asks how I knew Rosalyn did it, I can't help but smile. "Besides Momma, Rosalyn was the only person I ever knew to throw dried sage on her fires. Momma did it to keep the haints away, but Rosalyn wasn't scared of them. She just liked the way sage smelled."

His eyes are troubled. "Obviously, there's something we don't know about that night, something that would answer our questions."

Then I hear myself saying what I never thought I'd say to any of them. "Maybe if we can figure it out, Rosalyn can be at peace."

Give him credit, Linc doesn't look at me like I've lost my mind for saying such a crazy thing. Instead, he just nods like he, too, has heard strange noises at Moonrise and wondered if the place had ghosts. All he says is "I think you're right, Willa, my girl. But I also think this should be another of our little secrets, don't you? At least for the time being. Let me think on it, and you do the same, then we'll put our heads together and see if we can come up with some answers, okay?"

I nod in agreement. I don't tell him that I've thought on it for over a year now, and it don't make no more sense to me now than it did then.

7

helen

MR. JUSTICE

The month of June has come and gone when Emmet makes his pronouncement: Okay, Honeycutt, enough is enough. Don't know about you, but I've got to get my ass back to work.

He's right; we've taken off to frolic way longer than either of us planned. A couple of weeks, we'd said originally, then back to the salt mines. I *have* to work on my cookbook—the publisher is already bugging me for a draft—and Emmet's ready to get back on the air with his news commentaries, plus the big documentary he's doing. Our fun in the sun is over.

After agreeing that we're ready to settle into a routine, Emmet and I take our supper to the veranda to watch the sunset over the lake. Unbelievably, it's the first time we've had the entire evening alone since we got to Highlands. We discuss how different the sunsets are here from those in south Florida, which are dazzling enough to take your breath away. I tell Emmet how fitting it seems that mountain sunsets are more serene and peaceful. Witnessing them is a spiritual experience for me; I feel closer to God and more connected to the universe than I've ever felt.

"Uh-oh," Emmet says, grinning at me over a forkful of chicken-and-melon salad. "When I hear a Cracker talking like that, I know a convert is in the making. Around here it's known as mountain fever. Soon the heart I thought was mine will be lost to these hills."

"Oh, you'll always run a close second," I tease, and Emmet chuckles. To my great surprise, he tosses his napkin on his plate, gets up from his chair with a loud scraping on the stone terrace, and comes around the small wrought-iron table to where I'm seated. With my own forkful of salad suspended halfway between my plate and mouth, I watch in bewilderment as he reaches for my hands to pull me from my chair. The fork clatters to the ground; chicken-and-melon salad lands on my sandals; and before I have a chance to protest, Emmet has taken my face in his hands and kissed me, long and hard.

My fingers laced around his neck, I pull back and say weakly, "My goodness, Mr. Romance. Where did *that* come from?"

"You ain't seen nothing yet," he says in a low voice. "We got time for a quickie before the next course?"

"A *quickie*? Jesus, Emmet!"

"Although you've obviously forgotten, Honeycutt, we're newly-weds. We're expected to jump into the sack at all hours of the day or night at the slightest provocation."

"What did I do that was so provocative?" I dare ask.

"Went on and on about connecting to the universe," he murmurs as he draws me closer. "Turns me on when you talk dirty." I giggle and he adds, "And reminded me how little you and I have connected since we've been here."

What a fool I've been to think he hasn't noticed me turning from him night after night, feigning sleep and ignoring his overtures! I lean into him and say, "I hate to tell you, but there's not a next course."

"You wanna bet?" Emmet says as he leads me inside.

———

EMMET HAS EVEN more surprises in store for our evening alone. As soon as the sunset begins to fade, he leads me to the boathouse, down a steep wooded pathway that's slippery with moss and rocks, and overhung with gnarled laurel branches. Ever since we've been here, he tells me, he's wanted us to go on a twilight boat ride. He's showing me Moonrise from Looking Glass Lake, where the photo I liked so much was taken. Emmet's undergone a subtle change since we've been in Highlands, I've noted. His resistance has given way to an unmistakable love of the place, which his grief had apparently suppressed. It appears that I'm not the only one with mountain fever.

"You think the lake is something at sunset," he says as he gets the rowboat out and holds it steady for me to crawl into. "Wait till you see it this time of the day. Not a sight you're likely to forget."

As soon as we push off from the dock, I see what he means. The water, the mountains, the sky, and even the cold mist surround us in an eerie silver light, so unexpected it's like floating across a lake of an unknown world. Although I offer to help, Emmet rows solo, saying he needs the exercise. I seat myself in the bow and watch the boat part the pewter waters in gentle, rolling waves. Except for the splash of the oars, the only sounds come from the frogs and cicadas. Rather than going down the lake where houses dot the banks, Emmet steers a short distance from the boathouse until we're almost directly in front of Moonrise, now high above us. Frowning in concentration with his eyes locked on our destination, he switches direction and rows even farther out on the wide, still lake. No longer the tender lover of our sunset supper, he's slipped back into his usual persona. "I think this is it," he mutters as he locks the oars in place and removes his camera from its case. "But I'll know for sure when I see it through the lens."

Looking remote and forbidding, Moonrise looms on the mountainside, dark and shadowy because we didn't turn on any lights before leaving. Emmet'd urged me to go back for a heavier wrap than my zipped sweatshirt, but I'd brushed him off. Now I wish I had listened. "It's *cold* out here," I whisper, shivering.

Without taking his eyes off the house, Emmet chuckles. "Why are you whispering? There's no one in the world but us, alone on a painted sea." He raises the camera chest level, looks down into the viewer, and begins to click away. Cameras hold so little interest for me that I've never taken a decent picture, but his expression is blissful, brow furrowed as he fiddles with the camera's strange doohickeys. On our daily outings with the gang, Emmet and Kit, who's also into photography, have taken some spectacular photos, which I'm content to admire without having to do the work.

After a couple of minutes, Emmet unlocks the oars and rows us a little farther out, moving the boat here and there until he finds the angle he's seeking. The boat rocks back and forth with a swishing slap that would be hypnotic enough to put me to sleep if I wasn't so cold. Hugging myself against the damp air, I sit and soak in the sight of Moonrise in the distance, where it looks both magnificent and creepy. After taking a few more shots, Emmet pulls a little digital number from his pocket. He likes the instant gratification of the digital, he mutters, and I nod politely.

Although I don't know cameras, it's obvious that the photo I found in Rosalyn's album was taken under less cloudy conditions than it is now. Darkness has fallen over the lake like a veil, and I stare up at the house, wondering if any of Emmet's shots are even turning out. I turn to ask him, but he lets out a yelp before I can open my mouth.

"Holy shit!" He jerks the digital camera away from his eye as though it burned him.

"What? What is it?"

He blinks at Moonrise with such an expression of surprise that I turn back toward it, halfway expecting the house to have ascended into the heavens or something. "*What?*" I demand again. The house looks exactly as it did before, just as dark and unwelcoming.

"You about ready to go?" he says, reaching for the oars.

"Oh, no, you don't. Not until you tell me what you saw."

"Nothing. It was just my imagination." He shrugs as he unlocks the oars without looking my way.

"Emmet!"

The sideways glance he gives me is a bit sheepish. "It was just weird, like a Hitchcock flick or something."

"*What* was?"

He looks up at the house, bemused. "I was looking through the viewer, getting the right angle, you know? And I thought I saw someone up there"—he points, and I follow his gaze—"in the windows at the top of the turret. Freaked me out for a minute, is all."

I turn my head to look toward the bank of windows high above the turret, which must lead to the attic, but I see nothing there, or in any of the other windows in the house. Not a shadowy figure, not a curtain stirring, nothing. Swallowing hard, I say, "It was probably a reflection from the lake."

"Yeah." Slowly and carefully, he begins rowing us toward the dock.

"Emmet, wait," I gasp. "I see it, too. Look!"

With the oars motionless, he tilts his head and squints. "Naw, there's nothing there. But I thought . . ."

His voice trails off, and I crane my neck one way and the other, frustrated. He's right: whatever shadow I saw—or imagined I saw—simply isn't there. Glancing his way, I blurt out, "Do you think it was a ghost?"

Emmet shoots me a scornful look and begins rowing again. This time he rows purposefully, leaning forward as he rotates the oars toward me in a wide swing. He's getting us back to the boathouse in a hurry. I cling to the side of the boat and keep my eyes on Moonrise as we move through the water, but darkness has fallen so quickly that the unlit house is only a silhouette. When I turn myself around in the bow, the wind hits my face like an icy slap. I shiver and pull up the hood of my sweatshirt to cover my head. Hearing clicking noises, I glance over my shoulder to find Emmet propping the oars on his knees while he puts the camera back into its case. Catching my eye, he picks up the oars to continue our flight over the silver lake.

"Couldn't resist one more shot of the House of Usher, huh?" I tease, but he shakes his head.

"What I couldn't resist was getting a picture of my wife with her hair tossed by the wind, and the moonlight turning it to pure gold."

I look up at the night sky hanging heavy with dark clouds. "What a charming, poetic image, my darling. Only thing, there's no moon tonight."

"If there were, it'd turn your hair to gold," he insists. "Don't be such a damned literalist."

"That's sooo purty, but could you please row faster? I'm freezing my behind off."

"And you claim to be more romantic than me? Bullshit." Emmet rows in silence for a moment, then says abruptly, "It appeared to be a woman in the windows."

I shiver, both from the cold and the surprise of his statement. "Could you tell what she looked like?"

"No. Just something about the shape made me think that."

I dare not ask him the obvious question, if the woman he saw was the one whose portrait hangs in the room below the window. I start to say something about the figure I saw in the garden but try another angle instead, purposefully keeping my voice light. "Emmet?

Don't you think . . . I mean, old houses can be haunted, and . . . well, you could've seen some kind of spirit, couldn't you?" When he doesn't respond, I glance over my shoulder to watch him maneuvering the rowboat next to the dock.

"Don't start that crap, Helen," he says with a snort. "Hop up on the dock and help me get this baby in."

In the yellow beam of his flashlight, we climb the pathway to the house, with Emmet planting his feet, then taking my hand to guide me through the rough spots. "You look miserably cold," he says. "I'll get you a fire going as soon as we get to the house, okay?"

It's become something of a joke with us. Try as I might, I cannot build a decent fire. When I give in and ask Emmet to do it, he gripes and says if I want a fire every damn night before bedtime, I've got to learn to do it myself. With a smile, I say, "Sounds great, but first I want you to check out the attic, make sure no ghosts are floating around up there."

He groans. "Aw, shit, I should've never said anything. You've decided now that the house is haunted, haven't you?"

"Well . . ."

Emmet stops so abruptly that I stumble. "Promise me that you won't say anything to the others about me seeing a fucking ghost at Moonrise. I'll *never* hear the end of it."

"If you promise to at least consider the possibility."

Emmet narrows his eyes. "Do you want a fire or not?"

"You mean I have to earn it? Cheater."

He stops the climb to grin down at me. "I'm glad I found you, Honeycutt. I still can't believe you were dumb enough to marry me."

"How could I resist? You came so highly recommended."

With a chuckle he says, "Me and you . . . it's been one hell of a ride, hasn't it?"

At the top of the path, he places an arm over my shoulders as we cross the mist-shrouded driveway to the house, and the promise of a warm fire.

——

THE CHEMISTRY BETWEEN Emmet and me came as a surprise to both of us. When I was growing up, my daddy started a fire in the grill by dousing the charcoal with lighter fluid and throwing a match on it, then jumping back when it leaped into flame. It's a perfect analogy for what I experienced with Emmet Justice. It was heady, delicious, exciting, all the more so because it was so unexpected, and, yes, unwanted. When we met, I was a divorced, middle-aged woman starting a new career that had suddenly, and surprisingly, taken off; and I had a son who was in his final year of college. The last thing I wanted was a relationship—the *very* last thing. After several long, exhausting years of dealing with a volatile soon-to-be ex-husband, I had finally found some peace and contentment in my screwed-up life.

Our relationship came at an even worse time for Emmet, and he had less business than I did getting into one, considering the shape he was in. But when do any of us get to choose our destiny, or tell fate that it's not a good time for us? Oh, we think we do, of course. I certainly did for most of my life, up until the moment I fell so hard for Emmet Justice that I couldn't imagine living without him. Before then, I'd seen myself as a scrappy kid who'd had to make her own breaks because nothing had ever been handed to me on a silver platter. To mix my metaphors a bit, if I'd sat around waiting for luck to open any doors for me, I'd still be sitting.

Unlike Emmet's group of friends, I wasn't born into a world of ease and privilege. Far from it. Instead, I was raised in a lower-class neighborhood in Orlando, by parents who were as blue-collar as they come. They were also decent and hardworking folks who struggled to raise a growing family with very little resources. We scraped by fairly well until my father, a union pipe fitter, became disabled with diabetes. Just starting high school, I took over the running of the household and raising of my younger siblings—as well as the care of my father—while my mother was forced to seek full-time employment. Untrained and uneducated, the only work she could find was cooking in a greasy-spoon café, where she fed her misery with the food she dished up, and brought the fat-laden leftovers home to us. Over time, my mother grew bitter and obese, my father obese and wheelchair bound. It doesn't take a shrink to point out the connection between my role in the family and the career path I took.

I pieced together enough scholarships and financial aid to attend the University of Florida, but staying in was a struggle. While other coeds enjoyed campus life, I was either working a job, attending classes, or studying to keep my grades up. The science courses I took in order to become a registered dietician were difficult and demanding, but I was determined to make something of myself. In my final semester, I was doing my clinical work at the hospital when I met a handsome young resident and fell in love for the first time in my life. A smooth-talking charmer, Joe Synder was everything I'd dreamed of as a lonely teen stuck tending to a sick father and a houseful of hungry siblings. Blinded by love (and thrilled that I'd snagged a doctor to boot), I was so taken with Joe that I overlooked his less appealing qualities and told myself he'd change once he settled down.

After Joe and I married, he signed on with a hospital in Miami, where I assumed we'd be deliriously happy. The first few years we were happy enough, especially after our son, Adam, was born, but it was not to last. Unusual for his profession, Joe was not a particularly successful doctor. He was difficult to work with, jealous of his colleagues, and careless with his work habits. Dismissed from the prestigious Miami hospital, he became a "doc-in-the-box" at a twenty-four-hour clinic in an immigrant neighborhood, a big step down for him.

The longer we were together, the more demanding and critical Joe became, and the more I tried to excuse his behavior. I blamed it on the long, grueling hours of the clinic, which required night and weekend shifts. In addition, I had such low self-esteem that I read-ily agreed with him about my numerous faults and inadequacies. We'd been married twelve years when I discovered his first affair, but it would not be his last. I took Adam and left; teary-eyed, Joe begged my forgiveness and enlisted Adam's help. That became a pattern, which caused me a lot of heartache and a couple of bleeding ulcers. Because I'd once loved and admired Joe, and been so sure he'd change, his actions wounded me deeply. I would eventually learn that love doesn't always die a natural death. It can be killed by betrayal and disillusionment.

When Adam left for college, I filed for divorce. By then, neither Joe nor I loved the other, and our lives were miserable. Conse-quently, I was shocked when Joe fought the divorce as hard as he did, pretending to be heartbroken. The truth was, he was deter-mined to hang on to the assets he'd hidden away from both me and the IRS that my lawyer was about to uncover. He also fought to keep his sleazy affairs from coming out, not wanting our son to find out the kind of man he was. For a year or so, I spent more time in a Miami courtroom than at home. Had it not been for insuring my son's future, I would've taken nothing from Joe Synder and never looked back. I lost lawyers because of my unwillingness to fight for my needs rather than Adam's; they couldn't possibly understand that material things meant nothing to me by then. Survival of the spirit was a stronger need. Despite my concessions, Joe fought the judgment and took me back to court over and over.

I'd probably be sitting in court today had it not been for an amazing stroke of luck, a job offer from Fort Lauderdale, which got me out of Miami, and away from the ex-husband from hell. When Adam was a child, I'd been mostly a stay-at-home mom, working part-time at a diabetes clinic. After my divorce, one of the dieticians at the clinic moved away and recommended me for her extra job, a once-a-week spot on the health segment of the local news, demonstrating healthy cooking techniques. The pay was deplorable and I was terrified of being on TV, but I took it. By a quirk of fate, it turned out that I'd stumbled onto one of those rarest of things, a job I was made for. I not only enjoyed it, I was good at it once I learned to manage my fear of the camera. I took classes at the local culinary school and got even better. The zeitgeist was right; the latest craze was for healthy cooking. To my further surprise, I received a job offer from a TV station in Fort Lauderdale that was adding a cooking spot to its noontime show. I jumped at the chance to get out of Miami.

The chance to start a new life doesn't come often, but that's what my move to Fort Lauderdale felt like. It took a while to find myself again, but I'd been lost for a very long time. I rented a small town house, and I'd come home to it thinking this must be what someone newly released from prison feels like. I'd forgotten what it felt like to go home without a feeling of dread in the pit of my stomach. Slowly, I began to see things as though for the first time, with eyes no longer dulled by despair at the mess I'd made of my life.

Because Joe had been a better father than husband, Adam remained close to his dad, and I didn't begrudge him their closeness. When Joe remarried as soon as our divorce was final, I didn't begrudge my son's fondness for his new stepmother and her kids, either. But I felt something like despair when Adam set his sights on medical school in Baltimore, so far away from his doting mother. Another bitter pill to swallow, but over time, it went down much easier. During my childhood, I'd learned that life could bring you to your knees. In middle age, I was finding that you didn't have to stay there.

It took me a couple of years, but I began to gain some confidence in myself, peace of mind, and enjoyment in the simple pleasures of everyday living lost during my marriage. Then, with the force of a category-five hurricane blowing in from the tropics, Emmet Justice came storming into my life.

His reputation preceded him. Everyone in the television business, even newcomers like me, knew of Emmet, or had seen his newscast. In his younger years, he started out as an intern at a fledgling CNN company, and worked his way up to become the most popular early-morning anchor in Atlanta, an enviable position he held for three decades. A respected but much smaller station like Fort Lauderdale would've never landed such a hotshot newsman had it not been for the tragedy that made a change necessary for him. CNN's top anchorman needed out, and the station manager where I worked was a former classmate of his. Emmet was lured to Fort Lauderdale by the offer of a one-year contract, and free rein with his program. In exchange, he'd help run the newsroom until a new director was secured. Those of us in the newsroom knew little else about our new boss, but we were intimidated by him before he even arrived.

———

THE COOKING SHOW host is usually a TV station's most popular employee. Within a few days of his arrival in Fort Lauderdale—at the end of summer and the beginning of a new broadcast season—Emmet had joined the group who watched my spot on the noon show, then hung around afterward to pig out on the leftovers. It was a ritual known as the feeding frenzy, and I enjoyed the easy camaraderie as everyone scrambled and jousted one another for the best goodies. The first time Emmet stepped out of the dark wings of the set to join us, an awkward silence fell over us like a sandbag. His staff was both in awe of and fearful of him, and they had spread the word: Their new boss was every bit as tough as he looked. His tactics were the same he used on the unsuspecting suckers he interviewed—first he disarmed you with that effortless charm of his, then he moved in for the kill. Poor Emmet; his attempts to win over his colleagues with friendly banter weren't enough to override the intimidation factor.

Every time Emmet appeared, the others would scatter as though a hawk had swooped down on a henhouse, leaving me alone with him. Since it was my set I was stuck, so he honed in on me. And each time, I'd become flustered and unnerved by his razor-sharp wit and those clear-colored eyes he aimed at me like lasers. He grilled me about the food I'd prepared as though I were Fidel Castro and he'd been granted the interview of a lifetime. I'd later find it was the same intensity with which he approached everything.

This went on for several days, then one afternoon I was on the set later than usual prepping for the next day's show. Emmet stopped by on his way out, a well-worn briefcase in hand. "You're working late, Honeycutt," he said breezily. "Any vittles left for a poor beggar?" Because the two of us were thrown together at the feeding frenzies, we'd become friends of sorts, though I was far from comfortable with him. Despite that, he intrigued me. I sensed a heavy, lingering sorrow about him, and saw him as a tragic figure who covered up his grief with a brittle air of nonchalance and glib repartee. If I hadn't heard that he'd recently lost his wife and moved to Florida to recover from his grief, I'd have never suspected he was anything other than the usual cynical newsman, and hardnosed, demanding boss.

Sorry, I told him, but my production crew had beaten him to the leftovers. Evidently someone had tipped him off as to the other way I fed my colleagues: If you begged pitifully enough, I'd dig

through the fridge and find something for your supper. Because of
the station gossip, I knew Emmet fit the profile of those who rou-
tinely asked for a doggie bag: single people, mostly men, who
couldn't cook and grew tired of eating out. I've always been avidly
curious about the lives of others, and had found that a television
station was a goldmine of gossip. A few days earlier, I'd been in the
lounge when some of the women employees speculated about our
newly hired news commentator, and I'd listened with curiosity. It'd
surprised me to hear so many of the slick, gorgeous young women
pronounce Emmet hot. One of them caught me off guard by asking
what I thought. When I asked if she meant good-looking, she and
her peers had a good laugh at my expense. "Oh, Helen," she'd said
with a giggle. "You're so *cute*. I'm asking if you think he'd be good
in the sack." The way they were regarding me, it was obvious they
considered me way too old to remember what being in the sack was
like. One of the older women had retorted, "You young girls let that
man be. He's still grieving the loss of his wife, and the last thing he
needs is y'all coming on to him."

"Let me take you to dinner," Emmet suggested with a winsome
smile I hadn't seen before. "I'm making an effort to get to know
everyone on the news team. Plus, you've fed me since I've been
here, so I owe you."

I couldn't think fast enough to get out of it, so I stammered,
"Oh! Well . . . o-okay. Sure."

As we drove our separate cars to a nearby place I'd suggested, I
berated myself. What on earth was I doing, going out with that man?
Although it was hardly a "date"—at my advanced age of forty-five I
cringed even thinking the word—I'd avoided going out with anyone, even casually, since my divorce. And for the Intimidator to be
my first was unbelievably dumb of me. When I parked at the restaurant, I considered making a run for it.

Emmet selected the wine, but asked me to choose the food.

When we raised our glasses of a very nice Viognier, his eyes met mine and I quickly looked away. Then we both spoke at once and laughed as we tried to apologize at the same time: "Sorry! You were saying? No, you go first . . ." I had a sinking feeling that the evening was going to be worse than I'd feared.

And it might have been, had not the silver-tongued devil disarmed me, exactly what I'd promised myself on the way over wouldn't happen. Following an awkward silence, Emmet leaned forward and said earnestly, "Listen, Honeycutt, I've got to tell you . . . I'm scared shitless."

I stared at him, aghast. "Scared of *me?*"

With an impatient snort, he said, "Of course you. Who'd you think I meant, the waiter?" He frowned as he reconsidered his answer. "Okay, not of you, exactly, but of . . . ah, hell—you know what I mean."

I did, though his admission surprised me. Guiltily, I realized that I'd thought only of my own feelings and not considered his, a recent widower who had just relocated to a strange place. Even so, it was impossible to imagine him being scared of anything. Not him. The idea was so ludicrous that I told him so. He laughed, and I found myself laughing with him. "Sweetheart, you just don't know," he said, sitting back as the waiter brought the entrées I'd chosen, lime-infused, charred sea bass on a bed of jicama-mango slaw.

"Tell me more," I said, emboldened by the couple of glasses of wine I'd gulped down. "What is it that scares Emmet Justice?" Barbara Walters would've been proud of me.

Later Emmet would tell me that no one had ever turned the tables on him. By the time we'd finished dinner and moved on to dessert, swapping bites of a lemon-mint sorbet (mine) and a spiced rum custard (his), I knew his story. I learned about his upbringing in Charlottesville, where his father was a well-respected newspaper editor and his mother a museum curator ("We were far from wealthy but certainly comfortable," he'd admitted when I probed). He also admitted being ambitious and driven, and I prodded him to tell me about his meteoric rise to the top of his career. To my surprise, he was disarmingly honest in telling his story, and spared me none of the less-appealing details of his character—or so it seemed. Building his career, he was utterly ruthless and "took no prisoners in the process," as he phrased it, something he now regretted.

Over cappuccinos, Emmet brought up the loss of his wife. I'd avoided questioning him, knowing her death was the source of the sorrow he tried to cover up. It should've been him, he told me flatly. Revered by everyone who knew her, Rosalyn had been a wonderful person. He'd met her at a CNN function in Atlanta, and had fallen for her at first sight. He hadn't deserved her, a fact he'd known throughout their marriage, yet it hadn't stopped him from being a rotten husband. At that startling admission, I busied myself with my coffee so he couldn't see my expression. I didn't doubt it one bit; a man like him would be difficult to live with, and I felt for his poor wife. No one would've blamed Rosalyn if she'd left him a long time ago, Emmet added in a weary voice. He was impossible to live with, emotionally unavailable, and a shitty father to their only child.

"Were you at least faithful?" I asked, shocking myself at the audacity of such a question. "Oh, God! Please forget I said that, Emmet. Normally I'm not so bold. Or so rude, either."

He flinched, but dismissed my apology with a shrug. "You've heard all about what a shit I am. No point in holding back now." In the same expressionless manner, he admitted that he hadn't been the most faithful of husbands earlier in their marriage, but Rosalyn had laid down the law on that issue. She could live with a lousy husband, but not a cheating one.

Emmet went on to say that his grief was compounded by the guilt he felt, which had caused his breakdown. After his wife died, he'd hoped to salvage a relationship with their daughter, whom he hardly knew since his career had always come before family. The years of neglect had taken their toll, however. Although he'd reconnected with his daughter, their relationship felt tenuous and forced, overly but falsely polite, and uncomfortable for both of them. All of these things had been major factors in his move from Atlanta.

"I'm a fucking mess, Honeycutt," he said matter-of-factly. There was a genuine regret in his eyes, a self-reproach I wouldn't have thought him capable of. "A ruthless bastard who neglected, cheated on, then lost the only woman he's ever loved. And I have a kid who's a young adult now but barely knows her own father."

I sipped the cappuccino, then licked whipped cream from my lips. "What is it you fear most, then? Living the rest of your life like you've lived the first—what?—sixty-something years?"

He smiled the winsome smile again. "Ha. That's what hard living does for you. I'm not as old as I look, although I will be sixty this year." I cringed at my faux pas, but he didn't notice. He was pensive, frowning as he stared into space. "Naw, it's not that I'm afraid of. Why would I be? It's familiar territory. All I've ever known. It's the opposite that scares me more."

"Really?" I leaned toward him, intrigued. "What does that mean?"

With a shrug, he said, "I don't know for sure, but I think it has something to do with how I manage to screw up everything that matters most to me. I seem to have a genius for it."

I thought for a minute, mulling that over. "Wasn't it Nelson Mandela who said that we don't fear failure as much as we do success? But that's not you, Emmet. You've found plenty of success. It doesn't sound like you've found much else, though."

"Whatever it is," he said gruffly, motioning for the check, "I've never talked about it before, not like this. You got me good, and I was supposed to be getting to know you. You ever get tired of cooking, sweetheart, I'll hire you as a newscaster in a New York minute."

In the parking lot, Emmet held the car door open for me while I thanked him for treating me to dinner. When I cranked up, he leaned in, arms propped on the window. "You're a nice girl, Helen Honeycutt," he said. "If you weren't, I'd ask you out again."

I stifled a laugh and said, "Emmet? I think I know now what it is that you fear most."

"Oh, crap. Do I want to hear this?"

"Probably not. But give it some thought, okay? Here's my theory: Since your wife died, you've been forced to think about how you've messed up your life, and why, and what you've uncovered scares you. You don't strike me as the introspective type."

"Shows what you know. I spend hours every day in the lotus position, navel gazing."

"I'd be surprised if you've spent ten minutes in your whole life doing so. You've been too busy ferreting out the secrets of others."

"If you're implying that I'm less than perfect, then you're way off track."

I rolled my eyes, but persisted. "I'm only saying this because I've been through some of the stuff you talked about earlier. You know, in my marriage."

"So you were a lousy spouse, too," he teased. "Did you cheat on him?"

"No, but I wish that I had," I replied tartly.

He let out a hoot of laughter. "Not only a nice girl but a spunky one, too." He stared at me with his laser look, but his gaze softened. "What a fool that poor bastard was, to let someone like you get away."

"Oh, God," I groaned. "I may be out of practice, but I know a line when I hear one. Especially one that old."

At least he looked abashed. "I'm out of practice, too. I thought I made it up."

I put the car in reverse and gave him a little good-bye wave. "I've got to go now. Think about what I said, okay? And thanks again for dinner."

He didn't move from the window. "Want to do it again sometime?"

"No. I'm too nice, remember?"

"And too young. You deserve better. I'm a fucked-up, jaded, irascible old man."

"Remind me why I should go out with you, then?"

"I like your sass, Honeycutt. Sure you don't want to give it a try?"

"Good night, Emmet."

He had no choice but to jump back when I pressed the button, rolled up the window, and backed the car out, smiling. When I looked in the rearview mirror, he lifted his hand. After I pulled onto the highway, another glance showed that he still stood there, looking off into the night pensively with his hands in his pockets. Ever since the gossip in the lounge, I'd wondered what the younger women had seen in Emmet that I'd missed, and now I knew. It was the very thing that had made me so uneasy with him. His appeal was not in his looks, but in his intensity. That pent-up energy that radiated from him might be disconcerting, but it was also magnetizing.

————

THOUGH I DIDN'T know it then, that night marked the beginning of our relationship. After our dinner together, I'd found myself thinking about Emmet quite a lot, and decided I'd be a fool to have anything else to do with him. There had been a dangerous spark between us. I'd barely survived one toxic relationship, and if I let myself get into another one, I'd deserve whatever happened.

The next time I was prepared (or so I told myself) when Emmet stopped by my set on his way out, with the same greeting as last time. "Hey, Honeycutt! Any leftovers today?"

"I've got a couple of veal chops someone needs to take home." I kept my voice breezy and my back to him as I looked through the fridge.

"If I said I'd rather take you to dinner, would that be another tired line?"

"Of the worst kind," I said shortly. "Let me wrap the cutlets for you." I took them out and put them on a piece of waxed paper, avoiding his eyes. "Pop 'em in the microwave about a minute each, but no longer. They're already cooked, so—"

"Will you share them with me?" he interrupted, and persisted even after I said no as politely as I could. "Then will you come with me to a new place I heard about? You like Thai food?"

"Love it, but that's not a good enough reason to go there tonight. I'm tired, and I'm outta here."

"What if I give you a better reason?"

When I said it had better be a good one, he withdrew a stunning bouquet of pink rosebuds that he'd been holding behind his back. "How about this?" he said. "I've been doing some research on you, and here's what I've discovered: You have a weakness for flowers of all kinds, especially the fragrant ones. Because you're so thrifty, you rarely indulge and buy them for yourself. How am I doing so far?"

"How did you find that out?" I squealed.

"Trade secret," he said with a wink. "Which I only share over Thai food. C'mon, Helen—I'm lonely, and don't want to go by myself. I've told you that I'm lousy at relationships, so I won't come on to you, okay? I had a good time with you the other night, is all. Besides, nobody else here can stand me."

I couldn't help it, I laughed. In spite of my resolve, he'd gotten to me again.

"And I've a new line to try out on you," he added.

"Let's hear it first."

Without missing a beat, he said, "You're the most interesting woman I've met since moving here, but it's more than that. You're also the best-looking."

Handing him the bouquet to hold, I began untying my apron. "You had me at most interesting, but best-looking was a nice touch. I need to change, so why don't you pick me up at my place in half an hour?"

As I'd done to him last time, Emmet interrogated me over dinner. But he did it so artfully that I rather enjoyed it. He was no less inquisitive than at the feeding frenzies, but this time I found his interest beguiling rather than repellent. He made me feel like the most fascinating person he'd ever known, and who can resist that? Like everyone else he set out to captivate, I spilled all my secrets, and our coffees grew cold as we talked late into the night. When our waiter finally told us that they were about to close, I felt a pang of disappointment. For the first time since I'd moved to Fort Lauderdale, the prospect of returning home depressed me. I had cherished my solitude, but maybe too much so. The dark side of solitude, as I'd discovered, was loneliness.

Outside of my town house I unlocked the door, then told Emmet good night, thanking him again for a lovely evening. Saying he'd enjoyed it, too, he leaned in to kiss me lightly, even chastely, on the side of my mouth. Good move, I thought; not a brotherly peck on the cheek but not a lip kiss, either. When I looked up to tell him so, our eyes locked, and we stared at each other like a couple of those moonstruck characters in old movies, Cary Grant and Deborah Kerr, Humphrey Bogart and Ingrid Bergman. Before I could stop myself, I moved toward him. My arms went around him, and he pushed me against the door where we writhed and thrashed and panted, struggling for breath between our moans and the most passionate kiss—and moment—of my life.

When we pulled apart, gasping, I was horrified at my response to a man I'd not even liked until tonight, when he turned on the charm. Was that all it took for me to give up my hard-earned self-reliance? I wondered. In disgust, I rushed inside and slammed the door in his face. Later we'd laugh about that move; at the time neither of us found it funny. He waited for a couple of minutes before rapping on the door. "Open the damn door, Honeycutt," he demanded.

When I opened it and peered over the safety chain, Emmet hooted. "You won't need that. I don't like this any more than you do. I warned you it was a bad idea, if you recall."

I stared at him in astonishment. "You warned me *what* was a bad idea?"

"Us," he said impatiently. "I should've never asked you out again."

"And I should never have accepted," I retorted, stung. "So we're in agreement. End of discussion."

"Fine." He rubbed his face, then ran his fingers through his wiry, gray-streaked hair. He looked exhausted and exasperated. I had the door halfway closed when he added, "And I should not have brought you the fucking flowers, either."

Sighing, I leaned my head against the doorframe. "Look, Emmet, what do you want from me?" When he didn't answer, I went on. "Because if it's a one-night stand, or a one-month stand, or whatever, I'm not interested, okay?"

"I told you that I'm no good at long-term relationships," he stated matter-of-factly.

"Who said anything about long term? I don't want *any* kind of relationship with you!" My voice got so loud that he waved his hands to shush me.

"Goddamn, Honeycutt—keep your voice down! Somebody will call the police." This time when I started to close the door, Emmet stuck his foot in. "Let me come in, and we can talk this out like two reasonable, intelligent adults."

I shook my head. "No. Absolutely not."

"Why not? You're afraid to, aren't you?"

He was too clever for me, and I rose to the bait. I reached up to unhook the chain, then flung open the door as though daring him to come in. And with that move, I sealed our fate. The door slammed shut, and before I realized what was happening, he'd pinned me against it yet again. The difference was, this time both of us knew there was no turning back.

———

OUR SURPRISING ATTRACTION had flared so suddenly, and so passionately, that I expected it to die out just as quickly. Because neither of us was interested in getting involved, both of us fought doing so. We would agree that it would *not* do, that neither of us wanted it to, that we could walk away from each other without looking back. Which didn't prove to be the case. Throughout that fall, we were only apart for a few days here and there. When Christmas came, I wiped out my savings to take Adam on a trip to New York for the holidays, then convinced Emmet that he should be with his daughter on her first Christmas without her mother. Plus, I thought being away from him would help me sort out my feelings. It shocked and dismayed me how much I missed him, and we talked on the phone for hours, like lovesick teenagers. Adam was highly displeased that I'd gotten so involved with such an unsuitable man, a widower of less than a year with a reputation. Couldn't I see that this was a rebound relationship, and bound to cause me nothing but heartache? I understood and sympathized with his worries, since I shared them. Figuring his mother was having a midlife crisis, my son begged me not to do anything impulsive. I could only promise that I'd try.

I was glad for the caveat, because it turned out to be a promise I didn't keep. A belated Christmas gift awaited me in Fort Lauderdale. Returning to my town house on New Year's Eve, I'd walked into a profusion of flowers covering almost every surface in my apartment, their fragrance so sweet it took my breath away. Before picking me up at the airport, Emmet had bribed the supervisor to let him in with pots of gardenias, lilies, mock orange, and, of course, roses. I was so moved that I surprised both of us by bursting into tears.

Despite his skills at interrogation, Emmet was unable to get anything out of me. Nothing was wrong, I cried in exasperation. I was just tired from the trip, and he should *not* have done such an extravagant thing.

In a light, teasing voice, Emmet said, "If I didn't know better, I'd swear you missed me. Is this your way of telling me you care?"

"Oh, please. You wish. Just leave, Emmet. I'm exhausted, and need to go to bed."

"Sounds good to me."

"No!" I shot back so quickly that he held up his hands in surrender. At the door, he paused. "What should I do with your ticket, then?"

That got my attention. "Ticket?"

"The station's sending me to the Keys on New Year's Day, remember? I got you a ticket, too."

"That's *tomorrow*!" I gasped. "I couldn't possibly go, even if I wanted to. I just took several days of vacation time."

"The news directors have approved your absence."

Aghast, I stared at him. "Without even asking me?" Then it hit me. "You're teasing, aren't you? No way the station would let me off so soon, and for that length of time. You'll be gone a week, right?"

With a shrug, he said nonchalantly, "Everyone was happy to let you off once I told them we were going on our wedding trip."

Unusual for me, I was speechless. When I found my voice, I stammered around before yelping, "You told them *what?*"

Again, he shrugged elaborately. "Do you have a better suggestion? While you were gone I discovered that I can't be without you for a day, much less a whole week."

"You're unbelievable, Emmet," I said with a sigh. "You've skipped a few steps in this process. One, if you've even said that you were in love with me, I missed it—"

"That one's easy. You've brought me out of my despair, and given me a reason for living. Of course I love you. What else did I forget?"

"How about asking if I wanted to marry you before booking me a spot on our wedding trip?"

He rolled his eyes. "It's a waste of time asking questions when you know the answer. Neither of us *wants* this. But with you, Honeycutt, I think I can get it right. Hell, I have to get it right this time. I don't have a choice, because I want to be with you every day, every minute, for the rest of my life." He stopped, and looked at me helplessly.

"You've still missed the most essential step. You haven't asked me if I felt the same."

Emmet glanced at me sheepishly. "Yeah, I was afraid you'd get to that one." Seeing my expression, he rubbed the back of his neck wearily. "Okay, okay. I didn't ask because I was afraid of what your answer would be. I was hoping I could skip that part, and by the time you noticed, it'd be too late."

I didn't call Adam until it was a done deal, and Emmet and I were on our way to Key West. I feared his disapproval too much. Even worse, I feared he'd persuade me to come to my senses, and I didn't want to. Of course it was impulsive, and I was crazy to marry a man I'd known only four months and been involved with less than three. Not only that, Emmet was a widower fifteen years my senior, and had admitted to being a lousy, unfaithful husband. I knew only the barest facts of his former marriage, even less about his late wife's death. But I'd done everything right with Joe, from a formal engagement to a church wedding, and our life together had still turned sour. I'd been so miserable for so long I'd forgotten what happiness felt like until Emmet had come into my life. Many years ago, I'd believed in happy endings. I wanted to believe again.

8

tansy

SOME ELEMENTARY
SLEUTHING

After I got home from the poetry reading, I was too wiped out to do more than thumb through the pages I'd torn from Rosalyn's notebook. As my quick perusal in the loo had indicated, the scribbles were disappointing, seeming to contain little of interest about Rosalyn's final days. But I knew her well enough to hopefully pick up clues by going over her notes with a Sherlock Holmes–like intensity. (Elementary, my dear Watson.) Rosalyn's Day-Timer had been found, but it held only facts. It was the little thoughts and reminders she jotted down in her notebooks that told the true story of her busy days. She was so bad about making notes to herself in Atlanta traffic that Emmet had given her a hands-free recorder and told her if she didn't by God use it, he'd throw away every damn notebook she bought. Of course she didn't, nor did he make good on his threat. The irony doesn't escape me, that Rosalyn survived a lifetime of Atlanta's horrendous traffic only to skid off an isolated road in the one place she'd found peace and tranquillity.

On the following morning, I take out the notebook pages for a closer study. Towel-wrapped from my shower, with slicked-back hair still dripping a bit on my shoulders, I put on my reading glasses and sat on the side of my bed. Some of Rosalyn's notes to herself are unreadable; others made no sense. The ones that do aren't especially interesting, or only slightly so: *Return blouse to B-dale's. Take A's pkg to fedex—ask about return label. Remind E to call TT.* (Ted Turner? Hmm . . . wonder what about?)

Although Rosalyn absolutely refused to e-mail or text, her notes are textlike in their brevity and acronyms. Most abbreviations I can figure out; others I puzzle over. Rosalyn often called me Tans, so when I read *Return bk to TS—ask if she read his latest— better written*, I know TS is me, even if I don't remember the reference or the book. Many of the notations aren't reminders but simply thoughts, maybe a quote she heard on NPR. If I hadn't known her habit of grabbing for the notebook whenever she heard something quotable, I would've puzzled over *Time to say goodbye* (a Broadway song?), or *The earth laughs in flowers* (Emerson?). There are a few lines of poetry, and notes to herself about her garden club presentation on nocturnal plants.

It's the final pages I go over and over. Nothing is dated, but I can put together a time frame on some of them because I'm familiar with the references. I remember when she returned a blouse she got for Christmas, and the package sent to Annie after she'd exchanged some of her gifts. I also know which notes refer to various social events: the Swan House Ball coming up in April, Saint Clements Castle's Valentine's Day Celebration; and the final event referred to, an exhibit and reception at the High Museum, only a week before her death. After the notes about possibly buying a new dress for that event (which she did), and seeing whether Emmet was able to attend (he wasn't), her jottings become more cryptic. Oh, great, Rosalyn, I mutter to myself, I get to the good part and you go mysterious on me.

It's the references to NK, mostly on the final pages, that puzzle me. Rosalyn and I ran in the same circles and knew most of the same people, except for some of her and Emmet's CNN crowd. *Call NK, check date. NK—going or not? Don't forget ask NK about time in M.*

(in March, or May? Moonrise?). I look back through the previous pages without finding any mention of NK, leading me to wonder if he or she was a new acquaintance. Previously I noted several K's (Kit, the two of them going to lunch or somewhere) and N's (Noel, with similar notations), but this is the first combination of the two letters. I might've assumed the unknown person to be a new caterer, perhaps, except for the final entry: *NK—so many lies! Trust gone. Will I ever know the truth? Talked NK. Must go to M and find out.* It's not just the wording that grabs me. In contrast to the other notations that are scribbled haphazardly across the narrow pages, this one is scrawled as though it was written in great distress. The word "lies" is heavily underlined, and I have trouble making out the last word because it's smeared. Was the smear caused by teardrops? Strange, since Rosalyn was never much of a weeper.

I go downstairs still puzzling over it, then quickly rearrange my expression when I spot Noel breakfasting in the garden. It's downright impossible for me to keep anything from him. He not only knows me too well, I'm also a notorious blabbermouth. But I dare not tell him what I've done. How can I explain something to him I can't explain to myself? Yep, you heard me right, Noel—I tore up a little book that most likely held Rosalyn's last writings, and that should've been handed over to her daughter. Then I hid it from the rest of you, who loved her as much as I did. And why did I do such an outrageous thing? Damned if I know.

I can't help but smile at the sight of Noel at the table under the wisteria bower, looking as if he's having tea with Queen Elizabeth. Linen tablecloth and napkins, china plates, OJ in crystal carafe, toast in sterling rack. It's easy to see why so many of my friends assume Noel's gay, despite his previous marriage and numerous courtships with some of Atlanta's most desirable women. It used to catch me off guard when folks asked me which way he swung, until I came up with the perfect comeback. Now I raise my eyebrows in surprise and shoot back, "Why, darling—what a *straight*forward question."

When I drag myself down the stone steps to join Sir Clements for breakfast, I see that he isn't quite dressed for his soiree with Her Majesty, since he's still in his pj's. Only Noel would wear crisp charcoal-and-white pinstriped pj's that perfectly match his charcoal cashmere robe, making me feel downright shabby in black jeans and a tee. He looks so cute, so *Noel*, that I lean over and kiss his cheek before singing out, "Good morning, Bubba. Any grits and sowbelly left for me?"

Noel gets to his feet and pulls my chair out. "Sorry, old thing. Afraid you'll have to settle for scones and clotted cream."

"Ah, well. Be hard plowing the back forty on a breakfast like that, but hey—if it's good enough for his lordship, I'll make do."

Noel gives me one of his patented wry looks. "Nice to see the old Tansy back. I've grown quite tired of your moroseness."

"Don't start that again," I snap, then take a deep breath to compose myself. I have no intention of sparring with him; he'll get all haughty and self-righteous, and I need him in a good mood this morning. Shaking out my napkin, I force a cheery-o smile and say, "Pour me some coffee, would you, love? And might as well fix me a scone while you're at it. I've got the hangover from hell, thanks to that marvelous Moët you served at the reception last night. I consumed a whole bottle by myself."

Noel passes my coffee in a china cup as delicate as dragonfly wings. "Of course we had to serve the finest champagne. How often do we have the honor of hosting a Pulitzer Prize recipient?"

I make a face at him. "One time too many. And you know good and well she got better treatment than any of the Nobel recipients we've entertained in Atlanta, including a former president. But of course, she'd expect nothing less."

Noel hands me a hot scone smothered in clotted cream and

topped with some of Willa's wild plum jam, as fine as anything I've ever gotten in gourmet shops. Maybe better, since Willa sees no need for trendy additions like French tarragon or Asian peppers. Noel asks what I thought of the reading, thus launching our favorite breakfast pastime, rehashing the events of the previous evening. Over scones and coffee, we dissect the outfits, behaviors, and carryings-on of the guests at the Bascom last night, honing in on our favorites. When Noel asks if Frank Grimes ever found me, I shrug casually and tell him about Frank finding Rosalyn's notebook. Piling more jam on my scone, I shake my head sadly when I tell him that the pages were blank. Noel's response is, Ah, yes, Kit told him about that but he'd forgotten, being a tad hungover himself. Shame, isn't it, that Rosalyn didn't have a chance to write in it? We might've learned more about what happened the night of the accident. But doesn't look like we'll ever know, does it?

After that, I have to wait a bit, throw in a couple of catty re- marks about Kit finally hooking up with Jim Lanier, before asking Noel what I've been dying to since I came downstairs. Noncha- lantly, I reach for the silver coffeepot. "Noel? I've been meaning to ask you—I was going over my notes for the Fall Fling, and found a couple of things I couldn't quite make out. Who do we know with the initials NK?"

Noel wrinkles his brow and looks off into the garden. "Hmm. Ned Kelly at Fernbank, maybe? Natalie Cohn—no, wait; that's a C. And who was that woman we worked with on the Olympic Commit- tee, Nancy Somebody? King, I'm thinking. And don't forget, there's Nelson Kennedy."

"Don't think I know him."

"Yes, you do. Investment banker—tall, good-looking chap? Rosalyn always said he looked like Tom Cruise on stilts. I think you dated him a couple of times."

I shake my head. "If so, he didn't make much of an impression. Anyone at CNN?"

For a moment I think I've gone too far and aroused his curiosity, but Noel merely pushes a floppy lock of hair off his forehead before saying, "Only one I can thing of is that Greek guy, Nick, who used to work for Emmet. Wasn't his last name Kirakus? Poor guy was so smitten with Rosalyn that it ended up costing him his job. He made such a fool of himself at the New Year's dance last year that we thought Emmet would punch him out, remember?"

I certainly do, but reach over to put my hand over Noel's. "Dear boy, that was the year before. *Last* New Year's—or thereabouts— Emmet was in the Keys getting himself a new wife."

Noel flinches and closes his eyes. I squeeze his hand, then say with a groan, "I didn't realize we knew so many NK's. Now I'll never figure out who the notes refer to."

He folds his napkin and places it to the side of his plate. "Oh, probably just one of your many lovers." He smiles as he pushes back his chair to leave.

Out of nowhere, the thought comes unbidden; and though I don't say it aloud, it forms in my mind: *Or one of Rosalyn's*. It's a ridiculous thought, ludicrous, even; I'd swear on my mother's grave that Rosalyn never had a serious flirtation, much less a lover. True, Kit and I'd teased Rosalyn about that Nick guy, a hunk whom we called the Greek god, whose attraction to her cost him his job, even if indirectly. Being Rosalyn, she'd felt bad enough to have lunch with him after he got fired—then begged Kit and me not to tell Emmet—but that was it. Rosalyn with a lover is beyond comprehension. But once the thought of her unfaithfulness springs up like a poisonous mushroom, I can't let go of it until it plays out. Suppose, just suppose, that Rosalyn hadn't come to Moonrise to meet Emmet, as we'd surmised afterward. It never made sense to me, anyway. She'd known he was inaccessible, with a film crew deep in the mountains where cell service was practically nonexistent. Not only that, if she'd planned a spur-of-the-moment interlude with her husband, why pick a time when he'd be wiped out after a grueling assignment?

Inaccessible . . . spotty cell service . . . not exactly ideal conditions to arrange a rendezvous. At least, not with one's husband. On the other hand, with the snowy weather and icy roads, Emmet would never dream of Rosalyn going to Moonrise. An isolated house halfway up a mountain would be the perfect place to meet a lover, far from the prying eyes of nosy friends and neighbors. (Unimaginable for Rosalyn to meet at a hotel, even a five-star one.) The only one who might've seen her would be Willa, the most discreet of housekeepers. Or possibly Kit, except Rosalyn knew Kit was on a shopping trip with her contractor. But if, just *if*, Emmet had somehow found out that Rosalyn was there, and had gone to see why, might she not have made a run for it rather than have him catch her?

No, no—that makes no sense, either. Emmet had been as surprised as the rest of us to hear where the accident had occurred. My head is spinning in confusion, and I look up guiltily to tell Noel good-bye. I pat the hand he places on my shoulder as he stands beside my chair to kiss my cheek, off for a board meeting. I start to remind him to change before he goes, that the fusty old dowagers at the Bascom would never recover from the shock of having Lord Clements show up in his pj's. But the teasing remark catches in my throat, and I say nothing. Instead I sit blinking after Noel in further confusion, watching as he trips up the steps to the house.

When he leaned over me, his cheek next to mine, I smelled his delicious, spicy aftershave, noted the faint cut where he'd nicked himself shaving, felt the soft brush of his cashmere robe against my face. Then he was gone. But not before I saw it, right over my shoulder, the monogram on the pocket of the cashmere robe: *NKC*. Noel

Kingsley Clements. Both are old family names, and I remember the time when Mr. Clements told me that he and Noel's mother had argued over which one to call him. Then another memory hits me. Years later, all of us at Moonrise, with Rosalyn and I sitting on the sofa together. She looked at Noel to say, "Isn't Noel Kingsley the perfect name for him, Tans? So royal sounding! Suits him to a tee." Noel had stopped whatever he was doing to look at us quizzically, and Rosalyn had laughed and thrown a pillow his way. "Were your ears burning, N. K. Clements? Because we were talking about you, beautiful man."

I push away from the breakfast table in such a dither that I drop my napkin, slosh coffee on the linen tablecloth, and knock the cushion off the chair. By the time I stumble up the stairs to the safety of my room, I'm so furious with myself that I sprawl on the bed, arms and legs askew. Noel's correct, and I'm a fruitcake, crazy as owl shit. I should be committed—no, better yet, I should commit myself, right now. What is *wrong* with me, fantasizing in such a way about two of the most decent human beings I've ever known? Rosalyn cheating on her husband with *Noel*, one of the closest friends Emmet has? If it weren't so sick, it'd be laughable. And sick it is. I pull a pillow over my head with a groan. Someone in my demented state has no business playing Sherlock, and I make up my mind then and there to tear up the notebook pages and flush them down the toilet, soon as I can drag myself out of bed. It's unlikely we'll ever know what happened that awful night when we lost Rosalyn, but this is for sure: knowing won't change anything, nor will it bring her back. And speculation is making me crazier than ever.

9
willa

PAINTED LADY

Here I am, getting off later than I'd planned yet again. Don't know what's gotten into me, dragging my feet so bad these days when it comes to taking myself home. Got to where I plain hate the long drive, all the way out Buck Creek Road. Used to, I enjoyed passing by the waterfalls on the ride home, and sometimes I'd pull off the highway just to sit and stare at them. Now it makes me sad, seeing how pitiful they look. Bridal Veil Falls is near about dried up. If we don't get rain soon, I don't know what's gonna happen. Most of the crops are already gone, and my garden's never been this bad. Just about everything in these parts is burned up.

The other thing, I'm worried about getting home late and setting Duff off again. He's ill as a hornet these days, and I'm about sick of it. Sometimes, the only thing that keeps me from quitting Duff is to remind myself how different he is when he's not drinking. I grew up loving Duff Algood, thinking we'd marry one day. We was raised on land next to each other, and our mamas were distant cousins. Duff's a looker, too, and we have a big time together fiddling and singing. But he started playing at juke joints, then coming home drunk. Next thing I know, he's taken up the Algood pastime of making his own brew.

At first, Linc thought I was making it up when I told him about Duff brewing his own likker in my barn; he laughed out loud and said he couldn't wait to tell Noel. Once he saw I wasn't joking, he asked what was wrong. When I told him what that crap did to Duff—how it made him turn into a different person—Linc got all upset and said I had to make him stop. If homemade moonshine's not fixed right, he said, it doesn't just make you crazy. That stuff can kill you.

I've just made the turn off Buck Creek Road onto Little Buck when a butterfly makes a suicide dive into the front of my truck. I swerve as far over as I can—only a few inches leeway on Little Buck, the drop-off down the mountain's so steep—but I know the poor thing's dead. I've always hated to hit butterflies, even more so now that Linc's teaching me so many things about them. He's got me going around collecting them, and I about have a shoebox full. Some I'll fix to boards, and the rest I plan on framing. What I like are those frames with glass on both sides and a butterfly in the middle. There's several hanging in Linc's kitchen windows, the prettiest things I've ever seen.

As I feared, the butterfly's right next to the wheels, dead as a doorknob. I can't stand that I kilt something so pretty, but at least it's one I don't have. When I see that it's a Painted Lady, I'm downright excited, and pick it up ever so gentle. I can't wait to tell Linc. The black, white, and orange Painted Lady, with its little splash of pink underneath, is the one I particularly liked when I studied Linc's boards. He seemed kind of surprised, saying that the Ladies are so common, then laughed when I told him that I could identify.

I'm back to driving up the road when I recall what Linc says about where I live, and smile to myself. "Going to the McFee place is an adventure in time travel," he says. "Like going back a century or so to a simpler time and place." That pleased me a lot more than I let on.

Thing is, it's true. My property is hard to reach, it's so high atop Buck Mountain. And Buck's a real mountain, not a hill like the one

Moonrise sits on. You keep climbing the dirt road like you're ascending into the heavens, and just as you think you really are, the road crosses a rickety bridge over a gorge, where Little Buck Creek runs. Just beyond the bridge is the McFee forty acres. The old homeplace is squat in the middle of a grassy field, and under a spread of big old oaks.

It's near about sunset when I pull under the sourwood tree. I'm sure gonna have to get a move on to get everything done before dark. I keep the Painted Lady cupped in my hand when I climb the rock steps to the house, thinking I'll put it in a piece of Tupperware since the shoebox's about full. Last thing I want is to mess up its little wings. Like Linc's place, my house is one big room, with the kitchen in the back and the sitting room making up the front part. One difference with mine and Linc's place is, you have to go around the staircase to get to my kitchen. Because of that, I don't see Duff until I walk in. He's sitting hunched over the table, staring at me like he's about to spit nails. Before I can even say hey, he snaps at me. "Where you been?"

"Don't start on me," I snap back. "You know where I been."

"Damn right I do," he growls. "You've been at the Looking Glass Lake waiting on that cripple instead of home where you supposed to be, fixing my supper. I'm 'bout to starve to death."

I bend over to get the Tupperware from the cabinet under the sink. "Looks like you'll be starving a bit longer, big boy. You know all the chores gotta be done before we eat. If you've done your part, you'll get your supper sooner. Did you get the clothes on the line?"

Ignoring me, Duff bangs his fist on the table. "I'm hungry, by God!" he yells, and I whirl around, furious.

"What's got into you, Duff, yelling at me like that? If you think I'm gonna stand for being treated like the men in your family treat their women, you've got another thing coming."

He scowls like a thundercloud, but changes his tone to ask what's for supper.

"I'm frying up some pork chops and Irish potatoes," I tell him. "And planned on boiling that corn you pulled." Naturally there's no corn on the drainboard, so Duff drags his rear end up from the table. With a mighty sigh, he grabs his cap and starts out back to the cornfield. His hand on the latch, he stops to glance my way.

"What you putting in that Tupperware?" he asks, tilting his head curiously.

I tip it over to show him the Painted Lady. "Aw, I hit a butterfly with my truck soon as I turned off Buck Creek Road."

His eyes widen. "You gonna cook it?"

"Yeah, Duff," I say with a snort. "Thought I'd fix us some butterfly stew."

Duff gets all sullen and mutters under his breath, something about how he never gets his supper on time these days because of my foolishness. But when I take a step toward him, he's out the door like greased lightning, moving fast for such a big man.

––––

MY FIRST BUTTERFLY board is little, and don't look near as good as even the oldest one of Linc's, but Linc brags on it, anyway. The two of us went through my shoebox to decide which ones go on the board, and which to save for the glass. So far, I've picked out the Painted Lady, a Monarch, and another favorite, the Mourning Cloak, which Linc's gonna help me frame. A store downtown sells them for a hundred dollars with just one butterfly in it, and hundreds more if you group several butterflies together. Linc said I could sell them if I wanted to, start me a little "cottage industry," but I couldn't bear to part with them. It makes me happy, thinking how pretty those butterflies will look in my windows.

Mountain folks aren't much for fixing up their houses with pretty things like summer people do. Momma had her quilting and patchwork, but I never took to sewing. I like the outdoors too much, one reason why hunting butterflies suits me. Duff makes fun of me, but I don't care. At least I'm not hiding away in the barn making stuff that'll make you go blind or die. He's gotten even sneakier about his brew lately, and I about had a fit when I found out why. The other night, one of his buddies let it slip that Duff's been selling it to tourists over in Cashiers. It's a dry county, so there's always men wanting to buy likker for their fishing trips. Let one of them die from that poison of yours, I told Duff, and see where you end up. I wondered how come he hadn't worked much for Kit lately, yet always has plenty of pocket money.

I'm at Linc's, and he just woke up from his nap when Noel and Tansy drop in. My eyes about pop out of my head at the way they're dressed. Tansy's got on a bathing suit that looks like two strings tied over her privates. Since the robe she's wearing is made of something like fishnet, you can see her titties spilling over the stringed top, plain as you please. I blush at the sight of Noel in a bathing suit, a shirt tied around his shoulders, like I haven't seen him in one before. But Lord have mercy, that's one good-looking man!

The other day, Noel, Linc, and Tansy got to reminiscing about their picnics at the swimming hole on my property, at the foot of the waterfall just beyond the house. They used to swim there all the time, and I'd join right in. Let's do it again, Noel said. Next thing I know, we're all packed up and headed to the swimming hole. I keep trying to tell them I can't go with them, that we have preaching that night, with Duff and me singing for the laying on of hands. Tansy says great, they'll take Linc to get healed after we get done swimming. I can only imagine how shocked the church folks would be if I showed up with that bunch!

Come to find out, everybody's making a big deal out of the out-

ing, with Helen fixing a picnic to haul down there, which is quite a
hike. I give in, telling them I'll be right down soon as I go to the
house to get into my bathing suit. Duff's nowhere to be seen, so I
leave him a note to join us. Running down the road fast because the
sand burns my bare feet, I find myself getting excited. I love swimming, and it's been a long time.

Noel's already toted Linc down to the swimming hole because I
hear them laughing and carrying on when I turn off the road where
their cars are parked. A trail leads through a stand of laurel thickets
and straight down to the gorge, where Little Buck Creek runs. After
tumbling down the rocky gorge for miles, Little Buck suddenly
drops several feet over a broken ledge of rock to form the pool at its
base—a pool of the prettiest water, and no telling how deep. Then
the creek picks itself up to move on to flow into Big Buck Creek, a
ways beyond our property. Normally you hear the cascades before
you get there, but this year the water's so much lower that even the
sound's different. The air gets cooler and sweeter the closer I get,
and I pick up my pace.

Although I'm wearing a denim shirt of Duff's, with a towel
thrown around my shoulders, I'm self-conscious about my old
bathing suit, which has gotten way too little over the years. I come
through the laurel bushes to find everybody sitting around on
the big flat rocks surrounding the pool of water—except Linc,
who's perched on the seat his walker makes. They all holler and
call out to me, and I blush. It's silly to be so self-conscious all of
a sudden; I've been swimming with these folks no telling how
many times.

Linc motions to me, and I scramble over to the rock next to his
walker-seat. Bless his heart, his skinny white arms and legs look
like matchsticks, and I make up my mind then and there to get him
out in the sun more. We walk in the garden every afternoon, but
stick mostly to the shade because he's so pale. I should know better;

Momma used to say there wasn't much wrong with anybody or any-thing that a dose of sunlight wouldn't cure.

"We were just telling Helen about the plunge," Linc says with a wink. "Are you going to do it again, Willa?"

Tansy, who's on the other side of Linc and doing stretches, chimes in. "Yeah, sweetie. You go first and we'll follow."

I realize that they're talking about the time a few years back when every single one of us jumped from the top of the falls into the pool. It's hard to believe we actually did such a foolhardy thing, and I grin at them, remembering.

"Someone's got to take the lead, and Willa's the youngest," Emmet says. He's seated farthest away from the falls, next to where Helen has placed a couple of picnic baskets. Standing by him, Helen looks cute as a bug in a little embroidered top over her suit, short enough to show off her shapely brown legs.

Kit's sprawled on her towel next to Helen like she's sunbathing, except she's raised up on an elbow to watch everybody, sunglasses pushed up on her head and hair falling over her shoulder. I eye her, curious. She's gotten to where she's a lot nicer to Helen, which sur-prises me.

Kit studies Helen for a minute before saying, "Don't y'all think Helen should go first? It could be like an initiation rite to welcome her as one of us."

Judging by her expression, Helen's trying to decide if they're kidding, or what. Turning her head to me, she says, "Willa? Should I do the plunge?"

"I don't know what they've told you about taking the plunge, Helen, but only a pure-tee fool would do it," I tell her, which of course gets all of them hooting and hollering, swearing it was the most fun they ever had. Poor Helen blinks her eyes and looks even more confused.

"Emmet?" She prods him with her toe and demands, "You'd

better tell me the truth!" which sets everybody off again, howling with laughter. She stands with her hands on her hips, looking from one to the other, eyes narrowed. "Okay. I get it," she says finally. "Y'all are having me on, aren't you? Take the rube to the waterfall and dare her to jump off, break her fool neck, huh?"

Grinning, Emmet puts his beer down to reach for her hand, but Helen jerks away. He holds up his hands in surrender but he's still grinning, full of mischief, so she whirls around to point a finger at Linc. "You're the only one I trust, Linc. Y'all didn't actually jump from the top of that waterfall, did you?"

Before Linc can answer, Noel speaks up. "Obviously Linc hasn't told you how he got so gimped up, Helen."

"Not funny, Noel," Helen snaps. "Linc?" she repeats, her voice high.

Linc shakes his head at their foolishness. "I'm afraid it's true, my dear. And the person who's to blame has yet to say a word in her defense."

All eyes turn to Tansy, who's still stretching this way and that. She stops and sighs. "Oh, for Christ's sake," she says, throwing her arms way out. "Here's what happened, Helen. A few years ago we had a champagne picnic here at the swimming hole. Except for Willa, who has better sense, the rest of us started hitting the bubbly pretty hard—"

With a hoot, Noel interrupts. "Speak for yourself, old girl."

"Bull hockey," she hisses. "You were drunk as a lord, Noel Clements."

He looks insulted. "I won't stand for you telling Helen I got smashed on champagne. What does that do to my macho image? It was Emmet's thermos of vodka that did me in. You, too, if memory serves me right."

"I was the only sober one here," Kit butts in.

"Not true," Emmet says. "Rosalyn wasn't drinking." I notice

the others look at him kind of funny, then realize how come. Everybody in town talks about how he never mentions her. Most folks reminisce about a person they've lost, even if doing so makes them sad, but not Emmet.

Everyone falls silent, until Tansy picks up the story again. She tells Helen about the first time they took the plunge, and Helen listens wide-eyed. "Trust me, Helen—Kit's full of shit, as usual," Tansy says. "Just like the rest of us, she was high as a Georgia pine. There were six of us—neither Myna nor Poor Old Al came—"

Everybody butts in again to remind Tansy that Linc hadn't even met Myna then. At this rate she'll never get her story told, and I hide a smile.

It's Noel who shushes Tansy and picks up from there. "Let me tell you what really happened, Helen. First of all, Tansy was the one who dared the rest of us to do it. Big surprise, huh? Next thing we knew, Tansy had left her swimsuit in the laurel and was crawling butt naked up to that ledge—" He points to the top of the fifteen-foot high falls, and Helen gasps. "All of us yelled at her to come back," Noel continues, "but of course she ignored us. Being the knight in shining armor that I am, I went after her."

"All I wanted to do was strut around up there bare-assed," Tansy says, "until Don Quixote came charging after me." She shrugs her shoulders, holding her hands palms up. "What choice did I have? I jumped."

"Tell the truth, Tans," Noel says, arms folded, and she laughs and tosses her head.

"Okay, I slipped. That ledge is slippery as snot, and I was plunging down the falls before I knew what had happened. Nothing to do but hold out my arms and swan dive in." She stops to run her fingers through her hair. "Well, that's not quite true. Fortunately I had sense enough to flip and go in feet first. Otherwise I really might have broken my neck."

"Good heavens!" Helen's eyes are huge, then she starts to giggle. She prods Emmet with her toe again and says, "You liar. You told me all of you took the plunge."

"Oh, everyone did," Tansy tells her. "Even Willa."

This time it's me who grins and holds up my hands in surrender. "It's the God's truth, Helen. Noel jumped in after Tansy, and swore it was great. So Linc, Kit, and Rosalyn climbed up there, too, and when they told me Noel was right, well . . . I couldn't let a bunch of old folks show me up, could I?" Everybody laughs at that, but I add real quicklike, "I gotta tell you, though, I was scared out of my mind. Yeah, it was fun at the time, but I wouldn't do it again, especially with the water as low as it is now."

It's Kit who argues with me. "Oh, c'mon, Willa! The pool's so deep there couldn't possibly be any danger, and you know it. If Helen wants to do this, let her see for herself." Turning to Helen, she asks, "You don't want to be the only one here who hasn't made the plunge, do you?"

"Sure don't," Helen says. "I want to give it a try."

Without another word, she tosses off the embroidered top and starts toward the waterfall, prissing in her little white one-piece suit. When Emmet jumps to his feet to grab her arm, she shakes him off. I can tell that irritates him because he orders her to stop right that minute. Willa's right, he tells her, the water's too low for anyone to make the plunge today. Helen stops, but she bats her lashes and says to him in a mocking voice, "Are you telling me you're afraid of a big bad waterfall, Emmet? Afraid to make the plunge?"

Emmet says damn right he is, and okay, she's made her point—they shouldn't have teased her. The others chime in, serious now. Noel says, "We jumped off the falls, Helen, but we were drunken fools that day. It might've been fun drunk, but I wouldn't do it sober."

To my surprise, Kit gets up and walks over to join Helen. "Oh, please," she says in disgust. "You guys are being ridiculous. Come on, Helen—I'll go with you. Obviously our boys aren't brave enough."

Helen's face lights up when she sees Kit, and she follows her to the waterfall without a backward glance. I turn to see what Emmet's gonna do now. It's the water level I'm worried about, not whether or not somebody's with you for the plunge. Hands on hips, Emmet's watching with a frown, but he doesn't try to stop them. Neither does anyone else, so I wait, too. They're probably just calling Emmet's bluff, having a little fun with him. Helen don't know any better, but a priss-pot like Kit won't do this, I'm sure. Standing at the foot of the falls with Helen by her side, Kit's smiling like a possum as she unbuttons the hooded cover-up over her bathing suit. Though we can't hear them over the sound of the waterfall, she's obviously telling Helen how to climb to the top. Helen's looking up and nodding, but she looks scared—scared enough that I relax. She's just aggravating Emmet by pretending she's going to do this.

By the time the thought's out, Helen has grabbed hold of a bush growing on the embankment and started the climb up. In a split second, she's climbed to the top of the falls like a monkey shimmying up a banana tree. Standing with her cover-up still half buttoned, Kit stares after her openmouthed, like she's too surprised to even move. Everybody looks up and yells at Helen to come back, but she has nowhere to go, nothing to do now but perch on the rocky ledge of the falls. I remember how slippery that thing is, and can tell the minute Helen feels it, too. She looks over the edge and down below, and her face turns white as a sheet. Cussing a blue streak, Emmet has come over to stand at the foot of the falls where Helen climbed up, and where Kit stands looking helpless and scared. Listen, honey—take a step back real careful, Emmet calls up to Helen. When she totters like she's about to faint, Noel pulls off his shirt to go after her at the same time that Emmet bends down to unlace his shoes.

I don't wait for either of them. Before you can say jackrabbit, I've thrown off my shirt, pushed Kit out of the way at the foot of the falls, and crawled up that embankment fast. Below, everybody's yelling for me to hurry. Just as I get to the top, however, Helen's feet slip out from under her and she lets out a little cry. "Helen!" Emmet yells in horror. From my perch on the ledge, I watch helplessly as she goes over the ledge, tumbling through the air as if in slow motion. Can't nobody fall that far without going all the way under, and I can only pray I'm wrong about the depth of the water. When she hits, there's a loud splash as she disappears beneath the bubbly surface.

When she don't come up right away, I have no choice now but to jump in after her. I hit the surface of the pool hard, and the water's so cold it takes my breath away. As soon as I shoot upward and get my head above the water, I gasp for air like a trout on a riverbank. Scared now, I look around for Helen, but she's still nowhere to be seen. Tansy and Kit are standing next to Linc, yelling at me to find her and sounding as scared as I feel. Just as I catch my breath to dive under again, Helen pops up next to me like a cork. I see the shock in her eyes as she too gasps for breath. She reaches out for me, and I grab her hands so she can't go under again. Before I can ask if she's okay, there's a loud cry above us, and we look up to see Noel and Emmet jumping in, one after the other. Until then, I didn't realize they'd followed me to the top.

The two of them hit even harder than I did, with a splash that sends waves all the way to the rocks. Tansy and Kit start squawking like wet hens—and Linc yelps in surprise—when the water splashes them as well. When Noel and Emmet surface, both of them head straight for Helen with the fast strokes of those Olympic swimmers on the TV. Emmet looks more worried than I've seen him in a long time. With a yank, he pulls Helen away from me and starts fussing at her, yelling, "Goddammit, Helen—why wouldn't you listen to me?" I swear, I've never seen a man who don't act mad when he gets scared.

After Emmet helps Helen out, Noel, who's treading water next to me, puts a cold hand on my shoulder. "She's okay, right?" I don't need to answer him; we watch as Emmet wraps Helen in the towel Tansy offers. Helen tries to laugh the whole thing off, but I notice her stagger a bit when Emmet leads her back to the rock where the picnic's laid out. She's fine, she keeps telling everyone as she puts her little top back on, but I wonder. I don't say anything, even to Noel, but she hit hard, and stayed under longer than she should've. It worried me a lot more than I let on. Now that Emmet's dried off and pulled on a T-shirt, he's plopped down on the rock with a towel around his neck, breathing hard. Tansy's standing by sort of nervous-looking, like she doesn't know what to say—not like Tansy at all. Poor Linc watches them from his seat on the walker, unable to do a blame thing. It's Kit I can't figure out. She's taken her place on the other side of Helen, and her eyes dart from her to Emmet, back and forth. Worried as Kit appears, what I don't get is the smirk she keeps trying to hide. I can't help but wonder if she didn't taunt Helen on purpose, shaming her so she had no choice but to do what she did. She knows how bad Helen wants them to accept her.

I jump when Noel asks me if I'm getting out, like I've forgotten he was in the pool with me. "If ever an occasion called for a beer," Noel says with a shake of his head, "this is it."

When I tell him to get Emmet one, too, and fast, he swims to the side of the pool and pulls himself out in a hurry. By now I'm used to the cold, so I dog paddle over to the side closest to Linc. He's shaking his head like he can't believe what he just saw. "Willa, my girl," he calls out when I appear in front of him, "I salute you.

While everyone else stood around helplessly, you took charge to save the day."

"I was scared shitless" is all I can think to say. Me and him just look at each other, shaking our heads, then both of us laugh. Not much else to do at this point, anyway. The others are doing the same now that everything's okay, laughing and talking in relief as they pass around the beer and food.

Eyeing Linc, I say, "Before all this happened, I was thinking that it'd do you good to get in if the water wasn't so blame cold. Let's try it another time, okay?"

To my surprise, Linc struggles to his feet. "On the contrary, I'd love to get in. And I prefer cold water, which I find both invigorating and therapeutic."

He hollers for Noel to leave his beer and come help him get in. Noel obliges, though he tries to talk Linc out of it, as I figured. Brushing him off, Linc insists the cold won't bother him. I say he's got to keep his shirt on, at least, and let Noel take his glasses. After Noel helps him ease down into the water, I take over. When Linc takes ahold of my arm, Noel goes back to join the others, who are now digging into Helen's picnic baskets and acting like nothing happened. I tread water backward and lead Linc around the outside of the swimming hole, which ain't all that big. We have to move slow 'cause of his right side being so weak, and Linc frowns like it's hard work. When I ask if he's okay, he raises two fingers in a victory sign.

"Hey, Linc! Willa!" Tansy yells. She's wedged in between Noel and Kit, the three of them sitting on a rock with plates on their laps. Emmet and Helen are on the flat rock next to them, Emmet drinking a beer and Helen putting stuff from her baskets on a tablecloth. "BLTs!" Tansy calls out to me and Linc. "Made with turkey bacon—right, Helen?—but they're not half bad."

I look at Linc and giggle. He rolls his eyes and says, "Talk about damning with faint praise."

"You ready to get out and eat?" I ask.

"When you are. God, this water feels terrific! Just what the doctor ordered."

I can tell he's having him a big time, but I worry he'll catch his death. "Tell you what," I say. "Let's make one more trip around, then I'll get you out."

Linc nods. He looks cute without his glasses on, more like a regular person than a professor, though he tells me he can't see squat. "By the way, hon," he says without meeting my eyes. "When Myna comes home this weekend, we probably shouldn't mention this."

I nod instead of asking him if I have stupid written on my face. That woman would have my hide! There's a commotion from the others, and I turn to see what's going on. They're waving at somebody coming down the trail, and when the laurel bushes part, Duff sticks his head out. Noel calls, "Duff, my man! You're just in time for the picnic."

When I see how he's dressed, my heart sinks. Along with his good dungarees, Duff's got on the plaid shirt I ironed this morning, a string tie, and his best boots. He's all spruced up, too, with his beard trimmed and hair all slicked back. Surely it's not time for preaching! The sun's still way up in the sky, hanging over the hickory tree by the falls.

"I ain't studying no picnic, Noel." Duff says it in such a rude tone that I'm shocked and embarrassed. "I come to get Willa." He stands in the clearing with his hands on his hips, staying put instead of walking down to the swimming hole. Finally he yells out, "Willa? What you think you're doing, playing around with preaching an hour away? Me and you're singing tonight."

"I haven't forgot," I call back. The others, across the swimming hole from where he stands, have gone real quiet, all ears now. "But we got plenty of time."

Duff leaves his spot to lumber over to the rock where I left my towel and his denim shirt, which he snatches up. "I told you I wanted to get there early tonight so we could practice," he says.

Noel leaves the picnic to come help me get Linc out. Duff stands there glaring while the two of us struggle getting Linc back to his walker-seat. Just as I feared, he's been in too long because he's shivering bad, with his legs so trembly he can't hardly stand. His shirt's wet from the armpits down, and Noel starts unbuttoning it fast. "I can't help y'all," Linc tells us with a weak little laugh, "until I get my glasses on. I'm blind as a bat."

"Hang on a minute," Noel says. "They're in your backpack." With a nod of his head, he motions toward the towels and stuff hanging on a branch of a nearby dogwood tree. "Could you get the backpack for him, Willa? And grab a couple of those towels, too."

I run over to the dogwood so we can get Linc wrapped up, but Duff grabs my arm and yanks me around so hard that I let out a cry of pain. "Noel can take care of Linc," he says to me, real mean. "You're off duty now."

I hear Noel say, "Hey—take it easy!" But Emmet moves so fast I don't realize what's happened until he's grabbed Duff by the front of the shirt and gotten right in his face. In a calm but not-to-be-messed-with voice, Emmet says, "Let go of her, Duff."

For a minute it looks like Duff's gonna take a swing at Emmet, and my heart jumps in my throat. But Emmet don't even blink. To my relief, Duff turns loose of my arm with a little shove. Scowling something fierce, he throws my towel and shirt at me, and I catch them on reflex. Without another word, Duff turns on his heel and disappears through the laurel bushes. Weak-kneed, I close my eyes, and Emmet puts a hand on my shoulder. "You okay, hon?"

I nod, then glance over to see Linc gripping the handles of the walker so hard his knuckles are white. Noel's behind him with his hands on Linc's shoulders, as if to keep him from coming out of the walker and going after Duff himself. On the other side, Helen stands frozen in place, while Tansy and Kit hang on to each other wide-eyed. After everything else that happened this afternoon, I feel so bad about Duff upsetting them that I take off running up the trail, slipping and sliding on the rocks barefooted. They call after me, tell me to wait, but I don't look back. I'd die of shame if I had to face them now. I try to brush my tears away, but they keep welling up in my eyes so I can barely see where I'm going. Soft-spoken as he is, Linc's voice carries up to me as he tells the others: "Hey, guys— don't go after her. It'd just embarrass her even more, and she'll be fine. Trust me—after what I saw today, Duff Algood is no match for our girl."

LADY OF THE NIGHT

E mmet and the Bride aren't the only ones who have to work this summer. After our whirlwind first weeks of sightseeing—under the guise of showing Helen every twig and anthill in a hundred-mile radius of Highlands—and the picnic at the swimming hole, each of us settles into our own routines. To give the devil her due, Helen's been the most diligent in shutting herself away until she's put in several hours' work on the cookbook. Or her new show, maybe. It's hard to imagine her pulling off the latter, frankly. Even if I could accept Rosalyn being replaced by a health-conscious Cracker with bouncy hair and a perky butt, I'd still have trouble with the woman herself. I mean, that girl has a bad case of what used to be called nerves. She jumps if you say boo to her, blushes when we trash-talk one another, then laughs her nervous little laugh as though she knew we were kidding all along. Yet Emmet—one of the most caustic intellectual snobs I've ever known—looks at us as if to say, "Isn't she *adorable?*"

According to Willa, Emmet, too, stays closed up in his office most of the day. He rarely used his office before; refusing to have the house wired for Internet was Rosalyn's way of forcing him to leave his work in Atlanta. But these days he's back at it, working on a big documentary about the drought. When he's not closed up in his office, he's in Asheville, doing a remote broadcast of his show at one of their TV stations. Things have changed for the newly-weds, and I wonder how that's going. I have to handle the ever-discreet Willa just right to get any kind of information out of her. That's when I miss Miss Creasy the most. Closemouthed as she tried to be, I knew how to get the dirt from her.

I got to know Miss Creasy when I was ten, the same time Noel, Rosalyn, and Kit came into my life. When my mama finally left my charming cad of a father, who'd squandered her considerable fortune, she and I returned to her family home in Cashiers. Mama picked up her old life with the country club set of Highlands, where her friends, including Rosalyn's mother, set out to find her a new man. Glamorous, sophisticated, and fun loving, Mama didn't need help with that task, and quickly hooked up with Norton Clements, a most eligible widower. Where she did need assistance, however, was luring Mr. Clements to the altar. Although he returned Mama's affection, he was content with the status quo. Egged on by her friends, Mama determined to change his mind. If I'd followed her around and taken notes on her schemes to get herself wed, I could've learned enough to manage the operations of the CIA . . . or more appropriately, the KGB.

Watching from the sidelines, I figured out long before Mama and her cohorts did that Mr. Clements had no intention of remarrying. Mama's efforts to land him included bringing me, her poor fatherless daughter, on outings involving his poor motherless son. Mr. Clements doted on me; Noel and I became fast friends; still no proposal. Frustrated, Mama redoubled her efforts, and Rosalyn's mother, who reigned over the social scene both here and in Atlanta, put her resources to work. By the time Norton Clements got to Laurel Cottage for the weekend, Mama could track his every move.

Mrs. Harmon's role was to host endless soirees at Moonrise, placing Mama and Mr. Clements in the most romantic of settings.

As it turned out, Miss Creasy knew Mr. Clements well, since she supplied him with herbal concoctions for his rheumatism and other ailments. Try as she may, however, Mama couldn't pry any information from the housekeeper about her elusive suitor until an unexpected thing happened: Quite by chance, I became the conduit.

During the soirees, Miss Creasy often babysat me, Noel, and Rosalyn, entertaining us with tall tales and deliciously scary ghost stories. I was so taken with Miss Creasy that I became a special pet of hers, her devoted admirer. During my and Mama's daytime visits to Moonrise, I followed her around like a puppy. Listening to her stories was more fun than playing with Rosalyn, three years younger and a mere child to me. Rosalyn didn't mind because she usually had Kit to play with. Kit's parents were always at Moonrise in those days, with her father and Rosalyn's doing business together. The truth of the matter is, the Harmons practically raised Kit, their daughter's devoted playmate. Miss Creasy turned out to be a goldmine of information, and I'd tell Mama whatever she had to say about Mr. Clements. I was taught the fine art of subterfuge by my mama, but subtle prying I learned on my own.

Unfortunately, Willa's not as pliable as her mother was. She's much more like her daddy, the stereotypical taciturn mountaineer. Even so, I still manage to get a few juicy tidbits out of her. The other day I asked if Helen ever let her and Emmet sample the recipes she's working on for her cookbook, and Willa provided a surprising answer. I almost busted my butt getting up the stairs to call Kit, who answered on the first ring.

"Listen up, girl," I said. "Willa just revealed the most amazing thing about Emmet, and I wanted to let you know before I call the *Atlanta Journal-Constitution*."

"And what is that?" she responded.

"He is actually a human being."

"No, he isn't, Tansy. That's ridiculous."

"Get this. I found out how the Bride sunk her heart-healthy claws into him."

Kit hooted. "News flash. She got him the same way younger women with cute little butts and perky boobs have always gotten older men."

I couldn't let that one pass, even if it meant forfeiting a serve to the other team. "So speaks the voice of experience."

"Yeah, you ought to know," Kit shot back, then we both giggled. "Okay, I'll bite. But it'd better be good. I'm playing golf with Mr. Lanier, and tee time's in half an hour. What'd she do, drug him?"

"Sort of. Emmet told Willa that he fell in love with his new wife's cooking before he fell for her."

"So?"

"Kit! Remember that he was a broken man in a strange town, who lived in a sublet and didn't know anyone except the folks in the newsroom! So what does our little bride-to-be do but show up at his door with comfort food?"

With a sigh, Kit said, "What have I said since day one? That's been my worry, that she stalked him out and took advantage of his situation. But the rest of you bought their little romantic story, the struggling single mom who won the heart of the bitter old newsman—"

"Grouping me with Noel and Linc is *not* fair! You know I've had my guard up from the start."

"You've been better than the guys, certainly," she admitted. "But here's what really bothers me. Since Emmet's remarriage, it's tormented me, the way I've let both Rosalyn and Annie down. All of us have, Tansy. Rosalyn comes to me every night—"

"She *does*? You mean like a ghost at the foot of your bed?"

"I mean like the dearest friend I've ever had, closer than a sister—" Her voice caught, and she paused to regain her control. "Look, I've got to go, but let me say this. God knows, I've tried— all of us have—to accept that Rosalyn is not only gone and not coming back, but also that she's been replaced. If it were by some- one more like us, I'd still have trouble with it, maybe. But who is this unknown woman? She might be a low-rent little schemer for all we know. I can't bear to witness the man that Rosalyn loved be- ing duped, if that's what is going on. No wonder Rosalyn keeps appearing to me."

"Next time Rosalyn comes," I said a bit testily, "ask her what the hell she thinks we can do about it. I'm not exactly thrilled, ei- ther, but like it or not, we're stuck with the situation."

Kit wasn't so sure. "Not if Emmet comes to his senses. I wonder if Rosalyn's trying to tell me that she understands how grief led him to make a dreadful mistake, but he has to get out before he gets in any deeper. For Annie's sake, if nothing else. For all we know, that woman could take him for everything he has—maybe even squan- der Annie's inheritance, too."

That rang a chord with me. "You'd think not, but it sure hap- pened to my mother. I grew up hearing about the way my deadbeat dad duped her, spent all her inheritance. Both of us were left with nothing."

Kit knew the story as well, which toughened her resolve. "All we need is the right opportunity, Tansy, and I believe you and I could help Emmet come to his senses. We owe it to Annie. It's the only thing we can do for Rosalyn now."

——

BEFORE LONG, OPPORTUNITY presents itself. Out of the blue, I get a call from Emmet. If I need further proof that he's as smitten as a schoolboy with his first crush, he hands it to me. He's calling for a favor, asking me to take a message to Helen. He wants to let her know that he'll be getting in really late from Asheville tonight—something about a dinner with his colleagues—but her cell's turned off. He doesn't want her to worry, he adds, and I stifle a snort of disgust. At least I'm no longer the only crazy in the group; evidently the Florida sun short-circuited his formerly functioning brain. Sounding downright sheepish (*Emmet?*), he admits he forgot to let Helen know last time he ran late, and she got really upset. I bite my tongue, remembering the endless nights Rosalyn waited up for him, fearing the worst, and how dismissive he'd been of her worries.

Kit's and my afternoon walk, which we've just resumed, is the perfect time to deliver Emmet's message to the Bride. A daily power walk was something Rosalyn, Kit, and I started several years ago. We followed the same route so often that our timing was clockwork: Kit'd walk by Laurel Cottage where I'd join in without her even slowing down. Arms swinging and legs pumping, we'd make our way up the driveway to Moonrise, where I'd edge over to make room for Rosalyn to jump in. Last summer—our first without Rosalyn—neither Kit nor I could do it anymore. When she and I resumed walking a few weeks ago, we changed our route in order to avoid Moonrise altogether.

Today, we'll go to Moonrise, I decide, and head out. I also decide not to tell Kit until we're halfway there in case she refuses. Then I'd have to go back later, and alone, to deliver Emmet's message. I pass Linc's cabin without even pausing, which is difficult for me. My hovering over him is beginning to piss Linc off. The traitor has joined forces with Noel, with both of them calling me neurotic now. I'm surprised to see Willa's truck still there, way past her usual time. Something could be wrong, so I head down the driveway to find out, hovering be damned. I've taken only a few steps when I'm stopped by the sound of laughter coming from the porch. Recognizing Linc's voice, then Willa's, I beat a hasty retreat before they spot me.

Funny, I was pleased for Linc when Willa signed on to help him out; now it's Willa I'm happy for. They've formed a relationship that's touching to witness, the wise old professor with the wide-eyed acolyte. The other day I found them in the garden, Linc seated on his walker, and Willa kneeling beside a flowering buddleia. Their heads were bent together, her copper-red hair glinting in the sunlight, while Linc pointed with a pencil to one of the branches of the buddleia. She'd told me Linc was teaching her to use his camera, which was on a cord around her wrist. Plus, he was teaching her about butterflies. For years she'd helped maintain his garden without knowing that everything is dedicated to the luring of butterflies: the water features and dry pond for basking; salt blocks; old logs for hibernation; ground cover and host plants; an adjacent overgrown meadow.

That day Willa waved me over in great excitement, and I made my way curiously through waist-high beds of lantana, bee balm, phlox, and verbena. The movement of butterflies through the leaves made it look like their blooms had sprouted wings. "A Zebra Longwing," Willa said breathlessly when I reached the place where she crouched. "They're hardly ever seen up here, Linc says, but the hot weather has the poor thing off its course." I bent over to look. Ebony with zebralike markings on its elongated wings, the Zebra Longwing was aptly named. When Willa told me about the Longwing's unusually feeble flight pattern, Linc beamed with pride. For an uneducated mountain girl, she was a quick study.

I approach the Rutherford house with trepidation, afraid my expression will give me away, and Kit can tell how much the house appalls me. Like most Southern women, I was raised to ingratiate myself. Speaking one's mind was unheard of in a well-bred lady of my generation, as was having an unlady-like opinion. As Noel constantly reminds me, I flunked out of—or was kicked out of—that course, yet I still can't bring myself to tell Kit what I think of her newly remodeled house. Hypocrite that I am, I carry on as if the job had been done by Frank Lloyd Wright himself, while John Galt on acid is more like it. Kit has turned a quaint old house into an ultra-modern one, its great walls of glass reflecting the late-afternoon sun in a dazzling, almost blinding glare. The damn thing looks like a spaceship that got off course and crashed in a primeval forest, clearing out everything in its way. The Death Star, Noel calls it. He sees Kit's house as a metaphor for everything bad that's happening to this area he loves so much.

Far worse are the grounds, once as lovely as any in Highlands. The yard's plowed up and bone dry, though terraced and staked off for Kit's Oriental gardens. Japanese maples and tulips, weeping cherries and willows, plus several shrubs I don't recognize, stand with their roots encased in burlap sacks. As devoted gardeners, Noel and I were disturbed that Kit would remove indigenous plants and trees that have flourished here for years and replace them with such showy intruders. If Poor Old Al were still alive, she couldn't have done it. He indulged Kit in every way—as old coots who marry sweet young things do—but would never have allowed such a desecration to his beloved homeplace. Al was a good enough guy, but out of his league with a wife like Kit. As Emmet put it, Poor Old Al cast his line for a trout and reeled in a mermaid instead.

Waiting for me at the end of her driveway, Kit raises her eye-brows questioningly when I pivot and head back the way I came, motioning her to follow. Normally we pass her house, then go around the part of the lake that runs next to the highway. Not the most scenic route, but at least it's away from Moonrise.

"What's up?" Kit asks as she falls into step with me.

Arms pumping, eyes straight ahead, I pretend to be so into my pace that I wait until we're halfway to Linc's before saying, "Different route today." We usually speak in monosyllables as we walk, if we talk at all. Power walking doesn't exactly lend itself to conversation.

Kit glances at me but doesn't slow down. We pass Linc's and a further distraction, which I'd also counted on. I know Kit; get her going on something and we'll be halfway to Moonrise before she notices. Sure enough, she jerks her head around to say, "Why's Willa still at Linc's? Is anything wrong?"

"Nope. Heard them laughing when I passed by."

"*Laughing?*"

"Yeah, you know—that noise we make when we're having fun? Laughing."

"Why were they laughing?"

"How should I know? Maybe Willa was tickling him. Or maybe they were doing the big nasty. God, I hope so. Be good for both of them."

"*Tansy!* No, really—what were they laughing about?"

"I don't know, okay? I didn't stop to ask, but figured it was a good sign. Linc's doing so much better these days, don't you think? Probably because the Myna Bird's flown off."

We pass Laurel Cottage, and I keep walking. Kit doesn't look my way when she says, "We're going to Moonrise, aren't we?" Considering that we've left the dirt path that skirts the banks of the lake and headed up the driveway that leads right to the front door, I refrain from commending her astute observation. She says testily, "Tansy?"

I glance her way reluctantly. A good reason for keeping my eyes straight ahead: Power walking leaves me winded, sweaty, and red-faced. My thick, wavy hair gets so damp and unruly that by the time I'm home, I look like Medusa on a bad hair day. Plus, I've put on a few pounds this summer, which makes me feel like one of the ducks waddling around the lake, those of the broad-butted variety. I honestly believe that Kit could walk to Cashiers without breaking stride. I sweat while she glows moistly, her cheeks flushed and pink. Stringy tendrils escape my hairband and slap my face as her sun-streaked ponytail swishes against her back rhythmically. In a close-fitting tank and running shorts, she is long, lean, and beautifully muscled, her skin the golden amber color of wild honey. It makes me want to puke.

"Okay, what's going on?" Kit says finally, and I tell her about Emmet's phone call. I expect her to say that she's turning around, that I can check on his little wifey all I please but leave her out of it. Instead she gets quiet, and I cut my eyes her way to see her lips curving up at the corners. "Well, well! Emmet getting all chummy with the channel six news team, huh? Guess his dining out with colleagues is allowed now that Rosalyn's no longer around. She'd never have stood for it, but what the Bride doesn't know won't hurt her."

I stare at her in surprise. "What do you mean? Rosalyn wouldn't do any such thing! Oh, sure, she complained about Emmet going out drinking with the guys, but mostly because he lost track of time when talking shop—"

Kit waves me off impatiently. "Oh, for God's sake. You know what I'm talking about. That girl Emmet had a fling with at CNN several years ago, Carolyn, Caroline—whatever her name is. She's an anchorwoman at channel six in Asheville now."

It's my turn to scoff. "Don't be ridiculous. That Carol woman happened ages ago. And they might not have even had an affair. She had the hots for him, is all I remember. Rosalyn was so used to that kind of thing."

Kit's laugh is a sharp little bark. "If Rosalyn hadn't kept such a tight rein on Emmet, he would've worked his way through those eager little sluts at CNN the same way most of those guys did. Especially those at the top."

I'm a bit taken aback by her scornful tone. I knew that Emmet'd taken a hit with her for remarrying so quickly, but didn't realize she'd become so bitter. "Hey, sweetie—we don't have to do this," I say. "Let's turn around."

We're deep within the rhododendron tunnel now, halfway up the driveway, which is such a steep climb that we have to slow down. Kit glances around, then lowers her voice as though the bushes can hear us. "No. I've been meaning to come up here, anyway, when Emmet was gone. Pay a little social call on the new missus myself."

"You *have?*" We've had only two gatherings at Moonrise since the start of the season, one on the first night then the dinner to celebrate Helen's new show. Highlands is such a social town that most of us spend almost as much time in one another's homes as our own. Courtesy dictates that I should've called on Emmet's new wife long before now. Had circumstances been different, and a decent amount of time passed before the remarriage, I would have. Like Kit, I haven't been able to do it, though, courtesy be damned. It would've felt too disloyal to Rosalyn.

Kit stops and turns toward me, a no-no in power walking. The important thing is to keep the momentum going. "Get real, Tansy. Don't try to convince me that you were coming here out of concern. The other day, you and I talked about finding an opportunity to figure out if Helen's the conniving little schemer we fear. You were coming here to worm your way into her good graces, weren't you? Which, of course, could've been done without my help. Since you've included me, then as far as I'm concerned, we're in this together."

I open my mouth to protest, since it's *her* theory that once Emmet comes to his senses, he'll realize what a fool he's made of himself and rectify his mistake. Not only do I doubt that will happen, I also doubt Emmet'd be grateful to us for intervening. All I wanted to do was nose around, not do anything to piss Emmet off. But maybe Kit's right, and the two of us owe it to both Rosalyn and Annie to help him rectify what could be a serious error of judgment.

We find the Bride in the kitchen rolling out dough. She's so obviously—and ridiculously—pleased to see us that for a fleeting moment, I feel like a cad. Pasting on fake smiles, Kit and I tell her we just happened to be in the neighborhood, and the poor girl's response makes me feel even worse. Oh, she's spotted us walking every afternoon, she says wistfully, and longed to join us. But—she lowers her eyes, blushes slightly—she figured we had our own routine and wouldn't welcome intrusions.

Good manners dictate that Kit and I protest profusely and insist that she join us *any* time she'd like to, that we'd be *so* hurt if she didn't. Instead, an awkward silence falls. I change the subject by saying heartily, "So, Helen! What are you making that smells so good?"

She blinks those big brown eyes at me in confusion, as though she has no earthly idea what I asked. Our unexpected visit seems to have thrown her for a loop, and she stands frozen behind a little butcher-block table where she's rolled out a circle of dough on its flour-strewn surface, a rolling pin held aloft. I have to admit that she looks rather fetching in a bibbed apron over cutoff jeans and a halter top, her cheek smudged with flour. Her hair's damp and tousled, her face devoid of makeup and shiny with the heat of the kitchen. "Oh!" she says, then laughs that annoying titter of hers. "Forgot what I was doing! Please excuse me—I'll get cleaned up then get y'all a glass of iced tea. Goodness, where are my manners?"

This time Kit and I do protest, insisting that she mustn't stop what she's doing on our behalf, that we can only stay a minute. Helen's just as insistent that she'll do no such thing, waving off our protests with her floury hands. I stop her by pulling up a stool to the table, then motioning Kit to do the same. "Next time," I say firmly, "we'll sit on the porch and have a glass of mint tea like the proper ladies we are. Right now, I'd much rather watch you cook."

Helen eyes me with uncertainty, then glances over at Kit, who's joined me at the table with an insipid smile on her face. Feigning interest, Kit tilts her head prettily and leans forward as though she simply cannot *wait*. With a shrug, Helen says, "Well, okay . . . if y'all are sure. Actually, I'm working on some recipes for my cookbook—the chapter today is on appetizers—and would love some feedback. Normally Emmet's my guinea pig, but the problem is, he's hardly unbiased. He brags on everything. I love hearing it, of course—who wouldn't?—but to be truly helpful, I need honest critiquing."

Though honesty is a completely foreign concept to either of us, Kit and I promise to be frank in our assessments. Helen seems almost pathetically pleased, which brings on another twinge of guilt. If this keeps up, I'll have to go to the confessional after we leave. For being nice under false pretenses, five Hail Marys and three Our Fathers.

Helen resumes rolling out the dough, sprinkling flour here and there, and she tells us that Emmet has offered to help her with the wording of the narrative that introduces the recipes. "See, that's what scares me the most," she admits, fluttering her eyelashes. "My publisher doesn't want just another eat-healthy cookbook—which are a dime a dozen these days—she wants narratives leading into each chapter."

Propping her elbows on the table, Kit frowns. "What does that mean? Stories?"

Helen puts the rolling pin aside and brings forth a little doo-hickey that looks like a cookie cutter. Not that I've ever cut a single cookie, but I remember Miss Creasy using one to make her tea cakes. As she goes around the big circle of dough cutting out a dozen or so smaller circles, she says, "I'm afraid that's exactly what they want. And I'm absolutely petrified! I'm a dietician, not a story-teller." She glances up at us with a weak smile. "I have to keep reminding myself that Emmet will help me through it, much like he's helping me with my show."

Kit perks up at this, tilts her head again. "Really? It's hard to imagine Emmet helping anyone with a *cooking* show. As far as I know, he's never even boiled an egg."

Helen explains rather sheepishly how Emmet's helping her overcome her nervousness in front of a camera, as well as improving her presentation skills. Kit's lips turn up ever so slightly at the corners as she purrs, "How nice for you, having him as a personal coach! But you have to be careful, don't you? You know, in case your colleagues become jealous?"

"Oh, no. Not in our newsroom. Everyone gets along really well." Stepping over to the stove, Helen brings some small bowls to the table, then explains that she's making turnovers with variations on a goat-cheese filling. She wants Kit and me to try the different ones, then tell her which we liked best, without knowing which filling she used. We watch as she spoons stuff from different bowls into the center of the little circles, then folds the tops over to form turnovers, crimping the edges with her fingertips.

"So the obvious problem of being married to your boss doesn't bother you, then?" Kit persists. "I mean, if it were me, I'd be concerned that . . . well . . . the folks you work with might resent you. You know—think they see favoritism whether there's any basis for it or not."

Helen pauses to look at her in surprise. "I can't imagine anyone . . ." Her voice trails off, and her expression changes. "But I see what you're saying." Brow furrowed, she thinks it over, then goes back to the turnovers. "I appreciate that, Kit, I really do. It'll help me be on my toes from now on."

Kit sighs. "All I know is, Emmet's always telling us that more backstabbing and resentment takes place in the newsroom than anywhere else. Doesn't he, Tansy?" Before I can answer, she eyes Helen with a sympathetic look. "Main thing *I'd* worry about is what they might say about your getting your own show. Didn't you

tell us it was out of the blue, that no one had mentioned expanding
your spot before?"

I can tell by Helen's expression that it hits her like a punch in the
stomach. She's got the turnovers on a baking sheet, and she reaches
behind her to put them in the oven. I notice her hands shaking when
she sets the timer, then the way she falters before turning back to
the table to clean up her mess. "I hadn't thought of that," she says in
a choked voice, not meeting our eyes. When she wipes off the floured
tabletop, she scrubs it so hard the little table sways and almost top-
ples over.

Kit shrugs elaborately. "The good thing is, being aware of the
possibility will make you work that much harder, wait and see. Just
don't let it make you even *more* nervous. If I were you, Helen, I'd
learn the tricks of the trade from the master, then blow your detrac-
tors away when the time comes. Prove to them that you earned
your own show, and would've gotten it even if you hadn't married
a big shot at the station! It's the only way to handle that kind of
thing."

The timer goes off and Helen jumps. She takes the turnovers
out, puts half a dozen on a little plate, sits the plate in front of us. Kit
doesn't eat enough to keep a mite alive, but I snatch one up, starving. Her earlier enthusiasm dissipated, Helen says listlessly, "One
batch is goat cheese with figs, one black walnuts, and the other sourwood honey. Emmet suggested that this chapter be about local ingredients, and that I focus on finding healthy choices from what's
readily available, no matter where one lives."

Kit breaks off a microscopic-sized crumb and nibbles it. "What
a great idea! And if you're looking for local ingredients, some of
the plants in the moon garden can be used in cooking. I'm no cook
myself, but Willa's mother used them in remedies and all sorts of
things."

"No kidding?" Helen says, then turns her head to the gardens in the back. "I had no idea, but of course I'm not familiar with any of the plants back there."

Talking around a mouthful of hot goat cheese, I warn her that some of the plants in the moon garden are poisonous. I'm not sure she hears me, but before I can swallow and try again, Kit chimes in. "Ah, Helen?" Kit says. "I'd take full credit for Emmet's ideas on the cookbook if I were you. Don't give folks any ammunition, or they'll end up saying your hubby not only got you a show, he wrote your book as well. It's just awful how spiteful and jealous people can be, isn't it?"

———

I WAIT UNTIL we're deep enough in the rhododendron tunnel so that Moonrise has disappeared from sight before saying anything. Downhill, Kit walks even faster, pumping her legs like a drum majorette leading a parade. She's been smiling like the frigging Cheshire cat since we left the Bride glumly waving us good-bye on the front steps.

I glance over my shoulder to make sure the Bride isn't creeping behind us, eavesdropping, then say, "Jesus, Kit! You did quite a number on that girl. Remind me to never piss you off."

She's so pleased with herself that she doesn't even try to look innocent. Raising her chin high, she says smugly, "I was simply reminding her that actions have consequences."

"You'd better hope not," I say with a snort, "or you'll be hit with a shitload of bad karma."

Kit turns her head to glare at me. "Oh, please. If you're softening toward her, remember this: For all we know, she went after her boss man the way a certain kind of woman has always done. She got what she wanted and then some; now she's afraid she's not savvy enough to hang on to it. Which it doesn't appear she is, not having the confidence or the smarts to pull off her perks without

Emmet's help. It's becoming more obvious to me. He sets up his little bride in a cushy job, too besotted to see that he's setting her up to make a fool of herself. Never forget, this is the man whose scathing criticism has brought experienced TV veterans to tears. One thing he cannot tolerate is professional incompetence. Can you imagine what he'll do to a novice like her if she messes up?"

I could, and it wasn't a pretty picture. Glancing at her, I say, "I have to admit, the way you worked in that bit about Emmet's former protégée living in Asheville was brilliant. Did you plan it that way?"

Kit shakes her head. "It fell into my lap when you delivered his message. All I had to do was act surprised that the Bride allowed him to hang around with the Asheville crowd, then mention that was something Rosalyn wouldn't do. I'm sure you noticed how strange she acted when Rosalyn's name came up. Wonder what that's about. I almost asked if she'd seen her ghost in the gardens or something."

I struggle to control my expression so she won't ask me if I ever have. Instead, I ask, "You snooped around when you went to the bathroom, didn't you?"

"I'd *never* do anything like that," she responds piously. "Besides, snooping is your territory." We walk in silence for a minute, then Kit adds, "You'll have plenty of chances to snoop when you return to show her the gardens. I expect full credit for pulling that off, by the way. Clever of me, wasn't it, to tell her about the plants? Gave you the perfect opportunity to offer a tour."

"I wondered what you were up to!" I can't help but be impressed at her cleverness. "For a minute I thought you were hoping she'd eat a poison mushroom or something."

We giggle, but I remind her that the Lady of the Night, Rosalyn's favorite nocturnal plant, is a member of the deadly nightshade family. "That's the main thing I want to check on in the garden," I add. "I assume none of the Ladies survived; otherwise they'd be on the sunporch. Rosalyn always brought them in for the winter."

Kit nods. "True, but she took them in and out a lot, a secret her grandmother taught her, and why they'd survived so long. Remember?" Her face falls, and to change the subject, I reach over and give her arm a pat.

"You did good today, girlfriend," I remind her. "All and all, a successful visit, wouldn't you say?"

NIGHTSHADES

Forcing myself to stay awake until Emmet gets home from Asheville won't be a worry tonight. Almost midnight, and I'm huddled in bed wide-eyed, the coverlet pulled up to my neck despite the warmth of the night. The lamps on our bedside tables are bright, and I'd have a fire burning if I knew how. All the windows are raised and the lace panels pulled aside in a desperate effort to bring in light, even though it's dark as a tomb outside. The bad thing about open windows are the night noises: the moaning of the wind, the rustling of little animal feet through dried leaves, the scratching of branches against a screen. With every sound, I jump and cower deeper into my covers.

I seem to spend a lot of my time in bed lately, though not for the usual reasons, sleeping or lovemaking—both of which I miss. I was just getting better about sleeping in a strange place, getting used to the creaks and groans an old house makes settling down for the night, when Emmet started staying so late in Asheville. I'd never tell him, or anyone, but I'm afraid to be here by myself after dark. And after what happened this afternoon, I have a good reason to, and for hiding under the covers yet again.

After Tansy and Kit left, I went upstairs to see if Kit might've snooped around during a run she took to the bathroom before she and Tansy left. It's awful of me to think Kit might have been

snooping, but her reception of me has been so confusing, sometimes cool and other times overly friendly, like at the swimming
hole. She hadn't been joking about my taking the plunge as a form
of initiation; it was obvious to me that she wanted me to fit in, to
prove myself game for their little adventures. Instead I blew it, and
ended up having a tiff with Emmet. He was rightfully upset with me
for taking such a risk just to be accepted by the others, even calling
my concerns about Willa and the boyfriend—what was *that* about?
I'd demanded—nothing but a smoke screen to divert attention from
my foolhardy actions. My plunge into the swimming hole brought
on the first real spat we'd had in our marriage.

By the following day we'd made up and things were back to normal. I was touched that Emmet sent Tansy and Kit over with his message about being late tonight. Even their hint that he might be
reconnecting with an old flame while in Asheville didn't bug me for
long. After they left, I looked up the woman on the channel six
website—what wife wouldn't? I told myself—then was ashamed of
myself for doing so. Carol Lind Crawford, channel six's glamorous, hotshot anchor, was raven-haired and smoky-eyed, built like a
supermodel. Your basic nightmare, but Emmet'd always had women
after him. If I didn't trust him, then why were we together? Love
without trust was nothing but a sham, as I well knew.

When I was able to check my messages, I discovered that
Emmet wasn't out with the channel six folks after all. Instead, he'd
reconnected with Doug Somebody-or-Other, an old buddy from
CNN who teaches journalism at Western Carolina now. Sounded
like Doug has launched a campaign to lure Emmet back to this
area, kicked off by a big dinner with local journalists. I listened to
the message twice, intrigued. Despite the unfriendly atmosphere of
the house and my sleepless nights, I love this area and wouldn't
mind if we ended up staying. Fort Lauderdale has lost its appeal for
me and Emmet both.

A quick perusal of the upstairs showed no evidence that Kit had been snooping, and made me feel worse for my suspicions. How would I ever get close to those women if I didn't trust them? It was the same thought I'd had about Emmet, how loving relationships are only formed in trust. I hadn't lived in Fort Lauderdale long enough to form close ties—probably one reason Emmet and I bonded so quickly—so I longed for women friends. For that to happen here, I have to let go of my wariness, my sense of being watched and judged as inferior to Rosalyn. No wonder none of them liked me, I decided. I was skittish, distrustful, and neurotic enough to lie awake half the night imagining ghosts watching me.

When checking for signs of snooping, I'd gone down the hallway and stuck my head in the other rooms—just to check everything out, I told myself. Willa kept everything in perfect order. Although Emmet didn't like calling her the housekeeper, she served that role, and I'd loved not having to fool with domestic duties for the first time in my life. Funny, the two upstairs rooms that looked even halfway lived in, the master bedroom and Annie's, were at opposite ends of the long hallway. The two guest bedrooms in between were as formal and uninviting as those we saw at the Biltmore. They were interchangeable, too, one papered and furnished in dark shades of burgundy and the other in hunter green. I shuddered to think I'd planned on using one of them as my and Emmet's room after realizing we'd be in Rosalyn's bed otherwise. I can only imagine what fusty old ghosts the guest rooms would harbor!

I glanced inside Annie's room but didn't linger. When we'd first come here, I'd gone through her room looking for clues to help me understand her, with very little success. Not that the room wasn't full of possibilities; Willa'd told me about them crowding all of Annie's stuff in after the Atlanta house was sold. Annie had taken very little with her to the horse farm, where she had limited quarters. I'd seen nothing unexpected in her room at Moonrise, just the usual scrapbooks, mementos, trophies, and photos. I'd perused the ones on display but wouldn't allow myself to go through her closet or chest of drawers, regardless of what treasures they might offer in my longing to know my stepdaughter better. Don't push it, I told myself. Let her get to know you better, too, and hopefully one day a closeness would develop between the two of us.

I hesitated for a long time outside the door leading up to the attic. My first day at Moonrise, Willa had given me a brief tour of the attic. We'd laughed and joked about its spookiness, and I had no desire, nor reason, to go back. Anything that needed to be stored I left on the landing near the door, and poor Willa would take it up for me. There was one little thing, though. Ever since the evening that Emmet and I saw a shadowy figure in the windows above the turret, I'd been curious, yet not brave enough to explore the attic for answers. And if I had any sense, I'd wait until the next time Willa came over to do so. It was late afternoon, and I'd miss the sunset if I didn't get outside pretty soon. Absolutely no reason for me to go into the attic, especially since I was here by myself. Only an idiot would do such a thing, I grumbled, even as I started to climb the steps.

Afterward I would realize that my venture into the attic gave me a false sense of security. Leaving the door propped open and all the lights ablaze, I hurried over to the bank of windows above the turret, which was separated from the rest of the attic by a rail. From the outside, a reflection from the lake could make it appear that something—or someone—floated around up there, but it was impossible otherwise. What Emmet and I saw was nothing but an optical illusion, and I couldn't wait to tell him that I'd solved the mystery.

After checking everything out, even if quite hastily, I left the attic and went downstairs. Feeling proud of myself for my little adventure, I went to the kitchen to reward myself with a glass of wine. Because of my trip to the attic, I'd have to hurry. Darkness fell quickly in the mountains. I'd been brave enough for one day, and would now have to catch the last of the sunset on the porch rather than at my hideaway, as I'd originally planned.

Standing by the kitchen window, I'd looked out over the gardens. Tansy seemed pleased at the prospect of showing them to me up close and personal, and I was, too. And I was especially interested in using some of the plants in my chapter on local ingredients. Frankly, I was ashamed of the way I'd let the gardens spook me. Then I recalled the shadowy figure I saw out there, at the beginning of the summer. It was probably another illusion, like the ghost in the attic. And just as the thought formed, however, I saw it again—a dark figure moving through the gardens, then disappearing into the trees at the far corner. Without thinking it through, I ran out of the kitchen, through the side porch, and around the house. Had I been so influenced by the atmosphere of Moonrise that I hadn't considered possibilities other than a haunting, thus giving a burglar plenty of time to case the joint? After all, there were valuable antiques here. Highlands' crime rate was practically nil, making the police reports in the paper a hoot to read, but still. I had definitely seen something in the gardens this time.

Outside, I didn't even have to go to the far corner of the gardens to realize that I was wrong. I got into the middle and stopped, looking around in disbelief. There was absolutely nothing—or rather, no one—out there. Wild and overgrown though it might be, the garden's not exactly a jungle, and anything would've been visible, even crouched under a tree, or in the bushes. Sighing, I turned to go back to the house. A bed of unusual plants caught my eye, and I paused to inspect it. Bending over, I studied the leafy plants, which looked a lot like kale. I reached down to break off a leaf to take with me. Tansy could tell me if what I'd found was edible or not.

I'd just broken off one of the stems when a scream split the hushed silence of the darkening grounds. I straightened up and dropped the plant, my heart pounding like a hammer. All summer I'd heard stories of the panthers native to these hills, and how their cry sounded like the scream of a woman in distress. I looked around fearfully, trying to decide whether to make a run for the house or hide in the shadows of a nearby dogwood tree. As if a panther couldn't see me, regardless of where I hid! I broke out in a run, knowing I had to get inside. Even when I was at the house alone, I didn't lock the doors, but the minute I got inside, I slammed and locked the door behind me. Then I went from room to room, all over the downstairs, closing and locking any open windows. Tomorrow, in the light of the day, I'd raise them again.

———

IT'S NO WONDER I'm now huddled in my bed, I tell myself. I'm still jumping at every sound from outside. From the safety of my windows, I've searched the dark gardens a dozen times, making sure no panther lurks out there. Finally I wear myself out, and return to my bed to wait for Emmet's return. It's such a lovely, starlit night that I finally turn off the lamps, darkness and panthers be damned, and soon the night sky works its magic on me. I settle back on my pillows, finally relaxed enough to sleep. My eyelids grow heavier, but I fight to keep them open so I can relish the beauty of the night. It's so different here from Fort Lauderdale. On the Atlantic, the night sky is a vast thing of unfathomable darkness. From the shore, the stars appear to be pinpoints of ice in a frozen black void, the moon cold and indifferent. In the mountains, the stars look like candles carried by angels to light their way through the corridors of heaven, and the sliver of moon, a smile. Tonight, the mountains take me in, and sing me to sleep.

I'm not sure what time it is when I'm awakened by the touch of Emmet's lips on the back of my neck, his arm sliding around my waist. "Better hurry," I murmur, stirring. "My husband's on his way home."

"Shhh," he whispers, his mouth pressed against my neck. When I start to turn toward him, he tightens his hold and pulls me closer. "No, don't," he says. "I want you like this. God, it's been a long time, hasn't it?"

"Too long, except for the afternoon quickie," I reply. Then, "Ah . . . is this what they call spooning?"

Emmet chuckles. "Don't think so, baby." His breath is warm and sweet on the back of my neck as he wraps his legs around mine. "Spooning is a little less . . . invasive."

"A little less what?" When he groans, moving against me, I try to nudge him with my elbow, but I'm pinned in too close. "I didn't hear you," I say again. Speech is getting more difficult, however, as is breathing.

"I forget," he says hoarsely.

"Not a good time for conversation, anyway," I manage to say with a little gasp.

"Yeah. You might want to shut up," he suggests in a ragged voice.

When I gasp again, louder this time, he puts a hand on my mouth to muffle my cry of release.

Afterward we lie on his pillow, my head cradled on his shoulder. From outside the window comes the song of a faraway bird, the rustle of the wind moving through laurel leaves. Even the sliver of moon I watched earlier is gone, the night now dark and forbidding. Before Emmet came along to share my bed, I dreaded moonless nights. For the first time in my life, I found myself totally alone; something I'd wanted, longed for, even. But on moonless nights, the siren song of solitude became more of a dirge.

Half asleep, Emmet stirs and says, "I was beginning to wonder if we'd have to go to Florida to get our mojo back."

I reach for his hand on my shoulder and lace my fingers through his. "If what just happened was any indication, we can save ourselves a trip." He chuckles, and I clear my throat to say, "Sorry that I've been so unresponsive lately. I hoped you hadn't noticed."

"You've been preoccupied, which is different." He raises our entwined hands to kiss my fingers. "Good night, love. Hope we can do it again sometime. Gives me something to look forward to on my long drive home."

One thing about Emmet that comes from his unorthodox hours as a newsman: He can be speaking to you one second and asleep the next. After our lovemaking, I'm usually wide-eyed and wanting to talk, so I nudge him before he conks out. I won't tell him about the scream I heard, in case he dismisses it as yet another example of my overwrought imagination, but I have other things to share. "Sweetheart?" I say. "I haven't had a chance to tell you that I had a good visit with Tansy and Kit this afternoon."

"And you wanted to tell me because . . . ?"

"Because I saw it as a good sign. You know, that folks here are beginning to accept me—"

Eyes closed, Emmet cuts me off with a snort. "Jesus, baby. Would you let that go? And leave those two alone, Kit and Tansy. I know why they came here."

"They came for a visit, like folks in Highlands do when someone's new here." Except when it's your new wife, I don't tell him.

"Crap. They came to snoop around," he states flatly.

"It's only natural that everyone's curious about me. I'm not Rosalyn, but—"

Emmet removes his arm from around my neck and yawns. "You're not Rosalyn, Helen, and won't ever be. Surely you've got better sense than to waste your time or energy trying to be something you're not." He gives his pillow a punch before plopping down on it, his back turned my way.

"Oh, I know. But it's been hard on me, coming here, being compared to her . . ." My voice trails off. It sounds ridiculous, saying it like that, whiny and pathetic. Quickly I add, "That didn't come out right. You're the one it's been hard on, I know."

His brittle laugh holds no amusement. "No, you don't. You have no idea how hard it is for me."

I flinch and say, "Of course I don't. But I thought . . . or maybe hoped . . . that you'd gotten okay with being here. That you were happy here, even."

Emmet swings his legs over the side of the bed and rubs his face wearily. "I'm going downstairs to get a drink. Want anything?"

"Can't we talk about this?"

"I'm having a shot of vodka with a splash of tonic. Nothing to talk about."

"You know what I meant. We haven't talked about it since we've been here."

He sighs in exasperation. "It sure as hell won't be tonight. Or rather, this morning. I'm having a nightcap, then conking out. And I don't want to have a therapy session beforehand."

I raise up to protest, but his look stops me. Even in the darkness of the room, I can sense the distance in his eyes. The tenderness we shared only a short time ago is gone now, cold as the night air. Pausing by the door, Emmet says, "Before we came here, Helen, I told you that some things were better left alone. But you can't let it rest, can you? If you keep this up, I'm afraid that you'll end up getting hurt, and I won't be able to stop it."

He goes out of the room, and I'm alone again in the darkness of a moon-forsaken night, back where I was before his return and the sudden passion that aroused me from a much-needed sleep. That's when the thought comes to mind, so unwanted that I put a hand over my eyes to shut it out. For the first time, Emmet's asking me to leave things alone strikes me as odd. What doesn't he want me to find?

———

UP CLOSE, AND in the brightness of a sunny day, the gardens are unsightly, even creepy-looking, but hardly the forbidden swamp they appear to be in the eerie light of the moon. Tansy, Kit, and I have come to the gardens from the stone steps in back, off the sunporch. From a portico just outside the sunporch, the steps lead directly down to a wide terrace of mossy bricks. Everything out here has been neglected. Even Willa's gardening crew, who keep the other terraces and pathways on the grounds cleared of fallen leaves and branches, give the back of the house only a desultory sweep with their leaf blowers.

Branching away from the terrace are three walkways. The one I followed last night, searching for the figure I thought I saw from the kitchen window, is the central one that goes under a rose-draped arbor and into the gardens. The two others circle the house before coming together at the front entrance. The nocturnal gardens are on either side of the central walkway, with white-pebbled paths running through them to encircle fountains, goldfish ponds, and statuary. The layout is more symmetrical than it appears from my upstairs windows; seeing it from the terrace, I can admire the garden's design rather than focusing on its snaky-looking overgrowth of weeds and brambles.

The gardens have a different effect on Tansy and Kit, and for different reasons—or so I assume. When we came down the steps to stand on the terrace, Kit closed her eyes, reaching out for Tansy to steady herself. Throwing Kit's hand off, Tansy cussed a blue streak and kicked a loose brick, then kicked it again before glancing my way to see if I'd heard her muttering. I kept my face expressionless, pretending not to hear her call Emmet a cold, heartless bastard, among other things. I didn't tell her that I've heard him called worse.

I'm not really surprised when Kit murmurs, "I can't do this, Tansy," and goes back into the house. I look toward Tansy expectantly, wondering if she, too, will call off our expedition. Scowling, she stands with her hands on her hips, eyes narrowed and lips in a tight line. The saucy, sardonic Tansy—her usual demeanor—is intimidating enough; Tansy mad enough to kick bricks and give Emmet hell is not someone I care to mess with. She towers over me, a lean-muscled woman in sleek black running shorts and tee, her hair held off her face with a leather headband. Under her breath she mutters, "Bloody fucking *hell*!" and I stifle a startled giggle.

I compose my face when Tansy turns to me, hoping she doesn't notice how that stare of hers unnerves me. It's a trait she shares with Emmet, the piercing look that nails you with its directness. Emmet's gaze is laserlike but deliberate as he sizes you up, takes your measure, decides if you're fair game. Tansy, on the other hand, turns hers on you so suddenly you're caught off guard and unprepared to defend yourself. Her voice tight and incredulous, she says, "You've lived in the house more than a month, Helen, yet you haven't demanded that Emmet get this mess cleaned up?"

Her question is both accusation and indictment, and my face flushes in response. Hearing it aloud, I realize how ridiculous I must seem to her, how silly and pathetic, someone not just frightened by the strange noises and shadows of an old house, but also afraid of a *flower* garden. I mutter something inane, but Tansy waves me off like an annoying insect. Without another word, she turns and heads down the central walkway with long, determined strides. I hesitate for a moment before going after her. Should I remind her that she's supposed to be giving me a tour, or just follow meekly along? She mutters and curses under her breath, stopping every few steps to kick at vines or yank a handful of weeds from the ground.

"Oh, God, her plantain lilies," she groans as she kneels beside a weed-choked bed of tall, stately stems with glossy green leaves, bordered by ground-hugging plants unlike anything I'd ever seen. "And the gingers!" With her bare hands, Tansy tears at the grass that's overtaken the lilies but it's futile, the grass is so thick. With a cry of frustration, she gets to her feet and heads back to the path. Tansy's march through the garden, with me trailing in her wake, increases her distress with each step. The ground is parched and rock hard, but even in the worst drought in years, weeds flourish everywhere, running rampant between the stepping-stones and white pebbles of the pathways. And it's not just the weeds. Even I, who know nothing about gardening, can tell the plants that have survived are in such desperate need of pruning they're almost indistinguishable from one another.

I understand Tansy's anger at Emmet, but also see for the first time that his decision to let the gardens go to ruin was irrational and illogical, neither of which is like him. He'd told me about his breakdown, which I thought I understood. Emmet's a sensitive, feeling man who has always buried his emotions; after the tragedy they erupted and brought him to his knees. When he'd told me about that awful time of hospitalization and mind-numbing depression, he did so in the most unemotional of ways, as though it happened to someone else. Now I have to wonder if losing Rosalyn affected him worse than I'd thought.

The day I arrived, Willa explained to me the unique character of the gardens—most of the plants came from seeds and cuttings brought from England years ago, which had been carefully nursed and reproduced by generations of gardeners since then. Without Rosalyn's skill and expertise with the plants, it's unlikely they'll survive for long. But why let the gardens go to ruin? Why not allow someone else to salvage what they can, or keep them up on a smaller scale? It makes no sense, and the unbidden thought keeps popping up in my mind like the ugly, insidious weeds: It wasn't the decision of a rational man. I fear that the state of the gardens suggests a man unable to let go of his dead wife, in the most morbid of ways. Rather than maintain her gardens as a tribute to her, he has to see it in ruins, like his life without her.

Tansy surprises me by tilting over a leaf-filled birdbath as easily as if it were made of papier-mâché instead of stone. The gunk that spills out is dark and soggy, which I wouldn't expect since we've had so little rain. The magnificent fountain in the center of the gardens is also filled with leaves, but these are dry, brittle ones that dance in the air when a gust of wind whips through them. Tansy eyes the fountain in disgust before marching over to the reflecting pool on our right. There are two here, one on either side of the central walkway: long, shallow rectangles of black scummy water surrounded by waist-high plants and vines. To me, the pools are the sorriest sights of all. Willa told me how they were situated just so to capture the light of the moon, reflecting it from different angles. Someone had to study the path of the moon real careful to get them placed just right, she'd added. Seeing the pools from my window, I'd been disappointed not to see moonbeams in them, even if a bright moon was overhead. Now I knew why.

Tansy calls me, and I turn to see that she's stomped through a couple of weed-choked flower beds and is motioning for me to follow. I don't relish the thought since I'd foolishly dressed in my cutoff jeans and sandals, not exactly gardening attire, but I do it, anyway. She's at the edge of the garden on our right, near a rustic fence made of laurel branches. Because of the sorry state of everything here, I'm just now seeing the real symmetry. The gardens on either side of the central walkway are identical in design, mirror images of each other, from the plants and trees to the statues and pools. Funny—the uniqueness of such a design should be pleasing; instead, it strikes me as creepy. It makes the gardens too perfect, too *planned*, even, without the happy accident of an overzealous plant blossoming more profusely on one side than the other.

Tansy motions to a line of plants with big, floppy leaves, unremarkable except for the long green pods hanging from the limbs. "Surely you've heard of angel trumpet?" she demands. "Florida's full of them." I tell her that I do indeed know angel trumpet, and she nods in satisfaction. "Only plants here that seem to have actually thrived on neglect," she tells me. "They were in full bloom earlier in the summer and are getting ready for another blooming, as you can see. And at dusk, as I'm sure you know."

I didn't, but wasn't about to tell her so. The shame I felt at my ignorance of gardening was silly, part of the insecurity that Tansy's brash self-assurance brought out in me. I should tell her the truth, that I was raised in a concrete-block house with a minuscule, white-sand yard of Bermuda grass and sticker burrs. Flowers would've been an unheard of luxury in our hardscrabble household. In my adult life, Joe and I had lived in what's ironically known as a garden house, commonly seen in south Florida. Plenty of potted tropicals around the swimming pool in the central courtyard, but no lawn or garden, either. Among Tansy and her ilk, my ignorance is another mark against me, the sign of an outsider lacking in the knowledge essential for refined living.

The laurel fences are riotous with pale green vines that Tansy identifies as moonflower vines, a necessary plant for any self-respecting nocturnal garden. Those I've heard of, but refrain from telling her that I've never seen one in bloom. Moonflowers don't need any special pampering, she says dismissively, as though that made them less of an attraction. Before moving on, she points out other plants that do well in nocturnal gardens, and I repeat the lovely names aloud: evening primrose, night phlox, night-blooming jasmine. So many of them become fragrant after sundown, Tansy tells me, that the scent can be overpowering. The more she tells me, the more I want to see the gardens cleaned up and in their glory again. And the more I realize I'll never be the one to make it happen. The moonflower vine and angel trumpet might thrive without special care, but it's obvious that a garden like this has to have someone to tend it. And not just anyone, but a skilled gardener dedicated to preserving it. Even if Emmet okayed an overhaul of the gardens— which isn't a given, by any means—I can't imagine him paying what it'd cost us to keep them up. And for what? Who would see them, without Rosalyn to lead her garden tours? Emmet won't ever enjoy them again, and I'd only do so on our rare trips here. Any way I look at it, the famed gardens of Moonrise are doomed to become a thing of the past.

"Here's the main thing I wanted to check on," Tansy says as she motions for me to follow her toward the back of the gardens, and a copse of magnolias. "*Brunfelsia americana*. Commonly known as the Lady of the Night."

I inhale sharply, delighted. "Such a beautiful name! I've heard of those as well, but have no idea what they are."

Tansy seems pleased at my interest. She waits for me under a spreading magnolia tree, ducking to avoid the lower-hanging limbs. Tansy tells me that everything in a nocturnal garden is planted to reflect moonbeams, so most of the flowers are white. Even the foliage is important; it should either be pale and silvery enough to be reflective, or dark to showcase the blooms. I can only imagine how lovely magnolia blossoms must look under the light of a full moon.

Since I expected to see whole beds of the mysterious plants called Lady of the Night, I'm puzzled when Tansy tugs on a hanging basket in the branches and says, "Well, I'll be damned. This little booger's still alive." Pulling down another, then another, she clucks sadly and shakes her head. Over her shoulder, she says, "These were the highlight of the garden tour, and if you ever saw one in full bloom, you'd see why. They can literally take your breath away. The flowers are creamy white and five pointed, but the most unusual thing is their long, narrow throats." She holds her hands apart to indicate several inches. "Talk about angels' trumpets! That's what they look like, delicate little trumpets. And the fragrance can stop you in your tracks, it's so intoxicating."

We move on to the next magnolia, where she goes through the same ritual, pulling on the baskets hanging in the branches to inspect their contents. This time, however, she gets mad again and begins muttering to herself. "I *knew* I should've taken them home with me after Rosalyn died. Dammit! But I thought Willa was taking care of everything, never dreaming in a million years that Emmet would lose his bloody mind and not allow her to keep up the yards."

I stand aside as she checks out the dozen or so hanging baskets. So far, she's found only one plant that's survived in the months since they were last tended. Just as I think she's forgotten I'm there, Tansy whirls toward me with a stricken look on her face. Her eyes are even blacker in distress. "You have *no* idea what a loss this is, do you, Helen?" she barks at me.

This time I bristle at her accusatory tone, as though whatever she's upset about is somehow my fault. Before I can respond, she lugs a basket off its hook over the tree branch and staggers under the weight, since the basket is the size of a large pumpkin. Undeterred, Tansy cries, "Rosalyn left these outside for the winter! She has *never* done such a thing in her life—" Realizing what she's said, her voice falters in midsentence. "Oh, God."

Lowering her head, she stares at the round basket she holds in her arms as though she doesn't know what it is. Sticking up from the soil is a tall, scrawny plant that's obviously alive, though neither healthy-looking nor even remotely attractive. She pokes at the dry soil around the plant with a long red fingernail and says, "This thing looks like shit. And I have absolutely no idea what to do for it."

"Aren't you a master gardener?" I cringe as soon as it's out of my mouth, figuring she'll jump me for making her feel even worse. Instead she hoots and rolls her eyes.

"I have a framed certificate on the wall proclaiming my right to modestly call myself such a thing, as does Noel. But it'll take a miracle from the patron saint of half-dead plants to save this bundle of sticks." Leaning down, she places the basket under the magnolia, propped against the trunk to keep it from spilling over.

When she kneels to poke at the dry soil again, I dare ask, "Just what is it?"

The look she gives me is not for the faint of heart. "Jesus— didn't you pay attention to what I said? I told you, it's a Lady of the Night."

"*Brunfelsia americana*," I repeat, more to show off than anything else. The Latin I took in my training as a dietician comes in handy at times.

Tansy gives me another look, but this one's a bit more civil. "Do you know anything about the plants of the nightshade family?"

With a sigh, I shake my head and resist asking her if she's paid any attention to what *I've* said about not being a gardener. Then it hits me that I'm not as ignorant as I thought, and I answer her rather smugly. "Actually, I do. Potatoes, tomatoes, and eggplant are members of the *Solanaceae* family, genus nightshade, and they contain alkaloids that can cause digestive problems, among other things. A lot of flowering plants are also nightshades, but we didn't study those like the vegetables."

When she tells me that I should know more since so many of the plants are tropical, I sigh again, more exasperated this time. "Tansy— being a native Floridian hardly makes me an expert in all things tropical, you know."

"Obviously not," she scoffs. "But I assumed—wrongfully so, as it turns out—that you might know *something* about the flora and fauna indigenous to your native land."

I glare at her but hold my tongue. I remind myself that I had her number the first time I laid eyes on her—she's every bit as snotty as she appears. Noel is so much nicer. No wonder the two of them never married each other—he's got better sense than to saddle himself with such a sharp-tongued, know-it-all shrew.

"The nightshades are some of the most beautiful plants in nature," Tansy tells me, oblivious to my assessment of her, "but also some of the deadliest, as I was trying to tell you the other day."

"*Deadly?*" I'd bent over for a closer look at the hanging basket, but recoil with a little gasp. Tansy chuckles, then gets to her feet and brushes off her hands.

"Ever heard of belladonna? For centuries, its deadly poison has made it well known in literature and folklore, and rightfully so. Many of the nightshades are poisonous, which makes them even more fascinating to me."

Now why doesn't that surprise me? Curious, I ask, "What about the Lady of the Night? Is she—I mean *it*—poisonous, too?"

Eyes wide, Tansy replies in an ominous tone, "Oh, yes! Even the slightest touch of its leaves can cause death and paralysis."

"In that order?" I say drily.

Her grudging look tells me that I scored one on her, and she turns away. Over her shoulder, she says, "If I were you, I'd ditch the idea of using any of the plants out here in recipes. Don't let Kit fool you—her thing is Asian gardens. She doesn't know a damn thing about this one. Rosalyn tried to show her a few things, but it never took. Kit was eager enough to learn, but too impatient—and lazy—for all the hard work involved."

This time she doesn't motion for me to follow, so I stand by the displaced hanging basket with its weird little plant sticking up as though peering over the top. I watch puzzled as Tansy stops by a magnolia tree that's out of line with the others. Not only that, even to my unknowledgeable eye it's obviously a different kind from the ones where the baskets hang. I wonder if it's the umbrella magnolia I've heard about, which is indigenous to these parts, and decide it must be, since the clusters of leaves flare out like little umbrellas. Strange, with everything else being so symmetrical, that this tree should be different from the others not just in appearance, but also in placement. The umbrella magnolia hugs the corner of the gardens on the right, without a twin in the opposite corner. And it takes up more room, too, with its sprawling branches hogging a larger space than the other precisely placed trees. On the mossy ground underneath its canopy is a weathered stone bench, and what appears to be a small rock garden. Tansy has knelt beside it, and curious, I go over to see what she's doing.

As soon as I get closer I know, of course. I have a vague memory of asking Emmet once if Rosalyn was buried in Atlanta, and his answering only that she'd been cremated. I didn't dare ask what'd been done with her ashes—the question was too morbid, so I let it drop. What strikes me as odd is that he failed to tell me her final remains were here, at Moonrise. Maybe not initially, when I first asked, but perhaps after we'd made plans to spend the summer here; or, failing that, once we arrived. Surely he knew I'd stumble on this place eventually. I put the unwelcome thought out of my mind, that it was a callous thing to do, letting me find out this way. He could've told me.

Tansy gets to her feet with a hand to her throat. Her face is sorrowful, her eyes on the mound of stones laid out on the mossy carpet under the tree. It's obvious that the ground underneath the stones had once been disturbed, as though to dig a hole for a planting. If I'd come on it without knowing, that's what I'd think, that someone had changed their mind about a planting, replaced the dirt, and decided to make a rock garden instead. The stones, large and variegated in color, are too artfully arranged to be random. Quite beautifully so, actually; not in an exact pattern but more of an irregular circle, with a floral-like design in its center. Even so, I would've expected a marker of some kind, some acknowledgment, and I find myself strangely disturbed as I stare down at the final resting place of my predecessor. Without looking my way, Tansy says in a quiet voice, "We were supposed to finish it. Noel put the stones there, for the time being, you know, until Emmet and Annie could decide what they wanted."

"So . . . this is the place she wanted her ashes, buried under this tree?" It's rare for either of us to mention Rosalyn, at least to the other.

Tansy shrugs, and her shoulders slump forward. "Who knows? She'd written nothing down. After the memorial service, everyone agreed on one thing: Her remains should be at Moonrise. We talked about scattering her ashes around the gardens, but that seemed so . . . I don't know, impermanent. Emmet didn't much like the idea, anyway, so it seemed only right to bury them somewhere. Rosalyn planted this tree years ago, when she first began introducing native plants in with the exotic transplants. She liked that it stood out from the others, so we decided it was as good a place as any."

Frowning, I say, "But . . . why isn't there a marker or something? It's weird, not to have an indication . . ." I let my voice trail off, then realize that I would've known had I explored this part of the gardens earlier, by myself. True, it might've looked like a rock garden, but somehow I would have known.

Tansy is quiet for a long moment, then says rather briskly, "We kept waiting for Emmet to come back up here and see that something was needed. But . . . he fell apart, and of course we couldn't ask him then. By the time we could've, he'd moved away. And moved on, too. I did ask Annie, but she wanted her dad to decide. She hasn't been back here. She won't, now."

The final word stings, and I turn away. Tansy and the others know that Annie came to Fort Lauderdale for a brief visit, a few weeks after Emmet and I married. I hadn't really expected her to, and it was far from a satisfactory visit. Trying to make it so, we frantically filled the weekend with sightseeing. Anything to avoid being alone with each other, I realize now. Afterward, I could say that I'd spent time with Emmet's daughter, but couldn't say that I knew her. Not at all.

Tansy leans over to brush dirt off her knees, then she turns back to the central pathway. She's halfway to the fountain before I realize that she's returning to the house, and I retrace my steps to the magnolia with the hanging basket propped on its trunk. I lift it in my arms and find that it's not that heavy, just awkward. It's a wire cage, with dangling chains where it hung from the branch, and some sort of mossy lining that scratches my bare arms. Tansy's halfway up the stone steps when I reach the terrace, and I call out to her. "Tansy! You forgot the Lady plant."

She turns to blink at me in surprise, as if she doesn't know what I'm talking about. In a cold voice, she says, "I told you—I have no idea what to do with the thing."

"Well, I certainly don't," I retort. "Could you take it to Noel, then? Or some gardener friend of yours who might save it?"

She shakes her head. "No one can. It's a tropical plant raised from seedlings that Rosalyn's grandmother smuggled out of the West Indies. It's not supposed to live in this climate."

I stare at her, incredulous. "But it has! You said yourself that it's unbelievable in full bloom. You can't just let it *die*. It's the last one left."

I can tell that she's torn, and when she shakes her head again, it's not nearly as forceful as before. "I can't take it with me, Helen. I'm walking."

"I'll drive you—" I offer, but she holds up her hand to stop me.

With a scowl, she flaps her wrist toward an old metal lawn chair on the terrace. "Put it over there. It needs to be in the sun, anyway. I'll send Noel over for it."

Like a fool, I stand holding the oversized planter and staring at her. Finally I blurt out, "But—what about the marker? Will you—or maybe Noel and Linc—talk to Emmet about it?"

Her look is so scornful that I cringe, but she's the one who looks away first. Over her shoulder she snaps, "I suggest *you* talk to Emmet about it. But I can tell you, it won't be a pleasant conversation. You might want to butter him up first. But you're good at that, aren't you?"

She slammed back into the house before I realize she's gone, and when I go into the kitchen to wash my hands, I hear her calling to Kit from the hallway. She washed up before I came in, leaving a wet, soil-smudged towel in the sink. Grabbing a clean one from a nearby drawer, I scurry down the hallway, drying my hands as I go. I'll be damned if she and Kit are prissing off without so much as a fare-thee-well. I want to know what, if anything, Tansy plans to do about the gardens. And it's certainly not my place to do something about that disgraceful mound of rocks under the magnolia tree! No wonder I've been hearing night noises—it's probably Rosalyn, demanding a proper marker for her remains.

In the hallway Tansy stands with her hands on her hips, frowning, looking around in obvious irritation. Just as she mutters that Kit must've gotten tired of waiting, a noise on the stairway startles both of us, and Kit appears on the landing. I stare up at her in surprise as she makes her way down the stairs, her fingers trailing on the banister. If she's disconcerted at being caught where she has no business being, you'd never know it. Her step is light, the ponytail swishing behind her. "Sorry!" she sings out. "I couldn't resist looking out over the lake from my favorite perch on the landing."

The last time she was here, she'd disappeared as well, but to the bathroom. Her explanation seems to satisfy Tansy, however, who tells her to get a move on, that she's ready to go, but I'm still skeptical. It's true, the landing offers a panoramic view of the lake, but so does the turret room. I recall what Emmet said last week, that Kit and Tansy only came here to snoop around. I push those thoughts aside to wave them off, but this time I don't follow them to the front entry. Instead, I lurk behind the curtains in the parlor and watch them until they're out of sight, disappearing in the rhododendron tunnel. I have no idea what I'm expecting to see, unless it's the two of them high-fiving each other at having duped me. Disgusted with myself for being so paranoid, I leave my hideaway and head back to the kitchen to start a batch of apple turnovers.

———

EMMET HOLDS UP his plate for seconds of the pan-fried chops and gravy, and I breathe a sigh of relief. After wasting one too many expensive chops, I've finally figured out that flash frying before braising keeps them tender. And the hot pan drippings with a splash of wine makes an acceptable low-fat gravy. I've also learned to read Emmet. Though he'll eat anything I put in front of him and declare it divine, his gusto while doing so serves as the best critique. I'd been pleased when he returned from Asheville early today, and starving. Taking full advantage, I piled on his plate and waited until he was happily occupied to bring up my and Tansy's forage into the gardens that afternoon.

I'd thought about it while preparing dinner, and concluded that Tansy was right. I should be the one to approach him, in a straightforward manner, without emotion or accusation. Returning to my seat at the wicker table on the porch, I wait until Emmet's well into the second chop to give him a brisk, to-the-point rundown of Tansy's visit, and our exploration of the garden. As I expected, he keeps his eyes on his plate, busily cutting the pork chop and raking the pieces through the gravy. Without looking up, he says, "Yeah, you're right. It's become an eyesore. Ask Willa to get her crew out there and clean it up, okay?"

Keeping his voice even, he asks that the work be done on a day he's in Asheville. "All that racket . . ." he adds, spearing a tomato slice with his fork, and I nod, although we both know that's not the real reason. I clear my throat and plunge in.

"Emmet, under the magnolia tree, where . . . ah . . . the ashes are buried—"

"Oh, God," he says. This time he raises his head to give me a look, an eyebrow arched high. "Bad overgrown, I guess. Tell Willa to take care of that, too."

I shake my head. "It's not that. Don't you think there should be a marker or something . . ." I let my voice trail off, not sure how to put it.

He gets to his feet, tosses his napkin down, then heads for the kitchen, empty plate in hand. "Don't you want an apple turnover?" I call after him. "Or a cup of coffee?"

Emmet pauses to glance at me over his shoulder. "I'll have my coffee later. I need to call Annie and ask what we should do about the marker." He's gone without another word, and I release my breath slowly. Until then, I didn't realize I'd been holding it, waiting for his reaction.

———

MID-JULY, AND Annie comes for a visit. I try to act cool, but I'm in a dither. When she visited us before, I was on my own turf, and one very much to my advantage. Like most folks her age, Annie liked being away from the ice and snow of a mountain winter, and on the sunny beaches of south Florida. We filled her days with swimming, snorkeling, and sightseeing, the nights dining in local dives or high-end restaurants. This time I'm hoping the two of us can have some alone time. Once Annie announced her plans, however, every-one staked a claim on her, and I wasn't surprised to find the step-monster at the bottom of her list. Even less surprising was Emmet's unwillingness to intervene on my behalf, though I could hardly com-plain. His own relationship with his daughter is way too tenuous.

I longed for a friend to talk to, someone who knew Annie well enough to offer me some guidance. Tansy and Kit were being friend-lier, but I was still uneasy with them. When Noel and Tansy returned for the Lady of the Night, I told them about Emmet's change of heart concerning the gardens. Even though I was ridiculously pleased when Noel gave me a pat on the back and one of his dazzling smiles, Tansy's response of "See? All you had to do was butter him up, just like I said," felt more like a put-down. Their reaction to the news of Annie's visit was guarded. Or rather, Noel's was; Tansy appeared stunned that I'd also pulled that off, too—which I shame-lessly allowed her to think. No reason for her to know I had noth-ing to do with it. Kit, on the other hand, made sure I understood her standing in her goddaughter's affections. She immediately claimed Annie for lunches, trips to the spa, and shopping sprees, taking up as much of her visit as possible.

Earlier in the summer I might've turned to Willa for help, but that afternoon at the swimming hole changed things. I was terribly concerned about her. A few days after the incident, she had assured everyone that things were fine with her and Duff. At preaching on the previous Sunday, Duff had rededicated his life to the Lord. I was surprised that the others seemed pleased as well, even Emmet. He brushed off my concerns by saying they'd known Duff forever. Beneath the macho swagger, he was a good old boy at heart. Willa could handle him. I didn't buy it. I thought I knew Joe Synder, too, yet he'd turned nasty on me after our love soured. I saw the look on Duff's face when he grabbed Willa's arm, and it gave me a cold chill of recognition.

I'm reminded of Willa when Annie arrives driving a pickup truck, the windows rolled down and bluegrass music blaring from the radio. She even dresses like Willa, I notice, when she hops out in jeans, boots, and a gray T-shirt with BOONE HORSE FARM printed on it. I'd been watching for her all afternoon, annoying Emmet so much he closed himself up in his office. "Your son seems to like me okay, Honeycutt," he said before slamming the door, "but if he doesn't, tough shit. I refuse to fret over him like you're doing with my daughter. If Annie doesn't like you, it's her loss. Tell her to go jump in the damn lake."

As sometimes happens with girls, Annie looks more like her father than her mother. She has Emmet's clipped, springy hair and clear eyes, with the muscular build of an athlete. Her fresh-faced, outdoorsy look makes her seem more approachable than the sardonic, worldly crowd I've encountered here. Even so, I'm far from comfortable with my new stepdaughter, and find myself babbling like an idiot when we make our way up the staircase to her old room. Neither her stony silence, nor the disdainful gaze enough like her father's to make my blood run cold, stops my nervous chatter. Annie carries a duffel bag over one shoulder and a little fringed purse on the other, leaving me nothing to bring up but a shopping bag. I practically wrestled it from her hands in my eagerness to help, even though she told me to leave it, it was just some jars of local honey she'd brought us.

"Your room's all fixed up and ready for you," I gush foolishly, as if she'd expect it to be otherwise. "And Willa laid out some aged applewood if you want a fire tonight. I haven't mastered the art of starting a fire yet—or rather, I can *start* it, I just can't seem to keep it going. But I *love* having one, don't you?"

Forcing a polite smile, Annie looks around the room as she says, "I'm surprised y'all can have a fire here, even at night. Boone's a lot farther north, yet we've had the hottest summer on record."

"Oh, yes, Highlands, too," I assure her. "But it doesn't stop me from begging your dad to build a fire in our bedroom every single night. Nothing I love better than lying on a stack of pillows and watching the flickering flames of a fire. And the smell of woodsmoke is simply divine, isn't it? I told your dad, I've gotten so spoiled that we'll *have* to put a fireplace in when we return to Fort Lauderdale."

For God's sake, Helen, would you *shut up?* Not only have I shown myself to be a blathering idiot incapable of even building a fire, I've just reminded the poor girl that someone other than her mother now shares her father's bed. Could I possibly rub it in any further? Stealing a glance at her, I trip over the rug by the bed and have to grab the nightstand to keep from falling flat on my face.

"Oh, my—look at the dahlias," I gush when I straighten up the little table, righting the vase before Tansy's plate-sized scarlet dahlias spill out. There's only the hem of my skirt to mop up the sloshed water on the hand-painted table, so I give it a swipe and hope Annie doesn't notice. "Tansy brought the dahlias over this morning, to match the colors in your room, she said, but I haven't gotten back up here to see how she arranged them." I catch myself before telling her the reason why. I've been hovering by the door all day watching for her arrival.

Ignoring my chatter, Annie lays her duffel on the toile-covered stool of a skirted dressing table, then leans toward the mirror to run her fingers through her close-cropped, windblown hair. Her impatient sigh is so much like Emmet's that I feel a pang for the two of them, so much alike yet so far apart from each other. Feeling my eyes on her, Annie glances my way and says coolly, "Is Dad here?"

I blink at her in surprise, then realize to my dismay that I've greeted her, helped get her things out of the truck, and showed her to her room—as if she didn't know where it was—all without telling Emmet she'd arrived.

"Oh! Oh, yes, he's here. In his office, finishing up some work,

but I'll go get him. You know the room on the other side of the turret? Not the library but the little study? He's using that for his office
this summer. Let me run tell him you're here." But Annie shakes
her head and says that she'd rather wash up first, then go downstairs to see him.

"Has your dad told you that he's going to Asheville a couple of
days a week to our network affiliate there, doing a remote broadcast
of his show?" I ask, but rather than waiting for her answer, I add
breezily, "You know how he is—he could've taken the entire summer off, but oh no. I'm feeling guilty because *I* was the one who
arranged it with the station. Wish now I'd left well enough alone."

Annie's lips turn up ever so slightly at the corners. Keeping her
clear-colored eyes on her reflection, she fingers her hair and murmurs, "Channel six? Yeah, I'll bet you do."

I stare at her. "Why do you say that?"

Annie meets my eyes in the mirror, and I see—or imagine I
see—a flicker of pity. Surely she doesn't know about her father's
fling, or whatever it was, with that woman! If it happened several
years ago, she would've been a child. With a shrug, she says, "Oh,
it's just such a long drive for him. Channel six is way on the other
side of town, you know."

She turns from the mirror and moves to the bay windows overlooking the gardens. Because they form a little alcove with reading
benches underneath, the windows in her room are the only ones
unadorned by the god-awful drapes found elsewhere in the house.
The heavy lace panels are there, but Willa left them pulled back
when she aired out the room. Despite the absence of drapes, and
the added frills that identify the room as having been a girl's, it's as
dark and gloomy as the others. It's the gloominess I've come to hate.
Finally I couldn't take it anymore, and got Willa to help me take
down the drapes in our room. Why I feared that Emmet would object I can't imagine, except for my ridiculous fancy that Rosalyn's

ghost would appear to demand I put her curtains back. When Emmet came up to bed that night, he stopped in the door in surprise. "Whoa now, sweetheart," he said. "This much moonlight will make sleep difficult, won't it?" When I told him to trust me, we'd sleep better, he grinned at me with a twinkle in his eye. "It's not us I'm worried about. What about the bats hanging from the ceiling?"

————

ANNIE STARES OUT the windows at the gardens, her shoulders slumped. Lost in thought, she's there so long that I cross the room to stand beside her, wishing I could think of something to say. I've looked at the gardens often lately and tried to imagine how everything will look when the work is finished. Willa's crew wasn't able to get much done before Annie got here, but it's a start. At the other end of the long hallway from our room, her bedroom offers a different angle, and I see that it looks directly onto the right side, and the magnolia tree with its circular stones underneath.

Trying to make her feel better, I say brightly, "I'm looking forward to seeing the garden after Willa's crew gets everything back like it was. I've heard it was beautiful."

"It will never be like it was," Annie says dismissively.

Duly chastised, I hasten to say, "No, of course not. I meant . . ." I let my voice trail off, then wonder what the hell I *did* mean, and why I couldn't leave well enough alone. I can't, of course, and add, "I'm sure Tansy told you she was able to save one of your mom's most exotic plants—you know, the Lady of the Night? Tansy said your grandmother, or maybe it was a great-grandmother, brought the first seedlings from the West Indies. It's not supposed to bloom in this climate, but evidently it thrived, and was quite an attraction. She and Noel have it on their porch now, but plan on bringing it back once they get it healthy."

"Why would they do that?" She keeps her gaze focused

somewhere beyond the gardens, on the faraway mountains. Her face is impassive, closed against me. "No one will be here to see it."

Weighing my words carefully, I ask, "I don't suppose you ever see yourself . . . ah . . . living here one day? I mean, I know it's too big of a house for you now, you being young and single, but one day, when you have your own family, you might——"

She cuts me off in midsentence. "No. I hate this place, and I won't ever live here."

I'm taken aback by the venom in her voice, and I long to ask her why—why would she hate a place that her mother, whom she obviously revered, loved? Her sadness I can understand, but not the barely concealed anger that seethes just below her blasé demeanor. Or maybe I do. The thought hits me with a flash of insight that should've been obvious long before now. Anger is the shameful, unspoken part of grief—fury at the one we lost for dying and leaving us alone to deal with our pain. I was much older than Annie when my parents died, within a few months of each other, and I was furious at them for not taking better care of themselves. They had refused to listen to me, even though I had the skill and know-how to help them with their numerous health problems. For a long time I couldn't stand to go into their room, or handle the meager belongings they left behind. It hurt too much, and I gladly signed away my part of the sad old house to my brothers. Maybe Annie's hostility toward her father, and this albatross of a house, is a diversion from the anger she dare not express toward Rosalyn for leaving her motherless.

Annie turns away from the windows abruptly. Without so much as a glance my way, she dismisses me by saying, "I'd like to get cleaned up now. If you see my dad, tell him I'll be down shortly."

———

DESPITE THE ROCKY start, everything went far better than I'd dared hope with Annie's visit until the final night, and the birthday dinner. Her twenty-fifth was coming up; and over her protests, I insisted we make it an occasion. She hadn't mentioned her birthday, she snapped, because she didn't *want* anyone making a fuss.

For me, making a fuss was a matter of pride. I hadn't been invited to any of Kit and Tansy's outings with Annie, nor their social calls on the old guard of Highlands. There was one awkward moment, when Annie was going out the front door just as Emmet and I came in from our morning coffee on the side porch, and Emmet called out for her to hold up. When he demanded to know where she was going, all dressed up and looking so pretty, Annie sighed in exasperation, but seemed pleased at his compliment. Emmet was trying, I'd give him that, much harder than he had during her visit in Florida. Then, he'd been defensive about our marriage; now, in this place of painful memories, he was more sensitive to his daughter's feelings. Even so, I feared he might be teasing her about being dressed up, considering what she was wearing: a skinny ribbed tank that came halfway to her knees (and looked like a man's undershirt), a long ruffled skirt, several leather necklaces with peace medallions, and red cowboy boots. Both her ears had numerous piercings, usually unadorned, but today she sported a couple of dazzling diamond studs among the tiny silver hoops. She'd applied lip gloss and mascara, and tousled her hair with mousse. Despite the hippie getup, Emmet was right: She looked unusually pretty.

Kit and Tansy were picking her up for a champagne brunch at the Old Edwards Inn, Annie informed her dad. "To which I'm not invited?" Emmet cried in mock indignation. When she told him it was girls only, he turned to me, standing nearby and wrapped in one of his flannel robes. "Surely you're not wearing my robe to that ritzy joint, Honeycutt?" he asked.

I stole a glance at Annie. Her face flushed in embarrassment, but she remained silent. Forcing a smile, I fluttered my hand dismissively. "Can't make it this time, I'm afraid. I've got a chapter to finish before I can treat myself to a brunch or anything else." If Annie appreciated my letting her off the hook, she gave no indication. Instead, she scurried out the door before I could change my mind.

To salve my hurt at being left out, I focused my attention on the birthday dinner. I told myself that hosting a party for my stepdaughter was not only the proper thing to do, it was a loving, generous gesture on my part. In truth, it was yet another pathetic attempt to worm my way into everyone's good graces. I set myself up for a fall by ignoring the snubs and slights from Annie, including her insistence that her friends in Boone were having a party for her when she returned, and she didn't want me doing anything. I waved off her protests, and Emmet said it was something he'd like to do, too. When Annie grudgingly gave in, I went to work on the plans. My last dinner party had been a flop because I'd tried to impress everyone not only with my tasty-yet-healthy dishes, but also with the announcement of my show. The news of my show brought about jokes and innuendos of nepotism; and the piles of leftovers told me how tasty my healthy dishes really were. This time, I'd make a dinner so unforgettable it'd go down in Highlands history. I had no idea how close to that lofty notion I would come.

Emmet, of course, had no clue what his daughter's favorite dishes were. Just don't serve horsemeat, he advised, and I pushed him out of the kitchen in exasperation. I turned to Tansy, who was as flippant and unhelpful as Emmet. She advised me to call Kit.

I'd started to call Kit before Tansy, until a mean-spirited thought—unworthy of my generous, loving spirit—stopped me. I was afraid Kit might exercise her prerogative as godmother, and ask if she could help host the party. Which, when I called her, is exactly what she did. No matter how I tried to talk her out of it, Kit waved me off like an annoying bug. Even worse, she insisted on having the event at her house. Because of the remodeling, she hadn't been able to entertain *all* summer, she whined, so the dinner party

simply *must* be at her place. And it had to be in her Oriental gardens, which she'd been slaving over for *months*, and couldn't wait to
show off. It was perfect! Surely Annie would want to spend the last
evening of her visit at Moonrise, I'd argued, but without much conviction, since we both knew it wasn't true. No, no, Kit protested,
Annie was dying to see her house, just hadn't had time yet. Having
no choice, I gave in, and hung up with a sigh. It wasn't a total de-
feat: The party might be taking place at Kit's horror of a house, but
I was by God preparing the dinner.

By the day of the party, I'd convinced myself it was a good
thing, hosting the party with Kit. All summer I'd been looking for
an inroad with Emmet's friends; now it had fallen into my lap. Working together on the party, a camaraderie developed among us that
had been sadly lacking before. Everyone wanted to help, so I put
Tansy doing the flowers, and Emmet and Annie coming up with the
songs for Willa and Duff to perform at the party. Noel did double-
duty, taking Annie along on his outings with Linc, which kept her
away while I prepared the feast. I'd hoped she and I would work
together on the menu, but she'd just shrugged and said anything
was fine. Cinderella wanted no part of a camaraderie that included
the wicked stepmother.

Planning the party got me into the Rutherford house for the
first time. The house—part chalet, part pagoda—was as weird-
looking as it appeared from a distance. Sprinklers crisscrossed the
freshly seeded lawns day and night, Kit obviously indifferent to the
daily pleas for water conservation. The inside was grander than I'd
expected, though the furnishings too stark and modern for my taste.
Showing me around, Kit revealed something about herself that explained the decor: She was a licensed decorator with a design spe-
cialty in feng shui. I struggled for something nice to say, since "You
actually *live* here?" didn't seem quite appropriate. Compared to this
place, Moonrise was downright cozy.

I could've taken one look at Kit's kitchen and known she wasn't a cook. The kitchen of a real cook is the heart of the house, and usually warm, cluttered, and a bit messy. Kit's kitchen dazzled with stainless steel, copper, and recessed lights, but was so bare not even a coffeemaker sat on the slate counters. Since cooking wasn't her thing, Kit's interest in the dinner menu surprised me. Encouraged by her friendliness, I admitted my frustration trying to plan a birthday dinner with no input from the birthday girl. Kit wasn't much help, either, but she listened intently.

When I asked about Annie's previous parties, she told me that Annie had never liked being fussed over. "Remember," Kit said with an indulgent smile, "she's her father's daughter. So much more like him than her mother! Only during Annie's childhood was Rosalyn able to throw big parties for her, and she went all out. You know, with clowns and pony rides and that sort of thing. And Rosalyn always made a special cake, some kind of fancy Victorian thing like her mother had made for her. It looked more like a wedding cake than something for a child's birthday, lit with sparklers instead of candles. The kids loved it, though. It was always the hit of the party."

I sighed and shook my head. "I'm just doing a classic sheet cake with buttercream frosting since Annie wouldn't say if she preferred chocolate, or what. It won't be fat free, of course," I added, and Kit giggled.

"Believe me, Rosalyn's cake wasn't either, with all that frosting and decoration. Every year, Rosalyn would say never again, making it was such a pain. We laughed about how relieved she was when Annie got older and wanted a regular birthday cake, like the rest of her friends. Those Rosalyn was able to get from a bakery."

I told her that Adam had been the same way, only wanting what his friends had at their parties. And with boys, that usually meant hot dogs or tacos rather than fancy food. In the scrapbooks I kept during his boyhood, I dutifully recorded what I'd fixed for his parties, though it was never anything out of the ordinary. An idea came to me, and I leaned toward Kit eagerly. "Kit? Do you think Rosalyn might've done the same, kept some recipes or something from Annie's parties that I could look at, maybe get some ideas?"

Kit's face lit up. "I know she did! Why don't you check out the top drawer of the sideboard in the dining room? That's where Rosalyn kept her mother's and grandmother's cookbooks, as well as handwritten recipes and notes. If she recorded anything about special occasions, that's where it would be."

After I got back to Moonrise, I called Kit to report that I'd found some notes about birthday parties, but they must not be Rosalyn's. Most of them had references to "DB" scribbled in the margins. Kit laughed at my confusion.

"Oh, Rosalyn was always scribbling notes to herself in a coded language," she explained. "Sometimes she'd forget what her abbreviations meant. But I can help you with that one: Rosalyn called Annie Doodlebug until she got older and begged her to stop. So you've hit pay dirt." Her voice caught, and she added, "Poor Annie. Last summer her birthday was so hard, the first without her mother. I'm glad you found the notes, Helen, because I'm sure you'll find something in them to make this birthday really special for her."

12

tansy

BIRTHDAY PARTY

Kit's house looks a lot better at night, lit up with dozens of candles, than it does in the daytime. What doesn't look better by candlelight, though? I arrive early to check on the flowers, which I'd sent with Noel this morning. With everything so dry, our gardens had precious little to offer. Fortunately, Kit didn't want anything but an arrangement for the buffet table. I let myself in and call out to her, but no answer. One thing for sure, I won't find her slaving her hiney off in the kitchen. I told Noel that Kit's never turned on the burners of her stove, to which he responded, "Don't be ridiculous, Tans—of course she has." Then, with a frown, "What are burners, anyway?"

I still can't believe Helen was gullible enough to let Kit wheedle her into having the party here! Kit got all huffy with me, but I was with the Bride on that one. Annie's twenty-fifth should've been at Moonrise and hosted by her father and stepmother—which is what Helen is, like it or not. Instead Kit got a housewarming out of it, with an unpaid caterer who's furnishing every morsel of food and drink. One thing about Kit, when she wants something bad enough, she always finds a way to get it.

Hearing noises in the kitchen, I start that way when Kit calls down to me from upstairs: "Tansy, sweetie? Could you come here a minute?"

Although I've been inside several times lately, she's refused to let me go any farther than the entrance hall. Not until everything's finished, she insisted. This is the only house she's decorated using the feng shui she's trained in, and she's beside herself. I'm curious to see what all her feng shui fuss is about. So far, everything appears to be ultramodern. The wonderful "old Highlands" charm of the house is gone, replaced by two-story ceilings with skylights, shiny bare floors and glass walls, geometrically shaped windows and doors. Her sofas and chairs are made of lacquered wood and leather, with no cushions to soften their harsh lines, and the tables are acrylic and chrome. Everything looks about as comfortable as rocks.

I try not to gape as I climb the suspended staircase, then head down the hallway to the master bedroom. Barefoot, Kit waits for me in the doorway with a rueful expression on her face. "Can you believe it? My zipper's jammed." Throwing her head sideways, she lifts her hair and twists it off her neck before turning her back to me.

I lean in, squinting. "Sure is. And bad." The short black sheath, an expensive designer creation, is new, which surprises me. To hear Kit tell it, she's flat broke. Can't blame her for the dress, though, since it's drop-dead gorgeous, showing just enough cleavage to be provocative. I free the zipper and give her a pat on the shoulder. "What a great dress! New, isn't it?"

Kit lets her hair go and turns to face me with that sideways smile of hers that strikes me as coy sometimes, and sly others. "Oh, pooh—you've seen this old thing a dozen times." She's lying like a rug, but I know better than to call her on it. With another smile, she gushes, "But don't you look nice."

"I thought so until I saw you," I grumble.

"Well? What do you think of it?" With a dramatic sweep of her arms, Kit motions to her room. I look around curiously at the cathedral ceiling, steel-gray walls, and dark, shiny floors unadorned by rugs. The only furnishings are a platform bed with a built-in headboard, a long lacquered dresser, and an armless, U-shaped chair. Or I assume it's a chair. In the corner is a slender tree, potted in a planter the size of a washtub. The tree's lacy branches reach almost to the tall ceiling before swooping down as though taking a bow. I wander over to the floor-to-ceiling windows and look out at the darkening lake. "It's fabulous, girlfriend," I lie. "And what a view you have." Without the trees in the way, you can see as far as Moonrise.

Kit's moved to the dresser to finish primping. Eyes fastened on her reflection, she puts on the exquisite earrings Al gave her for their tenth anniversary, and I watch with admiration. The size of pennies, the drop diamonds are the perfect touch for the black dress. She meets my eyes in the mirror. "I haven't quite finished with the decor, but I'm pleased so far." Leaning down, she pulls on a pair of strappy heels. "Listen, Tansy—I've been dying to ask you. What's going on with Noel? He's sure been at Moonrise a lot lately."

With a shrug, I tell her that he's been picking Annie up, taking her with him and Linc on their outings, but Kit scoffs. "I don't mean that. When he brings her back home, he works in the moon gardens—"

"Yes, I know," I retort, and it comes out a little sharper than I intended. Kit gives me a knowing look, one eyebrow raised.

"You don't have to be so touchy. But I've noticed that he hangs around till dark, especially when Emmet's in Asheville. Or rather, only when Emmet's in Asheville." With a pencil, she outlines her full lips before filling them in with a rose-brown gloss.

"My God, Kit! What'd you do, press your nose to the window?"

"No, sweetie . . . I'll leave that to you. But some of what goes on over there is clearly visible to me, whether I intend to see it or not. Plus, Annie tells me things."

"So what are you saying? That Noel's at Moonrise diddling the Bride while Emmet's away, even though Annie's under the same roof? Or maybe the stud muffin's doing her, too."

"My, my." Again, Kit gives me the sly half smile, her eyes meeting mine in the mirror. "If I didn't know better, I'd swear you were jealous of our boy. And I'm not saying any such thing. But Annie tells me how tired she is of Noel singing Helen's praises all the time. He's a bit too eager in his attempts to make Annie like her."

I watch her in exasperation. "Oh, come on, Kit. Of course he wants Annie and Helen to get along. He loves Annie, and wants her to be happy. And he's delirious to be working in the gardens since Rosalyn never let anyone else touch them. I still don't get what you're trying to say."

Kit picks up a bottle and spritzes herself with Joy, her signature scent but one I've always detested. "I'm not trying to say anything. Just pointing out that Helen's getting close to Noel. And if we're right about her—and she turns out to be the user we fear—I worry that Sir Lancelot will be putty in her hands."

"Oh, please. Noel may be nice, but he's no dummy. If all the women who're after him formed a line, it'd stretch all the way to Atlanta. But he's got a great radar for feminine wiles, or he wouldn't have remained unattached this long. He goes to Moonrise to work in the gardens. Plus he's showing Helen some basic gardening stuff because she doesn't know squat, but wants to learn. End of story."

Satisfied with her appearance if not my reasoning, Kit gets up, and we start out the door together. She pauses to put a hand on my arm. "Just keep your eyes open, okay? That's all I'm saying."

———

I FIND HELEN in the kitchen, and pray she didn't overhear Kit and me talking. Her face lights up when she sees me, however, and I relax. Kit was behind me coming down the stairs, but she scurried off to check out the terrace, where the party's being held. "I'd offer to help, but trust me—you're better off on your own," I tell Helen. Seeing her covered in an apron, hair damp and face shiny with steam, I refrain from asking if she feels like Cinderella.

"I've got everything under control, thank you." Her tone is friendly enough, but she's obviously distracted. The new kitchen is exactly what I'd expect after seeing the rest of Kit's house, about as homey as a science lab. Even Helen's clutter of pots and pans, mixing bowls, and trays of food does little to make it more inviting. Helen's so intent on whatever she's chopping that I slip out unnoticed, relieved she didn't ask me to grab an apron and lend her a hand, in spite of my disclaimer.

Kit's been so mysterious about her terrace (which she calls her Oriental gardens) that I'm dying to see it, but I'm stopped by a loud banging on the front door, and have to retrace my steps. Willa's peeking through the glass panel on one side of the door, and Duff the other. He's forgotten his key, and they came early to get their speakers and instruments set up. I follow them through the house to the back. Carrying a smaller version of the big fiddle Duff carries, Willa looks around wide-eyed as she exchanges glances with Duff. "Told you so," he says in a self-satisfied voice. "Didn't I say it was the weirdest damn house you've ever seen?"

The two of them are all lovey-dovey again, just as I expected. Mountain women pander to their men too much to suit me; after her humiliation at the swimming hole, Willa should've dumped him. Instead, she probably went home and cooked him a . . . what? Corn pone? I'll give her this: Duff's hardly my type, but he's one good-looking man, with those tight jeans, and the broad shoulders straining his cowboy shirt. Tonight he looks especially hot in all black, à la Johnny Cash. We pass through the living room, dining room, and sunporch—all equally stark and uncomfortable-looking—and I open the French doors leading outside, since their hands are full. I stop so suddenly that Willa runs into me. "Sweet Jesus," I murmur. "Would you look at this?"

Duff grins at Willa, his face aglow. "I did most of the work in this here backyard," he tells her, then struts outside like he owns the place.

Instead of being impressed by Duff's boast, Willa responds with a snort. "Huh! This ain't what I call a backyard."

Kit's Oriental garden, a large flagstone patio surrounded by woven bamboo walls, is one of the most spectacular I've ever seen, here and abroad. Lining the walls are hundreds of exotic plants and newly planted trees, where so many paper lanterns hang they appear to have sprouted from the branches. The pergolas on either side are crisscrossed with strings of tiny lights twinkling like fireflies. In the middle is a magnificent water feature, a koi pond with a templelike fountain the size of a church steeple. The stone pond's underlit with greenish-blue lights—the same color, I realize, as Looking Glass Lake on a sunny day. No wonder Kit's broke.

Getting set up under one of the pergolas, Duff busies himself with the microphone and speakers, and I pull Willa aside to say in a lowered voice, "Did you hear that Myna drove over today? Even though she barely knows Annie, she dismissed her classes so she could come to the party."

Willa shakes her head and groans. When I, too, groan, we laugh together, then I wave her off to check on the floral arrangement. I don't tell her why I wanted her to know—nor why I think Myna came home. A few days ago, Noel returned from a visit with Linc, obviously troubled. It appears that Myna and Duff have something in common, he stated glumly—both are jealous of Linc's and Willa's affection for each other. "If Linc were physically able," Noel told me bitterly, "Myna'd accuse them of being lovers, I guess. Bloody hell! The last thing Linc needs is that kind of stress."

When Emmet arrives with Annie, Kit and I carry on as though

she were a child again, at one of her little-girl parties instead of a grown-up celebration. She looks adorable in her hippie-dippie dress and cowboy boots, but I feel bad for her, even all dolled up. With Rosalyn's gene pool to dip into, the poor thing turned out to look just like her father. No wonder she can't stand him.

Her arms linked through theirs, Kit gives Emmet and Annie a tour of the house, which takes about ten seconds since there's so little to see. Even so, Kit is happier than a pig in shit to have their attention. Eyes bright, Annie hangs on to Kit's every word, while Emmet's expression is neutral. He pauses in the kitchen to give Helen a peck on the cheek, but Kit scolds him. He shouldn't interrupt the chef at a critical point with her cream sauce, she teases, then whisks them out to the terrace.

We've made it across the patio, where Willa and Duff, fiddles flashing, are playing "On the Road Again," when the other guests arrive. The birthday girl is rescued from the old folks by the arrival of her friends, so I tell Emmet to grab us the best table before the young folks get it. At the appearance of Myna and Linc, I nudge Emmet with my elbow. "A whole blissful summer without the dragon lady," I say in a lowered voice. "I knew it couldn't last. God is not that good."

"What I need is a drink." Emmet sighs. "Bad." When he heads toward the bar under the other pergola, I call after him to bring me one, too—and make it a double.

Leaning on a pronged cane instead of the walker, Linc no longer moves like a tortoise, and I await him, thumbs-up, as he hobbles over the flagstones to our table. Myna, who was at his side when they came through the French doors, has thankfully disappeared, replaced by Noel. Poor baby spent the day running errands for Helen, including fetching and setting up the dozen or so tables and folding chairs that Emmet rented for the occasion. Because the table-cloths are also rented, I realize that the only thing Kit had to do was put the hurricane candles on each table, then wrap a bit of ivy around their bases. I certainly hope she didn't strain herself.

Noel and I get Linc seated so he can see everything, and I lean over him, my cheek pressed to his. He's been looking so much better, but tonight he appears tense. "Did Kit give you the grand tour?" I ask, and Linc smiles a weary smile.

"Including a lesson in feng shui. Before tonight, I thought 'fuhng shwey' was a kind of martial art."

"No, that's fung foo, or something like that," I tell him. Noel hoots, dodging the karate kick I aim at his derriere as he pulls up a chair next to Linc.

"Thank God. Emmet heads our way, bearing gifts." Noel nods his head toward Emmet, who's sidestepping the candlelit tables with a tray of drinks in hand.

"Where did Myna get off to?" I ask Linc.

He looks around puzzled, but Emmet appears with the drinks before he can answer. My martini's so dry that I gasp and strangle, which amuses Emmet. "Jesus, Emmet!" I shudder. "How'd you make this thing?"

"Trade secret," he says with a wink. "If I tell you, I'll have to kill you."

"No, you won't," I retort. "Another one of these and I'll be brain-dead."

Emmet takes a chair next to mine and holds up his glass for a toast. "Let's raise our glasses to our cohost and dear friend, Kit. All summer she's had us in tears with her tales of woe and destitution." He looks around the lavish terrace meaningfully.

"Come on," I say, unamused. "You know what a rough time she's having. It's gotten so bad she's had to sell off some of her belongings."

"From the looks of the rooms inside," Noel says, "she must've had one hell of a yard sale."

"Even sold the front yard," Linc adds, and Emmet throws back his head to laugh.

"Stop it, guys," I hiss. "I'll be afraid to go to the bathroom because y'all will talk about me."

Linc's face brightens. "Would you check on Myna while you're there, Tansy? I don't see her now, and she was a tad puny earlier. I'd feel better knowing she's okay."

Noel jumps up to pull out my chair. "Tansy'll be delighted to check on Myna for you. Won't you, love?"

With Linc seated across from me, I can't give Noel a murderous look, but I manage to dig my sharp heel into his foot. I've taken only a few steps when Emmet calls out to me. "Tansy?" I turn to see him holding up the tray, his eyes dancing. "Would you bring us a refill on your way back?"

Before I can tell him where he can put the tray, Linc speaks up. "Make mine a beer this time, honey. And for God's sake, don't tell Myna I've already had a martini—especially one of Emmet's."

After stopping by the bar and asking one of the bartenders to take a tray of Shirley Temples to the table of laughing hyenas near the fountain, I head back into the house. When I spot Kit by the buffet table, I smile at her in grudging admiration. Damn if she's not rearranging some of Helen's dishes as though she's slaved over them all day. Passing the kitchen, I see that Cinderella's still hunched over the stove, spoon in hand. One thing I've noticed about Helen: She's painfully awkward except with her cooking, then she becomes a different person, all poise and self-assurance. I have to hand it to her, she's going all out to make this a special evening for Annie.

The downstairs bathroom is nestled behind the suspended stairway. I knock on the door, then step back startled when it flies open. Myna glares at me, her hand on the knob. "What do you want?" she demands.

I fold my arms and tap my foot. "I heard dinner was being served in there, Myna. What do you think?"

To my astonishment, she grabs my wrist to pull me inside. "What the hell—" I yelp, but she waves her hand to shush me as she slams the door.

"Oh, for crying out loud," Myna says indignantly. "I just want to ask you something."

"Surely you could've picked a better place." I stop when I see how god-awful she looks. She's decked out in her usual witch clothes, but her hair is unkempt and her coloring ghastly. Maybe she is sick after all. To quote Oscar Wilde, let's hope it's nothing trivial.

"Do you have any idea what that hillbilly is doing to my husband?" Myna demands.

I know, of course, who she's referring to, but pretend otherwise. "Willa McFee!" she screeches when I appear puzzled, waving her arms so widely that I step backward and bump into the door-knob. "She's rubbing him down with some kind of mountain concoction she makes—" My hoot of laughter doesn't even slow her down, though her eyes flash me a warning.

Noel's not going to believe this, I think, but to her I say, "The mountain concoction is an old remedy of Willa's mother's, made solely with herbs. I'd think you'd be all about natural ingredients."

Myna looks vindicated rather than appeased. "I knew it! Just wait until I tell Linc's doctors."

Exasperated, I snap, "It's going to be a hard sell, considering how much better he's doing. Why can't you just let it go, and be happy about his improvement?"

She surprises me even further when her face crumbles, and she sinks down on the toilet lid. Alarmed, I kneel beside her and put a hand on her arm. "You're sick, Myna. Linc said you weren't feeling well, and sent me to look for you. Can I get you a cold washcloth or something?"

She screws up her face and puts a shaky hand on her forehead. "You don't fool me, Tansy Dunwoody. You'd be delighted if Linc left me—all of you would! You guys have never liked me, nor appreciated the culture I've brought into Linc's life. Believe me, there was precious little before."

"Linc's not going to leave you. Has he ever given you any reason to think so?"

"Not until she came on the scene," she spits out. "Now that's all I hear, how charmingly innocent she is, how eager to learn—"

I grab her arms and give her a good shake. "Surely you're not suggesting Linc's planning to leave you for Willa—that's ridiculous. Listen to me. It's true, they have a close relationship, but it's one of teacher and pupil. Willa's never had the opportunities the rest of us have, and you know it. You're a teacher—"

Jerking her arms free, she hisses, "I am not. I am a Pulitzer Prize–winning poet, who is forced by a society of ignorant, culturally deprived cretins to turn to the academy to support my art. And while doing so, I'm replaced in my husband's affections by a—a— milkmaid with big tits and an even bigger ass!"

I want to tell her that it's hard to pull off righteous indignation while sitting on a toilet seat, but it's not worth the effort. Instead I leave, and take great pleasure in slamming the door behind me on my way out.

Returning to the terrace, I lurk by the bar until I get Noel's attention. Motioning, I mimic dance moves, and he nods knowingly. Kit has gotten Emmet on the dance floor, the large flat area next to the fountain. She's bending his ear about something or other, and Emmet's smiling down at her. I like seeing them on good terms again. Noel meets me in front of the pergola, where Willa and Duff are playing "Georgia on My Mind." After my encounter with Myna, I need to dance, but the song's over by the time we get in place.

Noel gives Duff a signal, and he switches to a classic jig, "The

Irish Washerwoman." Waving us off, Emmet and Kit leave the dance floor and head for our table. Undeterred, Noel motions for Annie and her friends to join us. Forming a line, Noel and I, along with Annie and several of her friends, begin jigging around the fountain, locking arms and moving in unison like a scene from *Riverdance*. Darkness has fallen, and our shadows weave in and out of the dance line, lit up by the watery blue lights of the koi pond. The partygoers who sit the dance out applaud and whistle apprecia-tively, which of course eggs us on. By the time we've circled the fountain half a dozen times, I collapse in a nearby chair.

I look up to see that Noel, without missing a beat, has jigged over to grab Annie's hand. Arms linked, she and Noel move so fluidly in a sensuous weaving and twisting foxtrot that they look like professionals. The other dancers step back to let them perform by themselves, and I watch in admiration. It's not surprising that Annie, with all her years of riding, is such a graceful dancer, but Noel, whom I'm used to seeing in a ballroom, blows me away. The product of prep schools and Princeton, that boy can two-step like a rhinestone cowboy. Before long, Annie's girlfriends have formed a line for their turn with him.

Kit comes up and slips an arm around my waist. "You're crazy, you know," she says with a smile, her eyes on Noel and the girls.

"So I've been told. And fairly often, too. What now?"

She inclines her head toward the dance floor. "You're crazy if you let someone take that gorgeous man away from you again. You didn't do a thing to stop him when the countess lured him off to France. If he hadn't caught her with one of her lovers, he'd still be there."

"I did try to stop him!" I protest. "I warned him about her, re-member? I reminded him of what the British say."

"And what's that?"

In my best British accent, I say, " 'Lovely country, France. Pity about the French.' "

Kit laughs, then gets serious again. "You've got to tell Noel how you feel about him, Tansy, and stop pretending you're his bestest buddy. He has no idea that you've been in love with him all these years."

I shoot her a dirty look. "Don't start that crap again, Kit."

"I'm just saying . . ."

"Well, don't say anything. Instead, tell me if the dragon lady has resumed her rightful place by her husband's side. I'm afraid to look that way. She might turn me into a pillar of salt."

"Why do you think I left? And does she look god-awful, or what? What's going on, do you know?"

I shake my head wearily. "Oh, yeah, I know. But trust me, you don't want to hear it. By the way, is Cinderella planning to make an appearance, or will she remain chained to the kitchen?"

Kit wrinkles her nose. "She's so determined to impress everyone that she's martyring out. Absolutely refused to hire help, and won't accept any now. She's gotten it in her head that Annie's going to grovel at her feet in gratitude, then embrace her with half of Highlands watching. Which will never happen."

I regard her carefully. "One good thing has come out of Annie's animosity toward the Bride, though. She and her father are doing better, aren't they? I never expected her to forgive him for remarrying so soon."

Kit smiles sadly, a misty look in her eyes. "She knows he wasn't himself then. After being around the two of them for several days, she believes that her father will see that, too. Oh—and get this. Just yesterday, Annie told me that she prays he comes to his senses sooner rather than later. She's discovered that the Bride is gaga over Moonrise, and has put in for them to move here."

I blink at her in surprise. "Move here for good? You're kidding!"

Kit shakes her head. "Nope. Annie's overheard several things. Like Helen has fallen in love with the mountains, and Emmet's not returning to Fort Lauderdale."

"I never expected him to. It was just a one-year gig, wasn't it?"

"Yeah, but he can go back if he wants to. You know Mr. Hotshot—he can go to any station in the country. He's also had offers to return to CNN, or to take over the newsroom at channel six."

"Ha! The Bride better think twice about that one. Of course, guess Helen could give that anchorwoman a few tips on how to snag her boss. But what about the new cooking show she's so thrilled about? Surely she won't give that up, even for Moonrise."

Kit gives me a knowing look. "Annie heard her dad telling Helen about his offers, and assuring her that she could get the same show at either place, if he made it part of the deal. Which brought about quite an argument. Helen said only if she got it on her own, and if she ever found out that Emmet was responsible for her show in Fort Lauderdale, she'd resign. Nothing but bull, of course, but he doesn't know that—"

Before she can finish that tantalizing tidbit, Duff taps on the microphone to announce he's just gotten the signal from the lady of the house that supper is ready. Dive into the vittles, he adds, then they'll be back to play for some slow dancing. Over the applause, Kit says to me, "The lady of the house? That would be me, right? Yet I've barely spoken to Duff tonight, so Helen must've told him to say that." Jerking her head toward the house, she narrows her eyes at the sight of Helen, standing in the doorway with a triumphant smile as she waves her apron above her head. Spruced up for the party now, she looks great in an off-the-shoulder sundress, heels, and Rosalyn's stunning gold locket. Still Cinderella, maybe, but with the glass slipper in hand now. Chalk one up for the Bride, I think, but take care to hide my smile. Kit wouldn't be amused.

We're in the buffet line when Noel leans over to whisper in my ear, "Get a look at Duff, would you? Last we heard, he'd found Jesus. You'd never know it now, would you?"

I follow his gaze to the far corner of the patio, where Duff's trying to hide. Smoking a cigarette and chugging from something in a small paper sack, he keeps peering around the French hydrangeas to make sure Willa doesn't see him. When he flicks his cigarette on the newly laid slate, then steps on it with the heel of his boot, Noel groans. "Guess he missed Kit's feng shui lecture," I murmur.

I nudge Noel at the sight of Kit heading Duff's way furiously, and Noel suppresses a smile. Sure enough, we watch as Kit, pointing to the cigarette butt, tears into Duff as he cowers under her wrath. He's bound to know he's got a good thing going with her, so he appears to be sincerely contrite. Even so, I'm surprised to see her put a hand on his shoulder, and him leaning over while she whispers in his ear. Duff nods, and I follow his gaze to where Emmet stands with Annie. Whatever Kit's telling him he's in agreement, evidently, because he keeps nodding. Kit gives his shoulder a friendly pat before returning to her guests. As soon as she's out of sight, Duff lights another cigarette.

"Wonder what that's all about?" I ask Noel, who shrugs. Then, "Oh, well. Dish me up some of them vittles, Bubba. I'm starved."

Even if Helen hadn't joined us at the table, her face aglow at the praise she was gathering, I would've admitted that the birthday supper was amazing. She's prepared a huge spread, with something for everyone, young and old. If these dishes are any indication, I whisper to Kit, her cookbook will be a success. She's come a long way from her first tasteless dinner of the summer. Despite being heart-healthy and good for you, the buffet dishes are delicious enough to bring raves from some of Highlands's snootiest foodies.

Between bites, I steal glances at Annie. Exercising a father's prerogative, Emmet insisted she join us at the grown-up table, and she's sullen and snappish. Ignoring the chair he pulls out for her, she plops her fanny down next to Kit, as far from her father and stepmother as possible. It would break Rosalyn's heart to see Annie being such an unpleasant little shit. She was always so good-natured and well behaved, and never gave them any problems to speak of. Mother and daughter were so close that we thought losing Rosalyn would destroy Annie, too. Even so, the way she's channeling her grief into a growing resentment of Helen worries me. Linc's eyes meet mine, and his frown tells me he feels the same. At the beginning of her visit, Annie was cool and distant with Helen, but polite, at least. Now even that's gone. Noel puts his plate down next to her, and her sullen expression disappears. When she flashes him a radiant smile, I relax. With that notorious charm of his, Noel has a flair for easing even the tensest of situations.

Despite the presence of the golden boy, Annie refuses to respond to any of our dinner table parlays. Instead, she refills her wineglass so many times that Emmet pointedly takes all the wine bottles to his end of the table.

That gets her attention. In an acid-laced voice, Annie drawls, "Oh, you want the wine for yourself, Dad? What a surprise! Over-indulgence is so unlike you."

Emmet's eyes flash, but his response is mild. "Doesn't look like I'm the one who's overindulging, sweetheart."

Helen glances from one to the other in alarm, and I pray she's got sense enough to stay out of it. Instead, she titters and places a hand on Emmet's arm. "Oh, we're entitled to overindulge on our birthdays, don't you think?"

"No, I don't, Helen," he says coolly. If his tone doesn't warn her to butt out, she's braver than I think.

To everyone's surprise, Myna speaks up from the other end of the table. "So what are you getting for your birthday, Annie? The invitation said no gifts, but surely there's something you want." If it were anyone else, I'd assume she was trying to ease an awkward situation, but Myna is clueless. She leans forward and blinks at Annie like a curious bird, and I exchange glances with Kit and Noel, both of whom shrug.

Annie's answer surprises me even more than Myna's interjection did. Annie tilts her head and gives Myna an icy smile. "Well, Myna, the only thing I really wanted belonged to my mother, and this very morning, I asked my dad for it. But he's already given it to someone else. So it doesn't really matter to me what I get now."

Kit puts a hand to her throat. "Oh, honey! Rosalyn's things are in the attic at Moonrise. I'll be happy to go through them with you. Your mother would want you to have anything that was hers. Especially on your birthday."

Tactless as ever, Myna brays out, "So what of Rosalyn's did you want?"

If I were sitting closer, I'd clamp a hand over her mouth, since I have a sneaking suspicion I know the answer to her inquiry. I steal a glance at Helen, and the candlelight picks up the gleam of the golden locket around her neck. Although she looks distressed, what Annie's hinting at obviously hasn't hit her yet. If not, she's the only one. Next to me, I hear Kit's soft gasp, and Noel coughs discreetly and squirms in his chair. I dare not look at either of them, nor Linc, either. I steal a peek at Emmet, but his look is so fierce I quickly look away. Just when I'm sure he'll explode, we're saved by Duff's booming voice on the microphone. Suppertime over, folks, he announces. Choose your partner and hit the dance floor!

Accompanied by Willa's fiddling, Duff hugs the microphone and croons a bluesy rendition of "Red River Valley," while chairs scrape on the flagstones as the revelers take to the floor again. With a little bow, Noel holds out a hand to Annie, but Emmet, moving fast for an old man, beats him to it.

"Sorry, old chap. Exercising another of my fatherly prerogatives," he says breezily, and he's hauled his daughter off before she can protest. Good move, I think. Get her on the dance floor so you can chew her out for being so rude. The music's loud enough to keep her friends from hearing you.

Since Noel's partner was literally snatched from his hands, I turn to claim him for myself. I've always loved the song, and say what you will about Duff, the boy can sing. Especially with Willa harmonizing, and I'm swaying dreamy-eyed by the time I reach out for Noel. Damned if he's not already on the dance floor with Helen. Amazing how fast he got around the table, as soon as Annie waltzed off with her father. I try not to look Kit's way, but she sidles over with one of her sly looks. Under her breath, she murmurs, "Well, well. Someone's looking pretty pleased with himself."

I hate it when Kit's right because she tends to gloat, which I hate even worse. Backlit by the fountain lights, Noel and Helen sway past us, locked in each other's arms. She's smiling at him as though Prince Charming had just sprung to life, and damn if Noel isn't looking down at her moon-eyed, too. I've brushed aside Kit's outrageous suggestion of their budding attraction, but now I wonder. Unbidden and unwelcome, the suspicions I had after reading Rosalyn's notebook come back to me. The idea of Noel and Rosalyn I'd dismissed as ludicrous, but still. As well as I know Noel, he's always been a difficult read. He's a smooth one—wickedly witty, flippant, and blasé, yet revealing precious little about himself. As much as he likes women, I've never seen him lovesick nor head over heels. I'm sure he loved the countess, but if he suffered from their divorce, he kept it to himself. They remain friends, and he visits her and her kids whenever he goes to France. It hits me that Noel's unwillingness, or inability, to lose himself in another person is the secret of his appeal, even more so than his more obvious charms. The unattainable is always more desirable than the readily available.

When the song's over, Helen gives Noel a quick hug. I look

around for Emmet and Annie, and find that she's back with the young stud she danced with earlier. Emmet, on the other hand, has started toward Helen but stops when he sees her whispering something to Noel, their heads bent together. Noel laughs, and she flushes prettily, eyes luminous. When Duff taps the microphone to ask for requests, I return to the table. Since the crowd's mostly made up of Annie's friends, my choice of dance partners is limited, and Kit just beat me to Emmet.

I arrive at the table just in time to save Linc. Myna's about to drag him home, again pretending to be ill. I'd be sympathetic if she hadn't told me from her perch on the pot that she was not sick, just distraught. To annoy her, I muster up my sweetest Southern drawl and purr, "Oh, Myna. You look just awful! By all means, you should go to bed. Noel and I'll get Linc home. All of us who were at Annie's first birthday want to be here when she blows out the candles on her twenty-fifth."

Myna gets the best of me by saying to Linc, "Then I'll stay to share that moment with you, Poopsie. I know how fond you are of Annie."

Linc gives her a weak smile and pats her hand. "Not if you're feeling unwell, honey. You mustn't make yourself sicker on my account."

As expected, Myna insists that being with him is more important to her, and I turn away before I throw up on her granny boots. Willa and Duff strike up a duet of one of my favorites, "I Fall to Pieces," and I look around for another dance partner. Behind me, I hear Myna say snidely, "You'd think Willa would leave the singing to Duff. She plays the fiddle fairly well, but her voice is so twangy."

I pause on the pretext of adjusting the strap of my shoe, eager to hear Linc's response. Bad move, Yankee girl, I think with a smirk. A belle knows better than to put down a rival. It puts Linc in the position of defending Willa, which he does. "She sings harmony, my dear," he says testily. "And quite beautifully, too."

"Oh, really?" Myna says without bothering to lower her voice. "Perhaps her next song will be about a hillbilly girl who's after a married man. And one old enough to be her father, too."

She's pushed him too far. "That's enough, Myna," Linc says. "If you cannot control yourself, then you should go home. I intend to stay here and enjoy what's left of the evening. And don't think you'll pick up this argument when I come in, because I have nothing else to say."

Instead of looking contrite, she sneers. "I'll go home, all right. But you haven't heard the last of this, Linc Varner."

After Myna departs, Linc takes off his glasses to rub his face wearily. Getting upset is the worst thing for him, but I don't know what to do. Rather than call attention to his distress and Myna's abrupt departure, I look around for help. Noel and Helen are talking with Emmet and Kit, so I scurry over to tell them what's going on.

"What the hell—" Noel says when I burst into their group, waving a hand to silence their jabber. When I give them a quick rundown of Myna's actions, it's Helen who looks alarmed. Both Noel and Emmet dismiss my fears. "Not to worry, Tans," Noel says. "Linc won't allow her to keep bullying him. And she's not going to risk losing him by doing so."

When Emmet agrees, Helen frowns, unconvinced. "I hope you're right. Linc looks pretty rattled to me."

Emmet studies her before saying calmly, "Trust us, sweetheart. We've known him a long time. He's fine, I swear." Putting an arm around her shoulders, he says, "Relax, okay? Look, Duff's tuning up his fiddle for the next song. It's probably been a while since he's played Chopin's Sonata number three."

Kit giggles, but I'm too edgy to make light of this, and it's obvious that Helen is, too. It's only when Duff begins playing "Together Again" that I force myself to relax. Helen seems to as well, though she tells us that she's going inside to get the cake ready.

"You can't go yet, Honeycutt," Emmet says in a tone seductive enough to change any woman's mind. Sure would mine, especially the way he's looking at her. Jesus! What does that woman have, anyway? "I've put in a request for our song," he adds.

But Helen doesn't relent. She tells him that she can hear the music inside, and he protests, saying he doesn't want to dance in the kitchen. Helen looks alarmed and tells him to dance with me or Kit instead, but not to come in. She has a surprise coming up that no one can see beforehand.

After she's gone, I ask Kit if she knows what the surprise is. "No idea," Kit replies breezily, then eyes Emmet sideways. "Do you, Emmet?"

He shakes his head and turns to leave, but Kit grabs his hand and pleads, "One more dance, please?" On the dance floor, I notice that Emmet keeps glancing over Kit's shoulder toward the house until she pulls him closer with an exasperated smile.

When the song's over, Duff taps on the mike to say, "The young folks just requested that the party go on for another hour or so. Shoot, me and Willa can play all night if need be. That sound good to y'all?"

When Annie's friends cheer, I hear Emmet mutter, "Oh, no, you don't" as he breaks free of Kit's hold. Pushing his way through the young couples poised to dance, he strides over to the pergola and takes the microphone out of Duff's hand. Duff steps back, startled.

"Sorry, kids," Emmet says over the squeal of the mike. "Party's gone on long enough. One more song, then we're bringing out the cake." He searches the crowd until he spots Annie, and motions her to come forward. She starts to protest, but Emmet's expression is not for the faint of heart. He says briskly, "I'm claiming my daughter for the last dance, and picking the song, too." Then, to Duff and Willa, "Let's hear 'You Are My Sunshine,' okay?"

After the final dance is over and the applause dies down, Helen appears in the doorway to instruct us to gather around the table for the cake. The little round table is draped with a sheer silver cloth that glitters in the light of the lanterns, and even the sullen birthday girl gets into the spirit, all smiles when Kit pulls out her camera. Emmet has his, too, as do a couple of Annie's friends. Annie giggles at all the flashbulbs going off, then cheers with her friends at her father's announcement of champagne to follow the cake. When Noel and Linc join me, Noel suggests we stay on the edge of the crowd so the young folks can get closer. We move back, and I get between him and Linc to link our arms together. The gods have finally smiled down on the celebration.

It happened so fast that afterward, none of us were quite sure how everything blew apart. Helen brought out the cake to startled applause, followed by a lot of appreciative oohing and aahing. Kit would tell me later that she knew what would happen as soon as she saw the cake, but my first sight of it rang no alarm bells. Instead I gasped, "Oh my," and Linc said, "Fantastic," while Noel gave a low whistle of appreciation. The cake was a mile-high concoction of three tiers, each piped with yellow icing and decorated with spun-sugar roses. Instead of candles, it was topped with a ring of sparklers, which Helen lit as soon as she sat the cake on the table.

More applause and flashbulbs, then Willa and Duff raised their fiddles, poised to play "Happy Birthday." I looked around to see who'd lead the singing. Only then did I realize that something was wrong. Everyone had gotten dead quiet, and I heard Noel mutter. "What the hell . . ." I looked up at him in confusion, and when his eyes met mine, he jerked his head back to the table.

Annie stood in front of the table facing Helen, who was poised behind it with a box of matches in her hand. The sparklers flashed between them so it was difficult to see their faces clearly, but I noted that all the color had drained from Helen's. Annie's face was flushed red, her expression furious. "How dare you?" she cried, then her voice rose an octave higher. "How dare you do this to me, Helen? You are not my mother, and you will never be my mother. Do you understand that? Never!"

"What on earth?" Linc said, turning from me to Noel in bewilderment. I looked at Noel, then back at the cake, and it hit me. At that moment, I knew what Helen had done. So many years ago, but I could see it as plain as the scene playing out in front of us. Moonrise—Rosalyn always held Annie's little-girl birthday parties at Moonrise, and on the terrace in front of the moon gardens. As long as I could remember, Rosalyn made a big deal of Annie's birthdays, and the parties were spectacular. We teased her because she went to so much trouble, especially with the cake. Of course Miss Creasy did most of the work, but Annie didn't know that. She only knew that the cake was special because it was the only time her mother ever baked, and the cake was the same kind Rosalyn had as a child. Desperate to please Annie, Helen had duplicated the cake. But how could she have possibly known about it?

Leaning in, Noel whispered the same question to me, and I shook my head. She must've found an old photo, I replied in a terse whisper. Again, Linc asked what was going on, and I had to shush him to hear what was being said over the raised voices. Distraught, Helen kept stammering apologies, but Annie was too upset to listen. Instead she cried out, "You take my father, then my mother's house, and even the jewelry that belonged to her. Now you're trying to insert yourself into my most treasured childhood memories! What a cruel, cruel thing to do to me."

At that, Annie collapsed into tears. His camera falling on the table, Emmet moved quickly to console his daughter. As did Kit, with both of them reaching the weeping girl at the same time. Turning her back on her father, Annie covered her face with her hands and went to Kit instead.

A hand over her mouth, Helen turned and ran into the house. The crowd of onlookers, stunned into silence, suddenly started talking all at once. The only one of us with any presence of mind was Willa, who began fiddling one of their jigs from earlier on. Duff shrugged and joined in, thankfully filling the dreadful chatter with a lively tune that would have been terribly ironic, even mocking, had anyone noticed it. Noel snapped at me to get Linc seated, then he rushed into the house after Helen.

Rather than take Linc back to the table we occupied earlier, I pulled up a nearby chair, which he collapsed into, gripping his cane with both hands. Leaning over him, I took a deep, trembling breath. "Oh, God," I said. "What an awful thing to happen."

"I don't understand what that was all about," Linc said in bewilderment. "Why was Annie crying? And what did Helen do to upset her so badly?"

"Listen, sweetie," I said in a low voice, "I'll tell you later, but I need to check on Noel and Helen first. Will you be okay until I get back?"

"But . . . where's Emmet?"

"He's with Annie, he and Kit." It was the first time I'd seen Linc that confused since his stroke. Patting his shoulder, I promised to get him home as soon as I returned. As bad as I hated leaving him alone, I simply had to find out what was going on.

Passing the pergola, I tried to get Willa's attention, but she and Duff were putting away their instruments and didn't look up. Her brow furrowed in distress, Willa looked as if she couldn't get out of there fast enough. The rest of the party was breaking up as well, and in a hurry. The young guests shuffled out awkwardly without anyone to bid them farewell. Kit had taken Annie aside, and the two of them huddled together behind the pergola. Emmet stood next to them helplessly, his hands thrust into his pockets and his expression grim.

When I walked past the silver-clothed table where the cake stood, I noted that the sparklers had fizzled out, leaving only a faint whiff of smoke above them. Just a few minutes ago, their celebratory sparks had lit up the night, if only for a brief moment. Now they were cold and spent, charred sticks atop an overwrought cake. The image struck me as a fitting end to the evening.

WOOD NYMPH

I need to go by the Rutherford house—or what used to be the Rutherford house—to make sure Carlita's got the party mess under control, but I won't rest easy till I check on the folks at Moonrise. With a belated birthday present for Annie, I've got an excuse. A bad moon on the rise, folks around here say, and that's what it feels like this morning. A bad moon was hanging around these parts last night, that's for sure.

I use my key to let myself in the front door, figuring they might be sleeping after such a night. Hearing somebody in the kitchen, I call out to let them know I'm here. Nobody answers, so I head that way, wondering if it's the ghosts I hear, having their breakfast. Far as I know, the haints hadn't been heard from all summer, but last night was enough to bring forth anything, even the undead.

I stop in the kitchen door at the sight of Emmet hunched over his newspaper and coffee cup, deep in thought. Unshaven, with his hair a mess and baggy circles under his eyes, he looks like the pure-tee devil. I start to back out, but he spots me.

Emmet usually jokes around, teases me about Duff or something, but not today. He just says in a gruff voice, "You're not usually here on Saturday, Willa."

Without looking his way, I cross over to the sink. Don't know if he's got a hangover or just the blues from the party, but I'm not anxious to pass the time with him. Even when he's joking around and friendly, Emmet makes me nervous. I have to think quick, though, since I can't tell him I came by to make sure they hadn't all kilt each other. Instead I say, "Oh, just thought I'd stop by on my way to Linc's. Then I'm on my way to Kit's to see how the cleanup's coming."

Emmet's the one who's paying Carlita extra to clean on Saturday, and it's bound to be a pretty penny. I'm sure Kit won't lift a finger to help out, even with so much stuff to put away. Most of the dishes Helen toted over from Moonrise, and she was waiting to get them today. Her plan was to run the dishwasher and let the rest soak overnight, but I wonder if she even got a chance to. If not, Emmet's liable to find hisself taking out a bank loan to pay for the cleanup.

"Aw, you brought me a gift," Emmet teases, sounding more like his old self. "You shouldn't have."

"It's something I made for Annie." I untie the bow and take the framed butterfly out of the little bag, where it's wrapped in tissue paper. Emmet holds out his hand to see it. I can't help myself; I'm tickled he asked even if it means conversing with him. I'm that proud of my butterflies.

"You made this?" he says as he holds it up to the window. One of my smaller frames, it fits in the palm of his hand. "It's exquisite."

"Well, I didn't make the butterfly, just framed it in glass." He raises an eyebrow, and I realize what I said. I'm always saying stuff like that around him. If he was more like Linc, I wouldn't be so nervous. "I meant, it's a real butterfly. Linc's showing me how to frame the ones I've collected."

Emmet holds it this way and that to the light of the window. "So Linc's turning you into an amateur lepidopterist, huh?"

"I don't know about that, but he's sure teaching me a lot about butterflies. Things I'd never thought of in a million years."

He turns to peer at me over his reading glasses, and I squirm under his curious gaze. "Tell me two of the most interesting things you've learned."

Oh, Lord, why didn't I see that coming? It's what Emmet does instead of carrying on a normal conversation, like you're on his TV show or something. Clearing my throat, I say, "Well, did you know that butterflies can't fly if the temperature drops below fifty? That's how come they have to bask in the sun so much. But what interests me even more is their life cycle. You know—egg, caterpillar, cocoon, then butterfly? Except what I've always called a cocoon probably's a moth instead of a butterfly since butterflies usually spin a chrysalis instead. Oh—and get this. Most butterflies come out of their chrysalis in a week or so, but some species take years. Can you believe that?"

"It's obvious you're an eager pupil. Note I said pupil, not pupa."

I give him a knowing smile. "I figured you knew more than you were letting on. It's hard to be friends with Linc and not pick up a lot, I reckon."

Emmet's expression changes, and he's scowling again. "Willa? I need to talk to you about Linc." I must of looked startled, because he holds up a hand before I can say anything else. "He's fine. It's something else. Why don't you get a cup of coffee and sit down?"

I shake my head, though I'm not sure my legs will hold me up. Lord, what now? Emmet runs his fingers through his hair, then he sighs, loud. "I won't beat around the bush. Your time is valuable, and I've got to get to work on my documentary. Bottom line is, Linc married an asshole. Because he's Linc, he'll endure it as long—and as stoically—as possible. Certainly a lot longer than he, or anyone else, should. You and Linc have spent a lot of time together this summer, and guess who's jealous?"

"I been afraid of that." I close my eyes for a minute, then say, "I won't go back over there, then. Last thing I want is to cause him any trouble."

Emmet stares at me so hard I'm forced to meet his gaze, and he says in a harsh voice, "You'll do no such thing. Only if Linc asks you to leave—Linc, not Myna—are you to stop helping him out, you hear? That's not what I'm saying. Myna's a pain in the ass, but she won't do anything except make everyone miserable. More to the point, I'm concerned about Duff, and his reaction to your relationship with Linc. I fear his jealousy may be more of a problem than Myna's."

I finally hear what he's trying to tell me. "I can see how you'd be worried after seeing Duff show his tail at the swimming hole, Emmet. But trust me, he's not gonna do anything but act the fool." With a small smile, I add, "And like Myna, he's been doing that as long as I've known him, too."

Emmet studies me real hard, like he's trying to decide if I'm telling the truth, then he nods slowly. "Are you sure?" When I tell him that I'm sure, he seems satisfied, then pushes back from the table. Real businesslike now, he says, "Okay. I'm refilling my coffee cup, then back to work. But first, promise me that you'll come to me, or Noel, if Duff's behavior ever gives you any reason for concern. Will you?"

I promise, then tell him again that Duff'll be just fine. Handing me the butterfly frame, Emmet says, "Annie's not here now, but I'll make sure she gets her gift. She'll be delighted. Just leave it on the table if you want."

I'm longing to ask him about last night, about where Annie is, and if everything's okay, but I dare not. I can't leave without checking on Helen, though. Busying myself with wrapping the frame in its tissue, I say, "Uh, Emmet? I was hoping to see Helen this morning."

As I feared, his eyes go cold and flat, but he nods toward the door leading to the porch. "She's outside somewhere. Probably that place she goes at the end of the path. You know, with the willow furniture." Without another word, he leaves the kitchen and doesn't look back.

That's where I find Helen. She's wrapped in an old flannel robe, and she sits on the willow settee with her feet folded under her. Coffee cup in hand, she stares out over the lake, where a fog floats like a cloud. It's a cool morning, with the tiniest taste of fall in the air. Or maybe that's my imagination. As dry as it is, we'll be lucky if the leaves even turn this year. Middle of August, and still no rain.

Helen doesn't see me, and I sit on the settee without her even noticing. I brought Annie's butterfly frame with me, which I hold in my lap. I've got several others ready for the glue gun, and I want to pick out a pretty one for Helen. Maybe I'll give her the Black Swallowtail. They're common as gully dirt in these parts, but so pretty that everybody loves them anyway.

Helen reaches out and pats my hand without looking my way. "What do you have there?" she asks, and I hand the butterfly frame to her. It's a moth, not really a butterfly, but still one of my favorites. Wood Nymph, Linc called it, and I knew that was the one I had to give Annie. It's little and pretty, with silvery-brown wings. When I asked Linc what a nymph was, he leaned back in his chair and made his fingers into a steeple. "Well, you're a nymph, Willa, as is Annie." At first he teased me by not telling me what that meant, making me guess, then he said, "A nymph, Willa, is a beautiful young maiden. A creature of the woods and rivers. But more importantly, a Nymph—unlike larva—does not change forms as it grows. And that fits you even more."

I find myself telling Helen that stuff about the Wood Nymph, just blurting it out, when I show her the butterfly frame. She smiles, studying the butterfly in the same way that Emmet did, but her smile is so sad it about breaks my heart. Looking out toward the lake, where the fog's lifting, I say, "Helen? I felt bad for you last night, and it looked to me like everybody else did, too. None of us knew what it was about, though. How come Annie got so upset with you?"

She lets out a sigh, then rubs her face with both hands. "Oh,

Willa, honey. I wish I knew. Evidently when I made the same cake her mother made for her, she thought I was trying to duplicate things Rosalyn did for her. Even worse, she thought I was doing it just so she'd accept me as part of her life. Things like the cake, and the special times she and her mother had, are sort of sacred to her, now that her mother's gone, and she resents anyone intruding on them. No, that's not quite true. She resents me intruding on them. Or so I assume. She won't discuss it, or anything else, with me."

I frown, thinking about it. "So you don't really know Annie feels that way, you're just guessing?"

Helen's laugh comes out sounding bitter, though I can't say I blame her. "I'm not sure what part of 'you will never be my mother' I failed to understand."

Without thinking, I blurt out, "But what a dumb thing for her to say! Of course you're not her mama. Your boy—what's his name?"

Adam, she tells me, and I go on to say, "You're Adam's mother, but Emmet's not his daddy. His daddy's still around, right?" She nods and even smiles a little, watching me real close, and I add, "So he don't need Emmet to be one. But Emmet can still be a part of his life, and somebody he can love and respect. And you could be the same for Annie, if she'd let you. Even more so, because her mama's gone now. Looks like she'd see it that way! Seems to me that the more people we love, the more we have to love us back."

"You'd think so, wouldn't you?" Helen falls quiet for a while, then she says, "But it's more than that. If Emmet had married Kit, say, or Tansy—someone more like Rosalyn—Annie would have less trouble accepting her. It's me, Willa. She dislikes me, and rather intensely, it appears."

It's hard to argue with that, so I don't even try. If anyone doubted it, last night would of been proof enough. Helen raises her head to stare at a spot somewheres beyond the mountains, and her yellow-brown eyes grow darker. Without looking my way, she says in a low voice: "Rosalyn's still here, Willa. She walks the halls, and roams around the gardens, checking on her flowers. And she watches me with Emmet."

Her words make the hair on the back of my neck stand up, and I shiver. A rabbit ran over my grave. "You mean, like a ghost or spirit?"

She shrugs. "I don't know where we go after this life. None of us do, regardless of what we've been told. I can only hope and pray it's to some place of eternal rest, as we've been led to believe. But I have a feeling the dead don't rest until the ones they left behind let go of them. That's why Rosalyn's here—none of them can let her go. Maybe they'd have had an easier time of it if I hadn't come along when I did. With me in the picture, Annie, especially, was forced to let go before she'd come to grips with her loss." She stops herself, and wags her head back and forth. "I don't know. Maybe I'm just grasping at straws, trying to make sense of this."

"What does Emmet say about Annie feeling so harsh toward you?"

Helen sighs and closes her eyes. She looks about as bad as Emmet did, with dark circles under her eyes, and the little lines by her mouth more noticeable. "Emmet's shut me out again," she says. "I'm afraid he's not too pleased with me, either. But he won't talk about it, except to say that Annie was rude to me and he won't have it. She stayed at Kit's last night, which made him furious, and she's going back to Boone today. Emmet says if he has to bar the door and take the keys to her truck, she's not going anywhere until she apologizes."

"Well, good for him," I say, but Helen doesn't agree.

"I've begged him not to. It will just make her hate me more, and it won't change her mind."

"Maybe not, but it'll sure change her manners. It's awful, her pitching a fit like that. Especially after you went to so much trouble for her, fixing all that good food, and a pretty cake. Rosalyn wouldn't stand for that girl acting up, I can tell you. They were real close, but Rosalyn didn't spoil her, or let her behave like a snob."

Helen puts her face down into her hands and moans. "I don't get it, Willa! When Annie came to see us in Florida, things were tense, and awkward, but nothing like this. She and I were overly polite with each other, but friendly, at least. I fretted a lot more over her relationship with her father, assuming that things would get better between me and her over time. But after she came here, there was a drastic change. At first I thought it was because we were at Moonrise, and everything reminded Annie of her mother. That'd make some sense, at least, and maybe it was a factor. But where is her hostility coming from? It's as if someone has poisoned her against me."

It hits me that she's right. Turning my head away, I stare at the lake while thoughts spin around in my head. I've been hearing things lately, of course; mostly people saying Helen's some kind of Jezebel who took advantage of Emmet at his lowest point. Talk, talk, talk; it's all people do here—summer people same as the mountain folks—running their mouths. Don't matter if it's true or not, since nobody bothers to find out. The way Helen looks at that man tells me the real story. I don't care what anybody says, she's crazy in love with him, and he is with her. If folks would leave them be, they might make it. Lord knows, staying together is hard enough for anybody without all that crap working against you!

Helen puts a hand on my arm, and I jump. "Willa? You know something you're not telling me, don't you?" I try to deny it, and she gives my arm a little shake. "I won't say anything, I swear. But if there's anything I need to know that will help me with Annie, please tell me. She's going back today, and we won't see her again for a while, maybe not until Christmas. So if I can do or say anything to make things better, it needs to be today."

I chew on my lip, frowning, then say, "If I knew something

that'd help, I'd tell you, Helen. Only thing I know, somebody's been stirring folks up, saying stuff about you—"

"What kind of stuff?" she cries. "What do they think I've done? Okay, Emmet and I should've waited a decent time after his wife's death to marry. I feel bad about that, and can see how our haste could be disrespectful to Rosalyn's memory. If I had it to do over again . . ." She stops herself, then glances at me, her face flushed. "I don't know. Even if we'd waited a decent time, I wonder if I'd be accepted. I'm not one of them, Willa. I'm not from their world, and won't ever be. I can't be what Rosalyn was. If they hold that against me, well . . ." Tears shining in her eyes, she shrugs, and says it again, "I can't be Rosalyn."

I felt bad leaving Helen with what she had to face, but not a blame thing I could do about it. We were on the settee talking when she looked up in surprise. Emmet stood on the path, hands on his hips. I don't know what all he heard, and I didn't wait around to find out, either. All he said to her was, Annie's about to leave now, and she's waiting to apologize to you. Then he turned around and walked back to the house. Why he looked like Helen was to blame, I can't imagine. It's not her fault Annie acted like a spoiled brat. I could tell Helen was even more upset, but she got up and went after him. Before she left, she gave me a hug and a thank-you—for what, I don't know. I told her I'd ask around, see what I could find out. No, don't trouble yourself, she said, and in a way that made me think it wouldn't make any difference, no matter what. It worried me, because I had a bad feeling that she was right. When I asked her to take the butterfly to Annie, she looked at the little sack with its pretty bow like she'd never seen it before.

I don't dare go to Linc's, not after what Emmet told me. When I pass by his cabin on the way to the Rutherford house, I see his wife's car parked under the old elm. Far as I can tell, no one's stirring inside. Because she's home, everything's closed up tight as a tick. It's a shame, since I know how much Linc likes sunshine and fresh air. First thing he has me do is open up all his doors and windows.

I wish Myna hadn't decided she was jealous of me because I was so excited about seeing Linc today. Early this morning when I was feeding the chickens, I saw a Buckeye in the snapdragons. Good thing I still had Linc's camera so I could take pictures to show him. He's got lots of Buckeyes on his boards, but this one had such unusual coloring. I've never seen one like it. A real light shade of brown, which shows up the spots on its wings better than the dark brown ones Linc has. One thing about the Buckeyes, you can't mistake them for anything else. Just hope my pictures turn out good.

Praise the Lord, Carlita's got things under control at Kit's, and don't need me because her granddaughter's helping her. I don't make it back outside to leave, though, before Kit sees me opening the front door and calls out to me. I'd spotted her and Tansy having coffee together, but they didn't see me.

"Willa! You're just the person I want to see." Smiling her phony smile, Kit comes up to me like I'm her best friend in the world. "Listen," she says in that breathy voice of hers that sounds like she's been running a race. "I tried to call Duff to come help me out this morning, but couldn't reach him. So I need you to take some stuff to Moonrise for me. You're driving your truck, aren't you?"

"Since I don't have nothing else to drive, I guess I am." Standing in the doorway, I fold my arms and wait for what's coming next. If she thinks I'm hauling all of Helen's dishes over there, she's got another think coming. I'd do it for Helen, but last night I heard Noel telling her not to worry, he'd gladly bring them over. He had to check on something in the gardens anyhow.

Big surprise, that's exactly what Kit wants, for me to take a load of stuff to Moonrise. "There's no point in Helen coming over to-day," she says in that syrupy-sweet tone she uses when kissing up.

"The poor thing's bound to be exhausted. You'd be doing her a big favor."

"Maybe so, but I stopped by Moonrise on my way over," I tell her, "so I'm not planning on going back that way."

Kit's eyes get real wide, and she puts a hand to her throat. To give the devil his due, she's got real pretty eyes, even without a smidgen of makeup on. Barefoot, and in a skimpy little robe that barely covers her hiney, she looks every bit as good as she did all dolled up at the party. I've heard plenty of talk about her, with folks in town wondering why such a good-looking woman hasn't gotten hitched again. She don't date much, either, and I hear she's already dumped that Lanier guy. Some folks claim she's still in mourning for Al Rutherford, which is a crock if you ask me. I doubt she's ever loved anybody but herself.

I've never been able to figure that woman out, and don't know how come I waste so much time trying. I barely remember her from my childhood, with her and Rosalyn being a good twenty years older than me, but she was always around. Since Rosalyn loved her to pieces, she must've seen something good in her. I have to admit that Kit loved Rosalyn just as much, so maybe I'm being too hard on her. For a while, we didn't see much of her because she married some bigshot Atlanta lawyer. Next thing you know, she's divorced him and staying here with Rosalyn and Emmet for the summer. That's when she met Al Rutherford at the country club, him several years older than her and with grown-up kids. Rutherfords have been in these parts forever, but Al'd made money in the lumber business—which was about the only thing he had going for him. Sure wasn't much to look at. Next thing you know, he's dumped his poor old wife and married Kit. It was a big scandal, but folks ended up tolerating Kit because she poured so much of his money into local fund-raisers and things, currying favor. She might've married Al for his money, folks said, but she sure was generous with it. That might be, but I knew the other reason she married him. She wanted that house right across the lake from Moonrise so she could be here all the time, sticking her nose into Rosalyn's business.

I'm so lost in thought that I jump when Kit asks me, "So, how were things at Moonrise?"

I just shrug, not wanting to tell her anything. "Not much going on. I didn't stay long."

She steps closer and lowers her voice. Guess she doesn't want Tansy, who's disappeared in the bathroom, to hear her. "That was such a dreadful scene last night! I felt so bad for all concerned— Helen, Emmet, Annie, but especially Annie. Helen thought the cake would win her over, but it sure didn't work out that way, did it?" She sighs, putting a hand to her throat. "I just wish she'd checked with some of us before doing such a thing. We could've told her not to try to force things with Annie. Matter of fact, I did try to tell Helen. She knew the reason I insisted on having the party here, so Annie wouldn't be reminded of past parties at Moonrise. If only Helen'd listened to me! It will be an uphill climb between her and Annie now. I'll do what I can to help them, but it won't be easy."

Now why do I have a suspicion she's just telling me this so I'll spread the word? She oughta know better. Kit's watching me close, like she's waiting to see what I'll say about the party. Thankfully, Tansy shows herself, finally.

"Did I hear you say you've been to Moonrise, Willa?" Tansy asks. "I came over here to tell Annie bye, but she'd already gotten up and gone. Did you see her?"

I tell her no, but Emmet said she was fixing to leave for Boone, and Tansy nods. She and Kit both look sad and tired this morning, but Tansy especially. That's the other thing about Tansy; as sharp-tongued as she is, she can be tenderhearted, too. It's plain to see that she feels bad about the party. "I'll probably go with Noel this afternoon when he returns the dishes," she says. "To check on Emmet and Helen. Did you see either one of them, Willa? And were they speaking to each other?"

I tell her yes on both counts, then ask, "Why wouldn't they be speaking to each other?"

Tansy clucks and shakes her head. "Lord, honey, you missed quite a scene. Emmet was pissed with Annie and Helen both, Annie for being rude, and Helen for being so hush-hush about the cake. Which led to Helen getting upset because Emmet didn't take up for her."

"I'm with Helen," I say shortly, not caring if it makes them mad. "She was just trying to give Annie a birthday party she wouldn't forget."

"Well, she sure as hell did that, didn't she?" Tansy says it kind of hateful, which irritates me. I feel a headache coming on, and tell them I need to get home. I'm halfway down the steps, and they're saying good-bye, when I glance back to tell Kit I'm sorry about not taking the dishes to Moonrise. Tansy eyes Kit funny-like and says, "I told you Noel was doing that, Kit. Why'd you ask Willa to?"

I'd love to tell her why, that Kit has no respect for me or my time, but Tansy glances my way, gives me another little wave, and closes the door quick. Not before I hear Kit's answer, though. "You know why, Tansy," she snaps. I stop in my tracks so I'll know, too. Then I hear Kit say, "We need to keep him away from Helen, not encourage them to be together."

I crank up the truck in a state of shock. Surely to God those fool women don't think Noel and Helen have a thing for each other? If they've got that in their heads, it'd explain how come they have it in for Helen. But where on earth would they come up with such a stupid idea? Lord have mercy on me—what next?

14

helen

GARDEN SPELLS

I finally get it. When Noel first started coming over to work in the gardens, I went outside to watch mostly out of curiosity. As much as I admire the art of gardening, and certainly the results, I feel like I've missed out on some essential knowledge that's too late for me to get now. Despite all that, I've had a bit of a breakthrough, which I'm ridiculously excited about. Today, kneeling in the gardens with my hands in the dirt, I planted a caladium, a gift from Noel, then leaned back on my heels with pride.

After Willa's crew finished the basic cleaning of the back gardens, Noel and Tansy took over, but for whatever reason (Noel claimed laziness), Tansy dropped out. The first afternoon Noel came over by himself, he made a point of stopping by the kitchen to tell me what he was doing. Even though I had no idea what he was talking about—deadheading, pruning, fertilizing, repotting?—I liked being included.

Noel would later tease me about my tentative approach to his work in the gardens. The afternoon he sought me out in the kitchen, I was in the midst of the most challenging part of my cookbook, sweets. It's almost impossible to make anything sweet unless it's loaded with fat and sugar. After a batch of walnut meringue cookies came out of the oven, I took some outside to Noel, with a glass of peach tea. I'd done it before, leaving tea or lemonade on the ter-

race table for him and Tansy. Noel called out that he'd be there as
soon as he finished the hostas. Since the reflecting pools were in the
worst shape, he tackled them first. I sat on the steps to watch, curious. The next time he came over I left lemonade for him before
venturing a little farther out, going to one of the stone benches
to watch him dig up a bed of impatiens. Annuals, he said over his
shoulder, that he was replacing with perennials. Really? I thought
they were called impatiens, I told him, and Noel laughed. It was
a week or so later before I asked if there was anything I could do
to help.

Noel is the easiest person to be with I've ever known. It's not
fair to Emmet, I know, but the contrast between him and Noel is so
striking that I catch myself comparing them. Emmet's intensity is
what attracted me to him, yet it's the same thing that scares me off,
too. Since Annie's departure, we've formed an uneasy truce that
has me edgy and strung out. I was so upset after Annie's party that
I slept on the love seat in my office, which left me with a crick in my
neck and Emmet even more furious with me. Annie's apology
seemed genuinely heartfelt and contrite, but it did little to ease the
tension between her father and me. Although I returned to our bed
that night, I waited until he was asleep. We've been sidestepping
each other ever since, polite but distant.

Today, Noel and I are clearing out the vines around the reflecting
pool and lamenting the state of the garden. Just as he's about to get it
into shape, a new problem has arisen. At the beginning of August,
Macon County put out a decree of mandatory conservation. We've
joked about voluntary, but mandatory is no joking matter. Since
Highland's water supply comes from what's known as the Big Arm of
Looking Glass Lake, those of us who live on its banks have a front-
row seat to the low levels brought on by the drought. It's an ominous
sight.

"We're luckier than some when it comes to saving our gardens,"

Noel tells me. "We can haul water from the lake if we have to. Form a bucket brigade."

"I hope you're kidding," I say, shocked. We can see the lake from the side of the house, but it's not exactly a hop, skip, and jump from here.

"Not at all. Matter of fact, I've already toted several buckets for my roses. And I even filled the rain barrel in the hopes of appeasing the gods so they'll do it for me next time."

We smile together, and he tells me he's bringing the Lady of the Night back to Moonrise, now that she's revived. "Back where the old girl belongs," he says. He wipes his brow on his sleeve and grins at me.

"Don't, Noel," I say as I get to my feet and brush the dirt off my knees. I've finally learned to wear jeans, sneakers, and an old T-shirt when in the gardens. "Emmet and I will only be here a few more weeks." As soon as I say it, I realize how much I'm dreading the end of summer. I'll miss the mountains, more than I could've imagined. My face must've shown my distress, because Noel eyes me sympathetically.

"Oh? I've heard rumors to the contrary," he says with his easy smile.

"Yeah, me, too." I remember with a rush of guilt that Emmet had a meeting with the powers that be in Asheville yesterday, and I didn't even ask how it went. Things are so strained between us that he didn't volunteer anything, either. Kit rode with him to Asheville, so he filled me in on her meeting instead. Evidently her financial situation has gotten so dire that one of her and Rosalyn's sorority sisters, who's a decorator there, gave her some consulting work. Asheville's the perfect place for her feng shui crap, Emmet told me, and I'd giggled. It was the first light moment we'd shared since Annie's party.

"So, what's the story?" Noel asks, and I sigh.

"Well. Once word got out that Emmet was back in these parts, he started getting phone calls from the CNN folks. Thinking he could be had, I guess, Asheville began pulling out all the stops to get him there instead, so he's mulling things over. Oh, he could go back to Fort Lauderdale, of course, but Emmet's not all that crazy about south Florida, frankly. Once he got back here, it felt like home, and he wants to stay. Even so, he hasn't decided for sure."

Noel frowns, studying me intently. "What's to decide? You've got your new show coming up when—first of the year? Surely you two aren't considering a long-distance marriage, you in south Florida and Emmet either here or Atlanta."

"No. Actually, one of the reasons we married so quickly was Emmet claimed he was too old to dillydally around, and we wanted to be together." Blushing, I tell him what I haven't told anyone else, for obvious reasons. It not only sounds coy, but would add fuel to any rumors that I'd been out to snag the boss man. "I'm not a prude—don't get me wrong—but I nixed living in sin because of my son. Sounds silly, I know, but I didn't want him to think less of his mother."

"And your new show?" he reminds me.

"I've gotten kind of excited about it, strangely enough." When he wants to know why that's so strange, I laugh. "I'm camera-shy, Noel. Oh, I know I appear to be so poised and collected, but I'm jelly inside. At the beginning of the summer, Emmet started coaching me, and I feel more confident now. He thinks I can get on elsewhere, especially with the cookbook coming out. So if he doesn't want to go back to Florida, I'll be okay with it. I think, anyway. I'm mulling things over, too."

Leaning on the handle of his hoe, Noel looks toward the house. "Emmet's not in Asheville today, is he? I noticed his Jeep was gone."

"He's out working on his documentary. A news crew is in the area to film the segment on the drought. Emmet's taking photos,

too, and Kit asked to go with them and take her own. Do you remember the first of July, when Emmet went to the local waterfalls
and photographed the ones affected by the drought? He's getting
more pictures so he can compare them. If they turn out well, he'll
use them in the documentary."

I have another pang of guilt, remembering that Emmet asked
me to go with them today and I wouldn't do it. Maybe the tension
between us is more my fault than I've admitted to myself. He's also
asked me to go to Asheville with him, several times, but I've been
too busy. What other conciliatory moves have I blown off? Blackberries are at their peak, I'd told him this morning, so I was going
berry picking. In keeping with the concept of using local produce,
I have to come up with blackberry desserts. Willa said I'd better
move fast before the bears got them. Even after my refusal, Emmet
still tried to talk me into coming with them. Bound to be berries
where the film crew was going, he'd said. This evening when he
returns, I tell myself, I'll make things right.

"Listen, Noel, I've got to go," I say rather breathless. "I'm
heading out to Willa's to pick blackberries, and I've let the time slip
up on me."

"Don't drive all the way out there," he says as he gathers up his
gardening tools. "Come with me instead. I'll take you to the best
berry patch in Highlands. Even better, it can only be reached by
boat."

Noel had walked to Moonrise, so we take Emmet's canoe for
the berry-picking expedition. I've discovered canoeing this summer, finding it the perfect way to unwind after a day's work. Before
we leave, Noel tries to call Tansy to see if she'll join us. "So where's
Tansy?" I ask when we leave the dock and head out on the lake. He
takes the lead, with me paddling behind him.

Noel grins at me over his shoulder. "Believe it or not, she's working. Been on the phone and computer all day. The foundation's got a

big event coming up in mid-September that she's handling. She says to bring her some berries. Better yet, she wants you to make her a blackberry cobbler for supper. With loads of sugar, butter, and heavy cream."

I laugh, and we paddle in silence and in unison, our steady movement sending the canoe skimming over the dark green lake like a water bug. As we near the far side of the lake, Noel glances back to say, "I'm taking you to a blackberry patch near enough to the edge of the lake that we can pick from the boat. Curbside service." Turning back to face the bow of the canoe, he points. "Right beyond that little cove."

When we pass the cove, however, Noel stops paddling to stare in dismay. The berry patch is gone, cleared away for the construction of a new house. "Bloody hell," he mutters. We stare at the house in silence, and I wonder if he's thinking what I'm thinking. The cedar-shingled house is modern, with lots of glass and angular windows, yet it's designed to blend into the surroundings. Not only that, it's set back from the lake and almost hidden in foliage, with only the underbrush cleared out to preserve the indigenous trees and bushes. If only Kit had done the same with her house, it wouldn't be such an eyesore.

We end up tying the canoe at Noel's dock, then hiking behind Kit's house to another patch he knows about, near the foot of the mountain. When we get to the blackberry brambles, Noel inclines his head toward a rocky trail that leads up the side of the mountain, across a little inlet from Moonrise. "Let's leave our baskets here, Helen. There's an overlook I want to show you, where the view's incredible. It won't take long, and we'll pick on the way back."

When we get to the steepest part of the trail, Noel reaches for my hand to help me with the climb. The trail splits off, and he leads me through a rhododendron thicket to a clearing where a large, flat rock sticks out from the mountainside like a shelf. "From here, we have a bird's-eye view of Looking Glass Lake," he announces, and I gasp in surprise.

Hands on hips, Noel stands near the edge of the rock with a satisfied look on his face. I come to stand beside him, and he points out where we'd just been on the lake looking for the blackberries. Seen from above, Laurel Cottage, the Rutherford house, and Linc's cabin appear small and insignificant. Except for Kit's place, perched on its barren patch of ground, little more than the rooftops of the other houses are visible through the trees and branches. Looking Glass Lake is clear and glassy, still enough to mirror everything around it—trees, brambles, houses, docks. In the middle of the lake a fisherman sits in a small wooden boat, which in turn sits on a duplicate of itself, the fisherman and his mirror-self casting their lines simultaneously. Around the lake the rhododendron and laurel are dry and wilted, their leaves curled into themselves like little hands. Even so, it's a sight spectacular enough to take my breath away. "Thank you for bringing me here," I say with a smile.

"My pleasure." A strong wind playfully ruffles Noel's hair as he looks out over the mountains, squinting. "I thought you'd like it. It's one of my and Tansy's favorite places."

Keeping my eyes on the vista spread out below us, I dare to ask something I've been curious about ever since Emmet told me about Noel and Tansy's relationship. Surely he's much too well mannered to tell me to mind my own business. "Noel? Emmet told me that you and Tansy have known each other since childhood," I venture. "And you met right down there, at Laurel Cottage, right?"

Noel glances my way in amusement. He's too clever for me, of course. "Ah. You're curious about Tansy and me, and our living arrangement."

Blushing hotly, I put a hand to my mouth. "Oh, no—I didn't mean to imply—"

Noel throws back his head and laughs. "Of course you did,

Helen, and it's fine. Really. I'm surprised you haven't asked before now. Trust me, you're the only person in Highlands who hasn't." I'm too embarrassed to face him, but he seems unperturbed. Shrugging, he says, "It's true, Tansy and I love each other, and have since we first met. But we're like brother and sister, which we almost became. When she and I were adolescents, my father and her mother became an item."

"I heard that," I tell him, then blush again. If I already knew, then why ask, he's bound to be thinking. And the answer can only be one thing—pure and simple nosiness. I'm ashamed of myself, as nice as he's been to me, but I'm also dying to hear more.

"Tansy and I have been the closest of friends since day one," Noel continues. "We have that rarest of all things, I think, a deep friendship between a man and a woman. It's odd that we connected in that way instead of sexually, especially after we became hormone-stricken teens who were constantly thrown together, in plenty of tempting situations. And as adults, it's pretty much the same. Tansy's one of the most attractive women I've ever known, but I wouldn't trade our friendship for a hundred love affairs."

"That's not just rare, Noel. It's unheard of. Don't you think?" His gaze meets mine, and I think it should be against the law for him to wear a blue denim shirt, with those eyes of his.

"Oh, absolutely," he agrees. "But you know what? I don't think we'd still be together if we'd been lovers. It never would've worked out."

Intrigued, I turn my head to study him. "Why is that?"

"You might've noticed," he replies, "that Tansy's a tad difficult?" I can't help it, I giggle. Noel appears amused, and says, "Let me rephrase that. As lovable as she can be, Tansy's also caustic, bad tempered, and unpredictable. And those are some of her better qualities." He smiles, and I realize he's teasing. Or maybe not. Something hits me, and I wonder if I'm right.

"Okay, time to 'fess up. Aren't those the same traits that also attract you to her? Her feisty temperament, the fierce way she goes about everything? She's such a life force. Very much like Emmet, actually."

Noel appears taken aback, then nods. "You're right, of course. I'm so close to both of them that I haven't seen the obvious, how much alike those two are." He's quiet for a minute, then says, "Which makes you and I alike, then, in their attraction to us."

"Except for one big difference. You resisted temptation with Tansy. I didn't with Emmet." We laugh together, then fall silent, each in our own thoughts. Noel's take on his and Tansy's relationship makes sense, but I wonder if he's right. From our first meeting, I've thought that Tansy loved him—and not just as a brother—but wouldn't admit it, even to herself. Why is it so complicated, the love we have for one another?

Clearing my throat, I say, "Noel? Tell me more about Rosalyn. This whole summer, none of you have talked about her. I mean, not really."

"What do you want to know about her?"

I'm too ashamed to tell him the truth. I want to know if Emmet will ever get over losing her, and if she'll always come between us. I want to know if she'll end up tearing us apart. Instead I hear myself saying, "I don't understand what happened the night she died. I'm sorry if that sounds morbid, but what I've heard doesn't make much sense."

Frowning, Noel shifts from one foot to the other. Then, as though he's decided that I can be trusted not to repeat our conversation to Emmet, he says, "It doesn't make sense to any of us, either. Didn't at the time, doesn't now. There are things about that night we'll never know."

"What do you think happened?"

He shakes his head and lets out a ragged sigh. "Truthfully, I can't imagine. Rosalyn was the least impulsive, or impetuous, person I know. It was out of character for her to come up here on the spur of the moment, and without letting any of us know, even Willa and Kit. But . . . let's give her that. All of us do things from time to time that are out of character, of course."

"I'm sure you talked to Kit and Willa both afterward . . ."

"Of course. Willa heard from her briefly, but not Kit. Or rather, Kit noticed Rosalyn had called, but was busy and didn't call her back, which of course she'll always regret."

"So Kit was home but didn't see Rosalyn? Or notice lights on at Moonrise?"

He shakes his head. "She was home, but in and out, and out the night Rosalyn was here. At that point in the remodeling, she and her contractor were traveling around looking at various materials, slate for the floor, roofing choices, things like that. To tell you the truth, Helen, none of us have probed too deeply into the circumstances leading up to the accident. At first, we were dealing with the shock, then Emmet's breakdown . . ." He glances my way, embarrassed, and I finish the sentence for him.

"Then his sudden marriage. Tell me something else, Noel. Just how crazy did Emmet go afterward? I mean, I can understand—or think I can—how he'd fall apart, a man who'd spent his whole life denying his emotions. But some of his decisions—like letting the gardens go—seem so irrational that I have to wonder. I don't question him about that time, but it's beginning to eat at me. If Emmet won't talk to me about it, then . . . well, there will always be a distance between us." And Rosalyn will always come between us, I want to add, but don't.

Noel looks taken aback, then says hesitantly, "I think we're saying the same thing. Something's missing that might, or might not, explain a lot. But at this point I've got to wonder if it wouldn't be better to let it be. It's been over a year since the accident. Frankly,

I don't know what's to be gained from stirring things up. Oh, I know, you don't want secrets in your marriage, or subjects that are off-limits. For what it's worth, though, I think you'd be wiser to leave it alone."

Again we fall silent, looking off toward the distant mountains. After a long, uneasy moment, Noel says gently, "It's been a rough summer for you, hasn't it?" When I nod, he sighs, and says, "And I thought it'd be such a good time for all of us to be here together, after losing Rosalyn, and then Linc's stroke. If it's any consolation, it's been a strain for everyone. Tansy and I have been at odds, even before the summer. Then that stuff with Annie, the problems between Willa and Duff, and Myna's jealousy—everyone's on edge. Maybe it's middle-aged angst. Or just the human condition."

"It's the human condition," I say with a wry smile.

Noel looks up, his blue eyes scanning the sky. "This is going to sound really strange, Helen, something I'd normally only say to Linc, maybe. Anyone else would laugh."

"I can't wait."

"I've been thinking, if it would just rain! The drought has become a metaphor for the summer, and our angst—or whatever it is. I thought being here would be great. Now I think we were trying to recapture something that's gone. Like the rainfall, it's gone."

Before I can respond, Noel inclines his head toward the trail. "Guess we'd better pick some berries before it gets dark on us."

The dry, dusty blackberries are disappointing, smaller than I've ever seen. It won't be easy making a juicy cobbler with such pitiful little things. Tansy will be happy, though; I'll have to add tons of sugar and butter, which will exclude the recipe from the cookbook. Noel and I fill our baskets, anyway, and are coming down the path when he grabs my arm. "Shh," he says, pointing.

In the woods beside the path, a flock of wild turkeys take flight, flapping their heavy wings through the underbrush. It seems impossible that anything so ungainly can get off the ground, much less soar like swans, but they do. "Ten of them!" Noel says. "I've never seen that many at once."

"Let's think of it as a good omen, then."

After the flock disappears deep into the forest, we walk together down the pathway. Carrying our baskets, we emerge into the clearing behind Kit's house, where our hike up the mountain began. Noel stops so abruptly that I stumble against him, almost spilling my hard-earned berries. I look up to see Emmet's Jeep in Kit's driveway, across from the trail. It appears that he and Kit have just returned from the photo shoot, their cameras still on straps around their necks, and are heading toward her back door. "Hey, Emmet," Noel calls out. "Wait up!" Both Emmet and Kit stop at the sound of his voice, and turn to look our way in surprise.

Noel crosses the dusty driveway with me following behind. When we reach the back of Kit's house, he gives Emmet a friendly pat on the back in greeting, then turns to Kit and holds up the basket of berries he carries. "Since Helen and I had to trespass on your property to get to the berry bushes, love, you're welcome to take some of our pickings. Not a particularly appealing offer, I know, considering how bad they look this year."

"The berry bushes?" Kit echoes, as if she has no idea what the words mean.

He inclines his head toward the woods beyond the driveway. "You know, the blackberry bushes off either side of the mountain trail."

There's absolutely no reason for it to be an awkward situation, but somehow it is. Looking skeptical, Kit peers at the basket of berries, then over Noel's shoulder, toward the laurel thicket where he and I emerged. "Oh," she says finally. Glancing Emmet's way, she murmurs something about being confused since Emmet told her I'd gone to Willa's to pick berries.

Before I can explain, Emmet, standing with his hands on his hips, says to me, "You need a ride home, Helen?"

"The canoe's at Noel's dock," I tell him. "We brought it over, but I'll take it back."

"Go with Emmet if you'd like, Helen," Noel says, "and I'll bring it over."

I shake my head. "No, no . . . I love taking the canoe out, especially at sunset."

Noel turns to Emmet. "So, you get some good shots?"

"Oh, Noel, this drought's so scary," Kit says. I note that she's finally turned off the sprinklers in her yard, which have been running almost continuously all summer. "A lot of the smaller waterfalls are about gone. And our water level's at its lowest ever, the news crew was telling me. The situation's getting pretty critical, isn't it, Emmet?"

"It's been critical," he replies rather curtly.

"So we might be bathing in the lake this time next week, huh?" Noel smiles that lazy half smile of his, but Emmet isn't amused at his attempt to lighten the situation. Instead, he glances my way again, then announces that he's heading home. When he turns to go back to the Jeep, Kit thanks him for letting her tag along, then adds that she'll be ready at nine sharp tomorrow. Noel raises a hand and says, "See you, old chap."

After Emmet drives off in a cloud of dust, Kit glances from me to Noel. "Well. Emmet changed his mind about having a cocktail, but if you two will join me, I'll give Tansy a call as well."

"Sounds good to me," Noel says easily, putting a hand on her waist. "After you, my dear." Turning to me, he asks, "Helen?"

"Thanks, but I'd better get these pitiful little blackberries home. I promised Emmet a cobbler tonight."

Noel insists I take his basket as well, adding with a wink, "Don't forget that the rest of us like cobbler, too. Right, Kit?"

Kit's smile seems forced. "Who doesn't like blackberry cobbler?"

Even though her voice is light, I detect an undertone of what—anger? Something odd is going on, although I have no idea what it could be. I wave good-bye to them, thank Noel for taking me berry picking, and hurry down the road to Laurel Cottage for the canoe. As I paddle into the promise of a sunset which often turns the lake into fire, I try to shake off the foolish notion that I've done something wrong. Kit appeared to be angry—or irritated, maybe—because Noel and I were together, which is ridiculous. Since Noel has been coming over to work in the gardens, we've become friends. I can't imagine why Kit would care, one way or the other. Emmet seemed irritated as well, but at least he had a reason. After all, I wouldn't come with him on the photo shoot, saying I had to go to Willa's. Then I showed up with Noel instead. But the idea of his being jealous of me and his best friend is ludicrous. It has to be something else. With a shrug, I force myself to put it out of my mind and enjoy the serenity of the lake. Behind me, a cool breeze, carrying the sweet promise of fall, eases my passage to the other side.

When I get to Moonrise, Emmet is nowhere to be seen. I mix up the cobbler and put it in the oven with the lamb and potatoes I'd left marinating. Then I run upstairs for a quick shower. Still in my towel, I go to the big old dresser, and that's when I notice one of the drawers is slightly ajar. Strange, I don't remember opening it, but nothing seems out of place. With a shrug, I dress quickly and return to the kitchen. I poke a meat thermometer into the lamb, stick it back into the oven, and set the timer for ten more minutes. Pouring myself a glass of Chablis, I go to the side porch, where we've started having dinner every evening.

Emmet's standing on the porch taking in the last of the sunset, a martini in hand. I go to him and put an arm around his waist, remembering my earlier resolve to do my part toward easing the tension between us. Casually, he lays his arm across my shoulder, and I relax.

We sip our drinks and look out over the splendor of the lake. We watch until the sun is gone, the pink vanishes from the darkening sky, and the sound of tree frogs and cicadas fill the air. "You hungry?" I ask, and Emmet shrugs.

"I can eat."

"Uh-huh," I say with a smile. "It'll be ready shortly." The ringer goes off, and I go inside to take the lamb out of the oven. Returning, I tell him it has to rest before carving, so it'll be a few more minutes. I sense his tension again, which baffles me. Hoping to sound nonchalant, I clear my throat to say, "Emmet? Ah . . . this afternoon, things felt a little awkward when the four of us were at Kit's."

He turns his clear eyes on me, but they tell me nothing. It's his interviewer's gaze, sizing up his subject. "Why was that?" he asks in a flat voice.

I shrug. "That's what's so odd. I have no idea. Did you feel it, too?"

"Did I feel what?"

This time there's no mistaking the edge to his voice. I was wrong to interpret it otherwise. Swallowing, I say, "You know. The awkwardness."

He turns back to the lake. Night has fallen now, and the lake is a vast pool of darkness. There's no moon, no stars, only the heavy clouds that mask their light. When he doesn't respond, I ask again, "Emmet?"

Without turning to me, he says, "What do you want me to say? You're the one feeling awkward. If you want to talk about it, go ahead. But I'd rather not. I'd rather we ate dinner, and let it drop. I'm tired, and hungry." He finishes his drink and goes over to the bar in the corner. Glancing my way, he says, "Need a refill?"

My glass isn't empty but I hold it out anyway, and he comes

over with a decanter in hand. When I raise the glass to drink, I see he's poured red wine, mixed in with the Chablis. Following my gaze, Emmet takes the glass from my hand abruptly and turns around. "No, it's fine—" I begin, but he walks into the kitchen, where he pours the wine down the sink. When he returns with a glass of Chablis, I state the obvious. "You're upset with me."

"Why would I be upset with you, Helen?"

Because you're calling me Helen, I want to say. Instead, I shake my head. "I . . . don't know. For going berry picking with Noel instead of Willa?" As soon as I say it, I want to take it back, it sounds so ridiculous. Stupid, stupid! Nothing Emmet hates worse than stupid remarks like that. Even though I deserve it, I cringe at his snort of derision.

"Surely that lamb's ready now" is all he says.

Halfheartedly, we make small talk over dinner. Just moments ago we were enjoying the sunset together; now there's so much tension I hardly know what to say. Sticking to safe topics, I ask about the news story on the drought, and the photos he got of the waterfalls. Could he tell a real difference in those taken today and the ones from earlier this summer? Neither of us mentions Noel, nor the tension of this afternoon, whether real or imagined. Perhaps what I'd misinterpreted were the conciliatory gestures on Emmet's part, and he's still upset about the party, and the awful scene with Annie. I didn't believe then, or now, that he didn't blame me, despite his denials. He conceded that my intentions were good, but foolish. I'd been so damned determined to impress everyone, and force the issue with Annie, that I'd brought it on myself. Annie hadn't wanted a big party, but I'd insisted. Before we came to Moonrise, Emmet had warned me not to stir things up, but I'd refused to listen about that, too.

I should bring up the topic again and try to clear the air between us, once and for all. Letting it fester is the worst possible thing to do, but I can't seem to find the right words. If Emmet is intimidating at his warmest and friendliest, a remote, silent Emmet can turn anyone to stone. Pushing back my chair, I say lightly, "Why don't we see if my cobbler will make it into the dessert chapter or not?"

Later, we're clearing the table of our dinner dishes when I stop him. "Emmet, listen," I begin. He's half turned away from me, heading toward the kitchen with our plates in his hands. "Can you put those down and talk to me?" I ask. With a short, impatient sigh, he puts down the plates, then folds his arms. I raise my eyebrows in surprise. "Jesus! Look at your body language."

He reaches toward the table to pick up the plates again, and I grab both his arms to make him look at me. "Talk to me, okay?"

"No, Helen. You talk to me. What's this about, anyway?"

"You know what it's about, Emmet. You're obviously still upset with me about the party."

Emmet stares at me like a scientist who has just encountered a strange specimen under a microscope. This is me, I want to shout at him, the woman you claim to love. Stop looking at me like I'm someone you don't know. Dear God—what's happening to us? But it's no use. His face is guarded, wary.

"I've told you that I'm not mad at you about the party," he says brusquely. "And I see no reason to keep repeating myself. Matter of fact, I refuse to. You'll be doing both of us a great favor if you never mention that fucking party again."

"I'll do that," I say in a choked voice, "if you'll tell me what it is that you're mad about, then. Because something is obviously wrong, and it belittles me for you to claim otherwise."

For a long moment—too long—he says nothing, just stares at me with those cold eyes of his. And that's what they can be, I realize suddenly—cold. Before, I've called them sharp, penetrating, probing, inquisitive, everything but what they are, cold enough to freeze the flames of hell.

"This is absurd," he says. "You've convinced yourself that I'm mad at you, and you're reacting accordingly. Doesn't matter that I've told you it's not true—you're determined to be right, aren't you? Okay, fine. I'm mad at you. Now do you feel better?"

To my dismay, my eyes fill with unwanted tears. I've never been one to use tears to manipulate anyone, but if I had been, I haven't picked my victims very well. Joe regarded tears gleefully, the white flag that signaled triumph for him. Our arguments always went on until I broke. Emmet hates what he calls sappy emotions so much that he's never moved by anything remotely suggestive of self-pity. He mutters, "Oh, for God's sake!" as I turn quickly and leave the porch.

I stumble into the nearest bathroom to wash my face. The splat of cold water helps me see that Emmet's right. Because of our argument after the party, I imagined tension at Kit's this afternoon, and reacted accordingly. I'm just overdue for a good cry. I've never been much of a weeper, but sometimes it's the best way to release pent-up emotions. I dry my face, then straighten my shoulders and march out of the bathroom. This won't do.

Emmet's at the sink, banging around as he fills the dishwasher. I come up behind him and press my blotchy face into his back. With a sigh, he turns around and takes me into his arms. "Shh," he says. "It's okay, baby. It's okay."

"I can't stand this distance between us," I say, and he chuckles.

"Well, then. Let's see if we can't remedy that." He brushes my cheek gently then leads me upstairs to the bedroom, where both of us undress. After crawling in next to me, he puts a finger over my lips when I try to talk. "Hush now," he says. Our lovemaking is frantic, as though we're trying to hold on to something precious that seems to be slipping away from us. Afterward, he goes to sleep immediately. I lie awake for what seems like hours, trying to sort things out.

Like Noel, I long for rain.

I want to hear a gentle rain falling on the hard, dry ground beneath our open windows. I've forgotten the fresh-washed smell and the sweetness of the air rain brings. I've forgotten the coolness; the music of drops falling through trees, the playful way it shakes and stirs foliage in its passage to the earth. The sound, like the rustle of angels' wings, would be a soothing balm, what all of us need now. My eyelids grow heavy, listening for something that doesn't come.

Just before falling asleep, I remember that the next day—or to-day, if it's past midnight—is Thursday. Although I've made no plans to do so, I'll get up and go to Asheville with Emmet. I really don't need to, with my end-of-summer deadline looming, and he'd told me he wouldn't be back until late Thursday night. But still. Lately, I've had more important things to do than be with my husband. Surely our relationship deserves some of my time as well.

Emotionally exhausted, I sleep so hard that I don't hear Emmet get up the next morning. I climb out of bed disoriented since I so rarely oversleep, and think it's early morning. Instead, I've slept until nine o'clock, unheard of for me. There's something about nine—is that when Emmet's leaving this morning?—but I can't recall what. I stumble down to the kitchen to ask him, smelling coffee. He's al-ready had his, the mug he uses empty on the counter. Groggy, I retrace my steps, except I go out the front door instead of returning upstairs. The morning air is cool on my bare arms, and I move more gingerly over the cold stone of the front porch. The Jeep is gone, but I can hear it. If he's just leaving, I can catch him. Hurrying down the steps and waving, I see the Jeep in the driveway, leaving a trail of dust behind. But I'm too late. The Jeep disappears around the bend and into the tunnel of rhododendron just beyond the house.

15

tansy

WAITING FOR RAIN

It's finally happened. Noel has lost his bloody mind. What the hell does he think he's doing, carrying on a flirtation with Emmet's new wife? Emmet has been one of Noel's closest friends for thirty-five years. Thirty-five years! Well, give or take a few, but still. Noel and I met Emmet at the same time, at a big CNN gala, on the night Emmet and Rosalyn met. God, we were all so young and beautiful then, fresh out of college with the world at our feet! Emmet was not only CNN's rising star, he was the hottest thing in Hotlanta at the time, in more ways than one. Rosalyn, who'd always had more beaus than Scarlett O'Hara at the Wilkes family barbecue, was a goner after five minutes with the charming devil.

And now, unbelievably, Noel's willing to throw away all those years of friendship. The boy's no dummy—surely he knows what a risk he's taking, flirting with Helen like he's been doing. If Emmet notices, it won't just destroy his and Noel's friendship, it will blow our group apart. We've been through too much together to allow something like this to happen. And over a twitchy-tail little tart from Florida! I simply must find a way to stop it.

It was Kit who clued me in on the latest. We didn't get a chance to talk until the day after the photo shoot, when she and Emmet ran into Helen and Noel coming from the berry patch. Kit called me with a report, but initially, I didn't get it. Why was the fool in such a dither because Noel took Helen to pick berries, for God's sake?

Exasperated, Kit explained that Helen had lied to Emmet, told him she was going to Willa's, when all along she'd planned an outing with Noel. Because Kit's riding to Asheville with Emmet these days, she's privy to a lot more information than we've had before. Emmet was definitely suspicious, she reported. If nothing was going on between Helen and Noel, why would she need to lie?

Unlike Kit's time with Emmet, I'm alone with Noel all the time. Even so, I've got to be careful about pumping him for information. Through the years, Noel and I have maintained our unusually close bond by respecting each other's privacy. It's the only way such a unique relationship would've lasted so long. My interfering with his business is the one thing Noel won't stand for, and a surefire way to alienate him. I have no doubt of that, yet I've learned something in my soon-to-be sixty years: As the wise old rabbit says to the young one in *Watership Down*, "When they catch you, they will kill you. But first they must catch you." I won't let him catch me.

Kit's allegations have upset me more than I realize, yet I can never tell her why. It came from earlier in the summer, when I'd pored over the pages of Rosalyn's notebook and had the unsettling thought that Rosalyn and Noel might've had something going on. It was so outrageous that I chastised myself for even thinking it. Noel, whom I'd loved for the greater part of my life, was too fine a person to betray a friend. Or so I told myself. Now I wonder if I've ever really known him at all.

Noel is the last man I'd ever expect to lose his head over a woman, or allow himself to be used or manipulated. As soon as the thought enters my head, however, I realize it's not true. Emmet Justice would be even less likely, yet look where he is. And look how fast it happened, too—none of us knew what was going on until it was too late. We didn't even know he was seeing anyone, for Christ's sakes, much less seriously involved! I cannot let that happen with Noel. He's told me nothing about this developing relationship with the wife of his best friend—not one word. And that alone is telling. The last time he was at Moonrise working in the gardens, he returned with a dish of blackberry cobbler Helen sent, the perfect chance to say he'd helped picked the berries the previous day. Instead, he left to take Linc's portion to him, without so much as a fare-thee-well.

Linc! Why haven't I thought of him before? I've always confided in Linc, poured my heart out in a way I can't with anyone else, even Noel. I desperately need some time with my Zen master. Not only that, I've neglected him lately, as all of us tend to do when his beloved's in residence. She's gone now, at least for a couple of weeks, to finish up summer term. Now's the perfect time to visit Linc. Willa just left, and Noel's at a library board meeting. Leaping from my chair, I scamper up the stairs to brush my hair and replenish my makeup. No self-respecting belle would ever call on a neighbor without primping first.

My visit with Linc is thwarted in a most unexpected way. I arrive to find him in the butterfly garden. Because he's navigating the pathways so nimbly now with the help of a four-pronged cane, he's always out there. To my surprise, he's stumbling along with his cane in one hand and one of our water buckets in the other. Noel's been sharing our supply of lake water with him, meager because it's such a pain in the ass to tote back and forth. I sprint down the pathway to help.

"What are you trying to water," I demand, "and why didn't you let Willa do it?"

He inclines his head toward a birdbath hanging from a scraggly dogwood branch, which is also a watering hole for his butterflies.

"Aw, I forgot that one. It takes Willa a good hour to do all the watering because I'm so damn useless. Except to follow her around supervising. And I failed to even do that properly today."

"If I didn't know better, Dr. Varner, I'd think you were as fallible as the rest of us. Throughout this whole ordeal, that's the first thing I've heard you say what might—just might—be considered a complaint."

Linc hoots in derision. "Oh, bull hockey."

"And you're so eloquent, too." I dump the remaining water into the bone-dry birdbath, then take Linc's elbow to lead him back to the house. "I'll get the bucket back to Noel. He's making another run to the lake when he gets home. Who would've thought a graduate degree from Princeton would lead him to a career as a water boy?"

"Only in America," Linc says.

I release his elbow to put my arm around his shoulders, easy to do since he's slightly shorter than me—as is most everyone I know. "Was Myna still riding your ass about Willa when she left?"

Linc sighs. "Now what do you think? Myna means well, but she's tenacious to a fault. She ragged me the whole time, only to continue her harangue once she got back home. Fortunately there was a thunderstorm in Tuscaloosa, and she lost phone service."

"I can't believe those sinners got rain while the righteous of Highlands are perishing."

"The rain falls on the just and the unjust," Linc reminds me, and we laugh together.

We've gotten out of the dusty paths of the butterfly garden and are moving toward the cabin when I spot Emmet's Jeep flying down the dirt road that runs in front of our houses. Seeing Linc and me, he comes to a screeching halt. Sticking his head out the window, he tells us to come with him for a minute. While I'm escorting Linc to the road, Emmet turns the Jeep around, facing back the way he came. He hops out of the Jeep to open the passenger door, then barks at me, "Noel home? He didn't answer his phone, so I was heading over to look for him."

"He's in a meeting," I reply as I crawl into the backseat. "What's up?"

"Just wanted to show you guys something," he says tersely. Once Linc gets buckled in, Emmet takes off with a spin of rocks beneath the tires, and heads toward the highway.

"The four horsemen of the apocalypse just rode into Highlands?" Linc guesses.

"You're close," Emmet says.

In the rearview mirror, Linc catches my eye and we exchange puzzled glances. I shrug and lean back in the seat to bask in the rush of wind blowing in my face, cool in the late afternoon. It's a bliss I rarely indulge in, considering the havoc it wreaks to my 'do. Nothing on the social calendar tonight, however, so I let it rip.

A mile or so down the road toward the Cullasaja Gorge, Emmet pulls the Jeep over, onto a dirt clearing next to the lake. He puts an arm out his lowered window to point to the Looking Glass dam. "Tell me if either of you have ever seen it like this."

"Oh, my God" is all I can say, then add in a choked voice, "No. Never."

Linc looks at the scene for a long time, then he slowly shakes his head. "We're fucked."

No water flows over the dam.

Less than a mile down the highway, Emmet pulls over again, but this time I know where he's taking us. Bridal Veil Falls is barely a trickle. None of us say anything because there's nothing to say; we sit in the Jeep and stare upward at what used to be a sixty-foot waterfall. Finally I break the silence by asking Emmet, "Do you remember when we brought Helen here at the beginning of the summer? I said then that it was unusually slow. But nothing like this."

Emmet turns the Jeep around and pulls back onto the highway. Meeting my eyes in the mirror, he says, "At least the seriousness of the situation is finally getting everyone's attention, which is why I'm doing the documentary. I had to practically beg the news crew in Fort Lauderdale to let me do this, and it wasn't an easy sell, either. No one thought it was newsworthy until I showed them the clips of a shorter version I did for CNN, summer before last."

"I remember that one," I say with a shudder. "Scared the doo-doo out of me. That was when Lake Lanier was so low all of the docks were on dry land. And several other lakes shrunk so badly you could see the old cars and junk folks had dumped on the bottom."

He glances toward Linc. "There's a little town between here and Asheville, Linc—the name escapes me right now—where the water supply has always come from two wells. One's the main source, the other the backup. The main one's dried up, and the other's within a few feet of it. Not something anyone ever imagined could happen."

"My God," I say with a sharp intake of my breath. "It's just beginning, isn't it?"

Emmet nods, his jaw set in a tight line. "Linc's right, I'm afraid, Tansy. We're fucked."

———

NONE OF US want to go, but Noel refuses to listen to our groans of protest. He's treating all of us, he announces while waving a handful of hundred-dollar tickets, to the Highlands-Cashiers Land Trust summer fund-raiser. No surprise, Noel's one of the hosts, and insisted that everyone—even poor, gimpy Linc—has to show our support for local conservation issues, not to mention supporting our favorite host. "After all, what are friends for?" he says with a grin. Emmet offers to make a donation not to go. Although all of us

moonrise   273

are big supporters of the land trust, no one wants to dress up and go to yet another party.

We've been working in the gardens, but stop when Emmet orders us to come in and have a drink with him. On the side porch, Noel and Emmet mix martinis together, jocular as always. I wonder if Kit's conviction that Emmet's becoming disenchanted with his bride is just wishful thinking on her part. I've seen nothing to sway me. Out of character for me, I stay quiet and watchful—at least for a while. It's the first time since I found out about the berry-picking episode that I've had the chance to observe the unlikely love triangle (if Kit's to be believed). When I arrived with Noel to work in the gardens, Helen didn't look particularly happy to see me. But she rallied and tried to win me over with peanut butter cookies and iced tea. Normally that would do the trick, but not today.

I have an opportunity to study her while Noel tries to convince her how great the fund-raiser will be. First a wine tasting at the Old Edwards Inn, he tells her, followed by an elegant dinner, then a Neil Simon comedy by the local theater group. Helen follows his every move with her soulful eyes, but that doesn't really tell me much. She's a great one for that kind of thing, I've noticed, and does it with everyone. Enraptured, she hangs on to your every word as if you just descended from Mount Olympus to impart your wisdom to her and her alone. Maybe that's why the two hottest men in town are gaga over her.

If only I would've kept my mouth shut the rest of the evening! Walking back to Laurel Cottage, Noel casually remarks that it was a hard sell, convincing Helen to go, but worth it when she finally agreed. "She and Emmet need to attend another social event in Highlands. They haven't done so since the poetry reading, and Emmet says he's still pulling the daggers out of his back."

"What does he expect?" I say sarcastically.

"Tansy . . ." Noel begins, but I snap, "Don't Tansy me."

His jaw clenched, he says in a tight voice, "I've noticed you and Kit thrusting a few daggers his and Helen's way. Which shouldn't surprise me, but does, somehow."

"What's that supposed to mean, surprise you? You've known how I felt about him and the Bride all along." I don't tell him that I wavered a bit as the summer went on, but know now that my instincts were right. I'm back where I began, distrusting Helen more than ever.

Noel shakes his head wearily. "I don't want to fight with you. I'm tired of fighting, and I'm tired of . . . I don't know. Everything. Every. Damn. Thing."

"Jesus! What's wrong with you?"

He shakes his head again, and won't say more.

——

TONIGHT THE BIG event is upon us, and I'm in a snit. When we arrive at the Old Edwards Inn, Noel takes my hand to help me out of the car, but I pull it away. Emmet and Helen are bringing Linc and Kit, so Noel and I ended up driving over alone, and in sulky silence. Noel tried to make small talk, but I sat with my arms folded and head turned away from him.

Yet again, it was a call from Kit that set me off. She phoned from Asheville to say that Emmet insisted they leave work early to get back in time for the fund-raiser tonight. "I tried to convince him that it didn't matter if he and I ran late," she added. "Linc and Helen could ride with you and Noel. Get this, Tansy! Emmet said no, that he refused to allow Helen to go into that hornet's nest of gossips without him."

"Oh, puke," I said, but Kit told me to wait, it got better.

"My response was, don't be silly—she'd be with friends, not

alone. Well, Emmet calls Noel, who naturally says he'd be delighted to take her royal highness. When Emmet asks if Noel would do him a favor and keep the town gossips away from Helen, you're not going to believe what Noel said! 'Not to worry. I'll make sure Tansy's seated at another table.' Emmet laughed, but I can tell you, Tansy, Noel wasn't making a joke. I was in the car, and Emmet had the speakerphone on, so I heard him plain as day."

Noel and I are climbing the stone steps to the wine garden when he stops abruptly. To my surprise, he reaches out to push an unruly strand of hair behind my ear, smiles at me, then says, "You look marvelous tonight, old thing. Pity you're such a bitch."

"And pity you're such a jerk, old chap," I snap. "A jerk who's becoming a skirt chaser, something I would've never thought of you. You men have no idea how ridiculous you are, panting after your sweet young things, or how they laugh at you behind your back."

Noel's eyes flash. "Behind the back is your territory, isn't it?"

When I'm greeted by my favorite tree huggers, I force myself to put away my anger and try to enjoy the evening. Like everyone else, I hadn't wanted to come. The dog days of August, made more miserable by the unusually high temperatures, have me lulled into a lethargy I can't shake, and I hate the thought of going anywhere that requires heels. Highlands may be a sleepy little town by day, but it comes to life at night with a social scene that rivals Atlanta's. Forcing a smile, I make my way through the revelers as if I don't have a care in the world, stopping to hug and kiss and chatter. Gaiety is not hard to pull off in this setting. The wine garden is one of my favorite places, as understated in its muted, flower-lush beauty as a Matisse painting. On such a sweet-scented, starlit night, it's almost impossible for me to stay out of sorts.

Once I spot the wide array of wine at the tasting table, my spirits lift even more. I'm on my third glass when Kit and Linc join me. She barely has time to whisper, "Honey, wait until you see the

Bride. And, girl, do I have something to tell you about what she's wearing!" when Noel appears to kiss her cheeks in greeting. He turns to put a hand on Linc's shoulder, smiling his lazy smile.

"Professor Varner, some of the world's finest wines await your sophisticated palate."

"You mean I didn't have to bring my bottle of Thunderbird?" Linc deadpans.

Noel says, "Save it for another occasion. And since you've stayed sober as a Presbyterian all summer, I don't see why you can't indulge yourself tonight."

Linc studies the wine table. "If you promise to tote me home afterward."

"Tonight, I'm the designated drunk-toter. Why don't I make your first selection, then you're on your own." Just as he does so, his attention is drawn to the trellised entrance of the wine garden, where there's some sort of commotion. With a quick wave, Noel hurries off to perform his duties as host, and Kit says drily, "My guess is, Emmet and Helen just arrived. They let Linc and me out at the front entrance, then went to find a parking place."

Linc's puzzled. "Why would their arrival cause a commotion? Sounds like someone's knocked over a beehive."

"Or a hornet's nest," I mutter under my breath.

Kit groans. "Jesus, Linc, how blind are you? Surely you noticed that slip Helen had on."

"Her slip's showing?" he asks, blinking.

A glass of wine in hand, Kit leans next to my ear to whisper: "Here's what I've been dying to tell you! On the ride home, Emmet told me he'd bought Helen a new dress for the occasion. I teased him about his taste, but he said one of the women at the station helped him pick it out."

I stare at her in disbelief. "Surely not—"

Kit smiles smugly. "Yep. Carol Lind Crawford! I weaseled it

out of him. I asked if he knew Helen's dress size, and he said no, but his friend who picked out the dress figured it out."

"How the hell could she possibly know?"

"Exactly what I asked. And he explained that his friend looked on Helen's website and decided that Helen was a four."

"A four? Oh, God, I'm going to kill myself. Or go home and put on a burka, at least." I look at Kit in admiration. "So Emmet told you that his former girlfriend picked out Helen's dress, huh?"

Kit sighs impatiently. "Well, he never called her by name, but who else but Carol Lind Crawford would study her rival's website?"

Before I can remind her that we'd done so ourselves, Kit nudges me so hard with her elbow that my wine sloshes. I turn to see that Helen and Emmet have made their way to the other wine-tasting table. "Dynamite dress, you've gotta admit," I whisper, and Kit agrees. Both of us snicker when Linc, who's been too engrossed in the various vintages to pay us any mind, turns to Kit and says, "Ah, yes. I now see what you meant about the slip."

Helen's new dress is not much more than one, a shimmering silk the color of pale caramel, which perfectly matches her skin and eyes. As soon I see it, I know that Kit's mistaken about Carol Lind Crawford shopping with Emmet—no way in hell a rival would've picked out that dress. Kit nudges me again, and we watch as a slew of men surround Helen with their suggestions of which wines to sample. Standing in little clusters nearby, their wives stare at her balefully and whisper among themselves. Rather than being flattered by all the attention she's getting, Helen looks flustered and distressed. Noel, the gallant knight, charges in to rescue the fair maiden. Linking arms with Helen and Emmet, he brings them over to join us, and Helen fastens herself to Kit and me. "Heavens!" she says, red-faced. "Those guys must've gotten a head start at the wine table."

"Trust me," I drawl. "The only way to make it through this night

is to catch up with them. I've seen more drunks at one of Highlands'
wine tastings than at a Georgia football game."

Before long, all of us are mellow with wine, talking and joking
among ourselves as if none of us ever harbored an unkind thought
toward the other. A string quartet plays smooth, sexy jazz in the
background, and the scent of roses wafts through the night air. Our
little group merges and mingles with the larger crowd, only to break
off and make our way back to each other. The longer the wine tasting
goes on, the cozier the tasters get. Looks like Noel was right to insist we attend the gathering after all.

———

DURING THE CANDLELIT dinner at Madison's, the inn's ritzy
dining room, our wine-induced congeniality doesn't carry us through
the first course. The tension starts during the chilled lobster appetizers and soon becomes as thick as the butter in the cut-glass bowl on
our table. It starts when Noel smiles at Helen, who's seated next to
him, and remarks, "Great dress, love. I'm surprised you're not wearing the gold locket, which would look great with it. "

Linc chimes in. "It's such a remarkable piece of jewelry." In-
clining his head toward Emmet, he adds, "Remarkable enough that
our daring correspondent here risked life and limb to possess it.
Right, my man?"

With Emmet seated next to me I can't see his expression, but
there's a definite edge to his voice. "All for naught, Linc, since the
locket's no longer in my possession."

Linc chuckles. "Oh, I'm sure Helen will let you borrow it sometimes."

"Not with the khakis, though," Noel says. "Your white polo
would probably show it off better."

Emmet takes a sip from his water glass before dropping the

bombshell. "The problem is, it's no longer in Helen's possession, either."

I freeze with a forkful of lobster halfway to my mouth. All eyes turn to Helen, who appears to be on the verge of tears. She blinks several times, then says in a choked voice, "I-I made such a terrible mistake, y'all. I'm afraid the necklace is lost."

That gets our attention. Noel raises his eyebrows, Linc tilts his head like an owl, and Kit lets out a cry of dismay. "Lost? But—how?"

"I imagine the usual way," I say drily. Then to Helen, "Was the catch loose or something?"

"It's bound to turn up," Linc offers. "After all, it's not exactly the size of an earring."

Helen lowers her eyes and shakes her head vigorously. "It wasn't like that, Linc. I mean, I didn't lose it that way." She stops herself when a tuxedoed waiter comes around to remove the empty glasses.

Once the waiter's gone, Emmet says brusquely, "Let's move on to another subject. Nothing can be done about it, anyway."

Raising her eyes to him, Helen shakes her head again. "No, Emmet. I want everyone to know what happened, and how awful I feel about it. It's important to me."

Noel places a hand on her arm. "You don't owe us an explanation, love. Why don't we just enjoy the meal now?"

Her look is pleading. "I really need to do this, Noel. But of course I'll wait if—"

"Oh, for God's sake," I interrupt impatiently. I'm dying to hear, if they'll just shut up and let her talk. "Noel, you and Emmet are both wrong. Let Helen tell her story because it's obviously important to her. We're between courses, anyway."

"Thank you," Helen says in apparent relief. Although she glances around the table, I notice she passes over Emmet quickly. Can't say as I blame her. I can feel his pent-up anger as if it were heat radiating from his body. Now I understand why she was so distraught earlier. It was caused by the unwanted attention of her husband, not the gentleman callers.

"I did an incredibly stupid thing," Helen says. "I wanted to give the necklace to Annie for her birthday—" Kit gasps, and I want to strangle her. If I don't get to hear Helen's story, I will. Helen goes on in a flat voice, "Wanting to give it to Annie wasn't the stupid thing—"

It's Emmet who interrupts this time. "That's open to debate, sweetheart."

Her eyes flash. "Not to me." Turning from him, she says to the rest of us, "It only hit me later, after she left, that Annie had been trying to say she wanted the locket for her birthday. So . . . I boxed it up, and included a note saying I understood how much it meant to her." Her voice catches and she reaches for her water glass, holding up a finger to signal she's not through with her story.

"The locket's not lost, then," Noel says in relief.

"Yes, it is!" she cries out, then pauses to compose herself. "Okay, here's what happened. I took the box, along with some other things, into town to FedEx it—you know, at the office supply store?—not realizing they closed early on Wednesdays. I dropped the other envelopes—some cookbook edits for my publisher, things like that—in the FedEx box. The necklace needed extra insurance, of course, so I brought it back. The next morning, my purse was right where I always leave it, on the entry table. But the box, which I thought I'd put next to it, wasn't there."

Noel breaks our stunned silence by asking the obvious. "You mean it was stolen? Have you called the police?"

Helen shakes her head. "It wasn't stolen, Noel. Couldn't have been. My purse, which had a couple hundred dollars in it, hadn't been touched. Plus, I'd packed the necklace in a regular FedEx box, not

one that might've suggested jewelry to a thief. Someone would've
had to broken into the house that night and taken only an ordinary-
looking box instead of my purse or any of the other valuables at
Moonrise. It makes no sense."

"But you didn't lose it," Noel argues. "Unlikely as it sounds, it
must've been stolen." When Helen shakes her head even more ada-
mantly, he persists. "How can you be so sure?"

She lowers her eyes. "I was thinking the same way, Noel, absolutely sure I'd brought the box home and put it down next to my
purse. Finding it gone, however, I began to question myself. The
truth is, I was pretty . . . ah . . . rattled during that time, so maybe
I didn't. I retraced my steps, and searched my car thoroughly. Then
I began to wonder if I'd accidentally dropped it into the FedEx box
with the other things I sent."

Seated on her other side, Linc leans forward to say, "I'll bet
that's what happened! They can confirm a delivery, of course. I'm
sure you've checked with them—"

"Of course," she says dismally. "The label was completed, except
for the extra insurance, so it could've gone as it was. FedEx has no
record of it, but just in case, I called Annie, too. I didn't tell her what
it was, just that I'd overnighted her a package and needed to know
the minute it arrived. I waited a couple of days to hear back from her,
but never did . . ." She falters before adding in a rush, "This afternoon, Emmet called to say he was bringing me a new dress, which he
wanted me to wear with the locket. I sort of panicked, and left Annie
a message saying it was urgent, and that's when she called back. And
said she didn't get a package from me."

"Hold on." Linc looks really confused now. "You lost me,
honey. Why was it urgent that you talk to Annie today?"

"Now we get to the heart of the matter, Linc," Emmet says
tightly. "She had to. I was bringing her something to wear with a
piece of jewelry that I assumed she still possessed."

Kit turns to Helen, aghast. "You mean you hadn't told Emmet about losing the necklace, Helen?"

Helen appears too flustered to answer, so Emmet speaks for her. "She was afraid to tell me, knowing rightly how pissed I'd be. Not about her losing it—things like that happen. But if I'd wanted Annie to have the damn thing, I'd have given it to her. Helen thought if she could tell me how thrilled Annie was to have it, I'd be appeased—"

"That's not true," Helen butts in. "Annie wanted the necklace, and I wanted her to have it, is all. But I was distracted, and careless with it, and now it's gone. Emmet's filing an insurance claim, of course, but . . . the locket's still gone."

A glum silence falls over the table. As if on cue, the waiter serves our soup course, and pours another round of wine. I've had enough—more than enough—but notice that Helen lunges for her glass. Can't blame her, though normally she's not a lush like the rest of us.

"End of story," Emmet says as he butters a piece of crusty bread. "Soup looks great, doesn't it?" His tone makes it clear that the subject of the lost locket is closed.

We might've made it through the rest of our dinner if the conversation hadn't drifted into even choppier waters. And if the waiter hadn't kept plying us with wine.

With a glance toward Noel, Emmet spears a piece of prime rib and says, "Different crowd tonight, Noel. Mostly tourists?"

"In August, yeah," Noel replies. "The Highlands crowd comes out for our spring fund-raiser, but not too many still in town for this one." With a sly grin, he adds, "Why do you think I wanted you guys here? Didn't want to schmooze with a bunch of drunken strangers all by my lonesome."

"I have to admit," Emmet says between bites, "tonight's crowd made me miss the usual suspects, our friendly neighborhood gossipmongers."

I slam my glass down, harder than I intended. "What's it with you and our friends here, Emmet? They're your friends, too, which you seem to have forgotten."

He eyes me coolly. "You're a smart girl, Tansy. Bet you can answer that one on your own."

"If you're implying that our friends—the folks we've known and loved all these years—have turned against you, then you're misinformed. And paranoid."

Normally his fierce gaze would cower me, but I glare right back. I'm emboldened by the amount of wine I've consumed, more than I've had in a long time. A very long time.

"Do you think I give a good goddamn whether or not the whole state of North Carolina turns against me?" Emmet spits out. "What I resent is Helen being shunned because of what I did. None of this is her fault."

I didn't think it was possible for Helen to look more miserable. "Emmet," she implores, "please don't do this. I told you it's fine." Her eyes darting from one of us to the other, she explains herself with a heavy sigh. "When we talked about the possibility of staying here and not returning to Florida, I told Emmet I'd love to, and felt sure I'd be accepted in time." She glances his way, then back to us. "Emmet thought I was saying—ah, that you folks have been less than welcoming to me. Which isn't true, of course."

Noel pats her arm. "Hey, it's okay. We know it hasn't been easy for you, like you and I were talking about the other day. But you're right, things will get better. Trust me."

Kit nudges me under the table with the sharp tip of her shoe, then again when Helen looks up at Noel, her eyes bright with un-shed tears. "That means more to me than you'll ever know, Noel. You've been so kind to me."

That does it. I raise my empty glass high. "Here's to our golden boy, the patron saint of sad and lonely women everywhere." I motion grandly to the wine steward for a refill. "Bring us another round, my good man, so we can toast this paragon of Southern chivalry."

"I think you've had quite enough," Noel says between clenched teeth.

"Aw, come on, sweetie. I want everyone here to know that they're in the presence of a real live saint."

A couple of diners near us cut their eyes our way, and Noel's face flames as red as the roses in the center of the table. "Then you might want to speak a little louder. I'm not sure the people by the front door heard you."

The wine steward appears with yet another bottle of wine, and I hold out my glass. Emmet tries to wave him off, and I wag a finger his way. "Oh, no, you don't, hotshot. I want one more, then you can have the rest of the bottle. You can handle it. Unless you've already started on your nightly martinis, of course."

"Mr. Clements?" the wine steward asks nervously when I motion him to come around the table. After a furtive glance at Noel, who's staring at me helplessly, the poor fellow comes around to fill my glass. The others shake their heads when he offers the bottle, and Noel motions for him to take it away. He says something to the wine steward as he's leaving us, and I eye him suspiciously.

"What'd you say to him?" I ask.

"I was speaking to him, not to you," Noel says calmly. "I asked him to send our waiter with a pot of coffee."

"Why did I even ask?" I clap my hands together gleefully. "What else would we expect of our hero?" When I notice that Helen is looking at me in wide-eyed dismay, I lean toward her. "Aw, poor baby. Are you afraid I'll hurt his feelings?"

"Leave Helen out of this," Noel says under his breath. "It's me you're mad with, though I don't know what in hell I've done this time."

"Oh, yes, you do, asshole. You know exactly what you've done."

In an anguished voice, he says, "Tansy, please."

But it's too late. Unable to stop myself, I turn to Helen and say in a mocking voice, "And you know, too, little Miss Berry-Picker. You and Noel both, sitting there looking so innocent, know exactly what I'm talking about."

"Okay, Tansy," Noel says with a sigh of resignation. "Obviously, you're not going to stop until you unburden yourself. Since Helen and I know whatever it is I've done, why don't you enlighten the rest of the table?"

Beware of what you ask for. I point a finger at him and raise my voice. "You've become someone I don't know anymore, Noel Clements. You used to be sweet natured, and lovable, and someone I trusted. Now you've turned into a"—I pause, struggling for the right word—"a fucking *man*!"

I must've spoken louder than I intended, because every diner in the room looks our way as the whole place freezes into a stunned silence. Our waiter and the wine steward appear out of the service door, bug-eyed, and the hostess pokes her head in, a hand to her throat. Too mortified to look around the room, or face Noel, I cut my eyes toward Linc, then Kit, both of whom are speechless. Helen's gripping the edge of the table, poised to bolt, and I dare not look Emmet's way. Over the years, Noel and I've had plenty of fusses and shouting matches, but never in such a public—or elegant—place.

Emmet breaks the spell by signaling our waiter to bring the water pitcher, and fast. Once the flustered waiter hurries over to refill our glasses, and with water this time, the other diners return to their meals, resuming their conversations in hushed voices. By the furtive glances our way, I can only imagine what they're saying. The waiter leaves after a whispered consultation with Noel, and I reach blindly for my glass, my face burning. My throat's so dry I gulp down the water greedily, as does everyone else at the table. Then Emmet pushes his chair back and turns my way. I cringe, bracing myself for a well-deserved tongue-lashing.

He's quiet so long that I dare glance his way, only to find him regarding me with what appears, unbelievably, to be amusement. "You know, Tansy," Emmet says, his eyes dancing, "I've always known you were a spitfire. But drunk, you're hell on wheels."

END OF SUMMER

I'm so blue because summer's about to come to an end that I can't hardly stand it. Unlike most everybody I know, I don't like summertime that much, except for certain things, like the excitement in the air when the summer people arrive. And I love the waterfall and swimming hole, and how cool that clear, bubbly water feels running over my skin on a warm day. But that's about it.

Main thing is, I like cold weather better than hot—only it's not the cold I like so much as how it makes me feel. I love the trees just as much with their limbs bare as with their pretty autumn leaves, or the green ones in spring. Linc says he likes trees better without leaves because of the way they look next to the sky. He promises when winter comes that he'll come back to his cabin every chance he gets, so me and him can go walking in the woods and pick out our favorite trees.

But I know better. Partly because of my help (or so he says), Linc's gonna be able to teach some of his classes this year. He was on leave last year, so he's anxious to get back in the classroom. And I want him to, I really do. His students need him back where he belongs. He's trying to talk me into going off to school, even if it's just driving over to Western Carolina a couple of days a week. If their professors are anything like Linc, I might do it.

Our time together is coming to an end, though, and nothing

can stop it. Or maybe I'm down in the mouth because I've been so tired lately, which ain't like me. I'm near about dragging by the time I get home after work. Duff keeps asking me how come I'm so ornery these days. Instead of trying to explain, I just shrug. Duff's not the kind you can tell how you feel. When he asks what's wrong, he's expecting you to say a head cold, or upset stomach, maybe. He don't want to hear that you feel like busting into tears all the time.

When I get home from work, Duff's not around, and I recollect that he's doing some work for Kit. Truth is, I'm glad to have a little time to myself. I might sit a spell before starting supper. For once, I wish I could come home to a good meal fixed by somebody else. And the more I think about it, the better it sounds. I don't care if I'm tired and achy, I've just made up my mind—tonight, Duff and me are going into town for supper!

While I'm in the shower, I think about where we should go. I'll have to pick out a place beforehand since Duff won't go for nothing fancy—which rules out most restaurants in town—but he'll eat a steak. I recall Linc saying him and Noel went someplace the other night where they had a nice steak; I'll call and find out where. I can't decide what to wear, but finally settle for my good white pants, with the long, flowery blouse I got at the Walmart. Instead of braiding my hair, I pull it back with a barrette—my dressy look—and I'm good to go.

Downstairs, I pour me a glass of iced tea, thinking I'll sit on the front porch to wait for Duff. I forgot to soak the breakfast dishes, so I get that done first. Standing at the sink is a pleasure now that my butterfly frames hang in the windows. I put a whole string of them across the top, sort of like a curtain, and even Duff agrees it looks real pretty when they catch the light.

The sun starts sinking into the mountains while I'm sitting on the porch in Momma's old rocker. I love it out here, and don't sit and rock near as much as I'd like to. I used to, but my life got too busy. Sitting and rocking, that's the time when I think about settling down, marrying Duff like he keeps wanting, and having some babies. Funny thing is, I'd made up my mind that this summer should be my last one single since I'm getting so old, in my mid-thirties now. Good thing I didn't share that plan with Duff, because he had to up and start drinking again. Now I don't know what to do. Ever since I caught him drinking brew the other night, he's been sober, but I'm determined to see how long it lasts before I mention anything about us getting married.

Duff's old pickup comes up the driveway in a cloud of dust, then he pulls around to the back. I wave, but he doesn't notice me out here. He's not going to be particularly enthused about us going out to eat until he hears "a real nice steak," and "my treat." Then he won't be able to get dressed fast enough.

I remember to call Linc, and when I tell him what's up, he struggles to remember the name of the restaurant where he and Noel got the steak, then laughs about his brain fog. Making light of everything, turning it into a joke, that's the way he's handled his infirmity. "I believe it was On the Verandah," he says. "No, wait— that's where we got the shrimp and grits. Now where'd we get that damn steak?"

"It's not like you and Noel don't ever go out," I say. "Tonight, too, seems like you said earlier."

"Yep. My main man comes through yet again. He's anxious to avoid Tansy, so we'll go to the club. If she's feeling better, and has a muzzle on, she might come with us."

We laugh together, since Linc had told me about Tansy saying what she did at Madison's the other night. Bad as I felt for poor Noel, it liked to have tickled me to death, picturing the whole scene. "Wait!" Linc says. "That restaurant at Harris Lake has reopened, and it's exactly what you're looking for. You won't need reservations, but I'll call and ask them to hold a table with a view of the lake. What time is good for the two of you?"

"Uh . . . Seven? And much obliged for this, Linc. I haven't been out on the town in Lord knows when, so I'm kinda excited. And you wouldn't know me, all dressed up."

"You're a pretty girl, Willa, something I hope you'll give yourself permission to enjoy."

"Huh! I don't know about being pretty, but I clean up okay, I reckon." I smile, teasing him. I never know how to respond when someone says nice things to me. Mostly, nobody ever does.

"Well, enjoy being young and pretty when you can, my dear. And I'll see you Monday morning, okay?"

"See you then. Bye now."

I've just put my cell phone up and gotten to my feet when I see Duff standing in the screen door with his arms folded, leaning against the doorframe. Something's wrong, I can tell by his face. "Duff?" I say, reaching for the door handle.

Good thing I wasn't standing too close. When Duff kicks the screen door open, it barely misses me, and I step backward with a cry of surprise. Propped against the doorway, Duff appears sober, but he's mad enough to shit a brick. "What's wrong with you now?" I yell.

His face twists into that look I hate, when his eyes narrow to slits. "Well, well, well," he says in a nasty voice. "Look who's got herself fixed up all purty. Going out with your boyfriend, huh?"

"I was, but don't think so now. Not after you kicked my door like that. Don't you ever kick anything in this house again!"

"Didn't know I was home, did you? And you sure as hell didn't know I was listening to your sweet talk with Linc." He mocks me in a high-pitched voice: "Ohhh, do you really think I'm that purty,

Linc? Aw, honey, ain't that sweet? You're just the sweetest thing! I'll see you at seven, then."

Smacking his lips and batting his eyelashes, he makes kissy noises, and I yank the rocker around so I'm facing the front instead of looking at his ugly mug. When Duff's spoiling for a fight, best thing is to ignore him. "I don't have nothing to say to you, Duff Algood. As usual, you don't know what you're talking about, but that's never stopped you from running your big mouth. I don't care what you claim you heard—I said no such thing to Linc and you know it."

He's not sober like I thought, and most likely started drinking soon as he got home. I close my eyes, then rock back and forth as soon as he mocks me again. I close my mind to his hateful accusations until he finally wears himself out and goes back into the house, making sure he slams the screen door real hard behind him.

I don't know how long I sit in the rocker. The sun disappears, and it's that time of the day I love, when a blue mist covers the mountains like a soft blanket, bedding them down for the night. With a heavy sigh, I pull myself up from the rocker. If I weren't so exhausted, I'd stay on the porch till the stars come out. The moon's almost full, the last one of summer.

Inside, the house is dark and quiet. Duff's gone, like I knew he'd be. I heard him banging around when he first came in, looking for something to eat. He probably finished off the leftovers from last night, then went out to the barn to get good and drunk. He better hope that the little hideaway he fixed hisself out there is cozy, because he's not coming back into this house, except to get his stuff. But not even that tonight, I decide. We've never locked our doors here—nobody gonna come all the way up the mountain to rob folks like us—but tonight Duff will find the doors locked against him. Finally—after all these years—I've had it with him.

As soon as I turn on the overhead light in the kitchen, I see
what Duff's done to get back at me: My butterfly parade is gone
from the window. With a sick feeling, I walk across the kitchen to
the sink, hoping that the wire I strung them with came loose, and
they fell. No such luck. Just to be mean, Duff took them with him.

What Duff did was clever, I'll give him that. On the porch, I
turned my back to him and wouldn't give him the satisfaction of re-
plying to all that stuff he said about me and Linc. But he knew if he
took my butterflies, I'd have to talk then, to beg him to give them
back. Well, two can play that game. I was heartsick before; now I'm
so mad I'm liable to be bawling by the time I get to the barn, even
though I'm practically running to get there. It's dark out, the wax-
ing moon hidden behind a bank of heavy clouds, and I rush into the
barn, not caring how much racket I make. No more sneaking around
trying to catch Duff with his likker. He can drink the whole damn
still for all I care.

He's not only closed himself up in the little stall he uses as a
hideaway, he's bolted the locks, too. I bang and holler, but he won't
open up. Since the radio's playing fiddle music loud enough to wake
the dead, I wonder if he even hears me. The idiot took my butterflies to get me out here, didn't he? And now won't even open the
door to me. I head to the ladder and kick off my sandals before
climbing up to the loft. I used to climb to the top half-floor and spy
on Duff, trying to catch him making sour mash for his brew, sneaking around real quiet. But tonight I don't care if he hears me, so I
scamper around the hay bales and head to the back of the loft. It
hits me that I can outsmart him without having to beg. All I have to
do is see where he's put my butterfly parade, then wait till he leaves
to get them back.

Because I have to peer over the top of the stall, I can't quite tell
what Duff's doing, just that he's hunched over his workbench.
Something's spilt on the floor around him, and I figure he's mixing

corn mash again. It's no surprise to see the lid of his army trunk open, and an empty mason jar lying next to it. Moving a little closer, I see that he's not making mash after all; he's building something, and I wonder what it is. The radio's playing loud so I don't hear any noise, just watch curiously as Duff raises a hammer to whatever's spread out on the workbench in front of him. The hammer comes down in a smashing blow, and Duff steps back with an arm up to protect his eyes. I know then what he's doing.

"Noooo!" I don't realize that I've yelled so loud until Duff freezes, then looks up openmouthed to see me standing on the edge of the loft above him. On the workbench and around his feet are the bits and pieces of my frames, the shattered wings of the butterflies like splotches of paint spilt on the floor, yellow and orange and bright, bright blue. I start to yell and cry at the same time, then before I can stop myself, I'm crying so hard I can't see. I'm dangerously close to the edge of the loft and the dizzying drop below, though, so I stagger backward, reaching for something to grab ahold of. I don't see the bale of hay that trips me up, just hear Duff screaming my name as I fall over the edge and tumble to the wooden floor below.

———

MY EYES FEEL like they're glued together, but a light's shining over me so bright I couldn't open them if I wanted to. Somebody keeps calling me, and I can't answer because my throat's parched. If I could, I'd ask for a drink of water. "Willa? Can you hear me, Willa?" Yeah, I can, and I wish you'd get me some water, whoever you are. Then hush up so I can go back to sleep.

When I wake up this time, the light's still over me, but I can open my eyes without it hurting. I look up and see angels floating all around me. Pretty angels, too, watching like they're waiting for me to say something. Clearing my throat, I ask, "Did I die?"

They laugh and flutter around and tell me they're not angels, just my nurses. I'm out of recovery, they tell me, and into a room. Then the one by the door tells them to quit laughing, the doctor's fixing to come in. What do I need a doctor for, I ask them? I've never been sick a day in my life.

My eyelids get heavy again, but when I open them this time, there's a woman standing over me, tall and pretty with shiny black hair. "Tansy?" I say.

The woman smiles. "No, dear. I'm Jenna Leftowitz, your surgeon. I'm acquainted with Tansy Dunwoody, however, and play tennis with her occasionally. Let's get you propped up so you and I can talk, okay?"

She presses buttons on the bed that raise the head higher, then puts another pillow behind me, asking if that's comfortable for my shoulder. I see then that my shoulder's wrapped up in big white bandages. It don't hurt, though. Matter of fact, I can't feel it, or anything else. I'm so groggy I know that they put me to sleep, and I'm just now coming to. The doctor pulls up a chair, and puts on the little half-glasses hanging on a chain around her neck. She studies a clipboard and I study her. She looks to be about Tansy's age, but she's a black woman, with skin the color of coffee and cream. I'm scared to ask why she called herself my surgeon since I've never had surgery. Never been in a hospital bed, either.

She explains everything without me having to ask, and as she talks, it all comes back to me. I'm one lucky girl, Dr. Leftowitz says. If I hadn't been so robust and healthy, I could've been very seriously injured from a second-story fall such as the one I had. My back could've been broken, or my neck, and I might've been disabled, or even paralyzed. As it was, I landed in such a way that my left shoulder took the brunt of the fall, so nothing's broken except my collarbone, which she fixed. I suffered a pretty bad concussion, one reason my mind's so hazy. She ends up saying that except for being so bruised and banged up, I'm going to be just fine.

After she answers all my questions about the surgery to fix my shoulder, Dr. Leftowitz looks at me real hard and stern, like a schoolmarm. "Willa, I need to talk to you about the fall," she says in a no-nonsense voice. "I talked with your husband when he brought you to the emergency room—"

"Duff ain't my husband. Well, a common-law one, I guess. And if he brought me in as drunk as he was, I'm luckier than you know." I can't believe I blurted out such a thing, something I wouldn't normally tell no one. Must be the concussion.

The doctor nods like she already knew that. "My understanding was that his brother-in-law drove. It was pretty obvious the state Mr. Algood was in, which is one reason I want to verify his story. He stated that you fell from the top story of the barn, where you'd gone to throw down a bale of hay for the livestock. He wasn't with you, but outside the barn, where he heard you crying out as you fell. Is that the way your accident happened?"

I hesitate so long that she starts to look suspicious, so I nod and say, "Yes, ma'am, that's right." Nodding's a mistake, because doing so, I discover that I'm beginning to feel again. A sharp pain shoots through my head, and I wince.

Dr. Leftowitz reaches over to pat my hand. "Movement's going to bring on a pretty severe headache for a few days, but we'll give you something for that. We'll have to be careful with your medication, of course. Another way you were so fortunate—if you'd been any further along, a fall like you sustained could've caused you to lose the baby."

My mind's still hazy, and I can't remember everything that happened last night—was it only last night?—so I'm not sure I heard her right. My face must show my surprise, because the doctor says,

"From your expression, I assume you didn't know. You've only missed one period, right?"

I manage to nod my head, and this time I hardly notice the pain it causes. Is she saying that I'm pregnant? Before I can ask her, she goes on. "That's another reason I wanted you to verify the details of the accident. Something your husband . . . ah . . . Mr. Algood said when I told him that the fall didn't cause a miscarriage bothered me."

I close my eyes for a minute, trying to take it in. She told Duff about the baby? Oh, God. I have a sick feeling I know what she's going to say next. Dr. Leftowitz gets that stern look on her face again and says, "Mr. Algood told me that if you were pregnant, the baby wasn't his. Your personal life isn't my concern, Willa, but your well-being is. He was so angry, and so inebriated, that I demanded his brother-in-law remove him from the waiting room or I'd be forced to call security."

"The baby's his, all right," I say in a dead voice, but she holds up a hand.

"As I said, that's not my business. But I'm quite concerned about your safety. Unless something unforeseen occurs, I'll release you tomorrow. Before then, however, I can request the sheriff's office to send someone over so you can fill out a restraining order against Mr. Algood."

"I don't want it," I say.

"Perhaps not. Unfortunately, I've seen women who failed to do so, and ended up in worse condition than you are now."

I look her straight in the eyes. "I'm not talking about the restraining order. It's Duff's baby I don't want."

Her dark eyes meet mine, and we look at each other for a long minute. "Are you sure, Willa? That's a big decision, and one you might later regret, especially at your age. You're still a young woman, of course, but conception does get a bit more difficult the older you are. So many career women get to your age and begin to think now or never."

Even though the pain is so sharp that my eyes water, I shake my head, hard. "No, ma'am. Only thing I'd regret is tying myself to that man for the rest of my life. I don't want this baby. You can do it, can't you? I mean, since you're a surgeon, and I'm already in the hospital—"

Studying me, the doctor says, "I want you to know that I support your right to make your own decision. And you're correct: Should you decide to go ahead with the procedure, the simplest way would be while you're here, and no further along than you are now. And yes, I'll do it, if you choose. It can be done early tomorrow morning before your release." She gets to her feet and takes off her glasses. "For now, I'd advise you to call someone you trust, a close friend or relative, maybe your pastor, and ask them to come be with you. Since I don't want you moving around until your headache clears, I can make that call for you, if you'd like."

I'd never talk to any of my girlfriends about this, and certainly not Pastor, and I'm about to tell her so when I think of the perfect person. It sounds crazy, even to me, but I know who I can talk to, and who I want with me. "Could you call Tansy for me, then?"

If Dr. Leftowitz is surprised, or wonders why on earth I'd want a wild woman like Tansy, who's liable to say or do anything once she gets here, she don't let on. Instead she pats my hand and says, "I'll do it right now."

———

TANSY DUNWOODY IS one for surprises, more so than anybody I know. In the back of my mind, I must've been thinking of her as the perfect woman to talk to because she's been around the block so many times, and I knew nothing she heard from me would shock her. I also knew she wouldn't look down her nose at me, or tell me that I'm going to hell for even thinking about doing what I'm planning to do.

Tansy comes barging into my room with an armful of lilies from her garden, and a big, pretty vase. When she leans over the bed and kisses me on both cheeks, the armful of flowers ends up pressed between us, smelling like heaven, I smile for the first time since I came to this morning. After Tansy fixes the flowers and puts them by the window, she pulls up a chair and says, "What the bloody hell were you doing, climbing to the top floor of the barn in your condition?"

I can't help myself, I smile again at the sight of her flashing black eyes and tight-lipped mouth. When Dr. Leftowitz said that she wouldn't tell Tansy why I wanted to see her about me being pregnant and all—that she couldn't without my permission any-how—I told her she might as well bring me that permission slip. I knew she'd never get Tansy off the phone without telling her everything.

When Tansy goes on to tell me that I've got to take care of my-self now, I realize that the doctor didn't tell her everything after all. She didn't tell her what I was planning on doing about Duff's baby. "Oh, I know," Tansy continues with a wave of her hand, "you mountain women pride yourself on working as hard as your men even when you're pregnant, hauling hay and plowing the back forty or whatever. But you can forget that. For once in your life, Willa, you're going to be the one who's pampered!" I keep trying to inter-rupt her, but she goes on about me taking care of myself, and how my pregnancy will give her an excuse to come to Highlands more often, to check on me and make sure I'm behaving and taking care of myself.

Finally I have to near about shout to get her attention, which hurts my throat. But I've got to shut her up, or next thing I know, she'll have me a nursery decorated. "Tansy, listen to me, okay?" I plead in a hoarse voice. "The doctor wanted me to talk with someone about this, and that's why you're here. But I really don't want to talk, I just want to do it and get it over with. I'm not having this baby. Duff claims it's not his—" Hearing that, Tansy looks so mad I hurry on before she starts ranting against him. "He's just being a jackass, as usual. He knows I ain't been with another man, don't matter what he says. I can't have his baby, Tansy, and I'm not going to."

In her no-nonsense way, she says, "Of course not. You're not having Duff's baby. End of discussion."

Relieved, I sigh. "Then let's call the doctor back so I can sign the papers. She said she could do the procedure tomorrow. If you can come back then, Tansy, I'd sure appreciate it. But there's no point in you talking about me pampering myself and all that other stuff, okay?"

Tansy leans in so close that she's right in my face. "You're not having Duff's baby, Willa. You're having *your* baby. Being a single parent must be one of the hardest things in the world, but if anyone can do it, it's you. That's one thing I'd bet my life on."

This time I shake my head real slow, back and forth on the pillow. "I can't. You don't understand—"

She grabs hold of my hand. "You're right, honey. I don't. I've never had children of my own, something I'll always regret. But I'm not exactly the motherly type, so it's for the best. I'd feel bad for any kid who got stuck with me for a mama. But you're not like that, Willa McFee—not you. You'll be great, and think about the incredibly rich heritage you'll be providing your child! Hell, I couldn't leave mine anything but money and jewelry, maybe a few designer dresses. But you'll be bringing your child up on a mountaintop."

"But what about Duff?"

She waves her hand, kind of like Duff's a pesky bug that she's swatting away. "Oh, Duff. He'll be a thorn in your side, honey, until he either finds the Lord and doesn't lose Him for a change, or another woman to put up with his sorry ass. My guess is the latter, since men like him survive that way. It's none of my business—though everyone says that never stops me—but I imagine you've been supporting him for years. Once you take that away, I doubt he'll hang around long, child or not."

My thoughts are all in a jumble, which must show on my face, because Tansy squeezes my hand again, and gets up to leave. "You need to get some rest, so I'm going to leave you to think about what I've said, okay? Unless you want me to stay, of course—but I know you've got a lot to think about."

Even to me, my voice sounds weak and pitiful. "I'm still groggy from the surgery, so I don't know if I can even think straight or not."

Like she did when she first came in, Tansy kisses both my cheeks, then she smooths my hair back from my forehead as she smiles down at me. "You're the strongest woman I've ever known, even more so than your dear, sweet mama. I want you to get some rest first, then think about this, long and hard, when your mind's clearer. Don't pay attention to a thing I said if it's not what you want to do. You're the only one who can decide. If you make up your mind to do this, just have Jenna—Dr. Leftowitz—call me, and I'll be with you, holding your hand all the way. But if you don't, I still want to be called, because Noel and I are picking you up when you're released. We'll either put you up in our spare room for a few days, or send you home with someone who'll take care of you. And I'm not listening to any of your damn protests, either."

She's gone before I can protest or anything else, leaving a whiff of her sweet-smelling perfume behind. I need to think, and decide what I'm going to do, like she said, but for now, I'm too exhausted to hold my eyes open. Thoughts keep spinning round and round in my head, like the old windmill in the field behind my house, the one that powers the well. I start drifting off to sleep, thinking about that windmill, and the water supply at the farm. Daddy used to say that we had the deepest well on the mountain, and that we'd never be short of water, with enough well water for generations of McFees. He'd tell me that I was too young to know it, but one day, that'd mean something to my kids.

With the drought like it is, it means something to me now. Daddy's not around anymore, but I can picture him, plain as day, pumping water at the well. When I was a little girl, I'd bend down and try to drink the water as it gushed out of the pump, laughing when it splashed my face. With my eyes closed, it's not my daddy I see pumping out the water; it's me. And it's my child who bends down to catch the water in her hands, looking up at me and laughing. She's got red hair, and plump little legs, and freckles across her nose, just like her mama. She's my child, and I know now that Tansy is right. I'll raise my child on top of a mountain.

DREAMS AND VISITATIONS

My last days at Moonrise, I dream of rain. In my dream, I'm standing on the overlook again, with the spectacular panorama of the lake spread out below. It was Noel who led me up the trail, and he stands silent beside me. Dark, heavy rain clouds hang low over our heads, close enough to touch. I'm afraid, even with Noel there. There's no lightning or thunder, just an ominous silence that presses in on us. The dark clouds open suddenly, and rain begins to fall, hard. I stare down at the tranquil lake, and watch as it turns gray and whitecapped, like a storm at sea. The rain falls so hard that I'm soaked to the skin, and cold, so cold. I shiver, and turn to ask Noel to take me home. But he's gone, and a woman stands next to me instead. She's dressed in white with her blond hair in a low chignon, and I recognize her from the portrait in the turret room. It's Rosalyn.

You don't have a home, Helen, Rosalyn says to me. But I do, I tell her, even more afraid. Moonrise is my home now. I'm going away for a while, but I'll be back. She shakes her head. No, Moonrise is gone. See for yourself, she says, pointing.

I look to see Moonrise sliding down the side of the mountain, into the lake below. The house crumples under the force of the storm, and the ivy-covered stones that once held it together roll down the mountain to hit the lake with loud splashes, one after the other. Crying, I bury my face in my hands, but Rosalyn keeps shaking my shoulder, trying to make me look. It's gone, Helen, she says. Helen, can you hear me? Moonrise is gone. Helen?

It's Emmet who shakes my shoulder, and I awake with a start, my heart pounding. Trembling, I cry out, "Don't make me look!"

"That was some nightmare, sweetheart," he says. The room's dark so I can barely see his face, only that he's here, his hands on my shoulders. In a quiet voice he says, "I didn't want to wake you, but you were freaking out. Scared the shit out of me."

I put a hand over my eyes and fall back on my pillow, but Emmet, propped against the headboard, pulls me to him. "Need a glass of water or something?" I shake my head. I'm coming back now, throwing off the dream. "Want to tell me about it?" he asks, and I shake my head again, shuddering.

"An old superstition says if you tell a dream before breakfast, it comes true," I murmur, and Emmet chuckles. I remember another superstition: If you dream of the dead, the rains will come. I turn my face to the window, looking for light. Framed in the windows are the dark tops of the distant mountains, made ghostly by the moonlight. I was waiting up for Emmet when I fell asleep, anxious to hear how his meeting went with the powers that be of the Asheville station. "Did you just get in?" I ask him hoarsely, and he replies that he's been home only a few minutes. "I tried to call you all day," I add.

"It was a wild day," he says. "You awake enough to hear about it?"

I'm still shell-shocked from my dream, but I nod, anyway. It's a crucial day for both of us, the reason I waited up, and kept trying to call him. We're down to the wire, at the end of the summer, and Emmet still hasn't decided which of the job offers he'll take. He's been torn, unable to give any of the stations that're scrambling to get him the final word. Everyone has teased him, saying he's like a prize recruit unable to decide which sports team to sign with. Before the business with the locket came along to distract us, I'd convinced him that it was his decision to make, that I'd be fine with wherever. But it needed to be done now, before my new show was launched, so I'd have time to establish myself elsewhere. Emmet says, "I'm going to accept Asheville's offer, Helen."

My eyes have adjusted to the dark so I can make out his features. The cloud-shrouded moonlight has cast his close-cropped hair in pewter, making me think of the profile of an emperor on an old coin. I stare at him. "Really? I knew you'd pretty much ruled out Fort Lauderdale, but didn't expect Asheville to beat out Atlanta."

"It's the package they put together. When I went into the powwow today, I found Doug there, along with a couple of bigwigs from UNC. The station had come up with a cushy deal for me, but the college was icing on the cake. They offered me the Lawrence Woods Distinguished Professor of Journalism position. It's one of the most prestigious and sought after in the nation."

"That's wonderful!" I gasp, then a thought hits me. "But . . . you've said before that teaching didn't interest you. Matter of fact, you call academe the pasture where old journalists go to die."

"The Woods endowment is different, the reason it's so sought after. No classes, just lectures and seminars. And you know how I like to run my mouth." He falls quiet for a moment, then adds, "But note I said I was going to accept the offer, not that I'd done so. I told them I'd call tomorrow, after I'd talked with my wife. I have to be absolutely sure that you want to do this."

"I've told you that I'm fine with wherever. More than fine, I promise. I know you worry about me giving up my show, but I'll take it somewhere else. Believe me, at the beginning of the summer, I wouldn't have been able to say that. But I've gotten such positive feedback from my cookbook editor that I'm feeling pretty cocky now."

Removing his arm from my shoulder, Emmet settles back for a talk. "You know I had to get out of Atlanta after Rosalyn died, Helen, and Florida was the perfect place at the time. Even more so, once I met you. I thought that meeting you was the great surprise of my life, but coming back to the mountains has surprised me even more. As you know, I didn't want to, nor was I sure I could with all the memories this place holds. It was difficult at first, and we've had some rough moments, both of us."

Still have them, I think, but keep that poisonous thought to myself.

Emmet continues, saying that coming back here was necessary for him, evidently, in the same way it'd been for him to leave. "There are still plenty of unresolved issues for me here, one in particular that eats at me," he says. "But I'm coming to terms with a lot of things I couldn't even look at before this summer."

I hold my breath, not sure I'm hearing him correctly. Could it be, then, that we can be together—in this house—without Rosalyn's ghost between us? One of the issues with his taking the Asheville job was Moonrise, and whether we'd live here. It seems ridiculous, to have an empty house within driving distance of his work and not use it. Emmet says briskly, "It's too late for this much introspection, especially when I'm so wiped out. And you've got to be, too. Let's sleep on this, and we'll talk tomorrow, before I make the call to Asheville."

He leans over to kiss me good night, misses my mouth, and we smile together. After adjusting his pillow, he shifts to his other side, and is snoring within seconds.

———

I OVERSLEEP THE next morning, hardly surprising since I stayed awake for what must've been hours after Emmet came in and woke me from my nightmare. The frightening dream lingers;

when I step into the shower and turn my face up to the flow of water, I flinch in remembrance. I adjust the spigot so that the water's almost unbearably hot, the steam dense as fog. At least I'm not reminded of the coldness of the rain when I stood next to a dead woman in my dream.

A surprising visitor waits for me downstairs. Padding barefoot to the kitchen, I make my way across the cool tiled floor to the coffeepot, anxious for a jolt of caffeine to clear my head from the remnants of the dream. I dump out the dank coffee Emmet made so I can brew a fresh cup. I'm not sure where he is, either closed off in his office or out for his morning run. Although it's later than he usually runs, he probably overslept, too.

Then I remember he and Noel are helping out with Linc until Willa's able to return, so he's probably at Linc's. Cradling a cup of coffee in my hand, I wander as I sometimes do in the mornings to the sunporch off the kitchen. I've taken to having my coffee there while looking out over the gardens, smiling to see butterflies flitting around the closed-up blossoms in frustration. At night I watch out the bedroom windows, where I've discovered that ghostly moths, like shadows of daylight's bright butterflies, visit the newly opened blooms of the night-blooming plants. It's ridiculous now to think that when I first came to Moonrise, the gardens actually scared me. I told myself that the overgrowth and wild tangles of vines gave me the creeps—which was true enough, but hardly the reason I avoided them. In truth, the ruined gardens were too much of a reminder of Rosalyn, and the way her charmed life came to such a tragic end. It's impossible now not to think of the restored gardens as a metaphor for my summer here, and the way I've come to appreciate them for their unique beauty.

My flight of fancy comes to an abrupt halt when I open the door to let in the sweet-smelling morning breeze. It's the way I usually greet the morning, opening up the glass door first, then going around the room to raise the windows until the little sunporch is flooded with light. When I open the door this morning, however, I gasp and step back so quickly that the hot coffee sloshes on my hand.

Under the rose arbor leading off from the terrace, Rosalyn stands with her back to the house, her hands on her hips as she looks over her gardens. As in my dream, she's dressed in white, but today her golden hair is loose on her shoulders, and it catches the light of the sun. "Rosalyn!" I cry, frozen in place with my hand on the door handle.

At the sound of my voice, the woman turns, and I see that it's not Rosalyn after all, just a trick of the sunlight and my dream-dazed state of mind. It's Kit, wearing a short white tennis dress and outlined in the brightness of the early-morning sun. She looks nothing like Rosalyn, and I hope to God she didn't hear me call her name. She starts toward me, and I wait in the opened door instead of going down the steps to greet her. I don't want her to know that she gave me such a scare that my knees are weak.

Rather than come inside, Kit stands near the steps and regards me rather strangely. I have a sinking feeling I know what she's going to say. "God, Helen," she gasps, wide-eyed. "You thought I was Rosalyn?"

My face flushes as I try to explain myself. "I . . . ah . . . had a weird dream last night, with a woman in it who looked like that portrait of Rosalyn. You know, in the turret room? Guess it was still on my mind this morning when I saw you in the gardens."

My silly-me laugh falls flat, and Kit stares at me like I'm a bigger fool than she thought. Her level gaze unnerves me so much that I blurt out, "What are you doing here?" then flinch at the rudeness of the question. Way to go, Helen; after making so much headway with everyone, you show yourself not only to be a fruitcake but an ill-mannered one as well.

"Actually, I was looking for you," Kit says, to my surprise. Her friendliness toward me has been lukewarm at best, so on and off that I'm wary. Still regarding me sideways, she goes on to say, "I saw Emmet on his run, heading toward Linc's. So I knew I'd find you alone."

After the unsettling night I had, I don't exactly relish a tête-à-tête with her, especially since I'm fairly certain why she's here. She can hardly go to Tansy's to rehash our dinner at the Old Edwards Inn the other night, and she's bound to be dying to talk about it. She insists we have our coffee on the terrace rather than the sun-porch, which suits me fine. As I come down the steps with the tray, I remind myself that it's a good thing, the two of us sitting together in this spot. Last time Kit was here, she went with Annie to look at the place where they'd put Rosalyn's ashes, and to help her come up with an appropriate marker that wouldn't look like a tombstone. I thought their choice a good one: A stone craftsman in town is making a small, tasteful fountain, and engraving its base with a few lines that Annie composed, in tribute to her mother and the legacy of the gardens.

Kit and I fix our coffees in silence except for the usual polite inquiries: "Do you use cream? Is stevia okay? I can get the sugar if you'd rather have it." I close my eyes to savor the long-awaited sip, then open them to find Kit's gaze fixed on me.

"I wanted to come over to tell you how pleased I am that you and Emmet will be staying here. Emmet told me when we were coming home from Asheville last night. I asked if he dreaded going back to Florida, and he told me no, because he wasn't going."

"I didn't realize you were still riding with him." I don't tell her I've been so wrapped up in the completion of my cookbook that I haven't even asked.

"Oh, yes. I've been fortunate enough to pick up some other

assignments there," she explains. "It's been great to have Emmet chauffeur me. I hope he's not complaining about my tagging along."

"Of course not," I assure her automatically. I'm still wary of her, even though she seems genuinely pleased about our staying here. I wonder if she'll feel the same when she hears about my plans for remodeling Moonrise, making it my own. She, of all people, should understand that need, but I suspect that Moonrise will always be Rosalyn's, regardless of what's done to it. I haven't thought it out yet, but if we stay here, my plans are to remove everything dark and gloomy about the house, and let the light in. I'll preserve its unique character and history, but have no intention of keeping it as a museum and showpiece.

"Helen?" Kit's hesitant voice interrupts my reverie. "This isn't easy for me, but I have something to say." She pauses to put her cup down, then looks at me in distress. "Oh, Helen, I have a confession to make! When you came here at the beginning of the summer, I wasn't very nice to you, and I feel awful about it. I hope you'll allow me to explain." When I try to tell her it's not necessary, she holds up a hand. "No, please. I wouldn't blame you if you refuse to listen to me. I haven't been a friend to you, and for the worst kind of reason."

"Kit, you don't have to do this," I say more forcefully than I intended. "Really. All along, I've understood how close you were to Rosalyn, and how it hurt you to see me here, and with the man she loved. Believe me, I can only imagine how my presence must've felt like a desecration of her memory, especially since I came on the scene so soon afterward. So you don't owe me an explanation, or an apology, either."

Frowning, she shakes her head in obvious agitation. "But I do! I owe you both of those things. And what you say is so true, and very perceptive on your part. It hurt me terribly to see you—not you in particular, but anyone—where Rosalyn should've been. Every time I saw you, at Moonrise, or with Emmet, it reminded me that she's gone, and not coming back. It's irrational, I know, but feelings often are, aren't they? However, sometime during the course of the summer, all of us got to know you better, and I realized—all of us did!—that you're a good person, and good for Emmet. Even so, I still pushed you away, and wouldn't allow myself to get close to you. And the reason? I wasn't ready to let go of Rosalyn. Once I faced that, I was forced to admit that I had yet to accept her death. It was the shock of the accident, I suppose, that made it so difficult. And I'll bet that Annie has done the same thing, poor baby. That's not healthy, for me or her or anyone else. So I wanted you to know how sorry I am for making you feel unwelcome here."

We study each other over our coffee cups, her on the verge of tears, and me in astonishment at her turnaround. It's the first time all summer that we've had a real conversation, and it moves me a great deal. I don't know her that well, but she strikes me as the same kind of person Emmet is, one who keeps her emotions tightly reined. Even though she comes across as haughty, I suspect her aloofness is merely a facade, the way she hides her pain—the pain life brings to all of us. I can only imagine how much it cost her to come here, and admit that. To her I say simply, "I accept your apology, and appreciate it more than you know."

She relaxes visibly, and smiles such a shaky smile that I reach across the table to touch her hand. When she waves me off in embarrassment, I get up to take both our coffee cups, motioning that I'll go inside for refills. At the kitchen sink, I look out to see her wiping her eyes with a napkin. She seems genuinely shaken, and my heart goes out to her. I return with fresh coffee, determined to make small talk as a way of letting her know that she and I have taken the first step toward becoming true friends. She and I can never have the lifelong bond she and Rosalyn had, but there's no reason we can't be close.

We move easily to other topics, talking about our relief that Willa's on the mend, how much worse her fall could've been, and how nice it is that Tansy's taking care of her. Kit tells me something I hadn't heard yet, about Willa giving her sorry boyfriend the boot, and I admit my distrust of him. With a frown, Kit tells me how sorry she is about the locket. Although I appreciate her saying so, I really don't want to talk about it, so I purposefully move on to a lighter matter. We giggle together about Tansy's outburst at Madison's, even though it was far from funny at the time. Blushing prettily, Kit then tells me that she's seeing Jim Lanier again, serious this time, and that they're going on a trip to Saint Thomas in a few days. It's when we get to my and Emmet's plans that she grows serious again.

Frowning, she says, "Another reason I wanted to talk to you, Helen—Emmet told me yesterday how bad he feels about your upcoming show. My impression was, he's afraid you're giving it up for him."

I sigh in exasperation. "You can't appreciate the irony of that unless you knew how he had to talk me into it to start with. But I've finally gotten myself psyched up, and even a little excited, enough so that I'm willing to pursue the idea with another station. Though frankly, I'd be just as happy with another noon spot, or something similar. Matter of fact, it'd be easier with the cookbook coming out, so I'll probably put off starting a new show until spring at least. My publisher's lining up several speaking engagements for me, book fairs and other venues, which I can't do if I've got a show to launch. So if Emmet brings it up again, tell him I said that, would you? Maybe then he'll shut up about it."

"Absolutely." Her face brightens as she leans toward me. "You know what else you can do to make him feel better? He told me that he can get you another show, as easily as he got you that one, if only you'd let him. Maybe if you did—"

"Emmet said that?" I sit back in my chair as if I'd been punched in the stomach.

"Oh, yes—several times. So you might want to go along with him. But, of course, that's just a thought. I certainly don't mean to tell you what to do."

"No, it's fine," I say weakly. "I see what you're saying." What a fool I'd been, to think an inept, bumbling amateur like me could've gotten something like that on my own! I'd foolishly brushed aside the speculation, but I should've known better.

I force my attention back to Kit, who's prattling on about how much we'll enjoy this area, and how she'd never regretted her decision after Al's death to live here full-time. "Atlanta's a happening place," she says, oblivious to my stricken silence, "yet I'd never want to live there again. It's a tough commute from here, granted, but once or twice a week shouldn't be so bad."

It hits me what she said, and I look at her in surprise. "Atlanta? No, no—Emmet's taking Asheville's offer, Kit."

Her face drains of color. "Oh, Helen . . ." she says in a choked voice. Seeing my puzzled expression, she quickly recovers and says, "I misunderstood, then. He's taking the Asheville job, huh? That's . . . wonderful. What a surprise!"

"I was surprised, too," I agree absently. I'm still reeling from shock, the way Emmet deceived me by pretending to know nothing about my show, even agreeing to coach me for it. He meant well, I know, but it humiliates me to think that I not only bragged but also threw a party to celebrate. How everyone must've laughed behind my back!

It's only when I see Kit regarding me uneasily that I realize something else is going on. Her expression is so troubled that it alarms me. "Kit? What is it? You look upset."

She tries to wave me off, insisting it's nothing, until she finally says, "If I were you, Helen, I'd steer Emmet away from Asheville. Tell him it'd be easier for you to get on one of the stations in Atlanta, or whatever. Just don't let him sign on with channel six, whatever you do."

I'm so startled by the urgency in her voice I lean toward her. "Why not?" It hits me then, something she and Tansy told me earlier in the summer, about the newswoman there, the anchor who'd been Emmet's protégée, then his mistress. Although it made me feel guilty and disloyal, I'd looked her up on the station's website. I'd forgotten all about that.

"It's that anchorwoman, isn't it?" I demand. "Carol—" Suddenly I recall Emmet's muttered comment last night, that he still had an unresolved issue to work out. Could it be a former mistress? Another thought hits me, and I grab Kit's hand. "Has Emmet been seeing that woman in Asheville? You'd better tell me, Kit! I'd never tell him you said anything, but I need to know. Wouldn't you want someone to tell you, if you were in my shoes?"

She waves an arm wildly, as though erasing a board. "Of course he's not seeing her! As far as I know, their relationship is strictly professional, just the occasional lunch, or dinner—"

"Dinner?" I echo dumbfounded. "The times he's had to stay late"—I stop to search my memory—"he's either had dinner with you, or with his buddy Doug."

Kit blinks at me in surprise. "That's what he told you? It's true that I've joined him for lunch a couple of times, but not dinner. The times I've stayed late, I've dined with my friend Janice." Her eyes widen, and she says in a pleading voice, "But Emmet couldn't be seeing that Carol woman again. You've got to trust me on this, okay?"

"How can you be so sure?" I ask in a tight voice.

"Because he gave me his word that he wouldn't."

"Oh, yeah." My laugh is bitter. "And we know how trustworthy men are about giving their word, don't we?"

Her gaze holds mine. "This is different. He was too distraught at the time to even think about deceiving me. That's all I can say about it, except that I have good reason to trust him."

"You mean he said it after Rosalyn died, then?" I look off beyond the gardens to the mountains in the distance, taking it in, then I nod in understanding. "I see. You were afraid he'd turn to that woman, Carol, after Rosalyn was out of the picture. From what I gather, she's a woman who caused Rosalyn a lot of pain, so none of you wanted Emmet to end up with her. Instead, he moved to Florida, where he met me. Am I right?"

I look back, expecting her reluctant agreement, and find instead that she's shaking her head. "No. That's not it. If only it were that simple! But I cannot say more. Trust me, you don't want to hear it, anyway."

I shiver as though a cold wind had blown over me, despite the warmth of the morning. Try as I may, I cannot persuade her to say anything else. She's so anxious to get away from me and my questions that she gets up quickly, and her knees bang against the wrought-iron table. Grimacing in pain, she scurries over to the nearest pathway without even a backward glance my way. I jump to my feet to follow her, grabbing her arm just as she passes the rose arbor, where I first saw her this morning. "Kit—please! What's so bad that you can't tell me, or even look me in the eye? What did Emmet do?"

She looks at me, torn, until she spots something over my shoulder and lets out a gasp. "Oh, dear—there's Emmet in the kitchen! He'd kill me if I told you—"

"Told me what? Kit, please!" I plead, but it's no use. She's pulled away from me and disappeared around the house before I can stop her. Short of running her down, and risking Emmet's spotting us through the window, I have no choice but to let her go.

———

I'M NOT SURE how I'll make it through the day, nor how I'll face Emmet with my thoughts in such a turmoil as I try to sort out what Kit said in the gardens. Our hurried consultation before he made the acceptance call to Asheville helps; I couldn't have kept my composure through another long discussion. After verifying again that I was in agreement with his decision, Emmet gives me a quick hug, then disappears into his office. Only once does he reappear, right before the other call he has to make, to Fort Lauderdale. He finds me in the chaise on the side porch, the edits of my cookbook in hand. I didn't think I could concentrate, but editing proved to be the perfect distraction. I work on my cookbook as if composing the Magna Carta.

Tomorrow, with Emmet in Asheville, I tell myself, I'll deal with this. For now, I'm numb with shock. I simply can't take in what I heard, that the man I thought I knew so well has lied to me all summer, over and over. Although it belittles me to do so, I can overlook the lies about my show. After all, he did it to help my career. If he'd told me the truth, I'd have never agreed to the show, and he's helped me see I can do it after all, that with a little coaching I could even be good at it. His involvement with the woman at channel six is another matter altogether, not so easily overlooked. If their dinners together were strictly professional, why hadn't he told me about them? After all, I heard about his and Doug's dining out, the restaurants they went to, what they talked about. How could I not be suspicious, hearing that he's been having dinner with an old flame and purposely not telling me?

And what am I to make of Kit's cryptic statement before she spotted Emmet in the window, and left in such a hurry? After

Rosalyn's death, he promised Kit that he wouldn't see Carol Lind Crawford again. Kit implied that there was something else, something I'm better off not knowing. An awful suspicion hits me, and I think back to the time Noel and I were at the lookout, and I asked about the night Rosalyn died. No one knew where she was heading when she impulsively came here for the night, but Emmet was in the vicinity with a news crew. Was Carol part of the news crew, and did Rosalyn think she might catch them together? It would explain why she didn't tell any of her friends what she was doing here, and could also explain why she left so suddenly. Maybe she decided she'd rather not know that the man she loved was a cheat and a liar. If so, I can identify.

I'm startled out of my thoughts when Emmet comes to sit on the edge of a nearby chair and waves his hand to get my attention. He's about to call Fort Lauderdale, he says briskly, and wonders if I still plan to return there next week and stay until mid-October. The newsroom in Asheville needs him to start right away, while I have to work out the time remaining on my contract, six weeks or so. Of course I'm going back, I respond without looking up from the editing. What kind of recommendation would they give me otherwise?

We'll still see each other often, he reminds me, flying back and forth until the time's up. He then gets up to leave, but pauses by the door. With a frown, he stands watching me.

"What?" I say testily.

"You okay, Honeycutt?"

For a moment, our eyes hold. I see the bewilderment in his and lower my head quickly. "Just have to get this finished, is all," I mutter, and don't look up until I hear him leave.

We have another such moment at dinner that evening, earlier than usual since Emmet's taking supper to Linc. For once, he's too distracted to eat much. "Too much to do," he announces, "and too little time to get it done."

I pick over my soup, barely able to get any down. I look up to find Emmet eyeing me curiously, then he announces, "You look like shit, sweetheart."

I let out a hoot of laughter. "You know the way to a girl's heart, don't you?" Suppressing a snide laugh, I think, You can say that again.

He puts down his glass with a clang. "If you're as pissed off with me as you appear, might as well let me have it. Do it in a hurry, though. Being the devoted friend I am, I'm about to fix Linc's supper—or rather, heat up the soup and cornbread you made—and take full credit for it." Eyes glittering, he chews a piece of cornbread and adds, "Linc's reaction to Asheville was the same as yours, by the way. He's surprised I took their offer."

I murmur something inane, then lower my head to the soup bowl. Emmet goes on to say it was his work in Fort Lauderdale that made Asheville so appealing. CNN has gotten too big and impersonal, and he really enjoyed being at a community station. Before this morning, I would've listened adoringly, asked questions about his broadcasting local news as opposed to the broader scope, blah blah. Now I know what really appeals to him about channel six. Community, my ass.

It hits me then, that Emmet's had a mistress all summer, even while playing the loving husband with me. When we first met, he'd told me that had been his pattern in the past. If I hadn't been so blinded by love, I would've known the truth: Emmet is one of those driven, high-powered men who likes having a woman at home as well as one on the sly. And despite what happened with Rosalyn, he has not changed. I push away from the table, unable to finish my supper.

Seeing my half-eaten bowl, Emmet stands, then asks if I want coffee. When I decline, he puts a hand on my shoulder, looking down at me. "You're acting weird as hell. You sure you're okay with this?"

I get to my feet, shaking off his hand. "I've told you that I am, so please don't ask me again. I'm just tired, is all."

"But our staying here . . . it's what you want, isn't it?" he persists.

With our bowls and utensils in hand, I start toward the kitchen, then pause in the doorway to glance back at him. "I don't know what I want anymore."

He's taken aback, his eyes suddenly wary. "Jesus, Helen! How am I supposed to take that?"

With a shrug, I say over my shoulder, "Take it any way you want." The porch door slams behind me, and from the kitchen, I see him staring after me in astonishment.

18

tansy

FINDING NK

The morning after that dreadful night at Madison's when I embarrassed all of us, Noel knocked on the door, rattled the knob, and called my name so many times I finally had to tell him that yes, I was still alive. Sort of, anyway. He was heading into town for a meeting but insisted I call if need be, and he'd return. With a groan, I pulled the covers over my head and waited, yet again, for the sound of the front door closing.

It took me a while to rise from the dead. The first day, I spoke to no one except Noel, and only through a closed door. It wasn't until later that I was able to shower, have some lightly buttered toast and several cups of tea. The second day, I was finally able to rejoin the human race. Good thing, because that's when I got the call from Jenna Leftowitz. Willa was in the hospital after breaking her collarbone in a nasty fall, but she was fine, absolutely fine health-wise. Emotionally was another matter. On learning of her pregnancy, Willa was looking at her options. Could I come be with her as she thought things through?

After my visit with Willa in the hospital, I return emotionally drained, too. Willa's going to be fine—more than fine, I think, now that she's rid herself of Duff—but I don't know about me. I've got to figure out the best way to go about mending fences with

Noel, and the others, too. Considering how little practice I've had, it's hardly surprising I don't do it well.

What I need now is a brisk walk and some fresh air. The overlook, maybe, where Noel took Helen before the berry picking, would be the perfect place for a mind-clearing hike. As I pass Linc's cabin, I realize I need to let him know about Willa's fall. After my walk, I'll stop to tell him, and stay until Noel gets in. Linc's going to be upset to hear about Willa, but as relieved as I am to know that she's going to be okay—really okay, maybe for the first time in her life.

I've passed Kit's house and started up the pathway when I notice with a start that since her walls are mostly glass I can see straight into her bedroom. Kit's in there, seated at her dresser primping, and I try to remember if she has a date tonight. Probably so, since Mr. Lanier recently got in from Europe, a day too late to attend the wine tasting with her, thankfully. At least I only humiliated myself in front of my nearest and dearest. Not quite true, since Madison's was full when I dropped the f-bomb, but still. Most of those folks I didn't know that well, if at all. August is the same in Highlands as anywhere else; a month when the year-rounders depart, clearing out before the onslaught of tourists.

I'd been surprised when Jim Lanier and Kit resumed their courtship. He's smitten, even admitting to me he'd carried a torch for years, waiting for Kit between husbands like Rhett with Scarlett. Yet Kit's been so lukewarm toward him he'd become discouraged. They never were lovers, which I can't understand. In Highlands, Jim's second runner-up to Noel, like him in all the ways that count—looks, charm, wit, and money. So much more attractive than Poor Old Al, who looked like Uga, the Georgia bulldog. If you're going to marry for money, no point in having to put a sack over the poor sucker's head.

Wonder why Kit's getting ready so early, unless she and Mr. Lanier are going all the way to the High Hampton Inn for dinner.

Well, la-di-da. Maybe tonight's the night for Jim, at long last. Curious, I retrace my steps to the turn in the pathway where I'm able to see into her room. I'll know by what she's wearing if seduction is in the works, since I know how her scheming little mind works. I can see her plain as day, seated at her built-in dresser, but she's in her undies, bra and panties, which does little to satisfy my curiosity. Even she's not *that* obvious. Looks like she's finished her makeup and is deciding on jewelry now. She twists her hair up and clips it in place, baring her neck and shoulders. All right! If she chooses her diamond earrings and necklace, then it's a go. The pearls, and Mr. Lanier might as well keep his hopes down and britches up.

It's neither, but I can't figure out what she's fiddling with. She, Rosalyn, and I knew one another's jewelry almost like our own, even knew where each piece came from. "Wear the bracelet Noel brought you from Venice," one of them might say to me. In our circles, the real stuff is either a gift or an inheritance, and comes with a story. Kit holds a piece up to her neck, then turns her head this way and that as she studies her reflection.

She fastens the necklace, and her hands fall away. I let out a gasp of disbelief at what I see. Kit is wearing Rosalyn's locket. But that's impossible! I might've gotten smashed the other night, but not before hearing about its loss. Yet . . . if what I see is not Rosalyn's lost locket, then I not only got smashed, I went blind, too.

Despite the remnants of a nasty headache and queasy tummy, I take off for Kit's house at full speed. Letting myself in, I bound up the stairs and down the hallway to her room. When I burst in, Kit meets my eyes in the long, narrow mirror above the dresser. If she's even remotely surprised to see me, she doesn't let on. Coolly and deliberately, she unfastens the locket and carefully replaces it in its velvet-lined case. I recognize the case, too. It's the one Rosalyn got from her jeweler; Emmet had discarded the original when he hid the necklace in his camera to smuggle it out of the country.

"What the bloody hell?" I shriek, and Kit's reflection, as calm and unfazed as ever, smiles at mine in the mirror.

"Come in, Tansy," she drawls. "Oh, and don't worry about knocking. Just barge on up the stairs. *Mi casa es su casa.*"

I've made it across the room and grabbed the brown leather box before she can protest. When I blink in astonishment at the locket nestled in its velvet setting, Kit lets out a light laugh. "Your entrance was certainly timely, sweetie," she says, "since I was trying it on when you came in. I was going to tell you about it, though. There's no reason for you to look like you've seen a ghost."

"Tell me about what?" I yell. "How you came to have a necklace that was lost only a few days ago? What'd you do, hijack a FedEx truck? Christ Almighty, Kit!" Then it hits me, and I take the locket out of the box for a closer inspection. With a sigh of relief, I say, "It's a duplicate, isn't it?"

"Oh, no, it's the real thing," she says breezily. "Try it on."

The tee I'm wearing with my running shorts is low cut, so I hold the locket up to my bare neck in much the same way she'd done as I watched through the long glass panels of her room. She's right; it's the real thing. My fingers tremble, and I put the necklace back as though it had burned me. It's crazy; Kit and I handled all of Rosalyn's things after her death, both here and in the Atlanta house, packing them away. Yet this feels downright creepy, a sacrilege, as though I robbed her tomb. Kit watches me with an amused look. When I put the necklace back, however, her expression changes, and she gasps. "You're really pale, Tansy. You'd better sit down."

"Yeah. I had a few rough nights." I stumble to her bed and plop down on the gray silk comforter. My stomach roils, and I put my hand to my mouth, hoping not to be sick again. Kit looks alarmed and pushes back from the dresser. She goes to her bathroom, then returns in a silk robe and with a fizzy glass of water in her hand. "Alka-Seltzer," she states, and I take it gratefully.

Kit returns to her seat at the dresser and takes the clip from her hair. When her hair tumbles over her shoulder, she picks up a silver-mounted brush, all as casually as if I were merely paying a social call, and nothing unusual had happened. The Alka-Seltzer begins to work its magic, and I take a deep, cleansing breath. Then I say tightly, "All right, Kit Rutherford. You had better by God tell me what's going on."

She brushes her hair, her eyes on her reflection, then licks her fingertips to smooth down her eyebrows. "No need for the drama, Tansy-Wansy. It's really quite simple if you'd stop to think rather than jumping to conclusions. There's only one way I could've gotten the locket—short of hijacking a FedEx truck, that is. Which would've been pointless, anyway, since I had the locket in my possession. I took it to give to Annie."

Not comprehending, I say stupidly, "No, you didn't, idiot. Helen boxed the locket up to send to her . . ." When I falter in confusion, Kit watches me.

"Hang on, and I'll explain. After the party, Helen wasn't the only one who wanted Annie to have the locket, so I came up with a plan. Every time Helen left the house, I sent Duff over to look for the locket. My plan was to hold on to it until Helen discovered it missing, then claim I found it out in the gardens, or somewhere she'd been. Once Emmet saw her carelessness with such a treasure, he'd be forced to give it to Annie, which he should've done in the first place."

"Whoa!" It's not sinking in, which shouldn't surprise me considering the number of brain cells I burned out at Madison's. "Surely you're not telling me that you sent Duff Algood to steal a piece of jewelry from Moonrise?"

Kit shrugs. "I sent him to recover something that should've been Annie's, anyway. But Duff had no luck, since Helen was either wearing the locket or had it hidden where he couldn't find it.

Until the evening he was snooping around and found a box addressed to Annie. He brought it to me, and voilà! There was the locket."

I stare at her, aghast. "I cannot believe what I'm hearing! You mean to tell me that you see nothing wrong with your handyman snooping through Moonrise? That's mind-boggling."

Kit rolls her eyes. "It's no big deal. He's been doing it for years, actually. Rosalyn knew, and didn't mind. If I needed to borrow something and Rosalyn wasn't there, she'd tell me to send Duff over to look in the attic, or her closet, or wherever."

"That's different and you know it! Do I have stupid written on my face?"

Ignoring that, Kit giggles. "One time I'd sent Duff over for something, and Willa came in. He had a little fun with her, making her think the place was haunted. I don't know if he ever told her the truth or not." Seeing my expression, she puts her brush down to give me an exasperated look. "Don't make a federal case of this, for God's sake."

"Federal case?" I shriek. "I'll give you federal case—what the hell do you and that stupid oaf think will happen once Emmet files an insurance claim on the locket? You ever heard of insurance fraud? Those folks don't take kindly to being duped about the whereabouts of missing jewelry as valuable as that piece. I cannot believe this! I just cannot fucking believe this!"

Kit cringes. "Please, Tansy. I heard enough of your trash mouth the other night. I know everyone says it these days, but I find the f-word extremely offensive. My upbringing, I guess. My mother would've had a fit if I'd ever used such a vulgar word."

"Oh, really? Well, maybe when your mother visits you in prison, she'll bring you a copy of the Southern belle primer, if there is such a thing. And you can teach the inmates how to hold their pinkie when they're having their tea. My God, Kit!"

She looks at me as though I'm the one who's the lamebrain here. "I won't let it get that far, of course. Like I told you, I'll let Helen stew a bit, then the FedEx package, locket intact, will miraculously reappear. I'll send Duff to plant it under the seat of her car, maybe. I haven't figured out the details yet, but I'm working on it. My plan to get it to Annie will still work, though. Emmet's furious at Helen for giving it away, so he'll take it back, I'm sure."

I get it, then. It sinks in fully, and I shake my head in amazement. When I can speak, I say in a shaky voice, "So you hate Helen that much? I had no idea. Seriously. I know you resent her, which I can understand. And that you believe that she's using Emmet, and on the make for a replacement if need be. But this"—I stop, unable to find the words for how creeped out it makes me feel—"this is just plain cruel. I mean it, Kit. Just plain cruel."

"Cruel?" she sneers. "What about her cruelty to Annie? You know how that girl suffered from her mother's death, as close as they were. And to have to deal with her father's breakdown, then watch helplessly as someone takes advantage of him, like Helen has done? She's the cruel one here, not me."

I rub my face wearily, suddenly exhausted beyond words. I want to go home, and get back into my bed. And to call Noel. I need, rather desperately I realize, to talk to Noel. I put the glass down on the little bedside table, which is either topped with acrylic, or lacquered to such a high gloss that it couldn't possibly leave a ring on the wood.

"We haven't talked about Madison's," Kit says as I struggle to my feet. "When I checked on you the next morning, Noel said you were sleeping it off. Were you sick?"

With a hoot of scorn, I say, "Now what do you think? Of course I was. Which is why I need to get home now." Actually, it's not quite true. Except for the sudden onslaught of weariness, I'm better. But my mind's reeling from the shock of seeing the locket, and hearing how Kit ended up with it. Everything about the story makes me uneasy, but I can't process it here, with Kit nearby. I need some time to sort things out.

Kit stops brushing her hair to turn around on the stool, which is shaped like an upside-down U, and watch me as I make my way across the room. Her brow furrowed in concern, she says, "Oh, sweetie! Bless your heart, you look awful. Do you need me to drive you? Sounds ridiculous, I know, since it's such a short walk. But even that can be too much if you're nauseated."

I wave her off, halfway to the door now. "No, no, I'm fine. The walk will do me good. Besides, I interrupted you in the midst of some serious primping. Are you going out with Jim?"

Her face brightens, and she flushes prettily. Seeing her so often, I forget how beautiful she is. No, not beautiful, exactly. Rosalyn was the beauty of our group. Kit's appeal has more to do with her aloofness, that haughty, remote aura of hers. That kind of thing can be powerfully alluring.

"I am. He's taking me to the High Hampton," she says. "And you're right, I need to finish getting ready. And before you ask, I'm wearing the black dress. You know, that I wore to Annie's party? Jim hasn't seen it yet."

I nod toward the dresser. "Surely you're not wearing the locket with it?"

Kit smiles. "Yeah, right. I was taking it to my safe, the only reason it's out. You know, Rosalyn never liked the locket, but I always did. One time she said she wanted me to have it, not Annie, so that's why I was trying it on. And that's when you came in and freaked out." Still smiling, she inclines her head to a black velvet box next to the brown one. "To answer your question, I'm wearing my diamonds tonight."

I don't tell her about my earlier notion, that wearing the diamonds would suggest a seduction. It's normally the kind of thing we'd giggle about, but it doesn't strike me as particularly funny anymore. Instead, I feel real remorse for my friend Jim Lanier, a truly decent guy who has no idea he's being set up. Not that he'd mind the seduction; it's that he truly cares for her, and she'll make him think she cares for him, too.

When Kit puts her brush down next to the box holding the diamond jewelry, something catches my eye. I must've seen it dozens of times in the past, yet never paid it much attention. Nodding toward the antique silver brush with its yellowish bristles, I say, "You inherited that brush from your grandmother, didn't you? I've never noticed the engraving before."

Kit holds it up for my inspection. "It's the only thing I inherited from her, the sharp-tongued old biddy." Her rueful smile is more of a grimace, and she runs her fingertips over the design on the back of the brush. "Actually, that's not true. I inherited her name, too. Rosalyn used to tease me unmercifully, knowing how much I disliked both the name and the harridan who gave it to me, old Nellie Katherine Wilkins." Tracing the letters engraved on the back of the brush, she shudders.

NKW. It hits me then, with a jolt that runs through me like an electric current. The NK that Rosalyn referred to in her notebook is Kit, not Noel as I once feared. Of course! I reach for the dresser to steady myself, dizzy with shock, and remembrance. I remember it now—Kit and Rosalyn laughing when they told us stories of their girlhood, the tricks they played on each other, the thoughtless cruelty of children. Kit made up mean little rhymes about Rosalyn's chubby legs, which Rosalyn countered with taunts about the name Kit hated. "All I had to do to make poor Kit cry," Rosalyn told us, "was follow her around the playground chanting 'Nellie, Nellie, Nellie.' Which wasn't nearly as good as Kit calling me 'Rosy-Face,' but I wasn't as inventive back then."

"Tansy?" Kit gasps, getting to her feet. "You look faint again. Hang on and let me get my purse. I'm driving you home."

I turn so quickly I stagger, but straighten myself up before she can fetch her keys and insist on taking me. Forcing a cheery voice, I call out, "Absolutely not. I'm walking," and hurry out the door before she can protest. I'm halfway down the hall when she calls out to me, and begs me to come back if I feel faint, or to call her if Noel's not back when I get there. She'll come over if I need her. Mr. Lanier won't mind waiting for her. I have an absurd urge to laugh, and tell her that I'm sure he won't, since he's been doing so all these years.

Back in my bedroom, I close the door but don't lock it. I never have. Noel's not home yet, but he's always respected my privacy too much to intrude. Even the other morning when I refused to let him know I was okay, he didn't barge in. If it'd been the other way around, a closed door wouldn't have even slowed me down. Nor a locked one, either. Noel was right—I'm such a bitch, and it's a pity. Pity for him, anyway.

My knees are so weak that I sit on the side of the bed to open the drawer of my bedside table, where I keep the torn-out pages of Rosalyn's notebook. I keep telling myself it doesn't mean anything, that I'm grasping at straws in a futile attempt to clear up the mystery surrounding Rosalyn's death. If there's even a mystery to be cleared up, that is.

Something occurs to me, and I pause to take a steadying breath. I finally understand why Emmet got involved with Helen when he did. He wasn't being disrespectful of Rosalyn's memory; nor had he fallen victim to a cunning woman, as I so foolishly believed. Unlike the rest of us, Emmet understood at some level that he had to get on with his life, no matter what it cost. If doing so meant moving away, or losing himself in someone else, then so be it. Emmet's a survivor, and a life force, who simply did what he had to do.

More uncertain than ever, I clutch the torn-out pages and wonder if I should just tear them to shreds. If I'm right, and I really do have the key to deciphering the last notation Rosalyn made, will the truth be worth it? What will happen to us, the group of friends I've loved for so long, and so fiercely? Perhaps I'm wrong, and it's nothing. Maybe the missing puzzle piece with Kit's name on it won't even fit. I can't recall exactly how the final entry's worded, except that it says something about lies. My hands shaking, I take out the last page and read it again.

NK—so many lies! Trust gone. Will I ever know truth? Talked NK. Must go to M and find out. A lot of the puzzle pieces are still missing, but this much is clear: In Rosalyn's final days, something happened between her and Kit that destroyed her trust in the closest friend she'd ever had. It's not clear if Kit's lies caused the rift, only that Rosalyn couldn't rest until she uncovered the truth. Of what, I don't know, just that Rosalyn went to Moonrise, despite the late hour and bad weather, to find some answers.

It's the possible interpretation of the last two phrases that make my blood run cold. *Talked NK. Must go to M and find out.* If those were written together as it sounds, then it can only mean one thing. It was a conversation with Kit that lured Rosalyn to Moonrise that fateful night. If Rosalyn hadn't been so determined to uncover Kit's lies, she'd be alive today.

I rub my eyes wearily, a part of me wishing I'd left Pandora's box forever closed. Getting to my feet, I wander to the window to see if Noel's back. He's not, and my eyes travel unwillingly to Kit's house, the castle of metal and glass that Noel calls the Death Star. I picture her there, perched on her U-shaped stool and brushing her hair as she plans her next seduction. Other pictures come to mind, starting with older ones of Kit and Rosalyn together as young girls and going to the most recent, the two of them middle-aged women celebrating Christmas at Moonrise. For the first time, I see the Death Star as a distorted reflection of Moonrise, the evil twin across the lake, and the exotic terrace garden a counterpoint to Rosalyn's moon gardens. And I remember Kit as a child, Rosalyn's shadow who was always at her side, watching, watching. Her greenish eyes were fastened on her friend in admiration, true, but also in envy. Why hadn't I seen it before, the envy? Rosalyn the golden girl, who had everything, and Kit her shadow-sister, watching from the wings. Oh, my God, Kit. What have you done?

19

helen

FULL MOON

After a restless, troubled night, I awake heartsick, with such a headache that I'm unable to drag myself out of bed. I know what I have to do, though I can barely stand the thought. Now that I suspect what happened the night Rosalyn died, I've got to confront Emmet with my suspicions. Another thought occurred to me through the night, making it even more imperative that I deal with this revelation instead of turning a blind eye. If I'm right, and it was Emmet's cheating that brought Rosalyn to Moonrise that fateful night, then it puts everything in a different light. It explains Emmet's breakdown afterward in a way that nothing else has. His grief for Rosalyn was bad enough, but it was the guilt that almost killed him.

Even so, I can't go to Emmet with my suspicions and accusations until I've thought everything through. I've sworn to Kit not to reveal her as my source, and plan to keep my word. Somewhere over the years, I've concluded that a person is only as good as his or her word. And that's the problem with Emmet, I think as I put a hand over my eyes to block out the sunlight flooding the room. If he'd told me all this at any time during our relationship, I would've been hurt, of course, but at least I'd have known. I wouldn't have had to hear it from someone else. There's no reason to doubt Kit's story; she not only had nothing to gain by telling me, I practically had to drag it out of her. No matter how I look at it, it comes out the same: From the beginning of our relationship until now, Emmet has lied to me. And even worse, his lies to Rosalyn might have played a part in her tragic death.

I doze fitfully all morning, then startle awake when Emmet comes in at lunchtime to check on me. Groggy, I ask why he isn't in Asheville. He's supposed to attend some sort of press awards dinner tonight. Oh, he'll get there eventually, he replies; too many loose ends to tie up before he can leave. He fusses over me, bringing me tea and toast and a handful of aspirin. When he starts out the door, however, he stops himself and looks at me ruefully. "Helen? I thought you'd be relieved that the locket's been found. Surely you're not still obsessing about it."

I stare at him in disbelief. "I'm too relieved to obsess about it. Of course I felt like a fool, failing to see that I'd dropped the box in the garage, but at least you saw it."

I don't say what I'm thinking, that I searched the garage thoroughly—or thought I did. Because the package is small, Emmet surmised that strong winds from the lake might've blown it in the corner, where it had lodged. His finding the package after his return from Linc's late last night was a bright spot in the misery of yesterday. The other one, I haven't shared with Emmet yet. Before yesterday—and Kit's visit in the garden—I would have, and eagerly. When I called Annie to tell her that the locket was recovered, she sounded genuinely touched that I'd wanted her to have it. And even more surprising, she insisted I keep it. Her parting words were the most hopeful I've had from her since we met. She's been doing a lot of thinking, she told me, and she realizes she's been wrong about a lot of things. She and I need to spend some time together so we can get to know each other. Wherever her father and I decide to settle, she added, she'd like to come for a visit.

Ah, Annie . . . my stepdaughter. Yet another heartbreak of this summer, made even more poignant now by her possible turn-around. I can't even think about her now.

"Oh—one other thing," Emmet says, still poised in the doorway. "I'll call Tansy and tell her you're in bed with a headache, okay?"

I blink in confusion. "Tansy?"

"She called me to say that your phone's turned off, and she really needs to talk to you about something. Probably her moon party." He crooks his fingers to indicate quotes. Just yesterday, before my talk with Kit, he and I would've laughed together. There's a full moon, and Tansy's raring for us to take champagne to the gardens to say good-bye to summer. Not surprisingly, we've all teased her about witches and warlocks and moon magic.

"Would you let her know that the only way I can get rid of my headache is to sleep it off?" As far as I know, Tansy's still with Willa, but I can't have Florence Nightingale barging over here to see about me.

He says sympathetically, "You look like you're in a lot of pain."

Even though I awoke feeling a tad better, I nod in agreement. He's right about the pain. It's called heartache for a reason.

When Emmet pauses, eyeing me in concern, I close my eyes and turn my back to him. It's only when I hear the door close that I let out a sigh of relief. Last night I feigned sleep, pretending not to hear when he called my name and touched my shoulder. I knew he was looking for more of a reaction from me about him finding the locket, but I couldn't talk to him.

Lying in the bed and dozing fitfully, I come to a decision. It's the coward's way out, I know, but so be it. I have to return to Fort Lauderdale for six weeks, and would've done so regardless of whether Emmet decided on Asheville or Atlanta. The difference is, he would've gone with me if he'd signed on with CNN. They wanted him back anytime, no strings attached. Since he's signed up for the package Asheville offered, he has to stay here. The station would be fine with his starting whenever, but not the college and their prestigious appointment. Classes start next week. As it turns out, after this weekend I'm leaving to work out my contract in Fort Lauderdale, and Emmet's staying.

All I have to do is hang on a couple more days. The first of next week, I'll be in Fort Lauderdale. Being away from Emmet will give me the distance to think everything out before our confrontation. Faking it until then, pretending everything's okay between us, should be easy because everyone's preoccupied with the end-of-summer preparations. Not only will we be packing up, there's also a frenzy of activities in the works, including Tansy's moon party. When I get home, I can get my perspective and decide what to do next. *Home.* I've come to think of Highlands as home, I realize with a pang of sorrow, in a way I never did Fort Lauderdale. Now I know what Rosalyn was trying to tell me in the dream. It's an illusion, like my marriage to Emmet has been. I don't have a home here after all.

Having come to a decision, I drag myself out of bed with a heavy sigh. Thankfully, the nap and aspirin worked to ease my headache. If only it were that simple to recover from a broken heart! But I can't let myself think that way, nor let my anguish show. There will be plenty of time later, in the loneliness of the town house Emmet and I shared together, to fall apart. For now, I've got to put those hurtful thoughts out of my mind. It hits me that I was wrong about this being the coward's way out, leaving here without a confrontation with Emmet. It will take all the strength I can muster.

I can't let myself think about good-byes, either. Unwittingly, Emmet and I had already discussed our good-bye to each other, when we went over the pros and cons of his career choices. A drawback to accepting Asheville's offer, he'd told me, was our being apart for six weeks. Both of us agreed not to make a big deal of it. As far as the others go, it's been much of the same. Tansy hates good-byes and says she'll strangle anyone who starts that crap at the end of the summer.

I've pulled myself out of bed and stand by the window, deep in thought, when I spot someone coming up the driveway. Leaning out, I see that it's Kit, which rather surprises me. The way she'd scampered away from here yesterday, I wouldn't expect her to return so soon, especially knowing that Emmet's here. Or maybe she thinks he's already left. I'm sure she knows about the awards dinner at the Grove Park Inn tonight, and assumes he's there. As far as I know, he's in his office downstairs working on the documentary. He'd told me earlier, before I dozed off, that he was playing it by ear. He needed to be at the dinner, but if he ran late, it couldn't be helped. Either way, the inn was holding a room for him.

I hear Kit entering the front door and brace myself to go downstairs to greet her. Most likely, Tansy told her I was on my sickbed, and she'll come up here to check on me if I don't ward her off. At least I'll be able to practice the persona that's got to carry me through the next day or so—busy, distracted, absentminded. Not far from the real me, actually. It will be easier to pull off with Kit than the others. Noel, Tansy, Linc—even Willa, though she's much quieter about it—are too sharp-eyed to be fooled for long. Kit, on the other hand, isn't quick to pick up on nuances of behavior. It hits me that she's too wrapped up in herself to be empathic, an unkind thought I force out of my mind. She's making an effort, and I need to do the same.

I head down the hallway but stop in surprise at the top of the landing. Instead of Kit coming up the stairs, or going toward the kitchen to look for me, she disappears into the turret room without even looking around. I'm about to call out to her, but stop myself when I hear her footsteps echoing through the turret room, then in the library. The only thing beyond there is my office, then Emmet's, at the back of the house. Surely she's not looking for me there? Not once has any of them been in my office. Emmet and I keep our doors shut as a signal that we're working. Sometimes I forget, but Emmet's office is sacrosanct because of the sensitive nature of some of the news items he's privy to, so it's always closed up. When he first moved into my town house, he made it clear that his office was off-limits, both at home and at the station. Kit's known him much longer than I have, so surely she knows that.

Just in case, I go down the stairs to stop her, if that's where she's headed. The way she acted yesterday when she saw him in the kitchen, I wouldn't think so, but still. Since she's decided that she's my new best friend, maybe she got it in her head to confront Emmet about that anchorwoman. After all, she's done it before, on Rosa-lyn's behalf.

I'm too late to stop her. By the time I reach the hallway outside our offices, Kit has disappeared into the holy of holies, closing the door quietly behind her. With a sigh, I slip into my office in frustra-tion. My thoughts are running wild, and I cross the room to sit at my desk. Oh, well. Nothing to do now but let the chips fall where they may.

It's just as well that I ended up in my office, I think with a groan. Whether I like it or not, everything in here has to be packed up for my return to Fort Lauderdale. There are plenty of empty wine boxes in the carriage house for packing, but I've got to sort through my papers first. It's a huge undertaking that I dread worse than poison, but I'm here, so I might as well get started.

Waiting for my computer to shut down, I stand by my desk and try not to panic at the piles of paper that I've got to sort through. A breeze from the open window stirs them, and I hurry around my desk to lower it. The last thing I need is for the wind to scatter the damn papers all over the floor!

There's no way I could've planned what happened next, not

then or any other time. As I reach up to close the window, Kit's and Emmet's voices come to me as clearly as if the three of us were in the room together. All summer he and I have worked in our adjoining offices without disturbing the other, or being overheard while on the phone, even with the windows to both our rooms raised. The low rumble of his voice would tell me when he was deep in conversation, but I couldn't understand what he was saying through the thick walls, even if I'd tried. Until today.

"Goddammit, Kit," Emmet's saying, sounding as exasperated as I'd expect with her barging in on him. "You're not going to change my mind, so you might as well give it up. Besides, it's a done deal. I called both channel six and the college yesterday to accept their offers, and the others to decline. Period. There's nothing else to be said."

I should leave it alone, but my curiosity gets the best of me. Eavesdropping is shameful and degrading, but I can't help myself. I'm curious as to what approach Kit will take with him, if she'll bring that anchorwoman into it, or what.

"Oh, I think there's plenty more to be said," Kit says, startling me. It's not her words so much as the huskiness of her voice. From here, it sounds almost seductive, but I couldn't be hearing her right. Trying to butter up Emmet that way would be a big mistake, which I'd think Kit of all people would be savvy enough to know.

"Look," Emmet begins, and there's a definite edge to his voice. If she's not careful, he'll kick her out. "I'm not going through all that crap again, so don't start with me. You've got it in your head that I've got something going on with Carol, and apparently nothing I can say will change your mind. So think what you will. She's not the reason I'm taking the job, nor did she have anything to do with my decision. Surely you know I could see her from Atlanta or anywhere else, if I had a mind to do so."

"I certainly concede that," Kit retorts. "You not only could, but did."

They're silent for so long that I can feel the tension in the room, even from here. No doubt Emmet's giving her that cold stare of his, and Kit's probably giving it right back to him, and refusing to back down. She's got a lot of guts, give her that much, since not many of us can stand up to the Intimidator. It's Emmet who breaks the silence.

"I told you afterward, and I'll tell you now. Then I never intend to do so again, you hear?" he says harshly. "Yes, Carol was here that day. She wanted to see Moonrise, and we had some time to kill between shoots, so I brought her here for a tour. But that was it, just a day trip, where I showed her around. She didn't stay overnight. Do you honestly think I'd carry on an affair here, of all places? That's beyond ridiculous."

"Rosalyn didn't think so," she says, and I put a hand over my mouth to stifle a gasp. It's as I suspected. Or I was close, at least. Thinking through what Kit told me yesterday, I'd wondered if Rosalyn came to Moonrise on her way to Asheville, trying to catch Emmet with that woman. What I hadn't imagined was the two of them being here. Somehow, Rosalyn heard that Emmet had brought his old flame to Moonrise, and she came here to find out if it were true. And she must've found evidence that it was, and left in a tiff. It's the only explanation. Oh, God—what an awful thing for her, coming here in such a turmoil that she wasn't thinking clearly, and drove carelessly over roads she knew to be dangerous! And look at the price she paid.

"None of us knows what Rosalyn thought," Emmet spits out, and I cringe at the acid in his voice.

Kit sounds small, and defeated. "No," she says simply. I hear a muffled sob, a rustle as though she's turned away from him, then the sound of her footsteps, moving away from his desk. Even without seeing them, I can imagine what's going on, can picture Kit trying to leave the room before he notices her crying.

The sound I hear next is Emmet's heavy chair being pushed back from his desk and scraping on the floor, then the heaviness of his footsteps following her. His voice is soft as he says, "Hey, don't cry. Shhh, now." He's comforting her, probably placing an arm around her shoulder. All of us make Emmet out to be such a bear, but he has a tender side, too. He can be scornful if he suspects weeping to be manipulative, but never of genuine sorrow.

Kit's sobs are muffled, as though she's pressed her face into his chest or shoulder. Although I can't quite make out his words, I'm glad he's offering comfort to her. From what I've heard, the two of them clung to each other for solace after Rosalyn's death, but his marriage to me caused a rift between them. Maybe they can reconcile, finally.

I hear the shuffling of feet, then a gasp from Emmet. "Kit, don't," he says sharply, and I freeze. Her sobs have turned to moans, and the rustling noises lead me to believe that they're in each other's arms. In a ragged voice, Emmet says, "You know we can't do this."

"Emmet, please," Kit says. "You know how I feel about you—how I've always felt about you. No matter how I've tried, I can't love anyone but you."

"It can never work for us." He sounds almost as regretful as she does. "We've been through this, and both of us agreed it wouldn't."

"That was too soon after Rosalyn's death!" Kit says urgently. "She wanted us to be together, and you know it. She told us so, plenty of times. And even made me promise to take care of you and Annie if anything happened to her. That's all I've ever wanted—to take care of you, and love you. Surely you know that."

"So you've said. But you also claim to have put all that behind you. Just the other day, you told me you were marrying Jim—"

"Only because I thought you were seeing Carol again! I was

hurt, and angry, thinking you'd started up with her again, despite what happened with Rosalyn. It shames me to admit it, but I was just trying to hurt you."

"Well, it backfired on you, then. I was happy for you, sincerely glad that you'd come to love Jim and could move on with your life—"

"I've tried to, Emmet. Give me credit for that, at least. After our time together, that night in Atlanta . . . both of us agreed it was too soon. But I never dreamed you'd run off to Florida like you did. If you hadn't, we could've made it work. I know we could have, and so do you."

"But I did go to Florida," he reminds her. "And married someone else."

"You've admitted that was a mistake!" Kit cries, and her voice breaks into sobs again. "You told me so, and how she used you—"

"You know my temper, honey. I say all sorts of shit when I'm mad. Always have. I don't know where I stand with Helen right now. Things aren't good between us—"

"Of course they aren't! How could it not be? Please, Emmet . . . let's not lose what we had in Atlanta. You felt like I did—like I do—I know you did!"

I hold my breath, my hand pressed over my mouth, waiting for his response. Emmet lets out a long, ragged sigh, and I can picture him running his hands through his hair. "She's going to Fort Lauderdale, you know," he says finally. "Next week. It's a good time for us to be apart, and to sort out how we feel about each other. I haven't said anything to her yet, but I'm thinking it'll be the best thing for both of us, the way things are now."

This time there's no mistaking the sounds I hear, the shuffling, rustling sounds of lovers shifting in each other's arms. I close my eyes in an attempt to shut out the image of them with their bodies pressed together, her arms locked around his neck. Kit whimpers,

"Oh, Emmet. It's been terrible, being at odds with you. I need you. I don't know if I can stand it any longer."

"Yeah, you can, sweetheart," he says gruffly. "You've stood a lot worse." The tenderness in his voice cuts through me like a sword. Her response is muffled, making me wonder if he's leaned his head against hers, as he so often does with me. It's a gentle, affectionate gesture, taking me by surprise when I'm cooking, or distracted by whatever I'm doing at the time. Unless he entwines his fingers through my hair, that is, or lifts a strand to his lips. Then a seemingly casual gesture quickly becomes erotic. I move so suddenly from the window that I stumble and grab the desk for support. Unable to listen any longer, I leave my office and hurry down the hallway, then up the stairs to the bedroom. I stagger across the room to the bed, where I collapse in a heap.

After my collapse on the bed, I don't know how much time passes until Emmet comes in to check on me. I got up once to wash my face, then returned to bed clutching a damp washcloth in my hand. Huddled beneath a throw, I placed the cool cloth over my eyes and surprised myself by falling asleep, emotionally exhausted.

Emmet stands by the bed and calls my name until I stir. If I didn't know better, the concern in his voice would've fooled me. Had fooled me, I remind myself. How could I have been so wrong about him? Obviously, he's someone I don't know, nor have I ever known. Based on what I just heard, he and Kit had something going on after Rosalyn died. No wonder she hated me on sight. And Emmet—now I know that he ran off to Florida not only out of guilt for his part in Rosalyn's death, but also for his entanglement with her best friend. Emmet and Kit—of course! It explains so much.

"Helen? You okay?"

I shake my head, only to regret it when he sits on the bed next to me. I try to backtrack, to insist I'm fine, but he's not having it, and removes the washcloth from my eyes. "Can I see for myself that you're fine?" With great care, he folds the cloth and places it on the bedside table.

"Aren't you going to Asheville this afternoon?" I blurt out. It's a stupid thing to ask; he'd already told me he was.

Emmet's eyebrows shoot up, and he tilts his head to the side. With a shrug, he says carefully, "I'm not in a particular hurry to get there. If it weren't for the awards dinner, I'd wait until tomorrow. But I foolishly agreed to introduce some of the folks who're getting awards—"

"What's foolish about it?" I interrupt, and again, my question takes him by surprise.

"What's foolish about it?" he echoes. "Well, you're leaving Monday for Fort Lauderdale, and we could have more time together if I were going to be here tonight."

I lie back on my pillow, marveling at the cleverness of his response. As I just heard him tell Kit, he wants some time away from me, too. Why not just tell me so? A wave of anger sweeps over me as I recall his oft-repeated platitudes about truth in journalism. He's always saying that you have to look beyond the facts for the truth. The age-old question "What is truth?" is rarely answered by facts alone. Ironically, he's used his own rope to hang himself.

"But I certainly don't have to go if you need me to stay with you," he adds in the same gentle voice.

When I glance his way, the sight of him, with his frown of concern, hits me like a fist to the stomach. My anger at his betrayal is battling with the inevitable pain. Right now, the pain's pulled ahead. With a brittle smile, I say, "No. I don't need you to stay with me."

Neither of us says anything for a moment, then he rubs his face wearily. "Even so, I hate to leave you alone if you're unwell." He stops as though to gauge my reaction. "Are you feeling better?"

Before I can answer, a thought hits me. "Who're you introducing tonight?" As if I didn't know.

"Ah . . . just one of my colleagues at channel six."

He's watching me warily, and my eyes sting with sudden tears.
Please God, don't let me cry! Not while he's looking at me like that.
It'd be the ultimate humiliation. I hear myself say, "I'm sure she's
thrilled to have you doing the honors."

"Who?"

"Who do you think, Emmet—Tinker Bell the fairy? You know
who I'm talking about. That anchorwoman, Carol! You're doing
her introductions tonight, aren't you?"

"Carol?" he echoes in surprise. "I didn't realize you even
knew her."

"Let's just say I know of her," I say stiffly. "And that she used to
be your . . . ah . . . protégée." I load the last word with all the sar-
casm I can.

With a groan, he says, "Oh, Christ. I might've known the damn
gossips here would've told you about that. It's surprising they waited
so long to do so, actually, with her living in Asheville now."

I can't stop myself. I'm in no shape for this conversation, and
certainly had no intention of having it. But these things take on a
life of their own. "Ah, yes! Both of you in Asheville. Made it mighty
convenient, didn't it, for you two to get reacquainted?"

He pulls back, blinking at me. "Are you suggesting what I
think?"

"You're a smart man, Emmet. You figure it out."

"You're one to talk," he says curtly.

"Now that's a tad cryptic."

"Nothing cryptic about it," he retorts. "Unlike you, I have no
problem coming right out with it. I hadn't planned on bringing it
up—not ever—even though it's been eating at me. I'm talking about
you and Noel, Helen. Funny you'd make insinuations about me

when you've carried on a flirtation with one of my closest friends since you met him."

With a sharp, biting laugh, I say, "I won't even dignify that with a response. It's nothing but a smoke screen, anyway."

His pale eyes go cold. "I've heard the rumors, of course. Folks said you went after your boss, but you're looking at Noel as a replacement if it doesn't work out with me." Abruptly, he gets to his feet.

Blinded by fury, I cry out, "That's a horrible thing to say. How dare you! And how dare you listen to anyone who'd say such a thing about me?"

"Even if the talk wasn't going around," he says, "I would've figured it out on my own. I've seen the two of you together."

"You've seen nothing, then," I say snidely. Please stop, I say to myself. Please stop this! Tell him you aren't up to it now, that you're still feeling sick. Then shut your mouth, and don't open it again. In a short time, he'll be gone. But I can't do it, of course. It has to play out, and come to its terrible ending.

Emmet stands by the bed with his hands on his hips. "Listen, Helen. I don't give a flying fuck if you've gone after Noel, because I know he can take care of himself. What I don't like is being played for a fool."

"Oh, really? Then you know how I feel about you and that Carol woman."

"Would you stop calling her that? Her name is Carol Lind Crawford, and yes, years ago we had a brief fling, which I deeply regret. I'm not proud of it, Helen. But I'm not involved with her now, no matter what rumors you've heard. Period."

"I don't believe you," I sneer. "But the funny thing is, she's not even the one I need to be concerned about, is she? Just a short while ago, I was all in a dither about you and that woman, Carol. Since then, I've found out that she's just one of your many women."

"Good God! What have the gossips been telling you?"

"I didn't need to listen to gossip," I say nastily. "You're always saying that a good journalist goes directly to the source."

He looks perplexed before stating flatly, "I have no idea what you're talking about."

I put my hands to my temples, which are throbbing now, and hear myself say, "Yes, you do, Emmet. I'm talking about you and Kit."

"Kit?" He looks genuinely puzzled. "What does Kit have to do with this?"

"Evidently she has everything to do with it. I can't believe I was so blind. All along, you and Kit. My God!"

He throws his hands up in the air. "For Christ's sake! Who put the idea in your head that something's going on between me and Kit?"

"I heard you," I say, but speak too softly, and have to repeat myself. "A few minutes ago, I was in my office. And I overheard you talking to Kit in yours—" I stop at the look on his face.

"You did what?" Emmet's fury is a scary thing, and I instinctively recoil.

"I-I was in my office earlier, and I heard—"

He explodes before I can finish, his face livid with rage. "You eavesdropped, you mean? Goddammit! You listened to a conversation I had in my office? Have you been doing that all summer?" Cringing, I shake my head, but he's too furious to notice. "I thought you understood that anything that goes on in my office is private, regardless. I can never, ever stand for anyone snooping around in there, you hear me? I would never have married you if I'd known you were the kind of woman who snooped."

"You'd . . . never have married me?" I echo, but my voice catches in my throat. Swallowing hard, I try to turn away before he sees my traitorous tears, but I'm not quick enough.

"Oh, way to go, Helen," he spits out. "When all else fails, turn on the tears."

And with that, he slams his hand into the nightstand so hard that the lamp totters, then falls to the floor. At the sound of it crashing, Emmet stops his tirade and freezes in place. He told me once that the lamp's one Rosalyn treasured, a glass-globed antique of her grandmother's. He stares at it for a minute, then kneeling, reaches under the table to unplug it before he picks up the broken pieces with unsteady hands. Getting to his feet, Emmet holds the jagged lamp and stares at it blankly, as though it's a jigsaw puzzle he can't quite figure out.

I watch his actions as if from a great distance. As carefully as if he were handling a broken body, he places the remaining pieces of the lamp on a nearby chair. After a long and terrible silence, he turns to face me. I wonder if he realizes that he's holding his offending fist, red and angry looking, in the palm of his other hand. It has to hurt.

When he lets out a long, shaky breath and says, "Oh, God," I lower my head, unable to meet his gaze. "Helen?" he says when I bury my face in my hands. Serves me right, falling apart like this. I hadn't wanted a confrontation but went on with it, anyway. When I don't answer, Emmet starts pacing, the way he always does when stressed out. I can hear him walking back and forth, and know he's raking his fingers through his hair in agitation.

"Shit," he says finally. "Listen, Helen . . . I'm sorry, okay? Oh, God, I'm sorry! Look at you, and here I am, yelling at you like a madman, flinging a fit and breaking things . . . Jesus!" He sighs heavily. "Can you look at me?"

I do, but keep my hands cupped around my eyes, like blinders, not caring if I look ridiculous. The late-afternoon sun is so bright it hurts, and starts my head throbbing again. Standing at the foot of the bed, Emmet rakes his fingers through his hair and says, "I swear to you, I've never done anything like that before. I don't know what came over me. Oh, hell, that's not true. The thing is, I do know, and that's the problem . . ." He stops in confusion.

"I should've left it alone," I say in a ragged voice, but he doesn't hear me.

"Look . . . I'm going to Asheville now," he blurts out. "Instead of waiting any longer."

"Asheville?" I echo, as though I've never heard of it.

"Yeah. It'll be better for you if I go now." He says it without meeting my eyes. I can't respond, so I nod mutely. "Better for you," he repeats, "for me to go. Maybe we both need to cool down. I know what you heard, between me and Kit, and it's not what you think. But I doubt you want to hear that now—any of it. Both of us are so overwrought that the best thing would be to stop this before we go too far. Don't you think?"

I take a shuddering breath. The only thing I can say is "If you're going, you need to get there before dark." Irrationally, though, I don't want him to leave. If he goes now, he'll be running away rather than facing things, exactly what I'd planned on doing.

Even as I'm thinking that, Emmet heads toward the closet, his mind already made up. "I should call the inn and tell them I'm coming," he says matter-of-factly. "They overbooked because of the awards banquet, so I told them I'd let them know if I'd be running late. And I'll be back home tomorrow afternoon, okay?" Pausing before he opens the closet door, he throws me a sideways glance. "Do you need me to warm you up some soup or something before I go?"

I'll get something later, I reply, and his relief is almost palpable. My head's pounding, and the thought of food turns my stomach. Emmet pulls his overnight bag from the shelf, then throws in some of his things. He's such a careless, haphazard packer that I'd started doing it for him. He tosses the bag on a nearby chair, and I see a dress shirt and running shoes thrown in together and sticking out from the top of the unzipped bag.

Abruptly, he leaves the room, and I wonder if he intends to leave without even saying good-bye. Instead he reappears, carrying a glass of water and a bottle of aspirin. "You might need these," he says gruffly. "I'm leaving them on the table, okay?" He stands beside the bed for a moment, then leans over to kiss my forehead. When he smooths back my hair, I close my eyes, and tears trickle down my cheeks.

"We'll talk when I get back tomorrow," he says. When I don't respond, he adds, "Know this, though. I'm sorry as hell about all of this, Helen. I never meant for it to happen. Any of it."

"I know you didn't," I say in a choked voice. "And neither did I."

Our eyes meet and hold for a brief moment. The regret in his voice tells me the bitter truth, that whatever we once had is over. Emmet knows it, too, knows that we've crossed some invisible line of no return. And with that knowledge comes another terrible truth: When he comes back to Moonrise, I won't be here. I no longer have to wait until the first of the week to return to Florida. There's nothing to keep me here.

Emmet's eyes fall away from mine, and he turns away quickly. Before I can call out to him, he's walked over to pick up his overnight bag, his back to me. Then he leaves the room without a backward glance. The door I keep open for the breeze blows to with a loud slam, and I flinch.

————

IT'S THE MOON gardens I hate saying good-bye to, as much as anything else. I appreciate the irony, of course, smiling a bitter smile as I wander through them for the last time. Now that I've decided to leave, I can't bear to stay here a minute longer than I have to. If I hurry, I can pack up my car and get an early start in the morning. But first, one last look at the gardens. Much to my surprise, some of the night bloomers are finally coming through.

Noel's put the Lady of the Night in a larger planter and on a sunlit path, and he's brought over lake water every single day to keep it alive. Noel! My face burns in shame at the remembrance of Emmet's hateful accusation about my flirtation with his friend. Ever since the berry-picking incident, I suspected he felt that way, yet I'd convinced myself otherwise. Jealousy was for lesser beings, not Emmet Justice. Who on earth could've made him think such an awful thing? I wonder. It's not like him to listen to idle gossip. If nothing else, he's too good a journalist. Despite that, he let emotions sway his reason, and allowed himself to believe the worst about someone he once professed to love.

Forcing such hurtful thoughts out of my mind, I kneel beside the Lady of the Night to check for new growth. I told Noel it was foolish to bring her over here, even if Emmet and I ended up staying, but he wouldn't listen. Now he'll have to take it back to Laurel Cottage. I've learned since why the other plants were hanging in the magnolias when Tansy found this one, the lone survivor. Like me, they're not natives to this clime, and it takes a lot of care for them to survive a winter. On the days when temperatures plunged, Rosalyn brought them in to the sunporch, but she left them in the hanging baskets otherwise to help them acclimate to a cold habitat. Poor Rosalyn—she'd been in such a state on her last trip to Moonrise, she'd forgotten having left them out.

Yet another irony, I think. From the first time I heard her name, I've envied Rosalyn and wanted to be more like her—beautiful, poised, confident—everything that I'm not. We came from such different worlds that I couldn't possibly identify with her, I told myself. Instead, I was eaten up with envy of her—which is a terrible thing. Envy does something to your soul that's not very pretty, as I've discovered. Despite Rosalyn's seemingly charmed life, she suffered as we all do, and from everything the rest of us go through, including the heartbreak and betrayal even a privileged life can't

shield you from. The truth is, nothing can. I wish I'd known Rosalyn, I think suddenly. Crazy as it sounds, I think we would've liked
each other, maybe even become friends.

I think also of the woman who calls herself Rosalyn's best
friend, Kit Rutherford. I don't know what to make of her, much less
the conversation I overheard between her and Emmet. On the surface, it seems pretty clear: Kit's been secretly in love with the husband of her best friend, and came to believe he might return her
love with Rosalyn gone. It's what lurks beneath the surface that
puzzles me. I can't help but wonder if Rosalyn ever suspected Kit's
feelings for her husband. By his own admission Emmet wasn't faithful, yet it didn't sound like he and Kit had anything going on while
Rosalyn was alive. In Emmet's office, Kit alluded to a time afterward, perhaps when they turned to each other in a moment of grief.
It explains so much: Kit's hostility toward me, her coolness with Emmet for our marriage, even her final visit with me, when she planted
suspicions to turn me against him.

And that's part of my turmoil as well. I was all too ready to believe that Emmet lied to me about everything, and had been lying
all along. Now that I know what was behind Kit's overtures, I wonder how much of what she told me was intended to tear Emmet and
me apart. She refused to tell me what she knew about Rosalyn's
death—that Rosalyn came here to catch her husband with another
woman—but enough was implied that I could figure it out. I have
no doubt now that Kit did that intentionally. What a good act she
put on, pretending to be my friend! That's all it was, an act of contri-
tion intended to disarm me, to trick me into trusting her. Despite
the duplicity, I can even understand why she did such a thing. If
I've learned nothing else from this, it's that any of us can be so
blinded by love and desire that we become desperate, even irrational.

I get to my feet with my thoughts in a whirlwind of pain and
confusion, and glance down at the Lady plant regretfully. I'd so

looked forward to seeing it in bloom, inhaling the intoxicating fragrance I've heard about, learning to care for it myself. Brushing the dirt off my knees, I turn away abruptly. For whatever reason, it wasn't meant to be. Maybe an experience that uniquely beautiful only comes once in a lifetime, if at all. Despite the way things turned out, I can't help but see my time with Emmet that way. We had our moment in the sun, when we loved in a way I never imagined possible. It couldn't last, of course; nothing that dazzling can. I glance back over my shoulder at the Lady plant, a puny little thing struggling for life in a hostile environment, and I offer up a prayer for its survival. Even though I couldn't make it here, hopefully she will. One night, under the glow of a full moon, she might even bloom.

Because I've stopped to admire every plant, tree, and butterfly—or so it seems—it's taken me longer than I expected to walk through the gardens, and I haven't decided yet when to tell the others good-bye. They know I'm supposed to leave in a few days, but no one knows I'll be gone in the morning. As tempting as it is, I can't just take off without a word. I've grown too fond of them—even of the irascible Tansy—for that. Suddenly I remember Tansy's calls earlier about the moon party, and I go toward the house to listen to my messages.

I make my way down the pathway toward the house and realize I don't have a choice about my good-byes: Like it or not, I have to go to Laurel Cottage and Linc's cabin now, before it gets any later. Even though Moonrise is just beginning to feel like home—to welcome me, even—I don't relish the thought of returning in the dark to a big, spooky house that once scared the crap out of me. And I sure don't want to if it storms! For the first time all summer, thunderstorms are in the forecast. It might not be tonight, but they will come, we hear. As much as I've longed for rain, I hope it holds off until I'm long gone. One last thing I wanted to do was see the gardens at night, lit only by the moon. All summer, and this is the first time the gardens have been ready for the full moon. Scanning the twilight sky, I wonder. It's fairly clear now, but thunderclouds are building beyond the mountains. During the time I've been outside, the sky's gone from a startling, almost eerie blue to an ominous shade of gray. Something's in the air, something close and foreboding, which makes me uneasy.

Once I'm back upstairs, I listen to Tansy's messages, and there's one that puzzles me. Matter of fact, she's left the same message more than once. She's got to talk to me, and right away. It's going to sound odd, she says, but don't talk to Kit or see her if she comes over. Trust me on this, Tansy says in the last one. I can't, of course. After what I heard this afternoon, I don't trust her or Kit, either one. I'm not sure that I'll ever trust anyone again.

I'm holding the phone in my hand when it rings. I answer automatically, then want to kick myself when I hear Tansy's voice. "Helen?" she cries. "Oh, thank God. I was hoping you'd answer. Are you over your headache?"

"I'm fine," I say briskly, anxious to get this over with.

"Listen, I've got to talk to you—" she begins, but I stop her.

"I can't now. I'm leaving Monday, and I haven't even started packing—"

"You cannot leave here without talking to me first," she insists. "And this is much more important than packing, I can assure you. Didn't you listen to my messages? You know, about Kit?" When I tell her that I did, she demands to know if I've talked to anyone. After a slight hesitation, I lie and tell her I haven't.

"Good," she says with a sigh of relief. "Promise me you won't, and it'll give me time to get more information. It's probably just as well. Even if we talked now, I couldn't tell you much more than this: Something weird's going on with Kit that I haven't quite sorted out yet. But I have a really bad feeling about it." She stops herself, and I can picture her scowling, waving her words off. "Oh, hell! I'm not making a damn bit of sense, I know. I shouldn't have said anything until I found out more—but know this, Helen. You're the only one I've said anything to. I haven't even told Noel what I found out about her."

I close my eyes and sigh in exasperation. "Tansy, I have no idea what you're talking about."

"Of course you don't!" she snaps, as though it's my fault. "How could you, when I don't even know myself? Just . . . aw, hell. Just promise me you won't talk to anyone until we talk, okay? We might be over there tonight."

"Over where?" I echo, more bewildered than before.

"Moonrise!" she hisses. "Where'd you think, the Biltmore? Jesus, Helen! I told you, we're coming over to see the gardens in the full moon—"

"That's supposed to be tomorrow night," I protest. "When Emmet's here."

"That was the plan," she admits grudgingly. "But we can't see a full moon if it storms, can we? So Noel says we might have to do it tonight. We're waiting to see what the weather does. I'll let you know, okay?"

She's gone before I can say anything else, but putting my phone away, I realize it'd be better if they came over tonight. Our good-byes could be done without my having to leave here, then worry about getting back after dark, or in a storm. Having decided that, I turn to my packing. No point in trying to figure out what Tansy's up to. If so, curiosity might tempt me to trust her, and that's the last thing I can afford to do now.

I start in the kitchen. I bring half a dozen sturdy wine boxes in from the carriage house, more than enough to pack up what I brought with me in June. Or it'd better be; my car won't hold any more. I sure can't ask Emmet to ship them to me, though Willa would. Willa! I can barely stand the thought of leaving here without seeing her, especially with her recovering. I've talked to her only once since she got home from the hospital because Tansy's been so insistent that no one bother her. Suddenly that strikes me as a tad peculiar, even for Tansy. What if Willa is more banged up than she's letting on, and asked Tansy not to tell us? Or maybe her injuries are from something other than a fall—an abusive lover, perhaps? With a gasp, I grab the phone to dial Willa's number.

My fears are quelled by a hearty chuckle from Willa when I blurt them out as soon as she answers. "I'm fine, Helen—I swear," she assures me. "And Tansy's only doing what I asked her to. It's not that I didn't want to see none of y'all. Tansy thinks I oughta keep a low profile for a while. I don't know if you've heard that I broke it off with Duff, but I'm laying low until the dust settles."

"Yeah, I heard you kicked him out," I say, then add, "And I can't tell you how relieved I am, frankly. You're too good for him. None of my business, of course, but I hope you won't let him back into your life. I'm afraid he's off somewhere right now, plotting a way to get back into your good graces."

"I would be, too, except for what Tansy did," she tells me with a catch in her voice.

"Tansy?"

"I still can't believe it. Just a few minutes ago, Tansy called to tell she'd taken care of Duff, and he wouldn't bother me again, not ever. She found out that he did something illegal while working for Kit—Lord only knows what, or how Tansy found out—but she called Duff to tell him he'd go to the pen if she reported him. Stay away from all of us, Tansy told him. And Duff will, I know. Nothing scares him like the thought of serving time in the pen."

"Good Lord," I gasp. "That's brilliant of Tansy." Willa and I giggle together, then I clear my throat to say, "Listen, hon, I called to check on you, but also to tell you good-bye. I have to go back to

Fort Lauderdale next week. Or rather, I was supposed to. I've decided to start the trip tomorrow instead."

"Tomorrow? Oh, shoot. I hate to see you go," she says, which touches me. "But you'll be back in a couple of weeks, right?"

Closing my eyes, I remind myself that I have no choice. I have to lie to her, and to all of them, until I can get away, and get my life sorted out. "That's the plan," I say cheerily. It helps that we're on the phone, and not face-to-face. I'd have a lot of trouble looking into those clear, honest eyes of Willa McFee and flat-out lying.

Willa has her own little surprise for me before she goes. "When you come back, Helen," she says almost shyly, "I'll have something to tell you."

"Oh, no, you don't," I cry in dismay. "Tell me now, or my curiosity will kill me."

No matter how I beg, Willa won't say more, except that it's something good. And she's too superstitious to tell it yet, so like it or not, I'll have to wait. I give in, though I have a sneaking suspicion of what it might be. Since she's rid herself of Duff, I hope and pray she's found someone new who's worthy of her.

After Willa and I say our good-byes, I return to the kitchen with a vengeance, packing like a maniac. I won't let myself stop until I've got everything in the kitchen, then my office, packed up, the boxes sealed with brown tape. Then I drag them to the garage one by one, stacking them by my car for an easy getaway in the morning. I don't put anything in yet, not until I see how much I end up with, and figure out what goes where. My bedroom I'm doing last, so I can pack an overnight bag for two days of travel. Naturally I'm returning with more than I came with, though not a whole lot. The local pottery I picked up, mostly; gardening books Noel gave me; the shawls and wraps Emmet bought me for the cold.

Emmet . . . I can't go there, or I'll never get this done. I can't allow myself to stop and puzzle over his relationship with Kit, or my cryptic conversation with Tansy, or anything else. Soon I'll have all the time in the world to do so, to try to figure out how everything went so terribly wrong, and fell apart like it did. Out of nowhere, I recall a conversation I had with Linc a few weeks ago. He and Willa were in his gardens, and I stopped by to say hello after an afternoon canoe ride. Linc showed me an unusual black-and-white butterfly he called a Zebra Longwing. I knelt beside him to listen to his minilecture about its habitat, flight patterns, and such, which meant little to me. Instead, I watched Linc, amazed at the change in him since the time we first met. When he caught me studying him, I remarked that he looked happier than he'd been all summer. Linc's eyes held mine, then he said, "I've learned to be wary of happiness, Helen. We tend to get used to it and forget that the next heartache is already heading our way."

Outside, I scan the evening sky as I wait for darkness to fall. The sun has gone without leaving behind even a smidgen of its earlier glory. High over the mountains hangs a round white moon. A new moon comes up with the sun, Willa told me once, but a full moon rises at sunset. In the gardens, the evening primroses have yet to unfurl their delicate yellow blooms, even though the bed of sundrops opened up as soon as the sun disappeared. Standing on the pathway in the middle of the gardens, I look around in something close to excitement, despite my weariness and distress. It feels like I've been waiting for the full moon all summer.

The clouds come and go; just as I'm sure we won't be able to see the moon, they'll float away only to reappear moments later, dashing my hopes. The evening air still has that heavy, ominous feel to it that makes me uneasy. I need to check my messages, see if the party's on. After Noel checked out the weather report, he was supposed to leave me a message. Or I think that's what Tansy said. Turning, I start toward the house to find out.

I've made it almost to the rose arbor when I hear an odd noise from the far side of the house, and I stop, puzzled. Suddenly there's a Tarzan yell, followed by bursts of laughter and some kind of grinding noise. With a groan, I stand and wait until they make their appearance on the pathway that runs around the house from the driveway. The moon party is on.

Noel, Tansy, and Linc appear, and I stare in disbelief when I see what brought on their yelling and laughter. They've fashioned a makeshift rickshaw for Linc out of God knows what, with Noel pulling one side and Tansy the other. Linc whoops in delight; Noel's red-faced and straining with the effort of dragging the contraption over the pebbly pathway—the grinding noise I heard—and Tansy's trotting along beside him so easily she couldn't possibly be pulling her weight.

"What on earth?" I cry when they come to a halt before stumbling onto the terrace. "Where did you get that thing?"

Panting, Noel pretends to collapse while Tansy helps Linc down from the seat of the little rickshaw, brandishing his cane. Once she's got him steady on his feet, Tansy brings out a basket stashed under the seat. "Champagne," she announces. "For our end-of-the-summer toasts."

I ignore the basket and point to the rickshaw instead. Waving a hand, Tansy says dismissively, "Aw, it's an old pony cart Noel had in the garage. He's tried all summer to get Emmet to help him pull Linc around in it, but Emmet wouldn't do it."

Noel mops his brow with his shirtsleeve. "Emmet told me to bugger off, actually. Pity I didn't listen to him."

Linc crosses over to one of the terrace chairs and plops down in satisfaction. "I'm glad you didn't, my friend. That was the most enjoyable ride I've ever had."

"How did Noel talk you into pulling it?" I ask Tansy, wide-eyed.

Looking sheepish, she mutters, "Ah . . . it was my penance for the embarrassment I caused everyone at Madison's."

I'm not about to go there. Instead I turn to Noel and cry, "Surely y'all didn't pull that thing up the driveway! What'd you do, start yesterday?"

Grinning, Noel shakes his head. "We came over in rowboats. Linc and I in his, and Tansy and the pony cart in ours, pulling up the rear. The bad part was lugging the cart up from the dock."

I look at Tansy in astonishment as she makes her way to the table with her basket. "My God, Tansy! You did all that as penance?"

With a shrug, she says, "Beats a hair shirt, or flogging myself." Making a face, she reconsiders. "Well, maybe not."

I can't help myself; despite my sad, gloomy mood, I laugh and the others join me. From the basket on the table, Noel takes out a bottle of champagne and five plastic flutes. He looks my way and tilts his head toward the house. "Run fetch Emmet, love, so we can get this show on the road, so to speak. Since we arrived by water, we'll have to get back before the bottom falls out."

When I tell Noel that Emmet's in Asheville, it's Linc who speaks up. "He is? But . . . he told me just this morning that he didn't think he'd go."

Unperturbed, Noel pops the champagne and says breezily, "Yeah, me, too. But he probably felt too bad about skipping out on the awards dinner. That it, Helen?"

In a flat voice, I reply that yes, guess that was it. "So Emmet's getting an award?" Linc asks, but Noel shakes his head.

"Not this time, old chap. That newswoman who's one of Emmet's protégées—what's her name?—is, and he's supposed to introduce her."

Tansy flicks her eyes my way then back to Noel, aghast. "Ah, Mr. Sensitive? Have you forgotten that She-Who-Cannot-Be-Named needs to stay that way?"

Noel sighs in exasperation. "Oh, bloody hell, Tans. Don't be ridiculous. Need I point out that I know a bit more about that situation than you do? And as I've told you numerous times, that's old news. *Comprende?*"

My cheeks burn, but I dare not look their way. Instead I force myself to say in a cheery voice, "We'd better get on with the toasts, hadn't we?" I take a glass from Noel and look up at the grayish-black sky, cloudy again. "It's the first time all summer I've hoped the rain would hold off. I've been really looking forward to the full moon tonight."

Noel raises his glass. "Here's to the moon, then."

The four of us click our glasses together, then Linc hoists his for a twist on Noel's toast: "Fly me to the moon!" Although Tansy joins in, she doesn't offer up one of her own, which surprises me. That, and the way she keeps glancing at me anxiously. Despite her too-cheery facade, something has obviously upset her. Only when Noel nudges her does she raise her glass to say rather halfheartedly, "Ah, yes. A toast to the last moon of the summer."

Noel pours the last bit of champagne, and I clear my throat to say, "My turn." To my dismay, my eyes fill and I blink rapidly as I raise my glass. "It's been a wonderful summer, one I'll always treasure." My voice catches and I add quickly, "Here's to old friends, and new." After we drain our glasses and put them on the table, I hold up my hands in surrender. "Okay. This is going to be hard for me, so I'll make it short and sweet. Otherwise, I'm liable to cry, and we can't have that, can we?"

"Don't you dare start any sappy good-byes," Tansy hisses. "We agreed not to, remember? I'm no good at them."

"Such a surprise," Noel mutters. "You handle everything else so beautifully."

"I haven't forgotten, Tansy," I say, "and I agree with you. I'm no good at good-byes, either. Even so, I can't leave tomorrow without making the effort."

"Tomorrow?" Noel echoes, and I nod my head without meeting his gaze. Speaking rapidly, I remind him that I have to go back to Fort Lauderdale to fulfill my contract. Noel interrupts, saying they already knew that, so I repeat tomorrow. I have to go back tomorrow.

"Whoa, now," Linc says with a wave of his hand. "I still get confused fairly often, but tomorrow's Saturday, right? I thought you were leaving Monday, Helen—a week before the rest of us do."

They seem genuinely dismayed, and I find myself overriding their pleas that I stay through the weekend by claiming that I had it mixed up—I need to start back to work on Monday, I insist, not be traveling then. Which is a bold-faced lie, of course. If I'm not careful, I'll forget what's true, and what I've made up.

"What a shame," Noel says. "We've some things planned for our last weekend together. We'll just have to do them again next time you're here, I suppose."

I force a smile, but before I can respond, a sudden breeze blows away the clouds that have cloaked the moon in darkness, and the terrace is bathed in a pale, silvery light. I gasp, and each of us raises our head toward the heavens, and the appearance of the full moon we've been waiting for. The same breeze rustles the leaves in the garden, and brings with it a fragrance so sweet my breath catches in my throat. It's the moonflower vine.

"Well, don't just stand there, Helen," Tansy snaps, breaking the spell. "If you want to see the gardens in moonlight, you'd better do it quick."

She's right; the moon's out only for a short time as we wander the moonlit paths of the gardens, but I tell myself that's enough. It's magic for my last night here, and I'm grateful. The summer's almost gone, taking with it most of the night bloomers, but we linger over the ones that unfurl their colors for us. Linc identifies the Hawkmoths that I've watched from my windows, and I kneel before the riotous moonflower vine, inhaling its fragrance in appreciation. It's impossible, I tell Noel when he insists the perfume of the Lady plant puts the moonflower to shame. I look up to catch Tansy still studying me, but I can't read her expression.

When the clouds drift back over the moon, we return to the terrace in silence. Even before Tansy begins to pack up the basket, a heaviness settles over me, and I know the party's over. Scanning the skies, Noel announces, "I'm afraid we've seen all the moonlight we're going to see tonight, guys. Guess we should head back before the storm hits."

I'm standing beside him, and he turns to hug me, long and hard. "You'll be missed, my dear," he says as he leans over to kiss me lightly on the mouth. Because of Emmet's hateful accusations, I can't say what I'd like to, that I adore him, and will always hold his kindness to me close. Instead I go over to hug and kiss Linc, whom I can say those things to. I expect hugging Tansy to be awkward but it's not. Her dark eyes linger on mine, and I'm the first to look away.

Noel says, "Let us know when you'll be back, Helen, and we'll be here. I can drive over to T-town to pick up Linc if need be. Might even take the rickshaw." Eyebrows raised, he turns to Tansy. "I'm afraid Helen's missed saying good-bye to Kit, who must be off somewhere with Jim. Did you call her, Tans?" Before Tansy can answer, Noel looks at me with a shrug, oblivious. "Oh, well. I'm sure she'll be in touch, love."

"I'm sure she will," Tansy says briskly, her voice revealing nothing of our earlier conversation.

When Linc begins to make his way to the rickshaw, I cry out, "Surely you're not taking the canoes, Noel! Leave that fool thing here, and I'll drive everyone home."

"Naw," Noels says with a grin. "We prefer to travel in style. Right, my man?"

While Noel's helping Linc get settled in the seat, I see Tansy lean over to whisper something to them, and Noel nods. She leaves them abruptly to head back to where I stand on the terrace, and my heart sinks. I might've known she wouldn't leave without one last go at me. Sure enough, she takes my arm and pulls me into the darkness of the rose arbor, where Noel and Linc can't see us. "Tansy—" I protest, but her look stops me.

"You don't fool me, you know," she barks out. "Something's going on, and it's not pretty. You're leaving him, aren't you?"

I'm saved from answering by Noel, who calls out to Tansy to hurry with the girl talk, it's getting darker by the second. Without a pause, she yells, "Shut the hell up, Noel," then turns back to fire questions at me: "It's Kit, isn't it? You lied to me about not seeing her, didn't you? And if my hunch is right, she's told something that's got you running back to Florida like a scalded cat."

At one time, that would've angered me, but I shake my head wearily. "Look, Tansy, you're getting what you want, so why don't you just let it go? From the first day we met, you and Kit have wanted to see the last of me. Well, you're about to, so you can go celebrate at the country club, or wherever it is you society girls go for such things."

Her black eyes flash, and she sneers, "I'm right, then, and you're leaving Emmet. But he doesn't know, does he?"

"No. He doesn't know."

"You're such a coward that you'd run off without even telling him? Without having it out with him about whatever it was that Kit said? Which she probably made up, by the way. I warned you not to talk to her."

I'm shaking my head before she finishes, and I hold up a hand to stop her. "You don't know what you're talking about, but I've heard Noel say that's never stopped you. Yes, Kit told me some pretty unpleasant things about Emmet—or rather, she implied them—but that's not why I'm leaving. It's something else, something I've got to be by myself to sort out."

"Oh, bullshit," Tansy snorts. "Kit told you he's been seeing that anchorwoman, didn't she? I knew it!"

I rub my face wearily. "And you think I'm running off in a tiff, huh?"

She looks at me in disgust. "Well, aren't you? Emmet's a man, Helen, just like the rest of them. Rosalyn wouldn't stand for his little dalliances, and neither should you. Tell him to keep it zipped up, or else. But don't just run off without putting up a fight!"

"That's what you've wanted, isn't it? You and Kit, putting your heads together to come up with a way to get rid of me, doing everything you could to make me feel inferior to you—"

To my surprise, Tansy waves me off. "I won't insult you by denying it. I'm not one to hide my feelings, so yes, it's true. You weren't one of us, and I didn't like it. But most of all, you weren't Rosalyn."

I shake my head and shrug. "I won't ever be, Tansy."

Her voice is full of scorn. "No, you sure as hell won't. Rosalyn had more gumption than you'll ever have. She'd never run off and—" With a gasp, she jerks her head up to stare at me in disbelief. "But she did, didn't she? Someone must've told her the same thing . . ." Grabbing my arms, she shakes me, hard. "What did Kit tell you, Helen?"

I close my eyes and let out a shaky sigh. "She implied . . . that woman, Carol Lind Crawford, was here. Here, at Moonrise, with Emmet, and Rosalyn found out. So she came here to find out if he was seeing her again—understand, Kit didn't tell me this; I'm making some assumptions. Rosalyn must've found out that Emmet had lied to her and—"

With a sudden movement backward, Tansy drops my arms to place her hands over her mouth. "No," she says in a strangled voice. "It wasn't Emmet who lied to her. Oh, my God."

"What? It sounded like you said . . ."

To my astonishment, Tansy whirls away and leaves me standing there openmouthed, staring after her in bewilderment. "Tansy?" I call out, but she waves me off without so much as a backward glance. I take a step toward her but stop when she hurries over to the pony cart, where Noel and Linc wait in the darkness. "Let's get out of here," she orders Noel as she reaches down to pick up the handle. Oblivious to her distress, Noel says, "It's about time," and they start pulling the cart down the walkway. They don't see me standing in the shadows of the rose arbor, but I don't try to stop them, to demand Tansy tell me why she left me so abruptly. It's impossible to figure her out, and I'm too confused to even try. Not tonight, anyway. They disappear around the house, Linc laughing as they bounce him over the rough bricks of the walkway. I can hear them long after they're gone, even after they get into the boats and start their journey home. The crazy fools! My throat tightens as I hug my arms close. For a split second, the moon reappears and I step out of the rose shadows to study the sky, willing the clouds away.

I don't know how long I stand beside the arbor and wait, but the moon and stars stay hidden from my sight. Although my heart is as heavy as the clouds, numb with pain, I can't seem to leave the gardens. I have to go inside, have to finish the packing. Staying out here won't change anything. It won't change what waits for me inside, the finality of packing away my things and removing all traces of my presence from this place I've come to love. I take one last look around the shadowy, fragrant gardens, and sigh. This won't do. The moon's not coming back tonight, and staying out here won't change that. And besides, it's not the moon I'm waiting for, no matter what I tell myself. Prolonging this, I'm clinging to a time that's gone, and not coming back. Summer's over, and there's a melancholy touch of autumn in the night air.

20

tansy

STORM CLOUDS

Like it or not, I have to wait until Noel takes Linc home before I depart on my mission. Noel's already suspicious, eyeing me strangely and often, not even bothering to be his usual unflappable self. Not that he doesn't have good reason to be wary; after all, I was in quite a state when he got in from his meeting yesterday and found me pacing the floor. It was right after I'd found Kit trying on the locket, then seen the initials on her hairbrush. The odd thing is, I'd waited anxiously for him to get in, to tell him my suspicions about Kit, but decided against it. There was one more thing I had to find out first. So I told Noel that nothing was wrong with me. I was just in one of my funks. He knew better, of course. Finally he ran his fingers through his hair in exasperation—an uncharacteristic gesture for His Lordship—and told me I was driving him insane. When did I stop trusting him? I used to tell him everything, he said, ad nauseam, whether he wanted to hear it or not.

Poor baby. He really believes it, too—believes that I tell him everything that's going on in my life, that I share all my feelings with him. If he only knew.

For the umpteenth time, I wonder if ignorance is truly bliss. I liked it better when I didn't know about Kit, when I still loved her. Even after I saw her with the locket, and the awful suspicion started forming, I was still ignorant. Or at least, I could pretend to be. It was harder after I connected the monogram, NK, with the last entry in Rosalyn's notebook, but I could explain that away, too. After all, there was no real evidence of her duplicity, was there? Sure, it might look suspicious, and a person who didn't know Kit might jump to the wrong conclusion, but nothing was certain. And it's still not, I remind myself. There's still a big piece of the puzzle that's missing, and I won't rest until I figure it out.

If Kit did as I fear, and planted the same suspicions in Rosalyn's mind that she's done with Helen, then why? Oh, I know why she did such a thing to Helen (and it worked like a charm!) but Rosalyn? Kit would never have hurt Rosalyn, whom she absolutely idolized. Acknowledging that so-obvious fact, I bury my face in my hands and sigh, loud and long. I'm being ridiculous again. Despite Rosalyn's cryptic scribbles, it couldn't have been Kit who told Rosalyn that Emmet was at Moonrise with his mistress. If anything, she would've done the opposite—she would've tried to keep Rosalyn from finding out. My wild ideas are way off track, and I'm getting nowhere.

I wish I could let it go. It'd be so easy. Helen will return to Florida, leaving a very pissed-off Emmet behind. One thing for sure, he won't go after her, not with her sneaking off without letting him know. Being Emmet, he'll be so scornful of such a cowardly act that he'll say good riddance. Eventually he'll come to his senses, and admit the truth of the old adage: Marry in haste, repent in leisure.

The only way I can figure this out is by talking to Kit face-to-face, which I haven't been able to do. Before the moon party, I went over there to demand some answers. Her house was locked up with the garage door closed. I haven't seen her since she and Jim went to the High Hampton, but she's back, because her car's gone. Why hasn't she returned my calls or messages? She doesn't know I'm on to her about what she told Helen. Or rather, she doesn't know yet.

It's dark as sin outside, the moon hidden by heavy clouds, but I have to go to Kit's while Noel's with Linc. After leaving the lamp on and the door of my room closed so he'll think I'm reading, I grab my flashlight and head out. I'm almost to Linc's cabin when I see taillights in Kit's driveway, and a flash of chrome. She's just pulled into the garage. I speed up, passing Linc's without even bothering to peer in. Noel said he was building a fire, then they'd have a nightcap. He'd be there for a while.

I have no idea what I'll say to Kit when I see her. I can hardly tell her what I suspect her of doing to Rosalyn. She'll defend herself, probably say Rosalyn needed to know if her husband was cheating, but it doesn't wash with me. Of all people, Kit would know how it'd hurt Rosalyn, and friends never willingly hurt each other, right?

Just as I get to the driveway, I spot Kit in the garage, getting out of her car and heading toward the back door. When I call out to her, she goes inside as though she didn't hear me. Breaking out in a run, I sprint to the door and open it without bothering to knock. Like I did on my visit the other day, I barge in uninvited.

Kit's in the kitchen, pouring herself a glass of water, and my sudden appearance startles her so badly that she gasps in alarm. "Jesus Christ, Tansy! Don't you ever knock?"

She's so shaken that I'm immediately contrite, and hold up my hands in apology. "I didn't mean to scare you. But you won't answer my calls, and I really need to see you."

"I noticed you'd called," she says, avoiding my eyes, "and was going to call you back." She's lying, I can tell, and I'm even more convinced when she forces a nervous smile. "Listen, sweetie," she goes on, pushing a strand of hair behind her ear, "I don't mean to be rude, but I can't visit now. Jim and I stayed over at the High Hampton an extra day, and we're flying to Saint Thomas next week. I haven't even told you yet! But I've gotten really behind with my work, and there's some stuff I simply must finish tonight." With a sweep of her hand, she motions toward the table in the corner of the kitchen where she's left her briefcase and a pile of papers. "I was about to get started."

When I hesitate, she puts her glass of water on the counter and comes over to me, as though to lead me out of the kitchen. "Tell you what!" she says breathlessly, still smiling her fake smile. "Run on home now, and I'll come over tomorrow. Then I'll tell you all about Jim, and our upcoming trip, okay?"

She's trying to get rid of me, so I say tightly, "Don't worry. I'm not staying but a minute. I need to ask you something, then I'll leave. You'll have plenty of time to get your work done."

Her eyes flicker uneasily, but she still avoids my direct gaze. I imagine she's wondering if she should toss me out, or let me have my say. Settling on the latter, she motions toward two backless chrome stools pulled up to the counter. "I can give you a minute, but that's about it. Sorry to be so inhospitable, but it can't be helped."

I'm about to protest since I don't really want to sit down, but she perches on one of the stools, kicks off her heels, and crosses her long, shapely legs. She's dressed in a simple beige sheath with a long strand of pearls, which she twists around her fingers nervously. I pull out the other stool from the counter, slide the little flashlight into my jeans pocket, and face her. Might as well get this over with.

"Kit, this is going to sound strange, but I've got to talk to you about the night Rosalyn died."

Her eyes widen. "Don't tell me that you came over here and burst into my house like a maniac to talk about that? My God, I'm beginning to see that Noel's right. You're getting crazier every day."

Which really pisses me off, but I refuse to let her get to me. Before I can respond, she throws her hands up in the air. "I have plenty of questions about the night Rosalyn died, as you know better than anyone. For months afterward, I tormented myself in every way imaginable. I was eaten up with guilt, and—"

"Guilt?"

She shakes her head and sighs. "Irrational as it is, I kept thinking if only I'd been here, it wouldn't have happened. I could've gone over and kept her company, found out what was troubling her . . ."

"I think we both know what that was, don't we? She came to Moonrise to see if Emmet had that woman here." It comes out sharper than I intended, accusatory, and I hold my breath. I don't want her to kick me out before I get what I came after, but she merely shrugs.

"Well, each of us has our own theory, but no one knows for sure."

I study her before asking, "Didn't she tell you she'd leave him if he cheated on her again?"

This time Kit meets my eyes coolly. "Oh, she would have. In a heartbeat. You know that, too."

"Would you have told her if you found out he was? You know, thinking it was something she needed to hear?"

She stares at me in disbelief. "Of course not. It would've devastated her."

"Who told her, then?"

Again, she shrugs. "Maybe she had a hunch and was following up on it. My God, Tansy—what are you getting at? And why now, after all this time? It won't bring Rosalyn back."

I lean toward her urgently. "No, but it will always haunt us! Maybe if we find out what really happened, we can come to terms with it." Or maybe not, I remind myself. Maybe it will tear us apart. More determined than ever to get a response from her, I say, "Helen seems to think Emmet was here with that Carol woman, and when Rosalyn found out—"

Kit's eyes flash furiously. "So this is about Helen? I cannot believe what I'm hearing! Don't tell me Helen said something that's got you all riled up—" Again, she flails her arms dramatically. "You have truly gone off the deep end this time!"

I fold my arms and watch her. "You're the one who told Helen, Kit." When she starts sputtering a denial, I cut her off. "Oh, I know— not in so many words. What you did was imply enough that she figured out the rest. So you can cut the crap with me. What I want to know is why."

Her look is incredulous. "Do you even have to ask? You can act all pious now, Tansy, but you've been with me on this. You and I, we were the only ones who could save Emmet from himself. You did nothing, while I took it seriously. During the trips to Asheville, I helped Emmet see some things about his little bride that opened his eyes, including the way she was going after Noel. It broke my heart to hurt him like that, but he had to know. So yes, I admit it—I purposely said some things to Helen about Emmet's unfaithfulness. And it worked, too. She's leaving him. And by the way, I got Duff to return the locket, left it in the garage where Emmet would find it, not Helen. It was gone when I sent him back to check, so that worked out as I planned as well."

Her smile is smug and self-satisfied, but none of her confession surprises me. I figured she'd been working on Emmet, planting suspicions about Helen. I didn't need to come over here to have that confirmed, or to make sure she returned the locket. I tell her that, then add, "But what about Rosalyn, Kit? I know why you wanted to turn Helen against Emmet, but why Rosalyn?"

She jumps to her feet so suddenly that I instinctively pull back. Red-faced, she waves a finger at me and cries, "How dare you? I loved Rosalyn more than anyone in this world, so how dare you imply that I'd hurt her? I don't know how you got it in your sick little mind that it was me—"

"I know it was you. I found out from Rosalyn."

"That's a horrible, disgusting lie! If Rosalyn had told you any-thing, you would've said so long before now."

I shake my head to stop her. "I didn't say she told me, I said I found out from her. It was in the notebook—you know, that Frank Grimes gave me."

"That notebook was empty," she sneers, leaning over me.

I nod agreement. "The part I gave you was. I tore out the pages Rosalyn had written on."

The color drains from her face, and Kit sinks to the stool as though her legs can no longer hold her up. "Oh, God," she whis-pers. Her expression tells me everything I need to know.

Elbows propped on the counter, she covers her face with her hands. After a heavy silence, she comes clean. "I never thought Rosalyn would come flying up here like she did after I told her! When the trees were cleared away in front of my house, Moonrise was clearly visible, especially with their trees bare, too. I just hap-pened to see them—Emmet and a dark-haired woman. He was showing her around, and she was taking pictures. I knew who she was, of course—and watching them together, it was obvious that he was involved with her again. So I called him to say I'd seen them, and to demand he break it off before Rosalyn found out. You know Emmet, he insisted nothing was going on, that I was overre-acting. Then prove it, I said, call Rosalyn and tell her you have your former mistress at her house." Her voice breaks, and she squeezes her eyes shut, trembling.

"And when he wouldn't, you did it for him," I say with a sigh. "But what if you were wrong, and they weren't having an affair? Emmet was working in this area—maybe he was just giving her a tour of the house."

She shakes her head vehemently. "No. I didn't want to believe it, either, even after seeing them together, cozying up to each other every chance they got. It was only when Emmet called me back that I knew for sure. He asked me not to tell Rosalyn he'd brought that woman to Moonrise. Knowing how upset she'd be, I agreed, and he said they were leaving. But later, I found out he'd lied to me. I was going out of town, remember, and my contractor picked me up so we could get ahead of the bad weather. As we drove off, I saw a light on in Rosalyn and Emmet's bedroom—"

I interrupt her with a gasp. "But Emmet could've forgotten to turn it off before he left! That doesn't mean they were there together—"

Kit's look is so full of scorn that it stops me midsentence. "You didn't let me finish. Not only was a light on, a whiff of smoke was coming from the far chimney. You know as well as I do, Tansy, that the master bedroom has the only working fireplace on that side of the house."

She's right, and I slump back on the stool, taking it in.

Kit brushes away tears with the back of her hand. "I was so upset, so furious at him that I called Rosalyn immediately, which only made things worse. She refused to listen to me, and we had an awful fight. Because she didn't want to believe Emmet had betrayed her, she accused me of making the whole thing up."

I blink at her. "But . . . why? Why would she think you did such a thing?"

She shrugs, and tears roll down her cheeks unheeded. "She was just hurt, and lashing out, I suppose. You know, kill the messenger rather than hear the message."

I hesitate, thinking back to what Rosalyn wrote in her notebook: *NK—so many lies! Trust gone. Will I ever know truth?* Something doesn't add up. I understand Rosalyn being upset, not wanting to hear about Emmet's betrayal, but to accuse Kit of lying to her? To lose trust in a lifelong friend? I'm hotheaded enough to make accusations like that, but not Rosalyn. Not without good reason.

Why would she say *so many lies* if there hadn't been others? When I first got here, not five minutes ago, Kit looked at me without a moment's hesitation and lied to me. And she's lying to me now, I realize.

My reverie is broken when Kit suddenly raises her head to stare off into the distance. Her face is full of misery, her voice strangled. "I just wanted him to break it off with that woman. He'd sworn not to see her again, yet he flaunted their affair. Bringing her here, to Moonrise, made his betrayal even worse. He knew how seeing them together would hurt me."

"Hurt you?" I echo, startled.

Kit stares at me, her eyes cold. "Rosalyn. I said Rosalyn."

"No, you didn't. You said hurt you . . ."

"Jesus, Tansy—you are beyond pathetic," she spits out. "I know you're older than me, and bat-shit crazy to boot, but I didn't realize you'd gone deaf as well. You know good and well what I said."

"Yes. I do."

With her slip of the tongue, the last piece of the puzzle falls into place. I stagger to my feet, dizzy with the knowledge and my blindness at not seeing it until now. "You're in love with him," I say. "All these years, you and Rosalyn in love with the same man. It's why you've never been able to be happy with anyone else, isn't it? Including those poor fools you married."

It hits me that Kit didn't lie about one thing, saying she didn't want to hurt Rosalyn—she never considered Rosalyn's feelings at all. It was Kit who felt betrayed by the man Rosalyn loved, because she loved him, too. Her call to Rosalyn that day came out of spite and jealousy, not concern. And Rosalyn must've suspected as much. *So many lies!* If so, then Rosalyn didn't come to Moonrise to catch Emmet in a web of lies; she came to catch Kit. Something she found here must've confirmed her suspicions—the lamp wasn't on, maybe, or the logs in the fireplace cold. Whatever, Rosalyn was so devastated by the betrayal of her dearest friend that all she wanted was to run back home, maybe seek out the rest of us to share her anguish. But she never made it.

Kit breaks into ragged sobs, slumped on the stool with her face buried in her hands, her shoulders shaking roughly. "It should've been me," she cries. "He was supposed to turn to me after Rosalyn was gone! I could've been everything to him that she was. With Rosalyn gone, I was poised to step into her shoes. Don't you see that, Tansy? It should've been me at Moonrise, no one else! Emmet would've been mine, and so would Annie. Annie could be my daughter, too—mine and Emmet's!"

I watch her weep but make no move to go over to her, or offer her consolation. I should feel pity for her, but don't. She's lived out her life in the shadow of another woman, wanting what Rosalyn had and everything Rosalyn loved—including her husband and daughter. Pathetic, maybe, but forgivable had it not become an obsession. And that's what it became, a rather sinister obsession. As the truth of it hits me full force, I shudder with the knowledge. Kit doesn't love Emmet, not really, no more than she loved the other men she latched on to, or poor Jim Lanier, her latest victim. She only wants Emmet because he belonged to Rosalyn.

And I know this, too: ever since her childhood, her obsession has been with Rosalyn. I remember Kit as a child, her hungry eyes never leaving Rosalyn. The Harmons, pitying Kit's spend-thrifty, loser parents, took in a young Kit and practically raised her, giving her everything that their daughter had. While their daughter was kindhearted and beautiful in all ways, Kit—as I see it now—was sly, manipulative, and eaten up with envy. Instead of focusing on the gifts she'd been given, including such generous patrons, Kit wanted everything Rosalyn had, so much so that it took over her whole life.

And look at the lives Kit's obsession has shattered, including

Helen's, the latest. Although Kit didn't actually admit it, I'm sure she encouraged Duff to torment Helen every chance he got. Initially, she sent Duff over to plunder for whatever of Rosalyn's she wanted, things she feared would end up in Helen's possession otherwise. Knowing now what a shit Duff turned out to be, I'll bet he didn't leave it at that, merely sneaking in to do Kit's bidding. It infuriates me to think what he might have taken of Helen's, how he might've spied on her, or found other ways to torment her, not just out of meanness but also to ingratiate himself with Kit. And what was Helen's crime, after all, but to love a broken man enough to help him heal? And to try to become a part of his life, even with the odds against her? It's the ones who stood in Kit's way that deserve my pity, not her.

Absorbed in her misery, Kit doesn't notice when I stand to leave, nor when I linger a moment, wishing there was something damning I could say to her before I go. She thinks it's Emmet she'll lose if things don't work out, if she can't make him see that they belong together. I want to tell her that she's wrong. When you lose yourself, there's nothing else.

Leaving her house, I break into a run. There's a call I have to make, and I've got to do it now, before it gets any later. Otherwise, I'd stop by Linc's to see Noel. Once my call's taken care of, I'll return to Linc's. Tonight, after everything that's happened, I need to be with Noel, and Linc. After her betrayal, Rosalyn didn't make it home to gather her friends around, to allow us to comfort her with our love. But I will. Only a few steps away, they wait for me.

21

helen

RAIN

As I feared, the most difficult part of packing comes in the room Emmet and I shared, with its hideous old Victorian furniture. Everything here's a painful reminder, and I stop often to stifle a sob before making myself get on with it. I can't seem to stay away from the windows, either. I keep pausing to inhale the fragrance of the moonflowers, or to search for the few night-blooming plants—mock orange, jasmine, angel trumpet—in the cloud-shrouded darkness of the gardens. I remind myself that I've still got packing to do, then I leave the windows to open drawers or clean out the cubbyholes of the dresser. Catching a glimpse of the moon peering just above a drifting bank of clouds, I hurry over to watch, my packing forgotten.

Because I've dawdled, been distracted by memories and moon-light, it's much later than I'd hoped when the packing's finally done, my suitcases stacked by the door. I collapse on the bed, exhaustion having caught up with me at last. Tonight, exhaustion's a good thing since I need to sleep a few hours before my early start in the morning. I raise up on my elbow and look across the room to the leftover ashes in the fireplace. What I need is a fire to dispel the gloomy coldness of this room. Its bright flames might even thaw out the icy tundras of my heart.

In my nightgown, I work on starting a small fire, stacking the logs and kindling as I've seen Emmet do so many times, when I wanted a fire even on the warmest of nights and with the windows open, as they are now. To my amazement, the kindling blazes up long enough to grab the logs, and for the first time all summer I've made a fire that might actually burn for more than a nanosecond. Ridiculously pleased at my success, I stand watching as the fire sputters, flames, then spreads an amber glow over the room like warm honey.

Heavy-eyed, I return to bed, sure the flickering flames will lull me to sleep. The shadows a fire casts in a dark room are hypnotic, so I turn out the lamp and curl up under the covers. When I first came upstairs, I moved the broken lamp out of my sight, holding it gingerly as though it were a living thing, and brought the one from Emmet's table to my side. I can't let my mind go there, relive the ugly scene from this afternoon when he smashed the lamp. Instead I watch the slow-moving shadows the fire makes, and force those hurtful thoughts out of mind as I fall into a troubled sleep.

Well after midnight, I'm awakened by a noise so loud that I sit straight up in bed. It's ink-dark and cold, the fire long dead, and I blink in confusion. Before I can figure out what the noise was, there's another boom of thunder, and lightning splits the night in two. Rain! Throwing off the covers, I stumble out of bed to turn on the lamp. Nothing. Everyone's told me that Highlands always loses power during a thunderstorm. Except for the flashes of lightning, the room's so dark I can barely make out the outline of the windows. I pick up the brass candlestick on my nightstand, unused all summer, and grope in the drawer for the matches. It's futile; when I packed the contents of the drawer, I didn't see any. Crawling across the bed, I find a matchbox in the table on Emmet's side and breathe a sigh of relief, until I open it. Empty.

Cussing under my breath, I grip the candlestick and start making my way across the room, jumping at every clap of thunder and jolt of lightning. One good thing about furnishing a room with such big pieces of furniture, I don't have to worry about tripping over or running into them. Before I get to the fireplace, however, I remember using up the matches in my ineptness starting the fire, and I turn around. The ghostly-white lace canopy of the bed serves as a touchstone to help me find my way to the door, which I fling open in relief. My relief is short-lived when I face the eerie black-ness of the long hallway. I'm torn between feeling my way down the staircase, or returning to cringe under the covers in the dark. The rain I'll welcome when it comes, but I've always been terrified of thunderstorms. As long as I have candles to light the big spooky room, I'll be fine. Then I can watch the light show out the windows, safely across the room in my warm bed.

It's the brilliant, zagged flashes of lightning that illuminate the stairway enough for me to creep down it, feeling my way with the candlestick in one hand and banister in the other. I descend the stairs and reach the entrance hall with a sigh of relief, the floor cool on my bare feet, then put the candlestick on the long table under the mirror. I'll pick it up on my way back, after getting the matches. Now that I've made it, and don't have to worry about plunging down the stairs and breaking my fool neck, I might as well get the flashlight, too.

I'm not sure where it is, though, probably in the utility drawer by the stove. Feeling my way carefully, I hug the wall as I go down the back hallway to the kitchen. Even with the bay windows, the kitchen is as dark as the halls of hell, and I fumble my way to the stove. In the drawer I find a full box of matches but no flashlight. Oh, well. Gripping the matchbox like a talisman against the storm, I make my way across the kitchen to the porch on the side of the house, the one where we have our evening meals. From there, I can tell if the storm is going to blow away, or if I'm in for a bumpy ride the rest of the night.

Opening the door leading to the porch, I step out anxiously and look up at the heavy black sky. No rain yet, but the night air hums with tension, with thunder rattling the mountaintops. For the first time all summer, the smell of ozone fills the air. Beyond the driveway, the dark lake roils and ripples ominously, and a strong wind rustles through brittle bushes like the wings of hundreds of vultures.

A flash of lightning hits the ground close by the porch, then is followed by another flash so close that I scream and take off running down the hallway, the porch door slamming behind me. I'm more afraid of being struck by lightning than stumbling and falling over something in the hall. All I want is my bed. Even when I realize that I've dropped the matchbox, I don't stop my frantic run down the dark hallway. No way I'm going back for the matches now—I made my way down the stairs without them; I can sure as hell make my way back up.

Just as I burst into the entrance hall, lightning strikes something out front with such a deafening explosion that I cover my ears and scream again. The entrance hall is suddenly bathed in the flickering light of the storm, and I look up to see a dark figure looming toward me, outlined in the ghostly light from the glass panels on either side of the front door. With a loud cry, I fall backward and lose my footing, grabbing for the wall in a futile attempt to right myself. "Helen!" I hear as I'm grabbed up before I hit the stone floor, grabbed with a grip so tight that I close my eyes and let out another bloodcurdling scream.

"God Almighty," Emmet yells as he pulls me up. "I don't know who's making the most noise, you or the storm."

I've gone limp in his arms, but the sound of his voice surprises me so much that I push away from him wide-eyed. "Emmet! What are you doing here?"

He rubs his face wearily. "I live here, remember? And so do you, so you might as well get those damn boxes in the garage unpacked."

I stare at him as I rub my bare arms, smarting from his grip when he grabbed me to stop my fall. "You scared me!" I'm still reeling from the lightning and the shock of his sudden appearance.

"No worse than you scared me," he snaps back. Another flash of lightning illuminates his face long enough for me to see his expression. He's furious.

"So you were going to sneak off and leave me without a word," he says in a voice heavy with contempt.

I shake my head, then flinch at another boom of thunder. "No. I planned to leave you a note . . . or something. Then to call you, once I got on my way."

"Once you got far enough that I couldn't do anything about it, I suppose," he says tightly. "Or couldn't follow you to bring you back." Even in the dark, I can see the angry glitter of his eyes as he glares at me. "Know this, Helen. You will never get far enough from me that I won't go after you."

I swallow, and close my eyes tightly. "Emmet . . ." I begin, but he grabs my arm and shakes me.

"Tansy called me, and I drove like a lunatic to get here. Come on."

I don't have time to protest as he pulls me by the arm down the hallway toward the kitchen. "Where are we going?" I'm finally able to ask as I stumble through the darkness in my bare feet, too bewildered to ask more. His only explanation is "Can't see you in there."

Opening the side door, he leads me onto the porch where I just stood to check out the storm. Still no rain, but the wind has picked up, and it blows and howls and tosses the tall trees back and forth against the dark sky. When I realize where he's taking me, I cry out and struggle against him. "No, Emmet! I'm scared of storms, remember? I'd rather go back inside where it's safe."

This time a flash of lightning illuminates the bitter curve of his smile. "If only, sweetheart." His endearment is harsh, not loving. "If I knew a safe place, I'd take you there. But I can't, and you can't do it for me, either, because such a place doesn't exist. Not here, nor anywhere else."

I blink at him in confusion. When I open my mouth to ask what on earth that means, he puts a finger over my lips. "Just listen for a minute, okay? Then you can ask questions, all of them you want. Though I don't know how many I can answer."

"Go ahead," I say weakly, but I'm not sure I want to hear this. I hug my arms close, shivering. I'm not sure I want to hear this at all.

"Tansy called me," he tells me again, "a couple of hours ago. She caught me just as I was leaving the awards dinner, about to go up to my room." Holding my gaze so I can't look away, he adds, "Alone, Helen. I've been alone, every time in Asheville. You can either believe that, or not."

"It's something else, isn't it?" I manage to say.

He nods grimly. "It's about Rosalyn." He runs his fingers through his hair, then closes his eyes briefly, as though forcing himself to go on. "There's something I haven't told you about the night she died. All along, I've known why she came here. But I couldn't deal with my guilt, so I blocked it out. That's what you let loose when you overheard Kit and me talking in my office this afternoon, and why I reacted like I did. None of it was your fault. All of it was my anger, and my guilt."

I let out my breath slowly, trying to take it in. "I get the guilt— you'd brought a former mistress here, to show her Moonrise, right? And it started the chain of events that led to Rosalyn's death, and ended up being a secret held by you and Kit. But the anger? I mean, isn't that always a part of guilt, anger at yourself?"

Emmet flinches, and rubs his face. "Oh, yeah. No question, it's what brought on my breakdown. When Tansy called me earlier, and I learned more about what happened, what she found out from

Kit . . . well, that might've brought on another one. And probably would have, if I'd lost you, too. I pride myself on good judgment, Helen, yet I lost Rosalyn because I didn't use it. My talk with Tansy should've helped—at least I learned Rosalyn didn't come here to catch me cheating on her as I'd thought—but I'm not going to let myself off the hook. Not after I damn near did the same thing with you."

"But . . . wait a minute! I don't get it. What did Tansy tell you about why Rosalyn came here?"

Emmet looks beyond me, his eyes dark with pain, and the story comes spilling out. He tells me everything, the whole sordid tale of Kit and her obsession with Rosalyn, with wanting what her friend had so badly—wanting to be Rosalyn, even—that she was willing to go to any lengths to get it. Some of it I still don't understand, and whether he's leaving anything out intentionally or not I have no way of knowing. Instead he tells me how his and Rosalyn's life together had always included Kit as an integral part, almost like she was a family member. It sounds like Kit envied Rosalyn all her life, but I wonder when she fell in love with Rosalyn's husband. Was she waiting in the wings all those years, plotting to turn Rosalyn against the man she loved, or did she just seize the chance when it presented itself? How much had she worked on Rosalyn even before then, planting suspicions in her mind, and how did she misstep so that Rosalyn began to suspect her motives?

One thing I know, though Emmet won't say it, is Rosalyn wasn't Kit's only obsession. Kit must love him to the point of obsession, too. He talks instead of her apparent fixation on Rosalyn, which I don't doubt—and tells me how Tansy concluded that Kit came to want both Rosalyn's daughter and husband as her own. I'm in a perfect position to understand Kit's strong—and yes, obsessive—feelings for Emmet. I was dangerously close to losing myself in him as well, despite the hard-earned independence I'd finally found. I was willing to give it all up, the opportunity to be my own person, in order to be with him. All love has an element of surrender, I suppose, but not to the self. Never to the self, and if nothing else comes of this, I hope I've learned that. Emmet finishes by telling me how Kit put Duff up to all sorts of mischief, including taking the locket, then replacing it for him to find. Throughout the summer, in all sorts of ways, Kit has been working against me.

"Emmet?" I say, and he looks down at me curiously. I clear my throat to begin, but don't get the chance.

Both of us jump, startled, at the sound, one we haven't heard all summer—the sudden drumming on the roof of a downpour. The heavens open up, and the blessed rain comes down in torrents. Emmet and I turn to watch it together, then we work our way toward the edge of the porch, as if neither of us has ever seen such a welcome sight. The sound lifts my spirits and I cry out, "Finally!"

As we stand on the porch and watch the storm rage in front of our eyes, I'm seized by an utterly ridiculous notion. I have no idea where it comes from, but I know it to be true. If I can just feel the rain on my face, everything will be all right. I've been afraid of storms my entire life, a fear that has crippled me, and kept me cowering inside. Without thinking it through, I leave Emmet's side and cross to the back of the porch, where I grab an old windbreaker he left hanging there. After draping it across my shoulders, I return to take Emmet's hand in mine. He looks down at me with a surprised smile that disappears when I yank on his hand and repeat what he said to me earlier: "Come on."

"Whoa, now," Emmet yelps when I pull him down the rain-slick steps of the porch. He tries to make a grab for the laurel rail, but I hang on tight, and get him all the way to the walkway. Even as he sputters his protests, I pull him by the hand farther away from the house, to the grassy slope that faces the lake. It's too dark to see the lake, but we can hear the sound of the rain pounding it. Emmet's in a dress shirt and his good slacks, and I have on nothing but a thin nylon windbreaker over my nightgown. The rain comes down harder now, beating against us with such a force that I shiver violently, scared half out of my wits. The storm carries Emmet's voice to me when he cries out: "Have you lost your mind, Honeycutt?"

I take a deep breath and release my death grip of his hand. Then, with fingers wet and numb with the cold, I let go of the windbreaker, which I'd clutched to my throat. I don't have to remove it—the wind catches it, snatches it from my grasp, and tosses it aside.

I stand next to Emmet, huddled in the clearing with my silk nightgown flattened against me, soggy grass beneath my feet, and my hair streaming in my face. The rain pounds me so hard I almost topple. But I stand firm, legs apart and arms out for balance. The raindrops sting my skin on impact, like millions of tiny arrows. Then I don't feel them anymore. I keep my head down, and let the water pour over me. Opening my eyes, I raise my face upward, and ask the rain to wash away my fears.

AN INTERVIEW WITH CASSANDRA KING
AUTHOR OF **moonrise**

Q: *This year marks the 75th anniversary of the publication of Daphne du Maurier's classic novel* Rebecca. *While your book's not a retelling, it's certainly homage to that novel. Do you remember when you first read* Rebecca? *Why do you think this novel has endured?*

A: *Rebecca* is a beloved classic for many reasons. First of all, there's the mystery, the unanswered questions. Who was Rebecca, and why was she revered by everyone who knew her? Was she an angel, or a demon? And what about the narrator, who remains nameless throughout the book? Was she an easily frightened, overly imaginative wimp, or a terribly shy person unaware of her own strengths? And what about Rebecca's death? Was it an accident, or something more sinister? Then there's the delicious suggestion of the supernatural. I remember devouring *Rebecca* as a teenager, then searching out everything else Daphne du Maurier wrote. As a writer, I can now appreciate *Rebecca* for the author's masterful control of the story: the way the suspense draws the reader in, and the unforgettable characters.

For me, the creation of each book is its own story. Only afterwards do I look back and realize that so many things had to happen for the inspiration and creation to come together at just the right time. In this case, during a summer spent in a wonderful old house in Highlands, North Carolina, I stumbled on the grave of the owner's former wife in an overgrown garden. Although I was working on another book at the time, the book I was rereading during my down time was—coincidentally—*Rebecca*. From a serendipity of setting, place, and imagination came *Moonrise*.

Q: *It's often said that the past is always with us. The South truly loves its historic homes. And in many cities such as Beaufort and Charleston, South Carolina, their gardens are treasures often hidden behind walls. Do you believe that carefully preserving and honoring the past reflects a particularly Southern way of looking at the world? Are Southerners perhaps more attracted to gothic themes in fiction than the rest of the country?*

A: Let me answer the latter question first because my take on it influences the first. Southern gothic is a sub-genre of fiction, and for good reason. The lush, haunted landscape of the South is every bit as romantic as the wild moors of England and lends itself beautifully to the creation of a mysterious, darkly foreboding gothic atmosphere. Hidden, ruined or mysterious gardens add even more to such a landscape. As for our houses, the South is known for a particular kind of ancestor worship, which inevitably is tied into the "old home place." So yes, I think the South is about as gothic as it gets.

Q: *Family homes that pass from generation to generation carry the history of all the lives that have been lived within their walls. Do you believe there are such things as haunted places and ghosts?*

A: I should hope so, since my grandfather's house, where I spent much of my childhood, was haunted (and still is, as far as I know. Although it's no longer in the family, the present owners have reported strange happenings). I'm a strong believer in the past as a vital part of the present, however one interprets that. For me, our passage from one realm of existence to the other is fluid, transient, outside of time, rather than something that occurs at one particular moment in our life. I believe we exist in a spiritual world.

Q: *The stigma of divorce is, for many, a thing of the past. With the increase in the divorce rate, many more couples find themselves remarrying at midlife and having to adjust to blended families. In* Moonrise, *Helen is rejected not only by her husband's circle of friends but also by his daughter. Which do you think is harder to bear, and why?*

A: It depends on how you define family. Most of us expand that notion well beyond bloodlines or genetic ties, and close friends become like family to us. Certainly in a second marriage, efforts are made all around to expand the boundaries of the family unit. Helen and Emmet each have a child who has left the nest and started his/her own life, making for a slightly different situation (though not an uncommon one). Because Emmet's daughter has lost her mother, Helen wants to play a more significant role as stepmother than she might otherwise have done. However, the daughter's resentment is an obstacle that has to be overcome. From my observations, I don't think that's an uncommon situation, either.

Q: *The beautiful and lush Blue Ridge Mountains and the Highlands area of summer homes in particular play a large role in shaping the story. How important is place in your writing? When did you first discover Highlands, and what drew you to describe that place when you sat down to tell this story?*

A: Place is always important in my writing—almost a central character in some stories. In this particular book, I needed the mountain setting in order to create a particular mood. The story called for not only the majesty and beauty of the mountains, but also their remote loneliness: the way that mountains can feel so unattainable, forever out of one's reach. In the case of this novel, the setting came first, and the characters evolved from there. Highlands is a place of such incredible beauty that I've always been attracted to the area, drawn to the peacefulness of the Blue Ridge Mountains. Only in the past decade have we started spending a lot of time in the Highlands area, and I've been itching to incorporate the setting into a book.

Q: *Because you use multiple narrators, you're able to explore the arrival of the wealthier summer crowd from Atlanta and elsewhere from the point of view of Willa, a local mountain woman and housekeeper. Which of the multiple voices you used in telling the story was easiest to write? Which voice was most demanding?*

A: The use of multiple narrators seemed almost a necessity in this book. The plot centers on Helen's struggles with acceptance, rejection and self-actualization, so her point of view is essential, but I felt the best way to broaden the conflict between Helen and the group she's struggling to be accepted into was to allow the reader into their mind-sets as well. And then we have Willa, who offers her unique perspective on both groups. Willa was actually the easiest because she has a brogue—a folksy, simple way of speaking, heavy on idioms, that sets her apart from the other narrators.

Q: *In* Moonrise, *you've written about a circle of friends that includes not just women but also men. The relationship within each couple is unique. While friendship has been a regular theme in your previous novels, the women in* Moonrise *seem more capable of betrayal than in previous novels. Would you like to comment on this? And with the exception of your first novel,* Making Waves, *you've most often focused on friendships between women. Do you find it harder to write about men?*

A: Relationships are always complex, even the closest and most loving—or, perhaps, especially the closest and most loving. In this book, I wanted to explore that complexity in ways I haven't in previous novels. Yes, friendship is a beautiful thing, but how do we deal with rejection? We all experience rejection at some point in our lives, and it always hurts. And what about betrayal? I wanted to look at the darker part of friendships—what's often hidden beneath the amiable surface. How do friendships survive jealousy, lies, loss of trust? And if they do, what's left? All that intrigued me, especially as it applied to the relationships between men and women, both friends and lovers. I find it easier to write about men than women for some reason. I toyed with having a male point of view in this book in addition to Helen's and Willa's, using Noel or Linc as one of the narrators. But Tansy would not stand for it.

Q: *Did you find that you had to do more research on this novel than in past works?*

A: I believe more research often goes into a good novel than into nonfiction. In nonfiction, usually you're laying out the facts, reporting, presenting your research as it is. In fiction, your characters actually "use" whatever it is you've researched. For example, the butterflies—or more succinctly, the moon garden: If I were writing an article about a nocturnal garden, I'd describe it, present certain facts about it, et cetera. In this book, my characters work in it, walk in it, smell it, feel it—it has to be more real than whatever facts my research uncovered. Even so, I love the research that goes into a novel, and how you then figure out ways to work it into the story. It's one of the fun things about writing fiction.

Q: *What's the best and what's the most challenging aspect of living with another novelist, your husband, Pat Conroy?*

A: At this stage in our life together, we've ironed out most of the challenges of a two-writer household. At first, I was so fiercely determined to keep our identities separate that I bristled if anyone wrote about us in the same sentence. But the joys of living with another writer overcame my trepidations, and I now believe that writers should only marry each other. No one else should be expected to put up with us—the way we go off into our own little worlds while we're working on a book, and the way we can't wait to get back there. Pat and I are recluses at heart, and I suspect most writers are. Marry each other.

Q: *What is the next thing you are working on?*

A: I'm passionate about the preservation of the family farm in America, so I'm constantly scribbling ideas in my head for a book about a woman who was raised on a farm yet couldn't wait to leave it all behind. After life knocks her around a bit and breaks her heart, she returns to live off the land. Not quite autobiographical, but close.

If your book group would like Cassandra King to call in or make a virtual visit to your meeting, please send an email to assistant@ cassandrakingconroy.com with the date and time (EST) that your group is gathering, the novel of hers you will be discussing, the size of your group, and a contact name and phone number. Thank you.

CASSANDRA KING
ON PLANTING A
Moon Garden

Begin planning your nocturnal garden on a night with a full moon. Select a spot in your yard that gets the moon at night and plenty of sun in the daytime. Although the moon will illuminate your garden in bloom, it still needs sunlight to grow. To get the full effect of night-blooming plants, avoid planting your garden in spots that are illuminated by street lights or other artificial means.

Will you sit on a porch to enjoy the flowers and fragrance, or by an open window? Perhaps you have a patio or terrace for your evening viewing. For some gardeners, much of the pleasure of the nocturnal garden comes from the element of surprise; their gardens are tucked away in mysterious corners that call for a trek in the dark to appreciate them.

While night-blooming plants are basic to your garden, other elements are essential, too. Consider both annuals and perennials, planted a bit more haphazardly than in a daytime garden. Part of the charm of your nocturnal garden comes from the unexpected. Moonlight will soften and blur rigid, formal layouts. Silvery-leafed or variegated greenery can provide a lovely backdrop for highlighting the paleness of night flowers.

Some of my favorite flowers for a night garden are as follows: honeysuckle and jasmine, for their delicate flowers and summery fragrance; evening or river primrose, for the daintiness of their sweet blooms; white butterfly bush, for the night moths; mock orange, with its take-your-breath-away perfume, and of course the must-have moonflower vines, the showstopper.

Best of all, a moon garden is ideal for someone who, like me, is an inept gardener with a passionate love of flowers. By the light of a full moon, all is forgiven.